THE
ROYAL SECRET

THE
ROYAL SECRET

A NOVEL

LUCINDA RILEY

ATRIA PAPERBACK

New York   London   Toronto   Sydney   New Delhi

ATRIA
PAPERBACK

An Imprint of Simon & Schuster, Inc.
1230 Avenue of the Americas
New York, NY 10020

Originally published in 2000 in Great Britain by Pan Books, an imprint of Pan Macmillan, as *Seeing Double*
Updated and revised edition published in 2018 in Great Britain by Pan Books, an imprint of Pan Macmillan, as *The Love Letter*.

First Atria Books hardcover edition May 2019

ATRIA PAPERBACK and colophon are trademarks of Simon & Schuster, Inc.

For information about special discounts for bulk purchases, please contact Simon & Schuster Special Sales at 1-866-506-1949 or business@simonandschuster.com.

The Simon & Schuster Speakers Bureau can bring authors to your live event. For more information or to book an event contact the Simon & Schuster Speakers Bureau at 1-866-248-3049 or visit our website at www.simonspeakers.com.

Interior design by Kyoko Watanabe

10 9 8 7 6

Library of Congress Cataloging-in-Publication Data

Names: Riley, Lucinda, author.
Title: The royal secret : a novel / Lucinda Riley.
Other titles: Seeing double
Description: New York : Atria Paperback, [2018]
Identifiers: LCCN 2018049615 (print) | LCCN 2018052919 (ebook)
Subjects: | BISAC: FICTION / Contemporary Women. | FICTION / Suspense. | FICTION / Espionage. | GSAFD: Suspense fiction.
Classification: LCC PR6055.D63 (ebook) | LCC PR6055.D63 S44 2018 (print) | DDC 823/.914—dc23
LC record available at https://lccn.loc.gov/2018049615

ISBN: 978-1-9821-2127-3
ISBN: 978-1-9821-1506-7 (pbk)
ISBN: 978-1-9821-1507-4 (ebook)

For Jeremy Trevathan

Author's Note

I began writing *The Royal Secret* in 1998—exactly twenty years ago. After a number of successful published novels, I'd decided I wanted to write a thriller, within the setting of a fictional British royal family. At the time, the popularity of the monarchy was at an all-time low following the death of Diana, Princess of Wales. The year 2000 was also the Queen Mother's centenary year, with the official nationwide celebration taking place just after the book was to be published. Looking back, perhaps I should have paid more attention when an early trade review suggested that St. James's Palace wouldn't like the subject matter. In the run-up to publication, in-store promotions, orders, and PR events were inexplicably canceled and subsequently, *Seeing Double*—as the book was called then—barely saw the light of day.

My publisher then canceled the contract for my next book, and despite my knocking on numerous doors to find another, they were all closed in my face. At the time, it was devastating watching my career go up in smoke overnight. Luckily, I was newly married with a young family, so I concentrated on bringing up my children and wrote three books for my own pleasure. Looking back, the break was a blessing in disguise, but when my youngest started school, I knew I had to dig deep and find the courage to send my latest manuscript to an agent. I changed my surname to be on the safe side and, after my years in the wilderness, was ecstatic when a publisher bought it.

A number of novels on, my publisher and I decided it was time *Seeing Double*, as it was known in 1998, was given a second chance.

It is important to remember that *The Royal Secret* is, to some extent, a period piece. If I were to set it in today's world, the plotline would be totally implausible due to the advent of technology, especially in terms of the high-tech gadgetry now used by our security services.

Lastly, I wish to reiterate that *The Royal Secret* is a work of fiction, bearing no similarity to our beloved queen and her family's life. I hope you enjoy the "alternative" version, *if* it does manage to reach your hands this time . . .

Lucinda Riley
February 2018

KING'S GAMBIT

Opening move wherein White offers
a pawn to divert a Black pawn

PROLOGUE

London, November 20, 1995

"James, darling, what are you doing?"

He looked around him, disoriented, then staggered forward.

She caught him just before he fell. "You've been sleepwalking, haven't you? Come on, let's take you back to bed."

The gentle voice of his granddaughter told him he was still on earth. He knew he'd been standing here for a reason, that there was something urgent he had to do that he'd been leaving right until the last moment...

But now it was gone. Desolate, he let her half-carry him to his bed, loathing his wasted, fragile limbs, which rendered him as helpless as a baby, and his scattered mind, which had once again betrayed him.

"There now," she said as she made him comfortable. "How's the pain? Would you like a little more morphine?"

"No. Please, I..."

It was the morphine that was turning his brain to jelly. Tomorrow, he'd have none, and then he'd remember what it was he had to do before he died.

"Okay. You just relax and try to get some sleep," she said, soothing him, her hand stroking his forehead. "The doctor will be here soon."

He knew he mustn't go to sleep. He closed his eyes, desperately searching, searching... snatches of memories, faces...

Then he saw her, as clear as the day he'd first met her. So beautiful, so gentle...

"Remember? The letter, my darling," she whispered to him. "You promised to return it . . ."

Of course!

He opened his eyes, trying to sit up, and saw the concerned face of his granddaughter hovering above him. And felt a painful prick in the inside of his elbow.

"The doctor's giving you something to calm you down, James, darling," she said.

No! No!

The words refused to form on his lips, and as the needle slipped into his arm, he knew that he'd left it too late.

"I'm so sorry, so very sorry," he gasped.

His granddaughter watched as his eyelids finally closed and the tension left his body. She pressed her smooth cheek against his and found it wet with tears.

Besançon, France, November 24, 1995

She walked slowly into the drawing room toward the fire. It was cold today, and her cough was worse. Edging her frail body into a chair, she picked up the fresh copy of the *Times* from the table to read the obituaries with her customary English breakfast tea. She clattered the china cup into its saucer as she saw the headline taking up a third of the front page.

LIVING LEGEND IS DEAD

Sir James Harrison, thought by many to be the greatest actor of his generation, died yesterday at his London home, surrounded by his family. He was ninety-five. A private funeral will take place next week, followed by a memorial service in London in January.

Her heart clenched, and the newspaper shook so violently beneath her fingers she could hardly read the rest. Alongside the article was a picture of him with the queen, receiving his OBE. Her tears blurring his image, she traced the contours of his strong profile, his thick mane of graying hair . . .

Could she . . . *dared* she return? Just one last time, to say goodbye . . . ?

As her morning tea cooled, undrunk beside her, she turned over the front page to continue reading, savoring the details of his life and career. Then her attention was caught by another small headline beneath:

RAVENS MISSING FROM TOWER

It was announced last night that the famous Tower of London ravens have vanished. As legend has it, the birds have been in residence for more than five hundred years, keeping guard over the Tower and the royal family, as decreed by Charles II. The raven keeper was alerted to their disappearance yesterday evening and a nationwide search is currently taking place.

"Heaven help us all," she whispered, fear flooding through her old veins. Perhaps it was simply coincidence, but she knew the legend's meaning all too well . . .

1

London, January 5, 1996

Joanna Haslam ran full pelt through Covent Garden, her breathing heavy and her lungs rattling with the effort. Dodging past tourists and groups of schoolchildren, she narrowly missed knocking over a busker, her rucksack flying to one side behind her. She emerged onto Bedford Street just as a limousine drew up outside the wrought-iron gates that led to St. Paul's Church. Photographers surrounded the car as a chauffeur stepped out to open the back door.

Damn! Damn!

With her last iota of strength, Joanna sprinted the final few yards to the gates, then into the paved courtyard beyond, the clock on the redbrick face of the church confirming she was late. As she neared the entrance, she cast her gaze over the huddle of paparazzi and saw that Steve, her photographer, was in prime position, perched on the steps. She waved at him and he gave her a thumbs-up sign as she squeezed through the crush of photographers who were crowding round the celebrity who had emerged from the limousine. Once inside the church itself, she could see the pews were packed, lit by the soft glow from the chandeliers. The organ was playing somber music in the background.

After flashing her press card at the usher and digging for breath, she slipped into the back pew and sat down gratefully. Her shoulders rose and fell with each gasp as she fumbled in her rucksack for her notepad and pen.

Although the church was frosty cold, Joanna could feel beads of sweat on her forehead; the roll-neck of the black lamb's wool sweater she'd thrown on in her panic was now sticking uncomfortably to her skin. She took out a tissue and blew her streaming nose. Then, sweeping a hand through her tangled mass of long dark hair, she leaned back against the pew and closed her eyes to catch her breath.

Just a few days into a new year that had begun with so much promise, Joanna felt as if she'd been not so much chucked but hurled off the top of the Empire State Building. At speed. Without warning.

Matthew . . . the love of her life—or rather, as of yesterday, the *ex*-love of her life—was the cause.

Joanna bit her bottom lip hard, willing herself not to start crying again, and craned her neck toward the pews at the front near the altar, noting with relief that the family members everyone was waiting for had not yet arrived. Glancing back through the main doors, she could see the paparazzi lighting up cigarettes and fiddling with their camera lenses outside. The mourners in front of her were beginning to shuffle on the uncomfortable wooden pews, whispering to their neighbors. She hastily scanned the crowd and picked out the most noteworthy celebrities to mention in her article, struggling to distinguish them by the backs of their heads, which were mostly gray or white. As she scribbled the names down in her notepad, images of yesterday invaded her mind again . . .

Matthew had turned up unexpectedly on the doorstep of her Crouch End apartment in the afternoon. After the heavy shared revelry of Christmas and New Year, the two of them had agreed to adjourn to their separate apartments and have a quiet few days before work began again. Unfortunately, Joanna had spent that time nursing the nastiest cold she'd had in years. She'd opened the door to Matthew clutching her Winnie the Pooh hot-water bottle, clad in ancient thermal pajamas and a pair of stripy bed socks.

She'd known immediately that there was something wrong as he'd hovered near the door, refusing to take his coat off, his eyes darting here and there, looking at anything but *her* . . .

He had then informed her that he had been "thinking." That he couldn't see their relationship going anywhere. And perhaps it was time to call it a day.

"We've been together for six years now, since the end of uni," he'd said, fidgeting with the gloves she'd given him for Christmas. "I don't know, I always thought that, with time, I'd want to marry you—you know, tie our lives together officially. But that moment hasn't happened . . ." He'd shrugged limply at her. "And if I don't feel that way now, I can't see that I ever will."

Joanna's hands had clenched around her hot-water bottle as she had regarded his guilty, guarded expression. Digging in her pajama pocket, she'd found a damp tissue and blown her nose hard. Then she'd looked him straight in the eye.

"Who is she?"

The blush had spread right across his face and neck. "I didn't mean for it to happen," he'd mumbled, "but it has and I can't go on pretending any longer."

Joanna remembered the New Year's Eve they'd shared four nights ago. And decided that he'd done a bloody good job of pretending.

She was called Samantha, apparently. Worked at the same advertising agency as he did. An account director, no less. It had begun the night Joanna had been doorstepping a Tory MP on a sleaze story and hadn't made it in time to Matthew's agency's Christmas party. The word "cliché" still whirled round her head. But then she checked herself; where did clichés originate, if not from the common denominators of human behavior?

"I promise you, I've tried so hard to stop thinking about Sam," Matthew had continued. "I really did try all throughout Christmas. It was so great to be with your family up in Yorkshire. But then I met her again last week, just for a quick drink, and . . ."

Joanna was out. Samantha was in. It was as simple as that.

She could only stare at him, her eyes burning with shock, anger, and fear, as he'd continued.

"At first I thought it was just an infatuation. But it's obvious that if I feel like this about another woman now, I simply can't commit to you. So, I'm only doing what's right." He'd looked at her, almost beseeching her to thank him for being so noble.

"What's right . . . ," she'd repeated, her voice hollow. Then she'd burst into floods of coldy, fever-induced tears. From somewhere far away, she could hear his voice mumbling more excuses. Forcing open her swollen, tear-drenched eyes, she'd regarded him as he'd sunk down, small and ashamed, into her worn leather armchair.

"Get out," she'd finally croaked. "You evil, low-down, lying, double-crossing bloody cheat! Get out! *Just get out!*"

In retrospect, what had really mortified Joanna was that he'd taken no further persuading. He'd stood up, muttering stuff about various possessions that he'd left at her apartment and getting together for a chat once the dust had settled, then he'd virtually charged for the front door.

Joanna had spent the rest of yesterday evening crying down the phone to her mother, to her best friend Simon's voicemail, and into the increasingly soggy fur of her Winnie the Pooh hot-water bottle.

Eventually, thanks to copious amounts of Night Nurse and brandy, she'd passed out, only grateful that she had the next couple of days off work due to the overtime she'd put in on the news desk before Christmas.

Then her mobile had rung at nine this morning. Joanna had raised herself from her drug-induced slumber and reached for it, praying it might be a devastated, repentant Matthew, realizing the enormity of what he'd just done.

"It's me," a harsh Glaswegian voice had barked.

Joanna had sworn silently at the ceiling. "'Lo, Alec," she'd snuffled. "What do you want? I'm off today."

"Sorry, but you're not. Alice, Richie, and Bill have all called in sick. You'll have to take your days in lieu another time."

"They can join the club." Joanna had given a loud, exaggerated cough down the line. "Sorry, Alec, but I'm dying too."

"Look at it this way: work today, then when you're fit you'll be able to enjoy the time off owed to you."

"No, I really can't. I've got a temperature. I can hardly stand."

"Then you'll be fine. It's a sitting-down job, at the Actors' Church in Covent Garden. There's a memorial service for Sir James Harrison at ten o'clock."

"You can't do this to me, Alec, *please*. The last thing I need is to sit in a drafty church. I've already caught my death. You'll end up at a memorial service for *me*."

"Sorry, Jo, no choice. I'll pay for a cab there and back, though. You can go straight home afterward and email me the piece. Try and talk to Zoe Harrison, will you? I've sent Steve to do shots. Should make the front page if she's all dolled up. Right, speak later."

"Damn!" Joanna had thrown her aching head back onto the pillow in despair. Then she'd rung a local taxi company, and staggered to her wardrobe to find a suitable black outfit.

Most of the time she loved her job, *lived* for it, as Matthew had often remarked, but this morning she seriously wondered why. After stints on a couple of regional papers, she'd been taken on as a junior reporter a year ago by the *Morning Mail*, based in London, and one of the top-selling national dailies in the country. However, her hard-won but lowly spot at the bottom of the pile meant she was hardly in a position to refuse. As Alec, the news-desk editor, never ceased to remind her, there were a thousand hungry young journalists right behind her. Her six weeks at the news desk had been the hardest posting so far. The hours were unremitting and Alec—by turns a slave driver and a true dedicated professional—expected nothing less than he was prepared to give himself.

"Give me the lifestyle pages any day," she'd snuffled as she'd pulled on a not-terribly-clean black sweater, a thick pair of woolly tights, and a black skirt in deference to the somber occasion.

The cab had arrived ten minutes late, then had got stuck in a monumental traffic jam on Charing Cross Road. "Sorry, love, nothing doing," the driver had said. Joanna had looked at her watch, chucked a ten-pound note at him, and jumped out of the cab. As she'd hared through the streets toward Covent Garden, her chest laboring and her nose streaming, she'd wondered whether life could get any worse.

Joanna was snapped out of her reverie as the congregation suddenly ceased their chatter. She opened her eyes and turned round as Sir James Harrison's family members began to file into the church.

Leading the party was Charles Harrison, Sir James's only child, now well into his sixties. He lived in Los Angeles, and was an acclaimed director of big-budget action films filled with special effects. She vaguely remembered that he had won an Oscar some time ago, but his films weren't the kind she usually went to see.

By Charles Harrison's side was Zoe Harrison, his daughter. As Alec had hoped, Zoe looked stunning in a fitted black suit with a short skirt that showed off her long legs, and her hair was pulled back in a sleek chignon that set off her classic English-rose beauty to perfection. She was an actress, whose film career was on the rise, and Matthew had been mad about her. He always said Zoe reminded him of Grace Kelly—his dream woman, apparently—leading Joanna to wonder why Matthew was going out with a dark-eyed, gangly brunette such as herself. She swallowed a lump in her throat, betting her Winnie the Pooh hot-water bottle that this "Samantha" was a petite blonde.

Holding Zoe Harrison's hand was a young boy of around nine or ten, looking uncomfortable in a black suit and tie: Zoe's son, Jamie Harrison, named after his great-grandfather. Zoe had given birth to Jamie when she was only nineteen and still refused to name the father. Sir James had loyally defended his granddaughter and her decisions both to have the baby and to remain silent about Jamie's paternity.

Joanna thought how alike Jamie and his mother were: the same fine features, a milk-and-rose complexion, and huge blue eyes. Zoe

Harrison kept him away from the cameras as much as possible—if Steve had got a shot of mother and son together, it would probably make the front page tomorrow morning.

Behind them came Marcus Harrison, Zoe's brother. Joanna watched him as he drew level with her pew. Even with her thoughts still on Matthew, she had to admit Marcus Harrison was a serious "hottie," as her fellow reporter Alice would have said. Joanna recognized him from the gossip columns—most recently squiring a blond British socialite with a triple-barreled surname. As dark as his sister was fair, but sharing the same blue eyes, Marcus carried himself with louche confidence. His hair almost touched his shoulders, and wearing a crumpled black jacket and a white shirt unbuttoned at the neck, he oozed charisma. Joanna dragged her gaze away from him. *Next time*, she thought firmly, *I'm going for a middle-aged man who likes bird-watching and stamp collecting.* She struggled to recall what Marcus Harrison did for a living—a fledgling film producer, she thought. Well, he certainly looked the part.

"Good morning, ladies and gentlemen." The vicar spoke from the pulpit, a large picture of Sir James Harrison in front of him, surrounded by wreaths of white roses. "Sir James's family welcomes you all here and thanks you for coming to pay tribute to a friend, a colleague, a father, grandfather, and great-grandfather, and perhaps the finest actor of this century. For those of us who had the good fortune to know him well, it will not come as a surprise that Sir James was adamant that this was not to be a somber occasion, but a celebration. Both his family and I have honored his wishes. Therefore, we start with Sir James's favorite hymn, 'I Vow to Thee, My Country.' Please stand."

Joanna pushed her aching legs into action, glad that the organ began playing just as her chest heaved and she coughed loudly. As she reached for the order-of-service sheet on the ledge in front of her, a tiny, spidery hand, the translucent skin revealing blue veins beneath it, got there before her.

For the first time, Joanna looked to her left and studied the owner of the hand. Bent double with age, the woman only came up to her ribs. Resting on the ledge to support her, the hand in which she held the service sheet shook violently. It was the only part of her body that was visible. The rest of her was shrouded in a black coat that touched her ankles, with a black net veil shielding her face.

Unable to read the sheet due to the continued shaking of the hand that held it, Joanna bent down to speak to the woman. "May I share with you?"

The hand offered her the sheet. Joanna took it and placed it low so the old lady could see it too. She croaked her way through the hymn, and as it ended, the woman struggled to sit down. Joanna silently offered her arm, but the help was ignored.

"Our first reading today is Sir James's favorite sonnet: Dunbar's 'Sweet Rose of Virtue,' read by Sir Laurence Sullivan, a close friend."

The congregation sat patiently as the old actor made his way to the front of the church. Then the famous, rich voice, which had once held thousands spellbound in theaters across the globe, filled the church.

"'Sweet rose of virtue and of gentleness, delightful lily . . .'"

Joanna was distracted by a creak behind her and saw the doors at the back of the church open, letting in a blast of freezing air. An usher pushed a wheelchair through them and placed it at the end of the pew opposite Joanna's. As the usher walked away, she became aware of a rattling noise that made her own chest problems seem inconsequential. The old lady next to her was having what sounded like an asthma attack. She was staring past Joanna, her gaze through her veil apparently locked on the figure in the wheelchair.

"Are you okay?" Joanna whispered rhetorically, as the woman put her hand to her chest, her focus still not leaving the wheelchair as the vicar announced the next hymn and the congregation stood again. Suddenly, the old lady grasped at Joanna's arm and indicated the door behind them.

Helping the woman to her feet, then holding her upright by her waist, Joanna virtually carried her to the end of the pew. The old lady pressed into Joanna's coat like a child wanting protection as they came adjacent to the man in the wheelchair. A pair of icy steel-gray eyes looked up and swept over them both. Joanna shuddered involuntarily, broke her gaze away from his, and helped the old lady the few paces to the entrance, where an usher stood to one side.

"This woman . . . I . . . she needs . . ."

"Air!" the old lady cried between gasps.

The usher helped Joanna lead the woman into the gray January day and down the steps to one of the benches that flanked the courtyard. Before Joanna could ask for further assistance, the usher had ducked back into the church and closed the doors once again. The old lady slumped against her, her breathing ragged.

"Should I call an ambulance? You really don't sound very well."

"*No!*" the old lady gasped, the strength of her voice at odds with the frailty of her body. "Call a taxi. Take me home. *Please.*"

"I really think you should—"

The bony fingers locked around Joanna's wrist. "Please! A taxi!"

"All right, you wait there."

Joanna ran out of the gates into Bedford Street and hailed a passing black cab. The driver gallantly got out and walked back with Joanna to help the old lady to his vehicle.

"She okay? The old duck's breathing sounds a bit off," he said to Joanna, as the two of them settled the woman on the backseat. "Does she need to go to hospital?"

"She says she wants to go home." Joanna leaned into the cab. "Where is home by the way?" she asked the woman.

"I . . ." The effort of getting into the cab had obviously exhausted her. She sat there, panting.

The cabbie shook his head. "Sorry, love. 'Fraid I can't take her anywhere in that state, not by herself, like. Don't want a death in the back of my cab. Far too messy. Could take her if you come, too, of course. Then it's your responsibility rather than mine."

"I don't know her . . . I mean, I'm working . . . I should be in that church now . . ."

"Sorry, love," he said to the old lady. "You'll have to get out."

The old lady lifted her veil and Joanna saw her terrified milky-blue eyes. "Please," she mouthed.

"Okay, okay." Joanna sighed with resignation and climbed into the back of the cab. "Where to?" she asked gently.

". . . Mary . . . Mary . . ."

"No. Where to?" Joanna tried again.

"Mary . . . le . . ."

"Do you mean Marylebone, love?" the cabbie asked from the front seat.

The woman nodded with visible relief.

"Right you are."

The old lady stared anxiously out of the window as the cab sped away. Eventually, her breathing began to ease and she rested her head against the black leather seat and closed her eyes.

Joanna sighed. This day was getting better and better. Alec would crucify her if he thought she'd snuck off early. The story of a little old lady being taken ill would not wash with him. Little old ladies were only of interest to Alec if they'd been beaten up by some skinhead after their pension money and left for dead.

"We're nearly in Marylebone now. Could you try and find out where we're going?" called the cabbie from the front of the taxi.

"Nineteen Marylebone High Street." The clipped voice rang out crisp and clear. Joanna turned to look at the old woman in surprise.

"Feeling better?"

"Yes, thank you. Sorry to put you to so much trouble. You should get out here. I'll be fine." She indicated that they had stopped at a traffic light.

"No. I'll see you home. I've come this far."

The old lady shook her head as firmly as she could. "Please, for your own sake, I—"

"We're nearly there now. I'll help you inside your house and then go back."

The old lady sighed, sank further down into her coat, and said no more until the taxi came to a halt.

"Here we are, love." The cabbie opened the door, relief that the woman was still alive clear on his face.

"Take this." The woman held out a fifty-pound note.

"Haven't got change for that, I'm afraid," he said as he helped the old woman down onto the pavement and supported her until Joanna stood beside her.

"Here. I've got it." Joanna handed the driver a twenty-pound note. "Wait for me here, please. Back in a tick." The old lady had already slipped from her grasp and was walking unsteadily toward a door next to a newsagent's.

Joanna followed her. "Shall I do that?" she asked as the arthritic fingers struggled to put the key in the lock.

"Thank you."

Joanna turned the key, opened the door, and the old lady almost threw herself through it.

"Come in, come in, *quickly*!"

"I . . ." Having delivered the old lady safely to her door, Joanna needed to get back to the church. "Okay." Joanna reluctantly stepped inside. Immediately the woman banged the front door shut behind her.

"Follow me." She was heading for a door on the left-hand side of a narrow hallway. Another key was fumbled for, then finally fitted into the lock. Joanna followed her into darkness.

"Lights are just behind you on the right."

Joanna felt for the switch, flicked it, and saw that she was standing in a small, dank-smelling lobby. There were three doors in front of her and a flight of stairs to her right.

The old lady opened one of the doors and switched on another light. Standing just behind her, Joanna could see that the room was full of tea chests stacked one on top of the other. In the center of the room was a single bed with a rusty iron bedstead. Against one wall, wedged in between the tea chests, was an old armchair. The smell of urine was distinct and Joanna felt her stomach lurch.

The old lady headed for the chair and sank onto it with a sigh of relief. She indicated an upturned tea chest by the bed. "Tablets, my tablets. Could you pass them, please?"

"Of course." Joanna gingerly picked her way through the tea chests and retrieved the pills from the dusty surface, noticing the directions for use were written in French.

"Thank you. Two, please. And the water."

Joanna gave her the glass of water that stood next to the pills, then opened the screw-top of the bottle and emptied out two tablets into a shaking hand and watched the old lady put them in her mouth. And wondered if she was now okay to leave. She shuddered, the fetid smell and dismal atmosphere of the room closing in on her. "Are you sure you don't need a doctor?"

"Quite sure, thank you. I know what's wrong with me, my dear." A small, twisted smile appeared on her lips.

"Well then. I'm afraid I'd better be going back to the service. I have to file my piece for my newspaper."

"You're a journalist?" The old lady's accent, now that she had recovered her voice, was refined and definitely English.

"Yes. On the *Morning Mail*. I'm very junior at the moment."

"What is your name, dear?"

"Joanna Haslam." She indicated the boxes. "Are you moving?"

"I suppose you could put it like that, yes." She stared off into space, her blue eyes glazed. "I won't be here for much longer. Maybe it's right that it ends like this . . ."

"What do you mean? Please, if you're ill, let me take you to a hospital."

"No, no. It's too late for all that. You go now, my dear, back to your life. Goodbye." The old lady closed her eyes. Joanna continued to watch her, until a few seconds later, she heard soft snores emanating from the woman's mouth.

Feeling horribly guilty, but unable to stand the atmosphere of the room any longer, Joanna quietly let herself out and ran back to the taxi.

———

The memorial service was over by the time she arrived back in Covent Garden. The Harrison family limousine had left and there were only a few members of the congregation still milling around outside. Feeling really wretched now, Joanna just managed to take a couple of quotes from them before hailing another cab, giving up the entire morning as a bad job.

2

The bell was ringing. Again and again, it seared through Joanna's throbbing head.

"Oooh God," she groaned, as she realized whoever was at the door was determined not to take the hint and leave.

Matthew . . . ?

For a split second, her spirits rose, then sank again instantly. Matthew was probably still toasting his freedom with a glass of champagne, in a bed somewhere with Samantha.

"Go away," she moaned, blowing her nose on Matthew's old T-shirt. For some reason, it made her feel better.

The bell rang again.

"Bugger, bugger, bugger!"

Joanna gave in, crawled out of bed, and staggered to the front door to open it.

"Hello, sex kitten." Simon had the nerve to grin at her. "You look dreadful."

"Cheers," she muttered, hanging on to her front door for support.

"Come here."

A pair of comfortingly familiar arms closed round her shoulders. She was tall herself, and Simon, at six foot three, was one of the only men she knew who could make her feel small and fragile.

"I got your voicemail messages when I got home late last night. Sorry I wasn't there to play agony aunt."

"S'okay," she snuffled into his shoulder.

"Let's go inside before icicles start forming on our clothes, shall we?" Simon closed the front door, an arm still firmly around one of her shoulders, and walked her into the small sitting room. "Jesus, it's cold in here."

"Sorry. I've been in bed all afternoon. I've got a really terrible cold."

"Never," he teased her. "Come on, let's sit you down."

Simon swept old newspapers, books, and congealing Pot Noodle containers onto the floor, and Joanna sank onto the uncomfortable lime-green sofa. She'd only bought it because Matthew had liked the color and she'd regretted the purchase ever since. Matthew had always sat in her grandmother's old leather armchair whenever he came round anyway. *Ungrateful sod*, she thought.

"You're not in a good way, are you, Jo?"

"Nope. On top of being dumped by Matthew, Alec sent me out to cover a memorial service this morning when it was meant to be my day off. I ended up in Marylebone High Street with a weird old lady who lives in a room full of tea chests."

"Wow. And there's me in Whitehall, and the most exciting thing that happened today was getting a different kind of filling from the sandwich lady."

Joanna could barely raise a smile at his efforts to be cheerful.

Simon sat down next to her and took her hands in his. "I'm so sorry, Jo, really."

"Thanks."

"Is it over forever with Matthew, or do you think it's just a blip on the road to marital bliss?"

"It's over, Simon. He's found someone else."

"Want me to go and give him a good kicking to make you feel better?"

"Truthfully, yes, but in reality, no." Joanna put her hands to her face and wiped them up and down her cheeks. "The worst thing is that at times like this you're meant to react in a dignified manner. If people ask you how you are, you're meant to brush it off and say, 'I'm absolutely fine, thanks. He meant nothing to me anyway and him leaving is the best thing that's ever happened to me. I've so much more time now for myself and my friends and I've even taken up basket weaving!' But it's all *rubbish*! I'd crawl across burning coals if it would bring Matthew back, so that life can go on like normal. I . . . I . . . love him. I need him. He's mine, he be-belongs to m-me."

Simon sat with his arms around her while she sobbed. He stroked her hair gently and listened as the shock, grief, and confusion poured out of her. When she was all cried out, he gently released her and stood up. "You light the fire while I boil the kettle for some tea."

Joanna turned on the gas flames in the fireplace and followed Simon into the small kitchen. She slumped down at the Formica table for two in the corner, over which she and Matthew had shared so many lazy Sunday brunches and intimate candlelit suppers. As Simon busied himself making the tea, Joanna gazed at the glass jars lined up neatly along the worktop.

"I've always loathed sun-dried tomatoes," she mused. "Matthew adored them."

"Well." Simon took the jar full of the offending tomatoes and tipped them into the bin. "That's one positive thing to come out of this, then. You don't have to eat them anymore."

"In fact, now that I think about it, there were lots of things Matthew liked and I just pretended to." Joanna rested her chin on her hands.

"Such as?"

"Oh, going to see weird, foreign art-house movies on Sunday at the Lumière when I'd have preferred to stay at home and catch up on soaps. Music—that was another thing. I mean, I like classical in small doses, but I was never allowed to play my *ABBA Gold* or Take That CDs."

"I hate to admit it, but I'm afraid I'm with Matthew on that one," Simon chuckled, pouring boiling water over the tea bags. "You know, if I'm honest, I always felt Matthew was aspiring to be what he *thought* he should be."

"You're right." Joanna sighed. "I just wasn't impressive enough for him. But that's who I am: just a boring middle-class Yorkshire girl."

"I promise you, the one thing you're not is unimpressive. Or boring. Honest, maybe; down-to-earth, yes. But those are qualities to be admired. Here." He handed her a mug of tea. "Let's defrost by that fire."

Joanna sat on the floor in front of the fire between Simon's knees and drank her tea. "God, Simon, the thought of going through the dating process all over again is hideous," she said. "I'm twenty-seven, too old to start afresh."

"Yes, you're ancient, I can practically smell death on you."

Joanna smacked his calf. "Don't make light of this! It's going to take me ages to get used to being single again."

"The problem with us humans is that we fear and dislike change of any kind. I'm convinced that's why so many miserable couples stay together, when they'd be far better off apart."

"You're probably right. Look at me, eating sun-dried tomatoes for years! Speaking of couples, have you heard from your Sarah?"

"She sent me a postcard from Wellington last week. She's learning to sail there, apparently. Wow, it's been a long year apart. Anyway, she's back from New Zealand in February, so only a few weeks to go."

"You've been awfully good to wait for her." Joanna smiled at him.

"'If you love someone, set them free.' Isn't that the old adage? The way I see it is, if she still wants me by the time she arrives home, then we'll both know that it's right and for real."

"Don't bank on it. I thought Matthew and I were 'right' and 'for real.'"

"Thanks for your words of comfort." Simon raised his eyebrows. "Come on now, you have your career, your apartment, and me. You're a survivor, Jo. You'll come out the other side, you wait and see."

"That's if I still have a job to go back to. The piece I filed on Sir James Harrison's memorial service was crap. What with Matthew, and my awful cold, and that weird old lady . . ."

"You say she was living in a room full of tea chests? Are you sure you weren't delirious?"

"Yup. She said something about not being here long enough to unpack." Joanna bit her lip. "Ugh, it smelled so strongly of wee in there... Will we be like that when we're old? The whole thing completely depressed me. I stood in that room thinking that if this is what life brings you to, then what the hell is the point of struggling through anyway?"

"She's probably one of those mad eccentrics who lives in a dump and has millions stuffed away in the bank. Or in tea chests for that matter. You should have checked."

"She was fine until she looked at this old man in a wheelchair, who came to sit by the opposite pew to us during the service. She totally freaked when she saw him."

"Probably her ex-husband. Maybe *his* millions were stashed away in those tea chests," Simon laughed. "Anyway, sweetheart, I must be on my way. I've got some work to do before tomorrow."

Joanna followed him to the door and he clasped her to him in a hug. "Thanks for everything." She kissed him on the cheek.

"Anytime. I'm always there if you need me. I'll call you from work tomorrow. Bye, Butch."

"Night, Sundance."

Joanna closed the door behind him and drifted back into the sitting room feeling brighter. Simon always knew how to cheer her up. They'd been friends for all of their lives. He'd lived on the neighboring farm to hers up in Yorkshire with his family and even though he was a couple of years older than her, living in such an isolated environment meant they had spent much of their childhood together. As an only child and a tomboy by nature, Joanna had been thrilled to have Simon's company. He'd taught her to climb trees and play football and cricket. During the long summer holidays, the two of them had taken their ponies up onto the moors and played lengthy games of cowboys and Indians. It was the only time they'd ever fought, as Simon had always and most unfairly demanded that he live and she die.

"It's my game, we play by my rules," he'd insist bossily, a large cowboy hat swamping his head. And after they had chased each other across the coarse moorland grass, inevitably he would catch her up, tackling her from behind.

"Bang bang, you're dead!" he'd shout, pointing his toy gun at her, and she would stagger, then fall onto the grass, rolling around in pretend agony until she eventually gave in and died.

When he was thirteen, Simon had gone to boarding school and they'd seen less of each other. The old closeness had still remained during the holidays, but both had naturally made new friends as they grew up. They'd celebrated with a bottle of champagne up on the moors when Simon had won a place at Trinity College, Cambridge, Joanna going to university two years later at Durham to study English.

Then their lives had separated almost completely; Simon had met Sarah at Cambridge, and in her final year at Durham, Joanna had found Matthew. It wasn't until they'd both reconnected in London—coincidentally living only ten minutes apart—that their friendship had blossomed once more.

Joanna knew Matthew had never really taken to Simon. Apart from towering over him physically, Simon had been offered some kind of high-flying job in the civil service when he'd left Cambridge. He always said modestly that he was just an office bod at Whitehall, but that was Simon all over. Very quickly, he'd been able to afford to buy a small car and a lovely one-bedroom apartment on Highgate Hill. Matthew, meanwhile, had gofered at an ad agency before being offered a junior position a couple of years ago, which still only afforded him a damp bedsit in Stratford.

Maybe, Joanna thought suddenly, *Matthew is hoping Samantha's superior position at the agency will boost his* own *career . . .*

Joanna shook her head. She refused to think about him anymore tonight. Setting her jaw, she put Alanis Morissette on her CD player and turned the volume up. *Sod the neighbors*, she thought as she went into the bathroom to run a hot bath. Singing "You Learn" at the top of her croaky voice, the water pouring out of the taps, Joanna did not hear the footsteps along the short path that led to the front door, or see the face peering into the windows of her ground-floor sitting room. She emerged from the bathroom as the footsteps receded back down the path.

Feeling cleaner and calmer, Joanna made herself a cheese sandwich, drew the curtains closed in the sitting room, and sat in front of the fire, toasting her toes. And suddenly felt a faint flicker of optimism for the future. Some of the things she'd said to Simon in the kitchen earlier had sounded flippant, but they were actually true. In retrospect, she and Matthew had very little in common. Now she was a free agent with no one to please but herself and there would be no more putting her own feelings second. This was her call, *her* life, and she'd be damned if she was going to let Matthew ruin her future.

Before her positive mood left her and depression descended once more, Joanna took a couple of paracetamol and headed for bed.

3

"Bye bye, darling." She hugged him to her, breathing in his familiar smell.

"Bye, Mumma." He snuggled into her coat for a few more seconds, then pulled away, watching her face for signs of unwelcome emotion.

Zoe Harrison cleared her throat and blinked back tears. This moment became no easier, no matter how many times she went through it. But it wasn't done to cry in front of Jamie or his friends, so she put on a brave smile. "I'll be down to take you out to lunch three weeks on Sunday. Bring Hugo if he'd like to come."

"Sure." Jamie stood awkwardly by the car, and Zoe knew it was her moment to leave. She couldn't resist reaching out to brush a strand of his fine blond hair back from his face. He rolled his eyes, and for a second, he looked more like the little boy she remembered, and not the serious young man he was becoming. Seeing him in his navy school uniform, his tie done up neatly just like James had taught him, Zoe felt immensely proud of him.

"Okay, darling, I'll be off now. Ring me if you need anything. Or even if you just want to have a chat."

"I will, Mumma."

Zoe slid behind the wheel of her car, closed the door, and started the engine. She wound down the window.

"I love you, sweetheart. You take care now, and remember to wear your undershirt, and *don't* leave your wet rugby socks on for any longer than you have to."

Jamie's face reddened. "*Yes*, Mumma. Bye."

"Bye."

Zoe pulled out of the drive, watching Jamie waving cheerfully in her rearview mirror. She turned a bend and her son was lost from sight. Driving through the gates and onto the main road, Zoe brushed the tears away harshly and ferreted for a tissue in her coat pocket. And told herself for the hundredth time that she suffered more on these occasions than Jamie did. Especially today, with James gone.

Following signs for the motorway that would take her on the hour's drive back to London, she wondered once more whether she was misguided to confine a ten-year-old boy to a boarding school—especially after suffering the tragic bereavement of his great-grandfather only a few weeks before. Yet Jamie loved his prep school, his friends, his *routine*—all the things she couldn't give him at home. He seemed to be thriving at the school, growing up, becoming ever more independent.

Even her father, Charles, had commented on it when she had dropped him off at Heathrow yesterday evening. The pall of his father's death hung on him visibly, and she'd noticed that his handsome, tanned face was finally bearing signs of age.

"You've done so well, my darling, you should be proud of yourself. And your son," he'd said in her ear as he'd hugged her goodbye. "Bring Jamie out to stay with me in LA during the holidays. We don't spend enough time together. I miss you."

"I miss you, too, Dad," Zoe had said, then stood there, vaguely stunned, as she'd watched him walk through the security gate. It was rare for her father to praise her. *Or* her son.

She remembered when she had found herself pregnant at eighteen, and nearly died of shock and devastation. Just out of boarding school and with a place at university, it had seemed ridiculous to even contemplate having a baby. And yet, throughout the barrage of anger and judgment from her father and her friends, coupled with pressure from a completely different source, Zoe had known, somewhere in her heart, that the baby inside her had to be born. Jamie was the product of love: a special, magical gift. A love from which, after more than ten years, she had still not fully recovered.

Zoe joined the other cars streaking toward London on the motorway, as her father's words from all those years ago rang in her ears.

"Is he going to marry you, this man who's knocked you up? I can tell you now, you're on your own, Zoe. It's your mistake, you fix it!"

Not that there was ever any chance of marriage to him, she thought ruefully.

Only James, her darling grandfather, had remained calm, a quiet presence exuding reason and support when all those around her seemed to be screaming at the tops of their voices.

Zoe had always been James's special girl. As a child, she'd had no idea that the kind, elderly man with the rich, deep voice, who refused to be addressed as "Grandpa" because he said it made him feel old, was one of the most lauded classical actors in the country. She had grown up in a comfortable house in Blackheath with her mother and older brother, Marcus. Her parents had already divorced by the time she was three and she rarely saw her father, Charles, who had moved to LA. And so it was James who had become the father figure in her world. His rambling country home—Haycroft House in Dorset—with its orchard and cozy attic bedrooms, had been the setting for her most pleasurable childhood memories.

In semiretirement, only popping off stateside occasionally to appear in a cameo film role, which "brought home the bacon," as he put it, her grandfather had always been there for her. Especially after Zoe's mother had been killed suddenly in a road accident only a few yards from their house. Zoe had been ten, her brother, Marcus, fourteen. All she remembered of the funeral was clinging on to him and seeing his face set, jaw clenched, silent tears running down his cheeks as they listened to the vicar say the prayers. The service had been tense and bleak. She'd been forced to wear a stiff black dress, the lace irritating her neck.

Charles had returned from LA and tried to comfort a son and daughter he hardly knew, but it had been James who had wiped away her tears and hugged her as she wept long into the night. James had tried to comfort Marcus, too, but he had closed up and refused to discuss it. The grief Marcus had felt for the loss of his mother had been locked away deep inside him.

While her father had swept her up to live in LA with him, Marcus had been left at boarding school in England. It was as if she had not only lost her mother, but her brother too . . . her whole life all at once.

When she'd arrived in the dry, prickly heat at her father's hacienda-style house in Bel Air, Zoe had discovered she had an "Auntie Debbie." Auntie Debbie apparently lived with Daddy and even slept in the same bed as he did. Auntie Debbie was very blond, voluptuous, and not happy to have ten-year-old Zoe arrive in her life.

She'd been sent to school in Beverly Hills and had hated every moment of it. She'd rarely seen her father, who was too busy carving a niche for himself as a movie director. Instead, she'd endured Debbie's idea of child-rearing: TV dinners and wall-to-wall cartoons. She'd missed the changing seasons of England desperately and hated the harsh heat and loud accents of LA. She'd written long letters to her grandfather, begging him to come and fetch her so that she could live at her beloved Haycroft House with him, trying to convince him that she could look after herself. And that, really, she would be no trouble, if he'd only let her come back home.

Six months after Zoe had arrived in LA, a taxi had appeared on the drive. Out of it had stepped James, wearing a dapper Panama hat and a broad smile. Zoe still remembered the feeling of overwhelming joy as she ran down the drive and threw herself into his arms. Her protector had heeded her call and had arrived to rescue her. With Auntie Debbie banished to sulk by the pool, Zoe had poured out her woes into her grandfather's ears. Subsequently, he had called his son and told him of Zoe's misery. Charles—who had been filming in Mexico at the time—had agreed to let James take her back to England.

On the long flight home, she'd sat happily next to James, her small hand clutched in his big one. She had leaned on his firm, capable shoulder, knowing that she wanted to be wherever he was.

The cozy, weekly boarding school in Dorset had been a happy experience. James had always been glad to welcome Zoe's friends, either in London or at Haycroft House. It was only when she watched their parents' wide-eyed wonderment as they came to collect their children and shook hands with the great Sir James Harrison that she started to realize just how famous a man her grandfather was. As she grew older, James began to pass on to her his love for Shakespeare, Ibsen, and Wilde. The two of them would regularly take in a play at the Barbican, the National Theatre, or the Old Vic. They'd stay the night at James's grand London house in Welbeck Street, then spend Sundays in front of the fire going through the text of the play.

By the time Zoe was seventeen, she knew she wanted to become an actress. James sent off for all the prospectuses from drama schools and they pored over each, weighing up their pros and cons, until it was decided that Zoe should go to a good university and take an English degree first, then apply for drama school when she was twenty-one.

"Not only will you study the classic texts at university, which will give your performances depth, but you will also be older and ready to suck up all the information on offer at drama school by the time you get there. Besides, a degree gives you something to fall back on."

"You think I'll fail as an actress?" Zoe had been horrified.

"No, my darling, of course not. You're my granddaughter for a start," he'd chuckled. "But you're so damned lovely looking that unless you've got a bloody degree, they won't take you seriously."

They'd agreed between them that Zoe—if her A-level results were as good as expected—should apply to Oxford to study English.

And then she'd fallen in love. Right in the middle of her A levels.

Four months later, she was pregnant and devastated. Her carefully mapped-out future was in tatters.

Uncertain and terrified of her grandfather's reaction, Zoe had blurted it out over supper one night. James had paled a little, but had nodded calmly and asked her what she wanted to do about it. Zoe had burst into tears. The situation was so dreadful, so complex, that she could not even tell her beloved grandfather the whole truth.

All through that awful week when Charles had arrived in London with Debbie in tow, shouting at Zoe, calling her an idiot, and demanding to know who the father was, James had been there, giving her strength and the courage to make the decision to have her baby. And he had never once asked who the father might be. Nor questioned the trip up to London that had left Zoe drained and ghostly white when he'd picked her up from Salisbury railway station and she'd fallen sobbing into his arms.

If it hadn't been for his love, support, and complete faith in her ability to make the right decision, Zoe knew she would not have made it through.

At Jamie's birth, Zoe had watched James's faded blue eyes fill with tears as he'd seen his great-grandson for the first time. The labor had been early and so swift that there had been no time for Zoe to make the half-hour journey from Haycroft House to the nearest hospital. So Jamie had been born on his great-grandfather's old four-poster bed, with the local midwife in charge. Zoe had lain there, panting with exhaustion and elation, as her tiny, squalling son was lifted into James's arms.

"Welcome to the world, little man," he'd whispered, then kissed him gently on his forehead.

In that moment, she'd decided to name her baby boy after him.

Whether the bond had formed then, or in the following few weeks as grandfather and granddaughter took it in turns to get up at night and comfort a colicky, tearful baby, Zoe didn't know. James had been both a father and a friend to her son. Young boy and old man had spent many hours together, James somehow galvanizing the energy to play with Jamie. Zoe would arrive home and find them out in the orchard, James throwing the football for Jamie to kick. He'd take him off on nature hunts through the winding lanes of the Dorset countryside, teaching his great-grandson about the flowers that grew in the hedgerows and in their gorgeous country garden. Peonies, lavender, and salvia jostled for space in the wide beds. And in mid-July, the smell of James's favorite roses wafted through her bedroom window.

It had been a beautiful, tranquil time, Zoe simply content to be with her little son and her grandfather. Her own father was at the height of his fame, having just won an Oscar, and she rarely heard from him. She did her best not to mind, but still, just yesterday at the airport, when he'd hugged her and said he missed her, the invisible parental thread had tugged at her heart.

He's getting old too . . . , she thought as she negotiated the roundabout at the end of the motorway and headed for central London.

When Jamie was three, it had been James who had gently convinced her to apply for drama school. "If you win a place, we can all live in Welbeck Street," he'd said. "Jamie should be starting nursery a couple of mornings a week soon. It's good for a child to socialize."

"I'm sure I won't get in anyway," she had muttered, as she'd finally agreed to try for a place at the Royal Academy of Dramatic Art, only a short bicycle ride from Welbeck Street.

Yet she *had* got in, and with the support of a young French au pair, who collected Jamie from his nursery at noon and cooked lunch for both him and James, Zoe had completed her three-year course.

Her grandfather had then corralled his theatrical agent, plus a raft of casting director friends, to attend her graduation performance— "My darling, the world is built on nepotism, whether you're an actor or a butcher!" And by the time she left, she had an agent and her very first small part in a television drama. By then, Jamie was at school, and Zoe's career as an actress had subsequently blossomed. Although to her disappointment, it was the screen, rather than the stage—her first love—that formed her employment.

"My dear girl, stop complaining," James had reprimanded her

when she'd arrived home from a fruitless day on location in East London. It had rained solidly, and they hadn't managed a single shot. "You're employed, which is the most a young actor can hope for. The Royal Shakespeare Company will come later, I promise."

If Zoe had noticed her grandfather's slow decline over the next three years, she realized she had chosen to ignore it. It was only when he began to wince in pain that she had insisted he go to the doctor.

The doctor had diagnosed bowel cancer in its advanced stages; it had spread through James's liver and colon. Because of his age and frailty, a grueling course of chemotherapy had been ruled out. The doctor had suggested palliative care, to let him spend the time he *did* have left in a positive frame of mind, free of tubes and drips. If, as James deteriorated, that kind of equipment was needed for his comfort, then it would be provided for him at home.

Further tears filled Zoe's eyes as she thought of entering the empty house in Welbeck Street, a house that only two months ago had been filled with the pleasant aroma of Old Holborn tobacco, which James had smoked illicitly up until the day he died. In the last few months, he'd been very sick, his ears and eyes failing, and his ninety-five-year-old bones begging to be finally at rest. Yet his charisma, his sense of humor, his *life force*, had still filled the house.

Last summer, Zoe had made the heartbreaking decision to send Jamie away to school for his own sake. Watching his beloved great-grandfather deteriorate right in front of his eyes was not something she wished to put her son through. Because of their close bond, Zoe had known she must ease him into a life without "Great-James," as Jamie called him, gently, with as little pain as possible. Jamie didn't see the lines deepening on Great-James's face, nor the way his hands shook as they played a game of Snap, or how he'd fall asleep in his armchair after lunch and not wake until early evening.

So Jamie had gone away to school last September and had thankfully settled down happily, while Zoe had put her burgeoning film career on hold and nursed an increasingly frail old man.

One bitter November evening, James had caught Zoe's hand as she took an empty teacup from him. "Where's Jamie?"

"He's at school."

"Can he come home this weekend? I need to see him."

"James, I don't know whether that's such a good idea."

"He's a clever lad, more so than most boys his age. I've known since Jamie was first born that I wasn't immortal. It was obvious I was unlikely to be around beyond his early years. I've prepared Jamie for my imminent departure."

"I see." The hand clutching her own teacup had shaken like her grandfather's.

"You'll call him home? I should see him. Soon."

"Okay."

Reluctantly, Zoe had collected Jamie from school that weekend. On the drive home, she'd told him how ill Great-James was. Jamie had nodded, his hair falling into his eyes and guarding his expression. "I know. He told me at half-term, actually; said he'd call for me when it was . . . time."

As Jamie had run upstairs to see him, Zoe had paced the kitchen, worrying how her precious boy would react to seeing Great-James so ill.

That night, as the three of them ate supper in James's room, Zoe saw the old man had brightened considerably. Jamie spent most of the rest of the weekend ensconced in James's bedroom. When she'd finally gone upstairs and told Jamie they had to leave for school to arrive in time for Sunday curfew, James had opened his arms wide to his great-grandson.

"Goodbye, old chap. You take care of yourself. And that mother of yours."

"Yes. Love you!" Jamie had hugged his great-grandfather tightly, with all the abandon of a child.

They hadn't talked much on the journey down to Jamie's Berkshire prep school, but just as they'd pulled into the school car park,

Jamie had finally spoken. "I'll never see Great-James again, you know. He's going soon, he told me."

Zoe turned and looked at her son's serious expression. "I'm so sorry, darling."

"Don't worry, Mumma. I understand."

And with a wave he was off up the steps and inside.

Less than a week later, Sir James Harrison, OBE, was dead.

―――――

Zoe pulled up next to the curb in Welbeck Street, got out of the car, and glanced up at the house, whose upkeep would now fall to her. The redbrick building, despite its newer Victorian facade, had stood here for over two hundred years, and she saw the frames around the tall windows were in dire need of repainting. Unlike its neighbors, its exterior curved out gently, like a pleasantly full belly, and it reached up five stories, with the attic windows winking down at her like two bright eyes. Walking up the steps, she unlocked the heavy front door and closed it behind her, picking up the mail from the mat. Her breath was visible in the cold air of the house and she shivered, wishing she could retreat back to the comforting semi-isolation of Haycroft House. But work had to be done. Just before he'd died, James had strongly encouraged Zoe to take the leading role in a new film version of *Tess of the D'Urbervilles* directed by Mike Winter, an up-and-coming young Brit. She had only given her grandfather the script to keep him from boredom during his illness—it was one of many that were sent to her every week—and had never expected him to read it.

Yet, once he had, James had grabbed her hand. "A part like Tess isn't going to land in your lap every day and this script is exceptional. I entreat you to do this, dear girl. It will make you the star you deserve to be."

He hadn't needed to say "last request." She'd seen it in his eyes.

Without taking off her coat, she walked down the hall and turned the thermostat up. She could hear the clanking as the ancient boiler was brought to life, and prayed that none of the pipes would freeze in the deepening winter temperatures. Wandering into the kitchen, she saw wineglasses and dirty ashtrays were still stacked by the sink, left over from the drinks party–cum–wake she'd felt obliged to hold after the memorial service yesterday. She had perfected a gracious expression of gratitude as dozens of people had come to pay their respects and regale her with stories of her grandfather.

Half-heartedly, she emptied some of the ashtrays into the overflowing bin, knowing that most of the money from *Tess* would go to renovating the old house—the kitchen alone was in desperate need of an update.

The answering-machine light was blinking from the worktop. Zoe pressed "play."

"Zoe? Zoeeeeee . . . ??! Okay, you're not there. Ring me at home. Immediately. I mean it. It's urgent!"

Zoe winced at the slur in her brother's voice. She'd been horrified when she'd seen what Marcus had turned up wearing yesterday at the church—not even a tie—and he'd snuck off as soon as he could from the wake afterward, without even saying goodbye. She knew it was because Marcus was sulking.

Just after James had died, she, Marcus, and her father had attended the reading of his will. Sir James Harrison had decided to leave virtually all his money and Haycroft House in trust for Jamie until he was twenty-one. There was also an insurance policy to pay for Jamie's school fees and university education. Welbeck Street had been bequeathed to Zoe, along with his theatrical memorabilia, which took up most of the attic space at Haycroft House. However, he'd left her no actual cash; Zoe understood that he wanted her to be hungry and continue to pursue her acting career. There was also a lump sum of money in trust to set up the "Sir James Harrison Memorial Scholarship." This was to pay the fees of two talented youngsters who would not normally be able to attend a reputable drama school. He had asked that Charles and Zoe set the scheme up.

James had left Marcus £100,000; a "paltry token gesture," according to Marcus. After the reading of the will, she could feel the disappointment crackling like electricity from her brother.

She switched on the kettle, weighing up whether to call Marcus back, knowing if she didn't, he was likely to call her at some ungodly hour of the morning, drunk and unintelligible. However excruciatingly self-obsessed he could be, Zoe loved her brother, remembering her childhood with him and how sweet and kind he'd always been with her when she was younger. Whatever his more recent behavior, she knew that Marcus had a good soul, but equally, his penchant for falling in love with the wrong women and his very bad head for business had subsequently rendered him broke and very low.

When he'd left university, Marcus had gone to LA to stay with their father and had tried to make his mark as a film producer. Zoe had known from what her father and James told her that things weren't going as he'd planned. Over the ten years Marcus had been in LA, one project after another had crumbled to dust, leaving him and his benefactor father disillusioned. And leaving Marcus virtually penniless.

"The problem with that young man is that his heart's in the right place, but he's a dreamer," James had commented when Marcus had returned from LA to England three years ago with his tail between his legs. "This new project of his"—James had flapped the film proposal Marcus had sent him in hope of funding—"is full of sound political and moral ethos, but where's the story?" Subsequently, James had refused to back it.

Even if her brother had not helped himself, Zoe felt a sense of guilt for the fact that she and her son had been so favored by James, both in his lifetime, and in the recent will.

Cradling a mug of tea in her hands, she wandered into the sitting room and glanced around at the scuffed mahogany furniture, the worn-out sofa and the old chairs, their undercarriages visibly sagging with age. The heavy damask curtains were faded, with small vertical slits woven through the fragile material, as if an invisible knife had cut through them like butter. As she mounted the stairs toward her bedroom, she thought she'd try removing the threadbare carpets to see if the hardwood floor beneath them could be salvaged . . .

She paused on the landing, outside the door to James's room. Now that all the grim paraphernalia of life and death had been removed, the room felt like a void. She opened the door and stepped inside, picturing him sitting up in bed, a congenial smile on his face.

All her strength left her, and she slid to the floor, curling up by the wall, as all her grief and pain poured out in body-wracking sobs. She hadn't let herself cry like this up until now, holding everything together for Jamie. But now, here for the first time on her own, she cried for herself, and for the loss of her true father, *and* her best friend.

The ringing of the doorbell startled her. She stilled, hoping the unwelcome caller would go away and let her lick her wounds in peace.

The doorbell rang again.

"Zoe!" a familiar voice shouted through the letter box. "I know you're home, your car's outside. Let me in!"

"Damn you, Marcus!" she cursed under her breath, angrily swiping the last tears from her face. She ran down the stairs, pulled the front door open, and saw her brother leaning against the stone portico.

"Jesus, sis!" he said as he saw her face. "You look as wrecked as I do."

"Thanks."

"Can I come in?"

"You're here now, so you'd better," she snapped, and stood back to let him through.

Marcus slid past her and headed straight to the drinks cabinet in the sitting room, where he reached for the decanter to pour himself a healthy slug of whiskey before she had even closed the front door.

"I was going to ask you how you were holding up, but I can see it in your face," he remarked, falling back into the leather wingback chair.

"Marcus, just tell me what you want. I've got a lot to sort out—"

"Don't pretend you've got it so hard when good ol' Jim left you this house." Marcus swept his arms around the room, the whiskey sloshing perilously close to the rim of the glass.

"James left you a lot of money," Zoe said through gritted teeth. "I know you're angry—"

"Damn right I am! I'm this close—*this* close—to Ben MacIntyre agreeing to direct my new film project. But he's got to be sure I have the capital to begin preproduction. All I need is a hundred grand in the company account and I reckon he'll say yes."

"Just be patient. When probate comes through, you'll get it." Zoe sat back on the sofa, massaging her aching temples. "Can't you get a loan?"

"You know what my personal credit rating is like. And Marc One Films doesn't have the best financial track record either. Ben'll move on to something else if I hang about. Honestly, Zo, if you met these guys, you'd want to be involved too—it's going to be *the* most important film of the decade, if not the millennium . . ."

Zoe sighed. She'd heard plenty about Marcus's new project in the past few weeks.

"And we need to start applying for permits to film in Brazil soon. If only Dad would loan me the money until probate comes through, but he's refused." Marcus glared at her.

"You can't blame Dad for saying no; he's helped you out so many times before."

"But this is different, it's going to turn everything around, Zoe, I swear."

She paused and held his gaze. He'd really unraveled in the past few weeks, and she was becoming seriously worried about his drinking.

"I have no cash, Marcus, you know that."

"Come on, Zoe! Surely, you could easily remortgage this house, or even get a bank loan out for me just for a few weeks until probate's through."

"Stop!" She slapped her hand down on the arm of the sofa. "Enough is enough! Listen to yourself! Are you really surprised James didn't leave you his house when he knew you'd almost certainly sell it immediately? And you hardly visited him when he was ill. I was the one who cared for him, who loved him—" Zoe broke off, swallowing the sob that was threatening to escape her.

"No, well . . ." Marcus had the grace to look ashamed. He lowered his eyes and took a sip of his whiskey. "You were always his special girl, weren't you? I hardly got a look-in."

"Marcus, what's happening to you?" she said quietly. "I care about you, and I really want to help you, but—"

"You don't trust me. Just like Dad and Sir Jim. That's the real reason, isn't it?"

"Oh, Marcus, it's hardly surprising, the way you've been acting recently. I haven't seen you sober in God knows how long . . ."

"Don't you 'oh, Marcus' me! After Mum died, everyone was in bits over who would take care of precious Zoe! And who gave a toss about me, huh?"

"If you're going to drag up ancient history, then you can do it on your own time, I'm too exhausted for this." She stood up and gestured to the door. "Call me when you've sobered up, but I won't speak to you when you're like this."

"Zoe . . ."

"I mean it. Marcus, I love you, but you have to pull yourself together."

He stood up heavily, leaving his whiskey glass on the carpet, and walked out of the room.

"Remember, you're taking me to that premiere early next week," she called.

There was no reply and she heard the front door slam behind him.

Zoe wandered into the kitchen to make herself a cup of soothing chamomile tea, then surveyed the empty cupboards. A bag of crisps would have to suffice as supper. She searched through the heap of unanswered mail by the telephone for the invitation to the premiere for the film she had finished just before James became really sick. As she checked the details so she could text Marcus to remind him, the name at the top of the card suddenly came into sharp focus.

"Oh my God," she muttered.

She sank into a chair as her stomach did a 360-degree turn.

4

Marcus Harrison walked down the dank alley behind the twenty-four-hour betting shop on North End Road, and unlocked the door to the entrance of his apartment. He retrieved a pile of letters from his pigeonhole in the hall—each one no doubt threatening to pull out all his pubic hairs individually with tweezers if he did not pay the enclosed amount immediately—and climbed the stairs. He winced at the foul smell of drains, unlocked the door to his apartment, then closed it behind him and leaned against it.

He had a raging hangover, which had still not cleared, even though it was almost six the following evening. Dumping the bills on the worktop to gather dust with the rest, Marcus headed for the sitting room and the half-empty whiskey bottle. Pouring a hefty amount into a used glass, he sat down, knocked it back, and felt its comforting warmth flow through him. And wondered miserably where it had all gone wrong.

Here he was, eldest son of a successful, wealthy father, and grandson of the most lauded actor in the country. In other words, the heir to a kingdom.

Besides that, he was relatively handsome, ethical, kind—well, as kind as he could be to his geeky, weird nephew—and generally the type of person with whom success should walk hand in hand. And yet, it didn't. And it never had.

What was it his father had said to him after the memorial service, when Marcus had begged him to loan him the £100,000 until probate came through? That he was a "lazy inebriate" who expected everyone else to sort out his problems. God, that had hurt, really bloody hurt.

Whatever his father thought of him, Marcus knew he had always done his best. He'd missed his mum so much after she'd died that for the following two years her loss had felt like an acute physical pain. He'd been unable to express his grief—even the word "mum" had brought a lump to his throat—and the harsh world of an all-male British boarding school was not a place anyone could afford to look like a sissy. So he'd closed up and worked hard—for *her*. Yet, had anyone ever noticed? No, they were too busy worrying about his little sister. And when he'd decided to try his luck as a fledgling producer in LA, choosing projects he knew his mother would have liked because they "said something about the world," his films had bombed over and over again.

At the time, Charles, his father, had been understanding. "Go back to London, Marcus. The LA scene isn't right for you. The UK is much more receptive to the kind of low-budget art-house films you want to make."

To be fair, Charles had given him a decent amount to rent a place in London and live comfortably. Marcus had moved into an airy apartment in Notting Hill and begun Marc One Films.

Then . . . he'd fallen in love with Harriet, a long-legged blond socialite—he'd always had a penchant for pretty blondes—whom he'd met at one of Zoe's screenings. An aspiring actress herself, she'd been thrilled to be linked to "Marcus Harrison—film producer and grandson of Sir James Harrison," as the tabloids had quoted under their pictures in the gossip columns. He'd spent all his father's money on Harriet's expensive lifestyle, but once she had realized he was a "loser trading on his family name," she'd left him for an Italian prince. Marcus had had to crawl back to his father, who'd bailed him out of the heavy debt she'd left in her wake.

"This is the very last time I'm saving your hide," Charles had barked down the line from LA. "Get your life together, Marcus. Find a proper job."

He'd then met an old school friend who told him of an eco film project that he and a few other chaps in the City were backing. He'd offered Marcus the chance to produce it. Still smarting from Harriet's biting assessment of him and his career, he'd taken out a large overdraft for the necessary capital. Then he'd spent six months filming in Bolivia and had fallen in love with the isolation and grandeur of the Amazon rain forest, and the determination of the people who had lived in it for thousands of years.

The film had been a huge and terrifying flop and Marcus had lost every penny of his investment. In retrospect, he had to acknowledge that the script hadn't been up to much, that whatever the moral value of the film itself and what it "said," it also needed a great story—as his grandfather had once commented. So when he'd been sent a script a few months ago from a young Brazilian writer, and actually wept at the end, he'd known this was the film with which to make his mark.

The problem was that none of the banks would now touch him because of his appalling financial track record and his father had refused point-blank to "throw away" any more money. Everyone had lost their faith in him—just as he'd started to realize what it took to make an ethical but beautiful film, which he was sure would fill cinemas around the world, and might even win awards. The audience would be moved by the central love story, and would learn something in the process.

He was at his wits' end to know how to change everyone's attitude, and wasn't ashamed to admit how excited he'd been when his grandfather had finally popped his clogs. Even though it was obvious that all Sir Jim's affection had been for Zoe, Marcus was, after all, one of only two grandchildren.

But the reading of the will had not gone as expected. And for the first time in his life, Marcus felt real bitterness. His inner confidence and his optimism had disappeared in a puff of smoke. He felt like a failure.

Am I having some kind of breakdown? he wondered.

The telephone rang, breaking into his thoughts. Marcus picked it up reluctantly when he saw the caller ID flash up. "'Lo, Zo. Look, I'm really sorry about the other night. What I said was out of line. I . . . haven't been myself lately."

"That's okay." He heard her sigh heavily down the line. "None of us have. Did you get the text I sent you a few days ago? You have remembered you're taking me to this premiere tonight?"

"Erm . . . no."

"Oh, Marcus! Don't say you can't come now! I really need you."

"I'm glad someone does."

"Stop moping, have a shower, and meet me in the American Bar at the Savoy in an hour. My treat."

"That's big of you," he quipped, then added, "Sorry. I'm just a bit down, that's all."

"Okay. I'll see you at seven. We can talk then. I *was* listening to you the other night, you know."

"Thanks, sis. See you later," Marcus muttered.

That evening, with a second whiskey in front of him, Marcus sat at the bar in the dimly lit art deco lounge. When Zoe finally entered, wearing a black strapless evening gown with diamond drop earrings, every head—male or female—turned to admire her.

"Wow, Zo. You look radiant tonight," he told her, subconsciously brushing a hand over the wrinkled suit trousers he'd dug out of the laundry pile.

"Do I?" she asked nervously as she kissed him and sat down. She put a hand to her hair. "What do you think? I don't look too old-fashioned, do I?"

Marcus appraised his sister's sleek golden hair, which had been pulled back into some kind of fancy updo.

"You look like Grace Kelly, elegant and classy. Okay? Can I stop now?"

"Yes," she said with a smile. "Thanks."

"You're not usually paranoid about your looks. What's up?"

"Nothing, it's nothing. Get me a glass of champagne, will you?"

Marcus did as he was bid. Zoe raised the glass to her lips, drained half of it, and put it down on the table.

"God, I needed that."

"You sound like me, Zo," he said with a grin.

"Well, let's hope my half glass of champagne doesn't have the same effect on my appearance as that whiskey seems to have had on yours. You look dreadful, Marcus."

"To be honest, I feel it too. Any more thoughts on lending me that hundred grand?"

"Until probate's through, I simply don't have the cash."

"Surely you could borrow money on the strength of what's coming to you? Please, Zo," he urged her again. "If I don't stump up soon, the project's going to disappear from right under my nose."

"I know, I believe you. Really."

"Thanks. I mean, surely you must feel just a little pissed off with our grandfather too? Sorry, Zo, but what does a ten-year-old want with what must amount to millions of pounds? Can you imagine how much that will be in eleven years' time when Jamie turns twenty-one?"

"I understand how hurt you are about the will, but really, it's not fair to blame Jamie."

"No." Marcus drained his glass and ordered another. "I'm just . . . at the end of my tether, I suppose. Everything's going wrong. I'm thirty-four this year. Maybe that's it—maybe I'm suddenly staring middle age in the face. I've even gone off sex."

"Christ, now that is a sobering thought." Zoe rolled her eyes.

"You know"—Marcus waggled his Marlboro Light at her—"that kind of reaction is just what I expect from my family. You all patronize me, treat me as though I'm a child."

"Is that our fault? Let's face it, you have got yourself into some scrapes over the years."

"Yes, but now, when I have a cause I'm totally committed to, no one will believe or support me."

Zoe sipped her champagne and checked her watch. Twenty-five minutes before the premiere began—twenty-five minutes before she saw *him*, in the flesh . . . Her heart rate gathered pace and she felt horribly sick.

"Look, Marcus, we've got to be going. Get the bill, will you?"

Marcus signaled a waiter and Zoe took one of his cigarettes out of the packet.

"Didn't think you smoked."

"I don't. Often. Listen." Zoe inhaled, felt even sicker, and stubbed the cigarette out in the ashtray. "I've had an idea about how we might be able to sort out your problem. I'll have to speak to Dad about it."

"Then it's a nonstarter to begin with. Dad's as down on me as he could be."

"Leave it with me."

"What is it? Tell me now, Zoe, please. Let me sleep tonight," Marcus begged her.

"No, not until I've talked to him. Thanks." The waiter handed Zoe the bill and she tucked her credit card inside the leather folder. "How are you for the moment? Do you need some cash to see you through?"

"To be honest, yes," Marcus admitted, not able to look her in the eyes. "I'm down to my last few pounds and I'm about to be chucked out of my fleapit of an apartment for missing last month's rent."

Zoe reached into her clutch bag and drew out a check. She handed it to Marcus. "There. It's a loan, mind you. I took it out of my savings account and I want it paid back when probate comes through."

"Course. Thanks, Zoe. I appreciate it." He folded the check and slid it into his inside jacket pocket.

"Just don't spend it on whiskey, Marcus, please. Right, let's go."

The two of them took a taxi to Leicester Square, and crawled through the traffic at Piccadilly Circus.

"How big is your role in this?" Marcus asked her.

"Second lead. Even you might enjoy it. It's a good film—low budget, meaningful," she added.

The area outside the front of the Odeon in Leicester Square had been cordoned off. Zoe nervously tucked a strand of hair behind her ear. "Right. Here goes." She stepped out, shivering in the cold drizzle, and surveyed the crowd of eager onlookers. This was a production without a Hollywood star or special effect in sight, but she knew who it was they'd come to see. The huge poster on the front of the building was illuminated by numerous spotlights, Zoe's profile partly hidden by the lead actress's face—the curvaceous Jane Donohue.

"Blimey, wish I'd taken more of an interest while you were filming," Marcus quipped, looking up at the poster and the leading lady.

"Be nice when you meet her, won't you?" Zoe grabbed Marcus's hand instinctively as they walked onto the red carpet.

"When am I *not* nice to beautiful women?" he asked.

"You know what I mean. Stay close tonight, promise?" She squeezed his hand.

Marcus shrugged. "If you want."

"I want."

Flashbulbs popped as they walked into the foyer, which was buzzing with the usual first-night mixture of soap stars, comedians, and those famous simply for being famous. Zoe accepted a glass of wine from a tray and glanced around nervously. He'd obviously not arrived yet.

Sam, the director, pounced on her and kissed her enthusiastically. "Darling, sorry about poor Sir James. I would have come to his memorial service, but I was horribly caught up with all this."

"Don't worry, Sam. It was for the best. He was very poorly toward the end."

"Grief suits you, Zoe." Sam looked at her admiringly. "You look stunning tonight. There's a real buzz about the film, and doing this royal charity premiere was a stroke of genius by the PR people. We'll get oodles of newspaper coverage tomorrow, especially with you in that dress." He kissed her hand and smiled. "Enjoy, darling. See you later."

Zoe turned round; Marcus—despite her plea—had disappeared. "Damn!" She could feel the adrenaline pumping through her, making her head spin. And decided she had every right to behave in a cowardly and immature way. So she went and hid in the ladies' toilet, trying to calm her thumping heart. Just as the lights went down in the cinema, she crept into her seat next to Marcus.

"Where did you get to?" he hissed.

"The loo. I've got the runs."

"Charming," he sniffed, as the opening credits began to roll.

Zoe sat through the film in a daze. The thought that *he* was here, in the auditorium, possibly only a few yards away from her, breathing the same air as her for the first time in over ten years, sent such confusing, intense shafts of emotion through her that she doubted she'd make it to the end of the film without passing out. After all this time of telling herself it was some kind of adolescent fixation, she had to admit now that those sharp, deep feelings had still not left her. She'd used Jamie as an excuse for the lack of boyfriends in her life, not wanting to unsettle him with a string of different men. But tonight, Zoe knew she'd only been fooling herself.

And how exactly do you exorcise a ghost from the past? she asked herself. *You meet it straight on and look it deep in the eyes.* If she was ever to free herself from his invisible grasp, she had to destroy the fantasy that she had built up in her mind over the years. Meeting him again in the flesh, studying him for signs of imperfection, was the only hope of a cure. Besides, there was every chance he would have forgotten who she was by now. It had been a long time ago and he met so many people, especially women.

The lights came up with a roar of applause. Zoe gripped the seat with her hands, holding herself in it so she would not run away. Marcus kissed her cheek and squeezed her arm tightly.

"You were great, sis, seriously. Want a part in my new film?" he added.

"Thanks." Zoe sat paralyzed as those around her began to make their way out of the auditorium, all her earlier resolution leaving her.

"Shall we go straight home? My stomach really isn't good," she said as they finally stood up and followed the crowd outside.

"Surely you need to glad-hand for a bit? Suck up the praise? I was chatting to Jane Donohue while I was waiting for you to reappear from the loo and we agreed to meet at the after-party."

"Marcus, you promised! Take me home now, please. I'm really not well."

"Okay," he sighed. "I'll just go and find Jane to explain."

Zoe stood in the crowd, counting the seconds until Marcus returned and she could leave. Then she felt a tap on her shoulder.

"Zoe?"

She turned round, and felt the blood rush to her face. There he was, looking a little older, with a few creases beneath his warm green eyes, laughter lines etched into the skin on either side of his mouth. But his body seemed as trim in his dinner suit as it had been more than a decade ago. She gazed at him, thirstily drinking in every detail.

"How are you?"

She cleared her throat. "Well, thank you."

"You look . . . stunning. You're even more beautiful than you were." He spoke in hushed tones, leaning forward slightly to reach her ear. She smelled his scent, so familiar and frighteningly intoxicating. "And I enjoyed the film, by the way. I thought you were excellent."

"Thanks," she managed.

"Sir . . ." A gray-suited man appeared next to him and indicated his watch.

"I'll be along in a few minutes."

The gray suit melted back into the crowd.

"It's been so long," he said wistfully.

"Yes."

"How have you been?"

"Fine. Just fine."

"I read about your grandfather. Nearly wrote to you but I didn't know your, er, circumstances." He looked at her askance and she shook her head.

"I'm not attached," she said, then hated herself for admitting it to him.

"Look, I have to run, I'm afraid. Could I . . . call you, maybe?"

"I . . ."

The gray suit was approaching once more.

He reached out a hand to touch her cheek but stopped himself a whisper away from her skin.

"Zoe . . . I . . ." The pain was visible in his eyes. "Goodbye." With a resigned wave he was gone.

She stood in the crowded foyer, oblivious to everything except his walking away from her, leaving her for matters that took priority—just as they always had and always would. Yet her treacherous heart rejoiced.

Zoe stumbled back to the ladies' powder room to recover her composure. As she stared at her reflection in the mirror, she could see that the light in her eyes, which had flickered off so abruptly over ten years ago, had started burning once more.

Marcus was kicking his heels outside in the foyer. "Blimey, you *do* have a problem. Going to make it home?"

Zoe smiled and linked her arm through his. "Of course I am."

THE WHITE KNIGHT

The knight, with its L-shaped moves,

is the most unpredictable of pieces

5

Joanna was late again. Jutting both elbows out, she jabbed her way through the press of bodies on the bus and leapt onto the pavement at Kensington High Street just before the doors shut. Passing the identikit businessmen in black and gray suits and holding designer briefcases, she broke into a run, the cold morning air biting at her skin. Checking her watch, Joanna upped her pace. It had been a while since she had gone for a run, choosing instead to sit on the sofa and eat ice cream with *EastEnders* on the telly. At home in Yorkshire, she used to run five miles a day—up hills no less—and although she had tried to keep up the regimen in London, it simply wasn't the same. She missed the pure air of the moors, the glimpses of hares and peregrine falcons. The most exciting wildlife to see in London was a pigeon that still had both of its legs.

Joanna arrived wheezing at the front of the *Morning Mail* building. She stumbled through the glass doors and flashed her pass at Barry, the security guard, seated behind the desk.

"Hi, Jo. Cutting it fine, aren't you?"

She gave him a grimace and leapt into the open elevator, hoping that she wasn't sweating too much. At last, at ten past the hour, she collapsed at her overflowing desk and searched among the paperwork for her keyboard. She glanced up—no one seemed to have noticed her late appearance. Switching on her computer, she dumped the newspapers, magazines, old copy, unanswered letters, and photos in her in-tray. Telling herself she'd stay late one night this week to clear things up, she took an apple out of her bag and began to open her post.

Dear Miss Haslem . . .

"Spelled wrongly," she muttered.

I wanted to write and thank you for the nice piece you did about my son who had his Airfix model plane glued to his cheek. I was wondering whether I could ask you for a copy of the photograph that appeared with the article . . .

Joanna put the letter in the in-tray, bit into her apple, and opened the next one, an invitation to the launch of a "revolutionary" kind of sanitary towel. "Pass," she murmured, throwing that into the in-tray too.

The next was a large, creased brown envelope, addressed in spidery writing so indecipherable she was amazed it had even reached her. She tore it open and took out its contents. There were two further envelopes inside, with a piece of notepaper clipped to them.

Dear Miss Haslam,

I am the lady you helped home from the church a few days ago. I would like you to come to my apartment urgently as I don't have long now. I have enclosed two envelopes for you in the meantime, just in case. Keep them close to you at all times until we meet again. I'll have more for you when you come.

I am warning you, this is dangerous, but I feel you are a young woman of integrity, and the story must be told. If I have already gone, then you must talk to the White Knight's Lady. It's all I can tell you now. I pray you are in time.

I am waiting for you here.

I trust you, Joanna.

The signature beneath the writing was illegible.

Joanna read, then reread the letter, chewing thoughtfully on the apple. Throwing the core into the bin, she opened the smaller brown envelope and drew out a piece of cream vellum notepaper that crackled with age as she unfolded it. She scanned the page. It was a letter, written in ink in a flowing, old-fashioned hand. There was no date or address at the top.

My darling Sam,

I sit here, pen in hand, and wonder how I can begin to describe how I am feeling. A few months ago, I did not know you, did not know how my life would be changed, altered beyond recognition when I met you. Even though I accept we have no future—in fact, no past that any other can discover—I yearn for your touch. I need you beside me, sheltering me, loving me the way that only you can.

I live a lie and that lie will last for eternity.

I don't know for how much longer it is safe to write, but I put my trust in the loyal hands that will deliver my words of love to you.

Reply in the usual way.

Your true, true love.

The letter was signed with an initial. It could have been a "B," or an "E," an "R" or an "F"—Joanna could not decide. She breathed out, feeling the intensity of the words. Who was it to? Who was it from? There seemed to be no clues, other than that it was obviously a clandestine love affair. Joanna then opened the other envelope and drew out an old program.

The Hackney Empire is proud to present
THE GRAND AGE OF MUSIC HALL

The date was October 4, 1923. She opened the program and scanned through the acts, looking for names she recognized. Sir James Harrison, possibly, as his memorial was where she'd first met the old lady, or perhaps the old lady herself was one of the young actresses. She studied the faded black-and-white photographs of the performers, but there was no name or face that caught her eye.

She picked up the love letter again and reread it. She could only surmise she was looking at a letter written by someone who was, at the time, well-known enough for the affair to cause a scandal.

As the old lady had presumed, it had whetted her journalist's appetite. Joanna rose from her desk and photocopied both letters several times, then tucked them, along with the originals and the program, safely back into the innocuous brown envelope, which she slid into her rucksack before heading for the elevator.

"Jo! Over here!"

Alec caught her just as she was escaping to freedom through the door. She hesitated before walking back toward his desk.

"Where you off to? Got a job for you, doorstepping the Redhead and her lover. And don't think I didn't see you slink in here late."

"Sorry, Alec. I'm going to check out a story."

"Yeah? What?"

"It's a tip-off, could be good."

He looked at her, his eyes barely cleared from last night's hangover. "You got contacts already?"

"No, not really, but my gut tells me I have to go."

"Your gut, eh?" He patted his substantial belly. "One day, if you're lucky, yours'll be the same size as mine."

"Please, Alec? I did cover for you at the memorial service when I was dying."

"Okay, bugger off then. Be back by two, though. I'll send Alice to doorstep the Redhead until then."

"Thanks."

Outside, Joanna hailed a cab and directed it to Marylebone High

Street. Forty minutes later, she arrived outside the front door of the old lady's apartment. *I could have run here faster*, Joanna thought as she paid the driver, making sure to get a receipt for expenses, then she jumped out and went to study the bells by the door. She had a choice of two, both unnamed. She pressed the lower bell and waited for a response. No sound of footsteps came, so she tried again.

Nothing.

Joanna tried the top bell. Again her call went unheeded.

Once more, for luck . . .

Finally, the front door was pulled centimeters ajar.

"Who is it?" It was not the old woman's voice.

"I'm here to see the old lady who lives in the downstairs maisonette."

"She's not here anymore, I'm afraid."

"Really? Has she moved away?"

"You could say that, yes."

"Oh." Joanna physically drooped on the doorstep. "Do you know where she's gone? I got a letter from her this morning, telling me to come and see her."

The door opened a crack wider and a pair of female eyes peered out. "Who are you?" The warm brown eyes swept over Joanna's navy-blue woolen coat and jeans.

"I'm . . . her great-niece," Joanna improvised. "I've been away in Australia for months."

The eyes changed expression immediately and studied Joanna with what appeared to be sympathy. "Well then, you'd better come in."

Joanna stepped into the dark corridor and followed the woman through a door on the right of the entrance hall and into a similarly designed maisonette to that of the old lady's. Except this one was very much a home.

"Come inside." The woman beckoned her into the overwarm, cluttered sitting room and indicated a pink dralon sofa. "Make yourself comfortable."

"Thank you." Joanna watched the woman as she sat down in the chair by the gas fire. She reckoned her hostess was somewhere in her sixties, with a pleasant, open face.

"I'm Joanna Haslam, by the way," she said with a smile. "And you are?"

"Muriel, Muriel Bateman." She stared hard at Joanna. "You don't look nothing like your aunt."

"No, well, that's because . . . she married my blood great-uncle, if you see what I mean. Er, do you know where . . . Auntie is?"

"Yes, dear, I'm afraid I do." Muriel reached forward and patted her hand. "It was me that found her, see."

"*Found* her?"

Muriel nodded. "She's dead, Joanna, I'm really sorry."

"Oh. Oh no!" Joanna did not have to fake her shock. "When?"

"Last Wednesday. A week ago now."

"Bu-but, I got a letter from her this morning! How could she possibly be dead and still have sent this?" She fumbled in her bag and studied the postmark on the old woman's letter. "Look, it was sent on Monday of this week, five days after you said she died."

"Oh dear." Muriel blushed. "I'm afraid that was my fault. You see, Rose gave me the letter to post last Tuesday evening. Then, of course, with the shock of finding her the next day, and the police and all, I quite forgot about it. I didn't post it until a couple of days ago. I'm really sorry, love. I'll make some tea, shall I? You've just had a nasty shock."

Muriel came back with a tray bearing a teapot dressed in an orange tea cozy, cups, milk, sugar, and a plate of chocolate digestives. She poured the dark liquid into two cups.

"Thanks." Joanna sipped the tea as Muriel eased herself back into her chair. "Where did you find her? In bed?"

"No. At the bottom of the stairs in her entrance hall. All crumpled, like a tiny doll, she was . . ." Muriel shuddered. "I shall never forget the terror in the poor lamb's eyes . . . Sorry, dear. The whole thing's kept me awake for the past few nights."

"I'm sure it has. Poor, poor Auntie. She must have fallen down the stairs, do you think?"

"Mebbe." Muriel shrugged.

"Tell me, if you wouldn't mind, how she seemed in the past few weeks. With me being away and everything, I'm afraid I've rather lost touch."

"Well . . ." Muriel reached for a cookie and bit into it. "As I'm sure you know, your aunt had only been here for a few weeks. The maisonette next door had been empty for ages and suddenly, at the end of November, I see this frail little old lady arrive. And then, a few days later, all them tea chests—and she never got round to unpacking them. Personally, I think she knew she was a goner ages before she died . . . I'm ever so sorry, dear."

Joanna bit her lip, feeling genuine grief for the old lady, and waited for Muriel to continue.

"I didn't bother her for a few days, thought I'd let her settle in before I made myself known to her as her neighbor. But she never seemed to leave the house, so one day I knocked on the door. I was worried, see, with her being so frail and no one coming in or out of that awful, damp old place, but I got no reply. It must have been the middle of December when I heard a cry from the passage. Like a kitten it was, so weak and small. And there she was, on the floor of the passageway, in her coat an' all. She'd stumbled over her doorstep and couldn't get up. Naturally, I helped her, brought her in here, sat her down, and made her a strong cup of tea, just like I've made you today."

"If only I'd known just how frail she was," Joanna said, the lie slipping uneasily from her lips. "She always sounded so bright in her letters to me."

"If it's any comfort, we all say that after the event, dear. I had a bloomin' great big row with my Stanley and he went and dropped down dead of a heart attack the next day. Anyway, I asked your aunt where she'd moved from. She said she'd been abroad for many, many years and had only come back recently. I asked if she had relatives here and she shook her head, saying most of them were still abroad. She must have meant you, dear. Then I told her if she wanted bits of shopping done or medicines fetched for her, she only had to ask. I remember her thanking me very polite-like for my offer and asking if I'd get her some tins of soup. That's where she'd been going when she fell, see." Muriel shook her head. "I asked her whether she wanted me to call the doctor to see about her fall, but she refused. When it was time to take her back to her apartment, the poor old girl could hardly stand. I had to help her every inch of the way. Well, when I saw that miserable, miserable room that she lived in, with all them tea chests and that awful smell, I tell you, I was shocked."

"Auntie always was eccentric," Joanna threw in lamely.

"Yeah, well, excuse me for saying, but I'd reckon unhygienic, too, poor old biddy. Of course, I suggested I call social services, see if they could send someone in, get meals on wheels and a district nurse to bathe her, but she got so upset I thought she'd peg out then and there. So I left it at that, but I insisted I should have a key to her front door. I said to her, what if you was to fall again and the door was locked and I couldn't get in to help you? So she finally agreed. I promised that all I'd do was to pop in once in a while and check on her. She went on an' on about the key and keeping it safe and telling no one I had a spare." Muriel sighed and shook her head. "She was a funny old buzzard all round. More tea?"

"Yes, please. Auntie always did value her independence." Joanna gave in and reached for a chocolate digestive.

"Yeah, and look where it left her." Muriel sniffed as she topped up Joanna's cup. "Well now, I did pop in to check on her once a day from then on in. She was usually in bed, propped up with cushions, writing letters that I'd pop in the postbox for her, or sometimes dozing. I got into the habit of taking her some tea, or a Cup-a-Soup and a piece of toast. I didn't stay very long, I admit. The smell made me queasy. And then Christmas arrived. I went to see my daughter down in Southend, but I came back on Boxing Day. And sitting on the table in the passage was a card. I took it inside to open it."

Joanna leaned forward. "Was it from Auntie?"

"Yes. A beautiful Christmas card it was, you know, one of them expensive ones you buy separately and not in a pack. She'd written inside in ink, in that beautiful old-fashioned style of hers. 'Muriel, thank you for your friendship. I will treasure it always, Rose.'" Muriel wiped a tear away from her eye. "Made me cry, that card did. Your auntie must have been a lady—well educated. And to see her brought to that . . ." Muriel shook her head. "I went to knock on her door to say thank you for the card and persuaded her to come in to warm up by the fire with a mince pie."

"Thank you. You've been so kind to her."

"Least I could do. She was no bother. We had a nice chat, actually. I asked her about her family again, if she'd had kids. She turned dead pale, then shook her head and changed the subject. I didn't press her. I could see that over Christmas she'd got even weaker. There was nothing of her, just skin and bone. An' that terrible cough had got worse. Then, just after Christmas, my sister in Epping took ill and asked me if I could go and stay with her for a week to look after her. I went, of course, and got back only a couple of days before the poor old thing died."

"And she gave you the letter to post?"

"Yes. I went in to check on her the evening I arrived back. In a shocking state she was, shaking, jumpy as a cat on a hot tin roof. And her eyes . . . they had this look . . . I dunno." Muriel shivered. "Anyway, she handed me the letter, begged me to post it for her urgently. I said of course I would. Then she grabbed my hand and squeezed it, really tight, and handed me a small box. She asked me to open it, and there inside was a beautiful gold locket. Not my style, of course, too delicate for me, but you could see the workmanship was good and the gold was solid. Obviously, I said immediately I couldn't accept such an expensive gift, but she insisted I keep the locket, got really upset when I tried to give it back to her. Quite affected me it did. I went back to my own place and decided then and there that I was getting a doctor to her the next day, whatever she said. But the next day, it was too late."

"Oh, Muriel, if only I'd known . . ."

"Don't go blaming yourself. It's me that should have posted the letter immediately like she'd asked me to. But if it's any comfort to you, she passed away before it would have arrived. I found her at ten the next morning, lying at the bottom of her stairs, like I told you. Do you want a brandy? I could do with one, I tell you."

"No thanks, but you go ahead." While Muriel went into the kitchen to fix herself the drink, Joanna pondered what she had learned so far.

"I wonder what Auntie was doing at the foot of the stairs?" mused Joanna as Muriel came back. "If she was that frail, there was surely no way she could have climbed them alone?"

"That's what I told the ambulance man when he arrived," Muriel said. "He reckoned she'd broken her neck, and the big bruises on her head and her arms and legs said to him that she had fallen right the way down. I said then and there that Rose could never have got up the stairs alone. Besides"—Muriel shrugged—"why would she want to? The upstairs was deserted." She blushed slightly. "I went and had a peek once, just out of curiosity, like."

Joanna frowned. "That really is very odd."

"Isn't it just! Of course, the police had to be called and they all trooped in and started asking me lots of questions, like who she was and how long she'd lived there and stuff. The whole thing really upset me, it did. When they'd taken her away, I packed a case, called my daughter, and went to stay with her for a couple of days . . ." Muriel reached for her brandy. "I was only trying to do my best."

"Of course. Do you know where they took her?"

"To the morgue, I s'pose, to wait for someone to claim her, poor old thing."

The two women sat silently, gazing into the fire. Joanna was tempted to ask more, but could see how upset Muriel was. Eventually, she said, "I suppose I'd better go and see the apartment, decide what to do with Auntie's things."

"They've gone," said Muriel abruptly.

"What? Where?"

"I dunno. I told you I stayed down at my daughter's for a couple of days afterward. When I came back I let myself into her apartment, to lay the ghost as much as anything else, and the whole place had been emptied. There's nothing in there now, nothing at all."

"But . . . who would have taken everything? All those tea chests!"

"I thought that mebbe the family had been notified and come over to clear the place out. Have you got any family here that might have done it?"

"Er . . . no, I haven't. They're all abroad, like Rose said. There's only me here in England . . ." Joanna's voice trailed off. "Why has everything gone?"

"Search me," Muriel said. "I've still got the key. Want to go and take a look for yourself? Smell's not too bad now. Whoever took the stuff gave the place a thorough going-over with disinfectant too."

Joanna followed Muriel out of her apartment and into the passage, and watched as she unlocked the opposite door.

"Be glad when they get another tenant. A young family would be nice, breathe some life back into the place again. You don't mind if I leave you to it, do you? That place still spooks me."

"Of course not. I've disturbed you long enough anyway. Would you mind if I took your telephone number, just in case I need to get any other details?"

"I'll write it down for you. Come collect it when you drop the key back in."

Joanna stepped inside Rose's apartment, pulling the door behind her. She switched on the light and stood in the tiny entrance hall, looking up at the steep, uneven staircase to her right. And knew that the woman she had helped out of the church two weeks back was no more capable of mounting those stairs than a newborn baby. Slowly, Joanna walked up them, each step creaking noisily. At the top of the stairs was a small landing. Two deserted, damp rooms lay beyond, one on each side. She paced them, finding nothing save four walls and bare boards. Even the windows had been cleaned recently, and she looked down into a weed-filled courtyard at the back of the building. She left the room and stood on the landing, her toes on the very edge of the top step. The drop was no more than fifteen feet, but from here it seemed much, much further . . .

She walked back downstairs and entered the sitting room where Rose had lived for the last days of her life among her tea chests. She sniffed. There was still a faintly unpleasant aroma in the room, but that was all. As Muriel had said, the room had been stripped bare. Joanna got down on her hands and knees and crawled across the floorboards, looking for anything that previous eyes might have missed. Nothing.

She inspected the bathroom and the kitchen, then went and stood again in the hallway at the foot of the stairs, where Muriel had found poor Rose.

. . . I don't have long now . . . I am warning you, this is dangerous . . . If I have already gone . . .

A shiver of fear ran down Joanna's spine as she realized there was every possibility Rose had been murdered.

The question was, *why?*

———

The car parked across the street started its engine as Joanna came out of the front door. The traffic was solid all the way down Marylebone High Street. He watched her as she stood outside uncertainly for a few seconds, then turned to her left and walked off.

6

Joanna spent a long, wet afternoon in the driving rain, standing huddled with other journalists and photographers outside the Chelsea house of "the Redhead," as she was nicknamed by Joanna's fellow hacks.

The flame-haired supermodel, who was reportedly love-nesting with another female model, finally made a run for it through her front door. The flashbulbs popped as the Redhead broke through the crowd and ran for her waiting taxi.

"Right. I'm off to follow her," said Steve, Joanna's photographer. "I'll call you when I find out where she's going. My bet is the airport, so don't hold your breath."

"Okay." She watched the other photographers climbing onto their motorbikes, and the cluster of reporters dispersing into the rainy night. Groaning in frustration, she headed for Sloane Square tube station. All along King's Road, the shops were full of end-of-season sale signs—it felt as depressed with post-Christmas fatigue as she did. On the tube, she stared blankly at the advertising panels above her.

Doorstepping was such a thankless task. All that hanging around for hours, sometimes days, when you knew the most you'd get out of the person was "No comment." And it affronted her sense of basic human decency. If the Redhead wanted to have a rampaging affair with a *sheep*, for God's sake, surely it was no one's business but her own? However, as Alec constantly reminded her, there was no room for morals on the news desk of a national paper. The public had an insatiable appetite for all things salacious and sexy. The Redhead's picture on the front page tomorrow would sell an extra ten thousand copies.

At Finsbury Park, Joanna left the tube and headed for the escalator. At the top she checked her mobile. There was a short voicemail from Steve.

"I was right. She's on a plane to the States in an hour. Night."

Joanna tucked away her mobile and headed outside for the bus queue.

Too busy at work since her conversation with Muriel to think through everything she had found out, Joanna wanted to pick Simon's brain about it. She'd scribbled everything she could remember down on her notepad on the journey back and prayed there was nothing she'd forgotten.

Eventually, the bus arrived near Simon's apartment building. Joanna alighted, then walked briskly along the street, so lost in her thoughts she didn't notice a man melt into the shadows behind her.

Simon's apartment was on the top floor of a large converted villa at the crest of Highgate Hill, with wonderful views over the green spaces and rooftops of North London. He'd bought it two years ago, saying that what it lacked in square footage on the inside was more than made up for by the feeling of space on the outside. Living in London was an enormous sacrifice for both of them. They still held Yorkshire in their hearts, yearning for the peace, tranquility, and emptiness of the moors on which they had been raised, which was probably why they had both ended up only a ten-minute bus ride apart in a leafy outpost of London. Joanna envied his view here, but was content in her own quirky little apartment at the bottom of the hill in cheaper Crouch End. Granted, double glazing and a decent bathroom suite were luxuries her cantankerous landlord had never bothered with, but her neighbors were kind and quiet, which was worth a great deal in London.

Joanna rang the buzzer and the security lock opened. She trudged up the seventy-six stairs and, panting, arrived on the small landing that led to his home. The door was open, delicious cooking smells wafting out, with the sound of Fats Waller on the CD player.

"Hi."

"Jo, come in," Simon called from the small kitchen in one corner of the open-plan space.

Joanna plonked a bottle of wine down on the breakfast bar that separated the kitchen and the sitting room. Simon, face pink from the rising steam of a saucepan he was stirring, put down his wooden spoon and came to give her a hug.

"How are we?"

"Er . . . fine. Just fine."

He held her by the shoulders and looked at her. "Still pining for that idiot?"

"A little, yes. But I'm much, much better than I was. *Really.*"

"Good. Heard from him at all?"

"Not a word. I've put all his stuff in four rubbish sacks and left them in my entrance hall. If he doesn't come for them in the next month, they're going to the dump. I brought some wine."

"Well done on both counts." Simon nodded, reaching up into a cupboard above him to retrieve two glasses, and handing her a corkscrew. She opened the bottle and poured a healthy amount of wine into both of the glasses.

"Cheers." Joanna toasted him and took a sip. "How are you?"

"Good. Sit down and I'll serve the soup."

She sat at the table by the window, and glanced out at the spectacular skyline of buildings that formed the City of London to the south of them, their high, red-lit rooftops glowing in the distance.

"What I'd give to actually see the stars again, without any of this light pollution." Simon placed a dish of soup in front of her.

"I know. I'm planning to go home to Yorkshire for Easter. Fancy coming up with me?"

"Maybe. I'll see what's on at work."

"God, this is good," Joanna said as she hoovered up the thick black-bean soup. "I think you should forget about the civil service and open a restaurant."

"Absolutely not. Cooking is my pleasure, my hobby, and my sanity after a long day in the nuthouse. Speaking of which, how's your work?"

"Fine."

"Not stumbled on a major scandal recently then? Discovered a famous soap star has changed her perfume?"

"No." Joanna shrugged good-naturedly. She knew Simon had a passionate dislike for the tabloids. "But there is something I want to discuss with you."

"Really?" He wandered into the kitchen, put the soup bowls in the sink, and took out an exquisite-looking rack of lamb, with roasted vegetables, that had been resting in the oven.

"Yes. A little mystery I managed to stumble on. It could be something, or nothing." She watched as he filled two plates, then ferried the steaming food over to the table, accompanied by a jug of aromatic *jus*.

"*Voilà, mademoiselle.*" Simon came to sit opposite her.

Joanna doused her lamb liberally with the rich *jus*, then forked up a mouthful. "Wow! This is delicious."

"Thanks. So, what's the story?"

"Let's enjoy eating first, shall we? It's so weird and complicated that I need my full concentration to even know where to begin."

"Sounds intriguing." Simon raised an eyebrow.

After supper, Joanna washed up while Simon made coffee. Then she sat down in an armchair and curled her legs underneath her.

"Okay. Shoot. I'm all ears," said Simon, handing her a mug and sitting down too.

"Remember the day you came round to the apartment, and I was so distraught about Matthew dumping me? And I told you I'd been to Sir James Harrison's memorial service and sat next to that little old lady who almost keeled over, and who I had to help home?"

"Yes. The one who lived in a room full of tea chests."

"Exactly. Well, this morning at work, I received an envelope from her and . . ."

Joanna went through the day's events as chronologically and carefully as she could. Simon sat listening attentively, sipping his coffee every now and then.

"Whichever way you look at it, her death points to one thing," she finished.

"And that is?"

"Murder."

"That's a very dramatic assumption, Jo."

"I don't think it is. I stood at the top of the stairs she fell down. There is just no way that Rose could have got up them by herself. And why should she want to? The top floor was completely deserted."

"In these situations you have to think as laterally as you can. For example, have you considered that this old dear's quality of life was such that she really couldn't stand it any longer? Surely, the logical explanation is that she somehow managed to drag herself upstairs and committed suicide?"

"But what about the letter she sent me? And the theater program?"

"Have you brought them with you?"

"Yes." Joanna rifled through her rucksack and drew out the envelope. She opened it and passed Rose's letter to him.

Simon scanned it quickly. "And the other?"

"Here." Joanna handed the love letter to him. "Be careful. The paper's delicate."

"Of course." Simon slid it out of its envelope and read that too.

"Well, well," he murmured. "Fascinating. Absolutely fascinating." He brought the letter closer to his eyes and studied it. "Have you noticed these?"

"What?"

Simon handed her the letter and pointed to what he'd seen. "Look, all round the edge there are tiny holes."

Joanna looked and saw he was right. "How odd. They look like pinpricks."

"Yes. Pass the program, Jo."

She did so and he studied it for a while, then put it back down on the coffee table.

"So, Sherlock, what do you deduce?" she asked.

Simon rubbed his nose, as he always did when he was thinking. "Well . . . there is a chance that the old biddy was off her trolley. That letter could have easily been something written to her from an admirer, of absolutely no importance at all. Except to her, of course. Maybe her lover was an act in the music hall or something."

"But why send them to me?" Joanna looked doubtful. "Why say it was 'dangerous'? Rose's letter is pretty intelligently composed for someone who's supposedly lost their marbles."

"All I'm trying to do is to suggest alternatives."

"And if there are no plausible ones?"

Simon leaned forward and grinned at her. "Then, my dear Watson, it seems we have a mystery on our hands."

"I'm convinced that Rose wasn't mad, Simon. I'm also certain she was terrified of someone or something. But where on earth do I go from here?" Joanna sighed. "I was thinking that maybe I should show this to Alec at work, see what he thinks."

"No," Simon said firmly. "You haven't got enough yet. I think the first thing you have to do is establish who Rose *was*."

"How on earth do I do that?"

"You could start by going down to the local cop shop and spinning the same story you spun to Muriel, about being the great-niece just back from the land of koalas. They'll probably point you in the direction of the morgue, if she's not already been buried by her family, that is."

"She told Muriel her family were all abroad."

"Someone must have taken those tea chests away. The police may well have traced her relatives," Simon pointed out.

"Even if they have, it seems odd that those rooms were swept clean within forty-eight hours. Besides, I can hardly go down to the police station in search of an aunt whose surname I don't know."

"Course you can. You can say she lost touch with the family years ago, that she may have remarried since and you're not sure what surname she might go under now."

"Good one. Okay, I'll do that as soon as I can."

"Fancy a brandy?"

Joanna checked her watch. "No. I'd better be on my way home."

"Want me to spin you down the hill?"

"I'll be fine, thanks. It's a dry night and the walk will help work off my massive supper." She placed the letter and the program back in their envelopes and stuffed them into her rucksack. Then she stood up and headed for the door. "Another culinary triumph, Simon. And thanks for the advice."

"Anytime. But just watch yourself, Jo. You never know what you might have stumbled across by accident."

"I doubt my little old lady's tea chests contain the prototype to a nuclear bomb that could start World War Three, but I will," she laughed as she kissed Simon on the cheek. "Night."

Twenty minutes later, feeling better for the brisk walk down to Crouch End, Joanna put the key into the lock of her front door. Closing the door, she groped along the wall for the light switch, and flicked it on. She walked into the sitting room and let out a gasp of horror.

The room had been ransacked—there was no other word for it. Her floor-to-ceiling bookshelf had been tipped forward and hundreds of books were scattered across the floor. The lime-green sofa had been knifed, the material covering both frame and cushions violently ripped to pieces. Plant pots were overturned, the soil spilling out onto the floor, and her collection of old Wedgwood plates smashed in the fireplace.

Choking back a sob, Joanna ran through to the bedroom to find a similar scene. Her mattress had been ripped apart and flung aside, the divan underneath slashed and ruined, her clothes torn from the cupboards and drawers. In the bathroom, her pills and potions and makeup had been opened and flung into the bath, forming a colorful, congealing mess that any modern artist might have been proud of. The floor of the kitchen was a sea of milk, orange juice, and broken crockery.

Joanna ran back to the sitting room, huge, guttural sobs emanating from somewhere inside her. She reached for the telephone and discovered the wire had been wrenched out of the wall. Shaking violently, she searched through the wreckage to discover where she had left her rucksack and found it still in the hall by the door. Delving inside, she pulled out her mobile phone and, with fingers that shook so hard she dialed the wrong number three times, she finally reached Simon.

He found her standing in the hall ten minutes later, shaking and sobbing uncontrollably.

"Jo, I'm so sorry." He pulled her to him, but she was too hysterical to be comforted.

"Go in there!" she shouted. "See what the bastards have done! They've destroyed everything, *everything*! There's nothing left, nothing!"

Simon stepped into the sitting room and took in the devastation, before moving into the bedroom, bathroom, and kitchen. "Jesus," he muttered under his breath, stepping over the detritus to return to Joanna in the hall. "Have you called the police like I told you to?"

Joanna nodded and sank down onto the heap of Matthew's clothes that had spilled out of one of the slashed black bin bags in a corner of the hall.

"Did you notice whether they've actually taken anything? Your TV, for instance?" he asked gently.

"No, not really."

"I'll go check."

Simon was back a few minutes later. "They've taken the TV, VCR, your computer and printer . . . the lot."

Joanna shook her head in despair as they both saw the blue lights of a police car flashing through the glazed panel in the front door.

Simon stepped past her to open the door and went out to greet the police on the path outside. "Hello, Officer. I'm Simon Warburton." He dug in his pocket and produced an identity card.

"That kind of a job, is it, sir?" the officer asked.

"No, I'm a friend of the victim and she is . . . er . . . unaware of my position," he whispered.

"Righto, sir. I get your drift."

"I just wanted a word before you go in. This was a most frenzied and violent attack. The lady was out at the time, thank God, but I would suggest that you take this seriously and do as much as you can to find the culprit, or culprits, as the case may be."

"Of course, sir. Lead the way, then."

An hour later, after Joanna had been temporarily calmed by the brandy Simon had brought from his apartment, and had given as clear a statement to the police as her dazed brain would elicit, Simon suggested he take her to his place for what was left of the night.

"Best to leave the clearing up till the morning, I reckon, love," said the police officer.

"He's right, Jo. Come on, let's get you out of here." Simon put an arm round her shoulders and led her out of the front door, down the path, and into his car. She slumped into the front seat. Climbing into the driver's seat, he turned on the engine. As he pulled out from the curb, his headlights caught the license plate of a car parked on the other side of the road. *How very odd*, he thought as he swung the car left, and glanced into the darkened interior of the vehicle. It was probably just coincidence, he told himself, as he drove up the hill toward his apartment.

But he'd check it out tomorrow anyway.

7

The telephone rang just as Zoe had finished mopping the floor.

"Damn!" She sprinted across the kitchen, her footprints appearing on the damp tiles, and reached the phone just before the answering machine clicked on.

"I'm here," she said breathlessly, hopefully.

"It's me."

"Oh, hi, Marcus."

"Don't sound so pleased to hear from me, will you?"

"Sorry."

"I'm only returning your call, anyway," he pointed out.

"Yes. Do you want to pop round this evening for a drink?"

"Sure. Have you spoken to Dad?"

"Yes."

"And?"

"Tell you later," she replied distractedly.

"Okay. See you around seven."

Zoe slammed the receiver down and let out a howl of frustration. Time was running short. Next week she was off on location to Norfolk to begin shooting *Tess*. He only had the Welbeck Street landline number—neither of them had had mobile phones all those years ago—and if her grandfather had answered the phone, he'd called himself "Sid"; she couldn't remember exactly why, but they'd both giggled about it.

The fact that she wasn't going to *be* in London to answer it, coupled with the fact that she'd be in a small Norfolk village where he'd be so horribly noticeable, meant he wouldn't come to visit her anyway. And then it would drift and the moment would be gone. Zoe didn't think she could stand it.

"Please, *please* ring," she begged the telephone.

She glanced at her reflection in the corner of a mirror and sighed. She looked pale and drained. She'd done what she always did in times of high tension and crisis: she'd cleaned and scrubbed and polished and dusted manically, trying to wear herself out to keep herself from dwelling on the situation.

And . . . she had begun to realize she was totally unused to being alone, which wasn't helping either. Up until two months ago, there'd always been James to talk to. God, she missed him. And Jamie. She was only grateful that she *had* done as James had asked and accepted the part of Tess, especially as the call she so longed for looked more and more unlikely as each day passed.

Marcus rang the doorbell at half past seven that evening and Zoe greeted him at the door.

"'Lo, Zo."

She eyed him. "You been drinking?"

"Only a couple, honest."

"A couple of bottles from the looks of you." Zoe led Marcus into the sitting room. "Coffee to sober you up?"

"Whiskey if you've got it."

"Fine." Too weary to argue, Zoe went to the drinks cabinet, an ugly antique walnut thing, with heavy cabriole legs that she was always tripping over—and probably worth a fortune. She had to remember to call an assessor and update the inventory of the house contents for insurance, now that James was gone. Maybe she could sell some of the finer pieces to aid the house renovation. Finding the whiskey, she filled a tumbler a quarter full and handed it to her brother.

"Come on, sis. That's a bit of a stingy measure."

"Help yourself then," Zoe said, handing him the whiskey bottle and pouring herself a gin and tonic. "I'll just go and get some ice. Want some?"

"No thanks." He topped up the tumbler and waited for Zoe to return.

"Making yourself at home, then?" He motioned to the different art pieces on the wall.

"I just moved a couple of pictures down here from my bedroom to brighten the room up."

"Nice to have a legacy like this," he muttered.

"Not that again! Marcus, I hate to remind you, but Dad did give you enough money to rent your very nice apartment in Notting Hill a few years ago. On top of funding your many film projects."

"Fair point," Marcus agreed. "So, tell me what you and he discussed the other night."

"Well"—Zoe curled up on the sofa—"even though you've been totally ungracious over the business of the will, I can understand how you've felt."

"That's very perceptive of you, sister dear."

"Don't patronize me, Marcus. I'm only trying to help."

"I would have said you're the one doing the patronizing, sweetheart."

"Christ! You are so bloody impossible! Now, just shut up for five minutes, while I explain how I might be able to help."

"All right, all right. Go on, then."

"To be fair, I think the deal has always been that you were looked after financially by Dad, while Jamie and I were taken care of by James. And because I'm raising Jamie by myself, I think James wanted to make absolutely sure that whatever happened, we'd both be okay."

"Maybe," Marcus grunted.

"So"—Zoe took a sip of her gin—"given all the money's in trust for Jamie, there's only one area of the will from which I can legally and honestly extract some dosh for you."

"And that is?"

Zoe sighed. "I don't think you're going to like this, but it really is the best I can do."

"Come on then, shoot."

"Do you remember at the reading of the will, the bit at the end about the memorial fund?"

"Vaguely—although by then I was about to blow a gasket."

"Well, it's basically an amount held in trust to provide fees for drama school each year for one talented male and one female actor."

"Oh. You're going to suggest I use that and go back to college, are you?" Marcus quipped.

Zoe ignored him. "What Dad and I are suggesting is that we put you in charge of the trust and pay you a good salary to organize and administer it."

Marcus stared at her. "Is that it?"

"Yes. Oh, Marcus!" Zoe shook her head in frustration. "I knew you'd react like this! We're offering you something that will only take up a couple of months a year, maximum, but will at least give you a regular income while you try to get your film going. Yes, you'll need to do the initial promotion and get the media interested in it to help encourage applications. Then there'll have to be a week or so of auditions in front of a panel of your choice—I'm happy to come—and some administration, but really, it's money for old rope. You could do it standing on your head."

There was silence from Marcus, so Zoe decided to play her trump card. "It'll also make those that have doubted you in the film business stand up and take notice, help your reputation *and* the young future of British theater. There's no reason why you can't use the media coverage to raise your own profile and that of your production company."

Marcus raised his head and looked at her. "How much?"

"Dad and I thought thirty thousand a year. I know it's not the amount you need," she added hastily, "but it's not bad for a few weeks' work. And you can have the first year's salary up front if you want."

Zoe pointed at the folder on the table. "All the details on the trust and the amount we have to invest in it are explained in there. Take it home and have a look at it. You don't have to decide now."

He leaned forward and fingered the folder. "That's awfully kind of you, Zoe. I thank you for your generosity."

"That's okay." Zoe didn't know whether Marcus was being grateful or sarcastic. "I've really tried to sort something out for you. I know it's not the hundred grand you wanted, but you know that will come eventually."

Marcus stood up, sudden rage pounding through him as he glared at his sister's smooth, smug face. "Tell me, Zoe, where do you get off?"

"What?"

"You sit there and look *down* on me: the poor sinner who's lost his way but can be rescued with a bit of time and patience. And yet, *and yet*"—Marcus threw up his hands in disbelief—"it's *you* who's messed up, *you* who got pregnant at eighteen! So unless it really was the bloody immaculate conception, I'd reckon you know more about sin than I do."

Zoe's face drained of color. She stood up, shaking with anger.

"How dare you insult me and Jamie like that! I know you're angry, and desperate, and almost certainly depressed, too, but I really have tried to do everything I can to help. Well, this is where I get off. I've had it up to here with your pathetic self-pity. Now *get lost*!"

"Don't worry, I'm going." He headed for the door. "And you can stick your sodding memorial fund where the sun don't shine!"

Zoe heard the door slam behind him, and burst into tears. She was crying so hard that she only just heard the sound of the telephone ringing. The answering machine took the call.

"Er, hello, Zoe. It's me. I . . ."

She virtually vaulted off the sofa and sprinted into the kitchen to pick up the receiver. "I'm here, Art." His nickname was out of her mouth before she could stop herself.

"How are you?"

Zoe looked at her tear-stained reflection in the glass kitchen cabinets and said, "I'm well, very well."

"Good, good. Er, I was wondering, would it be too rude to invite myself to your place for a drink? You know how it is with me and I'd love to see you, Zoe, I really would."

"Of course. When would you like to come?"

"Friday evening, maybe?"

"Perfect."

"Around eight?"

"Suits me."

"Right then. I look forward to it. Good night, Zoe. Sleep well."

"Night." She put down the receiver slowly, not sure whether to carry on crying or to whoop for joy.

She chose the latter. Doing an Irish jig round the kitchen, she made mental plans to spend tomorrow beautifying herself. Hairdresser's and clothes shops were most definitely on the agenda.

Contemplating her complete and utter *shit* of a brother was not.

8

Marcus had fallen out of Zoe's house in Welbeck Street and ended up in some seedy Oxford Street nightclub, where he'd met a girl who—he'd been convinced at the time—was the image of Claudia Schiffer. When he'd woken up the following morning and glanced at the face next to him, he'd realized just how out of his mind he'd been. The bright makeup had slid down her face, and the dark roots of her peroxide hair were prominent against the white pillow she lay on. She'd lisped something in a heavy accent about taking the day off from work to spend it with him.

He'd gone to the bathroom and promptly been very ill indeed. He'd showered, trying to clear the cobwebs from his head, and groaned when he remembered just exactly what he had said to his sister last night. He was a first-class, low-down, rotten pig.

Insisting the woman in his bed refrain from playing truant from her job, he'd bundled her out of the apartment, and drunk large amounts of black coffee that burned in his acidic, complaining stomach. Then he'd decided to take a walk in Holland Park.

It was a crisp, frosty day, and the weathermen were predicting snow. Marcus walked briskly along the hedged footpaths, the ponds murky and still in the cold sunshine. Marcus pulled his jacket around him, glaring at anyone who made eye contact with him. Not so much as a squirrel dared approach him.

He let the lump in his throat turn to tears. He really didn't like himself anymore. Zoe had only been trying to help and he'd treated her appallingly. It had been the booze talking, yet again. And maybe she was right—perhaps he *was* depressed.

In retrospect, was what Zoe had offered him really so awful? As she'd said, it was money for old rope. He had no idea how much was actually in the memorial fund, but he'd bet it was substantial. He then pictured himself in the role of generous benefactor, not only to students, but maybe to struggling theaters and young filmmakers. He would become known in the business as a man with sensitivity, insight, and money to spend. And his mother would have most definitely approved of the project.

There was no doubt he could do with a regular income. Perhaps it would mean he could begin to take better control of his finances, live within a budget, then use his £100,000 legacy to put into his film company.

All he had to do was grovel to Zoe. And he'd mean it too.

After leaving his sister to simmer down for a couple of days, Marcus decided to call unannounced at Welbeck Street on Friday evening. Bunch of roses in hand—the last ones left at the corner shop—he rang the bell.

Zoe answered it almost immediately. Her face fell when she saw him.

"What are you doing here?"

He stared at his sister's subtly made-up face, her freshly washed blond hair shining like a halo. She was wearing a royal-blue velvet dress that matched her eyes and revealed rather a lot of leg.

"Blimey, Zo, expecting company?"

"Yes . . . no . . . I mean, I have to go out in ten minutes."

"Okay, this won't take long, I promise. Can I come in?"

She seemed agitated. "Sorry, but this really isn't a good time."

"I understand. I'll say what I need to here. I was a total pig to you the other night and I am truly, truly sorry. I'm not excusing myself, but I was very drunk. Over the past two days I've done some serious thinking. And realized that I've taken my anger and frustration at myself out on you. I promise I won't do it again. I'm going to get my act together—stop drinking. I've got to, haven't I?"

"Yes, you have," Zoe replied distractedly.

"I've seen the error of my ways and I'd love to take over the memorial fund if you'll still let me. It's a great opportunity, and now that I've calmed down, I can see how generous it is of you and Dad to trust me with it. Here." He thrust the flowers into her hands. "These are for you."

"Thanks."

Marcus watched as her eyes darted up and down the street. "So, do you forgive me?"

"Yes, yes, of course I do."

Marcus was staggered. He'd planned on a night of serious mea culpa–ing while Zoe extracted her rightful pound of flesh.

"Thanks, Zoe. I swear I won't let you down."

"Fine." Zoe surreptitiously glanced down at her watch. "Look, can we discuss this another time?"

"As long as you actually believe I'm going to change. Shall I come over next week to discuss it?"

"Yes."

"Okay. Do you have that folder handy by any chance? I thought I could take it home and study it over the weekend, think up some ideas."

"Okay." Zoe flew inside, took the folder out of James's desk, and ran back to the front door. "There."

"Thanks, Zo. I won't forget this. I'll call you tomorrow to make a date."

"Yes. Night."

The door was shut hurriedly in his face. Marcus whistled in relief, amazed at how easy it had been. He walked off along the road humming, as the first few flakes of snow began to descend on the streets of London.

"Evening, Warburton. Do sit down." Lawrence Jenkins, Simon's boss, indicated a chair placed in front of his desk. He was slim and dapper, dressed in an immaculate Savile Row suit, and wore a different-colored paisley bow tie for every day of the week. Today it was bright red. He had a natural air of authority, indicating he had been in the job for a long time, and wasn't someone to be easily crossed. His customary black coffee was steaming gently in front of him.

"Now, it seems you might be able to help us with a little problem that's come up."

"I'll do my best, as always, sir," Simon replied.

"Good chap. I hear your girlfriend had a bit of bother the other night at her apartment? Apparently it was ransacked."

"Not my girlfriend, sir, but a very close friend."

"Ah. So you're not . . . ?"

"No."

"Good. That makes the situation a little easier."

Simon frowned. "What exactly do you mean?"

"The thing is, we believe your friend may have been passed some—how shall I put it?—very delicate information, which, if it fell into the wrong hands, could cause us problems." Jenkins's hawklike eyes appraised Simon. "Have you any idea what this something might be?"

"I . . . no, sir. I have no idea. Can you elucidate?"

"We are pretty certain that your friend has received a letter that was posted to her by a person of interest to us. Our department has been instructed to retrieve that letter as soon as possible."

"I see."

"It's very likely she doesn't appreciate its significance."

"Which is what? If I may ask."

"Classified, I'm afraid, Warburton. Rest assured, if she does have it, it is absolutely imperative she returns it forthwith."

"To whom, sir?"

"To us, Warburton."

"Are you saying you want me to ask her if she has it?"

"I would try a less blatant tactic than that. She's staying with you at the moment, isn't she?"

"Yes." Simon looked at him in surprise.

"We checked her apartment over a couple of days ago, and the letter wasn't there."

"Tore it to pieces more like," he commented angrily.

"Needs must, I'm afraid. Of course, we'll make sure her insurance company is generous. Now, given it wasn't there, I would suggest that if she does have it, it may well be on her person, possibly at your apartment. Rather than subject her to more unpleasantness, I thought I could leave it to you to retrieve it for us. Rather fortuitous, really, you being her . . . friend. She trusts you, I presume?"

"Yes. It's what most friendships are based on, sir." Simon could not help the sarcasm that dripped unsolicited from his tongue.

"Then for now I'll leave it to you to sort out. Unfortunately, if you don't, then others must. Warn her off, Warburton, for good and for all. It really would be in her best interests to desist from further investigation. Righto, that's everything."

"Thank you, sir."

Simon left the office, angry and confused at being put in an impossible position. He walked back through the maze of corridors to his own section and sat down at his desk.

"You've been to see Jenkins?" Ian, one of his colleagues, came and perched on the corner of it.

"How did you know?"

"It's the glazed look in your eyes, the slightly slackened jaw." Ian smirked. "I think you need a good stiff gin to help you recover. The boys are having a shindig over at the Lord George."

"I was wondering why it was deserted in here."

"It is Friday evening." Ian shrugged on his coat.

"I might join you later. I have some bits and pieces to tidy up."

"Okay. Night."

"Night."

Ian left, and Simon sighed, rubbing his face with his hands. Admittedly, the conversation had not been much of a surprise. He'd already been aware that there was something odd about Joanna's burglary. Yesterday, at lunchtime, he'd gone to the car pool, smiled sweetly at the receptionist, and handed her the letters of the license plate he'd spotted outside Joanna's apartment the night before.

"Pranged it, I'm afraid. Only slightly, but it's going to need some minor repairs, although it's nothing urgent."

"Okay." The receptionist looked up the registration number on her computer. "There we are. Gray Rover, yes?"

"Yes."

"Right, I'll just get you a form. Fill it in and bring it back to me, then we'll process it."

"Will do. Thanks a lot."

The fact he'd known the license plate belonged to one of their fleet of cars was sheer coincidence. His own work car was N041 JMR. The number he'd seen on Wednesday night was N042 JMR. The chances were that the car pool had bought in quantity at the same time and that the license plates had been in numerical order.

Simon stared at his computer screen blankly, and decided to go home. Pulling on his coat, he waved a goodbye to the stragglers in the office who hadn't gone to the Lord George, then took the elevator down and exited Thames House through a side door. Deciding to take a stroll down the river before heading back to the apartment, he looked up at the austere gray building, many of the office windows lit up as agents completed paperwork. Long ago, he'd lost any guilt about lying to his friends and family about his job. Only Joanna took any interest in his work, and he made sure to make his tales of working at Whitehall as dreary as possible to dissuade her from asking further questions.

Given what Jenkins had said, it would no longer be so easy to put her off the scent. If this was now being handled by his department, he knew whatever it was Joanna had stumbled on was major.

And equally, that she was in danger as long as she had that letter.

———

As Joanna stirred the Bolognese sauce on Simon's hob, she watched the snow fall in fat white flakes from the panoramic window of his apartment. She remembered how, when she was a child up on the moors, the farmers had dreaded the snow, knowing it would mean long, hard nights rounding up the flocks of sheep and taking them to the safety of the barns, then the sad job of digging out those they'd missed a couple of days later. For Joanna, snow had meant fun and no school, sometimes for days, until the narrow lanes around her farmhouse had been plowed and were once more passable. Tonight, she wished she was once again snuggled up in her cozy attic bedroom, safe and untroubled by adult pressures.

When she had woken up on the morning after the burglary, Simon had insisted on calling Alec at the newspaper before he left for work. He had explained about the break-in as Joanna sat wrapped up in the duvet on the sofa bed, waiting for Alec to insist she turn up for work at the usual time. Instead, Simon had put down the receiver and said that Alec had been very sympathetic. He had even suggested that Joanna take the further three days that were owed to her from before Christmas, and use them to recover from the shock. And also set about the practical side of things, such as insurance, and the massive cleaning-up operation to make the apartment habitable again. A relieved Joanna had spent the rest of the day recuperating in bed.

This morning, Simon had sat down on the sofa bed and pulled the duvet cover off her.

"You sure you don't want to go home for a few days to your mum and dad?" he'd asked.

She'd groaned and rolled over. "No, I'm fine here. Sorry I've been moping."

"You've got every right to feel sorry for yourself, Jo, I just want to help you out. Going away might help."

"No, if I don't go back to the apartment today, it'll just haunt me."

She'd sighed. "It's like falling off a horse. You have to get straight back on, or else you never do."

The apartment had looked no better in the light of day, when she'd eventually forced herself to walk down the hill after Simon had left for work. The police had given her the all-clear, and she had passed on their report for the insurance claim. Then she'd steeled herself for the task, beginning in the kitchen, and setting to work on the stinking mess covering the floor. By lunchtime, the kitchen was back to normal—minus the crockery. The bathroom was gleaming and the sitting room had everything broken stacked neatly on the slashed sofa, waiting for the insurance assessor. To her surprise, the telephone engineer had turned up without her even contacting the company, and had rewired the line where it had been brutally ripped out of the wall.

Feeling too exhausted and miserable to contemplate the bedroom, Joanna had packed some clothes into a holdall. Simon had said he was happy for her to stay with him for as long as she felt she wanted to. And for now, she did. As she had reached down to stuff her underwear back into a drawer, Joanna had noticed something gleaming on the carpet, half hidden by a pair of jeans that had been wrenched from the wardrobe. She'd picked it up and seen it was a slim, gold fountain pen. On its side were the engraved initials *I. C. S.*

"Some classy kind of a thief," she'd muttered. Regretting having touched it and possibly disturbed the fingerprints, she'd wrapped it in tissue paper and carefully tucked it into her rucksack to hand on to the police.

Hearing the key in the lock, she poured some wine into a glass.

"Hi!" Simon walked through the door and Joanna thought how handsome he looked in his immaculate gray suit, shirt, and tie.

"Hi. Glass of wine?"

"Thanks," he said as she handed it to him. "Blimey, are you sure you're okay? You? Cooking?" he laughed.

"Only spag Bol, I'm afraid. I'm not even going to start competing with you."

"How are you?" he asked, removing his coat.

"Okay. I went to the apartment today . . ."

"Oh, Joanna, not on your own!"

"I know, but I had to sort things out for the insurance claim. And I actually feel much better having cleared it up now. Most of the mess was peripheral. Besides"—Joanna grinned and licked the wooden spoon—"at least I can get a new comfy sofa out of all this."

"That's the spirit. I'm going to take a shower."

"Okay."

Twenty minutes later, they sat down to eat the spaghetti Bolognese topped with generous amounts of Parmesan.

"Not bad, for an amateur," he quipped.

"Cheers, big ears. Wow, it's really bucketing down now," she said, glancing out of the window. "I've never seen London in the snow."

"Just means the buses, tubes, and trains will come to a grinding halt." Simon sighed. "Thank God it's Saturday tomorrow."

"Yes."

"Jo, where is Rose's letter?"

"In my rucksack. Why?"

"Can I see it?"

"Come up with something, have you?"

"No, but I have a mate who works in the forensics department at Scotland Yard. He might be able to analyze it and give us some information on the type of notepaper, the ink, and the approximate year in which it was written."

"Really?" Joanna looked surprised. "That's a pretty impressive friend."

"I knew him at Cambridge, actually."

"Oh, I see." She poured some more wine into her glass and sighed. "I don't know, Simon. Rose specifically said to keep the letter close to me, not to let it or the program out of my sight."

"Are you saying you don't trust me?"

"Of course not. I'm torn, that's all. I mean, it would be great to get some information on it, but what if it fell into the wrong hands?"

"Mine, you mean?" Simon gave her an exaggerated pout.

"Don't be silly. Look, Simon, she was murdered, I'm absolutely positive about that."

"You have no proof. A mad old dear who fell down the stairs and you're seeing *Tinker, Tailor, Soldier, Spy*."

"Hardly! You agreed with me that it sounded suspicious. What's changed?"

"Nothing . . . nothing. Okay, why don't we leave it like this? You give me the letter and I'll take it to my mate. If he comes up with anything, we'll take it from there. If not, I think you should drop the whole thing and forget about it."

Joanna took a sip of her wine, pondering the situation. "The thing is, I just don't think I *can* leave it. I mean, she trusted me. It would be a betrayal."

"You'd never met the woman before that day at the church. You've no idea who she is, where she's from, or what she might have been involved with."

"You think she might have been Europe's biggest crack-cocaine baron, do you?" Joanna giggled. "Maybe *that's* what was in those tea chests."

"Possibly." Simon smiled. "So, is that a deal? I'll take the letter into work on Monday morning and give it to my mate. I'm away on a god-awful boring seminar from Monday afternoon, but when I get back next week I'll pick the letter up and we'll see what he's had to say."

"Okay," she agreed reluctantly. "This 'mate' you know *is* trustworthy, isn't he?"

"Of course! I'll spin some story about a friend of mine wanting to trace her family heritage, that kind of thing. Do you want to go and get it, so neither of us forgets before Monday?"

"Okay," said Joanna, standing up. "It's ice cream for dessert. Can you serve it out?"

The two of them spent most of Saturday doing the remainder of the clearing up in Joanna's apartment. Her parents had sent her a check to help her buy a new computer and a bed while she waited for the insurance money to come in. She was touched by their thoughtfulness.

As Simon was going to be away for the next week at a "pen-pushing" seminar, as he joked, they'd agreed she would stay on at his apartment in Highgate.

"At least until you have a new bed to sleep in," Simon had added.

On Sunday evening, he locked himself in the bedroom, telling Joanna he had some paperwork to go through before the seminar. He dialed a number and the line was answered on the second ring.

"I have it, sir."

"Good."

"I'm at Brize Norton tomorrow at eight a.m. Can someone collect it from me there?"

"Of course."

"I'll see them in the usual place. Good night, sir."

"Yes. Job well done, Warburton. I won't forget it."

And neither will Joanna, Simon thought with a sigh. He would have to spin some excuse about the letter's being so flimsy that it had disintegrated during the chemical-analysis process. He felt awful betraying her trust.

Joanna was on the sofa watching *Antiques Roadshow* when Simon emerged from the bedroom.

"Right. All done and dusted. And let me give you a telephone number, for emergency use only, just in case you get into trouble while I'm away. You seem to be attracting it at the moment." He handed her a card.

"Ian Simpson," she read.

"A pal of mine from work. Good chap. I've given you his work and mobile numbers just in case."

"Thanks. Can you put it down by the phone so I don't lose it?"

Simon did so and sat down on the sofa next to her. Joanna put her arms round his neck and hugged him.

"Thanks, Simon, for everything."

"Don't say thanks. You're my best mate. I'll always be there for you."

She nuzzled his nose with her own, enjoying the familiarity of him, then out of the blue, felt a sudden sharp stirring low inside her. Her lips moved toward his and she closed her eyes as they kissed lightly, then deeper as their mouths opened. It was Simon who stopped it. He pulled away and leapt off the sofa.

"Jesus, Jo! What are we doing! I . . . Sarah . . . !"

Joanna hung her head. "Sorry, I'm sorry. It's not your fault, it's mine."

"No. I was as much to blame." He began to pace. "We're best friends! This kind of thing shouldn't happen, *ever*."

"No, I know. It'll never happen again, promise."

"Good . . . I mean, not that I didn't enjoy it"—he blushed—"but I'd hate to see our friendship ruined by a quick fling."

"So would I."

"Right then. I . . . I'll go and do my packing."

Joanna nodded and he left the room. She gazed at the television, the screen a blur through her damp eyes. It was probably because she was still in shock, vulnerable, and missing Matthew. She'd known Simon since childhood and even though she'd always acknowledged his good looks, the thought of taking it further had never seriously crossed her mind.

And, she promised herself, it never would.

9

On Saturday morning, Zoe lay in bed daydreaming. She glanced at the clock and saw it was half past ten. It was unheard of for her to be up later than half past eight—she usually left the badge of sloth to Jamie, who often required a forklift to get him out of bed during the holidays—but today was different.

It dawned on her that she was entering a whole new phase in her life. Up until now, she had been first a child, with natural restrictions placed on her freedom. Then she'd become a mother, a state that necessitated complete selflessness. And lately she had been a carer, helping and comforting James through his final weeks. But this morning, she realized, apart from her never-ending role as mother, she was freer than she had ever been in all her twenty-nine years. Free to live as she wished, make her own decisions *and* live with the consequences . . .

Although Art had left before eleven last night, and their lips had only met in a chaste kiss good night, she'd woken feeling wrapped up by love in the calm, contented way that one associated with a night of satisfying sex. They had barely touched, yet even the brush of his jacket against her side had sent desire tingling through her body.

When he'd arrived, they'd sat down in the sitting room and talked—at first both shy and uncertain, but soon relaxing into the easy intimacy of two people who had once known each other well. It had always been that way with Art, from the very beginning. While others around him treated him with deferential uncertainty, Zoe had seen his vulnerability, his humanity.

She remembered when they had first met, at a trendy smoke-filled club in Kensington, Marcus insisting they celebrate her eighteenth birthday with her first legal drink. Marcus had promised their grandfather that he would look out for Zoe, make sure she got home safe, but that had extended as far as Marcus's buying her a gin and tonic, and pressing some cash into her hand—"For the cab home. Don't do anything I wouldn't do!" And he'd melted into the crowd with a wink and a grin.

At a loss, she'd sat down on a bar stool and looked around her at the gaggle of people on the dance floor, laughing loudly and wrapping their bodies drunkenly around each other. James had always taken care to shield her while she was growing up, so, unlike most of her boarding school friends, she didn't have wild stories of nights out or experimenting with drugs in dimly lit toilets. Clutching the sweaty twenty-pound note Marcus had given her and feeling so uncomfortable that she decided she wanted to go home, she was just standing up from her stool when a voice stopped her.

"Oh, are you leaving? I was just about to ask if you wanted a drink."

She'd turned around to look up into a pair of dark green eyes, framed by a fringe of straight blond hair that seemed incongruous alongside the fashionable longer hair sported by the other young men in the club. He looked vaguely familiar to her, but she couldn't place him.

"No thanks," she'd said. "I'm not much of a drinker, really."

"Me neither." He'd broken into a relieved grin. "I've just shaken off my . . . er, friends. They were more keen on this place than I was. I'm Art, by the way."

"Zoe," she'd said, and had awkwardly stuck out her hand. He'd taken it in his and squeezed it briefly, sending a frisson of heat through her.

Looking back now, Zoe wondered whether, if she had recognized him then for who he really was, she would have left well alone. Would she have refused him when he'd asked her to dance with him again and again—the feel of his body pressed against hers sending all sorts of strange and wonderful sensations through her own . . . ? Then, finally, as the club was closing, allowing him to kiss her, swapping numbers, and agreeing to meet again the following evening?

No, Zoe thought firmly. She'd have made exactly the same decision.

Last night, they'd both steered clear of the past. Instead they had talked of nothing and everything, simply savoring each other's company.

Then Art had glanced at his watch regretfully. "I have to go, Zoe. I have a meet-and-greet in Northumberland tomorrow. The helicopter leaves at six thirty. You say you're filming in Norfolk for the next few weeks?"

"Yes."

"I can easily be up at our place there for a couple of nights. In fact, how about next weekend? Do you know yet where you're staying? I can have a car pick you up on Friday evening and bring you over."

Zoe had walked to the bureau and pulled out details of the small hotel where she'd be staying for the next six weeks. She wrote the information on a piece of paper and handed it to him.

"Perfect," he'd said with a smile. "I'll give you my mobile phone number too." He took a card out of his breast pocket. "Here. Please call me."

"Bye, Art. It was lovely to see you." Zoe had felt awkward, not sure how to end the evening.

"And you." And then he'd reached down for the briefest kiss. "See you next weekend. We'll have more time then. Good night, Zoe."

Eventually, Zoe got out of bed, showered, and dressed. She went shopping for groceries and came home having forgotten half of the things she'd gone out to buy. Dreamily, she played a record dating back ten years that she'd not put on the turntable since. She closed her eyes as the strains of Jennifer Rush's "The Power of Love" filled the room, the words as familiar to her now as they had been a decade ago.

On Sunday afternoon, she took a long stroll through Hyde Park, enjoying the snow-covered trees and walking on the white grass to avoid the treacherous icy paths. Returning home, she called Jamie at school. He sounded very perky, having just won a place in the under-tens' rugby A team. She gave him the number of the hotel she was staying at in Norfolk to pass on to Matron in case of emergency, and discussed where he and his friend Hugo would like to go for lunch in two weeks' time when she came to visit him. That evening, she packed much more carefully than she usually would for location filming, thinking about what she might need for next weekend. "Good underwear," she giggled, packing the La Perla set a friend had given her for Christmas, and which had never yet seen the light of day.

In bed that night, she allowed herself to consider the consequences of what she was beginning all over again. And the raw fact that, as before, there was no hope of any future.

But, Zoe thought sleepily as she turned over, *I love him*.

And love conquered all, didn't it?

———

On Monday morning, Joanna waved Simon off to work, relieved at his departure. After the Kiss, there'd been none of their usual easy banter, and tension had hung thick in the air. Perhaps a week apart would help, and she prayed they could settle back quickly into their old, comfortable friendship.

Joanna closed her mind to how she had felt about last night's kiss. It had been a very difficult few weeks and she was vulnerable and overwrought. Besides, there were other matters to attend to. And she'd been presented with the perfect opportunity: she had two whole days off.

As soon as Simon left, Joanna grabbed her rucksack and pulled out the photocopy of the letter, the program, and the note from Rose. As she did so, her hands touched cold metal and she retrieved the gold fountain pen. She'd forgotten all about it, what with everything else.

She turned it over in her hand, studying it. *I. C. S. . . .*

The initials rang a vague bell, but Joanna could not think from where. She sat cross-legged on the sofa bed, studying both the letters and the program. If Simon thought she was going to curtail her interest in this whole business, then he was wrong. Plus, he'd seemed agitated and nervous on Friday night, most unlike his usual self. Why was he so dead set on her not following this up?

She studied the letter yet again. Who were "Sam" and "the White Knight"? And who the hell had Rose been, for that matter?

She made herself a coffee and mulled over the few facts she had at her disposal. Was there anyone else who might know Rose's surname? Muriel? Maybe she had seen letters addressed to Rose. Surely Rose would have had to sign some sort of tenancy agreement when she took the apartment in Marylebone? Joanna dug out her notebook and flicked through it, searching for Muriel's telephone number. If she could garner Rose's surname it would make her trip to the local police station that much easier.

She picked up the telephone and dialed her number.

Sadly, Muriel was unable to help her with Rose's surname. She said she'd never seen Rose receive a single item of post, not even for utilities. The electricity ran on a coin meter and Rose had not had a telephone. She then asked about the address on the letters Rose had given her to post. "A couple of them were airmail letters. To somewhere in France, I think," Muriel said. *That at least fits*, thought Joanna as she remembered the instructions on the pill bottle.

Muriel did pass on the telephone number of their landlord. Joanna duly called the number and left a message on George Cyrapopolis's answering machine. But for now, it meant she would have to bluff her way through at the police station. She picked up her rucksack and left the apartment.

———

Joanna opened the swing door that led to the front desk of the Marylebone police station. The waiting area was deserted and reeked of stale coffee, the fluorescent lights highlighting the chipped paint and scuffed linoleum floor. There was no one at the desk, so she pressed the bell.

"Yes, miss?" A middle-aged constable strolled out of the office behind the desk.

"Hi, I was hoping someone here would be able to help me discover what's happened to my great-aunt."

"Right. Has she disappeared?"

"Er, not exactly, no. She's dead, actually."

"I see."

"She was found a couple of weeks ago in her apartment in Marylebone. She'd fallen down the stairs. The neighbor called the police and—"

"You think the call might have been taken by one of our officers?"

"Yes. I'm recently back from Australia. I'd got her address from my dad and thought I'd go and visit her. But when I arrived, it was too late." Joanna allowed her voice to break. "If only I'd have called round sooner, then . . ."

"I know, miss. It happens a lot." The constable nodded kindly. "I presume you want to know where she was taken, that kind of thing?"

"Yes. Only there's a problem. I've no idea what her surname might be. It's likely that she had remarried."

"Well, let's try and find her under the name you knew her by. Which was?"

"Taylor." Joanna plucked a name out of thin air.

"And the date she was found dead?"

"The tenth of January."

"And the address at which she was found?"

"Nineteen Marylebone High Street."

"Okay." The constable tapped into a computer on the desk. "Taylor, Taylor . . ." He scanned the screen, then shook his head. "Nope, nothing doing. Nobody of that name died that day, not that our station dealt with anyway."

"Could you try Rose?"

"Okay . . . We have a Rachel, and a Ruth, but no Rose."

"Those ladies both died on that day too?"

"They did. And there's another four local deaths listed here. Terrible time of year for the elderly. Christmas is just past, the weather's cold . . . Anyway, I'll check the address. If we were called to an incident that day, it'll be listed here."

Joanna waited patiently as the constable studied his screen.

"Mmmm." He scratched his chin. "Nothing there either. You sure you got the right date?"

"Positive."

The constable shook his head. "It might have been that another station took the call. You could try Paddington Green or, better still, the public morgue. Even if it wasn't us who dealt with the incident, your aunt's body would have certainly been taken there. I'll write down the address and you should pay them a visit."

"Thanks for all your help."

"No problem. Hope you find her. Rich was she?" He grinned.

"I have absolutely no idea," she said curtly. "Bye."

Joanna walked out of the swing door, hailed a passing taxi, and directed the driver to the morgue.

The Westminster Public Mortuary was an unassuming brick building next to the coroner's court on a quiet, tree-lined street. Joanna entered, not quite sure what to expect, and shuddered at Alec's favorite description of it as the "local meat factory."

"Can I help you?" A young woman on the front desk smiled at her cheerily.

What a god-awful depressing job, Joanna thought as she explained her story again.

"So the constable thought my great-aunt would probably have been brought here."

"Sounds likely. Let me have a look for you."

The young woman took similar details as the constable. She

looked up the name, the date, and the address. "No, I don't have a single Rose on that day, I'm afraid."

"Maybe she was using another name?" Joanna said, beginning to run out of options.

"I've put in the address you've given me and that's not showing anything up either. Maybe she was brought here a day later, though it's doubtful."

"Could you check anyway?"

The woman did so. "No, still nothing."

Joanna sighed. "Then, if she didn't come here, where would her body have gone?"

The woman shrugged. "You could try some of the local funeral homes. If there was family you were unaware of, they might have had her taken away privately. But usually, if there's been a death and a body is unclaimed, they'll end up here."

"Okay. Thanks very much."

"No problem. I hope you find your auntie."

"Thanks."

Joanna caught a bus back to Crouch End and went to her apartment to pick up her post. Her fingers trembled when she put the key in the lock, and as she closed the front door behind her, she thought how sad it was that what had once been her refuge and her sanctuary now made her feel the polar opposite.

Leaving swiftly and walking up the hill toward Simon's apartment, Joanna wondered whether the best thing might be simply to move somewhere else. Especially with Matthew gone, she doubted she could ever be comfortable there again.

When she arrived, she saw there was a message on the machine from George Cyrapopolis, Rose's landlord. Joanna picked up the telephone and dialed his number.

"Hello?" She heard a crash of crockery in the background. "Hello, Mr. Cyrapopolis? It's Joanna Haslam here. I'm your deceased tenant's great-niece."

"Ah, yes, 'ello." George Cyrapopolis had a deep, booming voice with a Greek accent. "What is eet you are wanting to know?"

"I was wondering whether Rose signed a tenancy agreement with you when she first moved into the apartment she rented from you."

"I . . ." There was a pause. "You're not the Eenland Revenue, are you?"

"No, I promise, Mr. Cyrapopolis."

"Hmmm. Well, you come 'ere to my restaurant and show yourself to me. Then we can talk, okay?"

"Okay, what is your address?"

"I at number forty-six on the High Road in Wood Green. The Aphrodite restaurant, opposite the shopping center."

"Fine."

"You come at five, before we open, okay?"

"Yes. See you then. Thanks, Mr. Cyrapopolis." Joanna put the telephone down. She made herself a coffee and a peanut-butter sandwich and spent the next hour calling every funeral home listed in central and north London. No Rose was recorded, either on that day, or two days after. "Then where on earth did they take her?" she mused, before calling Muriel once more.

"Hello, Muriel. It's Joanna. Sorry to bother you again."

"That's all right, love. Any joy findin' your aunt?"

"No, nothing. I just wanted to double-check who it actually was that took Rose away."

"I told you, an ambulance came for her. Said they were taking her to the local morgue."

"Well, they didn't. I've tried that and the police station and every single funeral home in the district."

"Oo-er. A lost body, eh?"

"Seems so, yes. And they didn't ask you if you knew of any family?"

"No. But I did tell 'em the old duck had mentioned they lived abroad."

"Mmm."

"Tell you what, though," Muriel chirped. "Have you tried the local registrar's office? I had to go there after my Stanley passed away. Someone would have had to register Rose's death."

"That's a good idea, Muriel. I'll try it. Thanks."

"Anytime, love."

Joanna hung up, then looked up the address of the local registrar's office, grabbed her coat, and left the apartment.

Two hours later, she emerged from Old Marylebone town hall feeling completely bemused. She slumped down on the steps outside and leaned against one of the large columns. At the registrar's office, she had tried every possible permutation that her information would allow. There had been three dead Roses registered in the two weeks after the tenth of January, but none at the right address and certainly not of the right age. A young baby, only four days old—just reading of her death had brought a lump to Joanna's throat—as well as a twenty-year-old and a forty-nine-year-old, none of whom could even conceivably be the Rose she was looking for.

The woman who had helped her said there was usually a five-working-day deadline to register a death, unless the coroner had not released the body. But as there had been no record of Rose's body at the morgue either, this seemed unlikely.

Joanna shook her head in agitation as she headed for the tube station. It was as if Rose had never existed, but her body *had* to be somewhere. Was there an avenue she still hadn't explored?

Emerging from the tube, Joanna walked along High Road—a mishmash of betting shops, restaurants, and thrift stores—looking for the Aphrodite restaurant. It had already grown dark, and she pulled her coat more tightly around her to ward off the biting chill. She caught sight of the restaurant's neon sign and opened the entrance door.

"Hello?" she called, seeing the small, brightly decorated interior was deserted.

"'Ello." A balding, middle-aged Greek man emerged from behind the beads strung across the doorway at the back of the restaurant.

"Mr. Cyrapopolis?"

"Yes."

"I'm Joanna Haslam, Rose's great-niece."

"Okay. Sit down?" He pulled two wooden chairs out from the table.

"Thanks." Joanna sat. "I am sorry to bother you, but as I explained over the telephone, I'm trying to find my great-aunt."

"What? You 'ave lost the body, ees it?" George could not stop himself from grinning.

"It's a complicated situation. All I wanted to ask you is whether my aunt Rose signed a tenancy agreement with you. I'm trying to discover her married name, you see. And I thought it might have been on the agreement."

"No. There was no agreement." George shook his head.

"Why? If you don't mind me asking? I would have thought it in the landlord's best interests to have one."

"Of course, usually I do." George removed a packet of cigarettes from the breast pocket of his shirt. He offered one to Joanna, who declined, then lit up himself.

"Then why not with my great-aunt?"

He shrugged and leaned back in his chair. "I place an advertisement in the *Standard* as usual. First call ees from old lady who wants to view. I meet her there that evening. She gives me one and half thousand pound cash." He took a deep puff of his cigarette. "Three months' rent up front. I know she was safe. I mean, not going to throw wild parties or vandalize the place, eh?"

Joanna gave a small sigh of disappointment. "So you wouldn't know her surname?"

"No. She said she deedn't need no receipt."

"Or where she moved from?"

"Aha!" George tapped his nose as he thought. "Maybe. I was at the building a few days after she move een. I see van coming. The lady—Rose, you say?—tell van men to put wooden boxes in apartment. I stand at the door and help men and I notice they have foreign steeckers on them. French, I theenk."

"Yes." At least this, coupled with the pill bottle and the airmail letters, confirmed where Rose had come from. "Do you know exactly when it was Rose moved in?"

George scratched his head. "I theenk November."

"Well, thanks very much for your help, Mr. Cyrapopolis."

"Not a problem, mees. You want to stay for some gyros? Very nice lamb, juicy," he offered in a cloud of cigarette smoke, patting her hand with his nicotine-stained one.

"No thanks." She stood up hastily and wandered toward the front door. "Oh, just one last thing." She turned to him. "Did you clear out the apartment after Rose had died? I mean, for new tenants?"

"No." George looked genuinely puzzled. "I went down a couple of days later to see what was happeneeng and poof! Everything gone." He regarded Joanna. "I thought eet was her family who had taken her theengs and cleaned up, but eet could not have been, could eet?"

"No. Well, thanks for your time anyway."

"That's okay."

"Have you rented out the apartment again now?"

He nodded sheepishly. "Someone called. No point haveeng it empty, was there?"

"No, of course not. Thanks again." Joanna smiled weakly and left the restaurant.

10

Joanna returned to work on Wednesday morning feeling deflated. In the past two days she'd got nowhere fast, had gathered no further information about Rose than she'd begun with, other than the fact she had almost certainly arrived from France. *Not quite enough to take to Alec and say I've uncovered a major scandal*, she thought. She'd even nipped out to the Highgate library, where, luckily, James Harrison's biographies had been on display on the front shelves. She had browsed through the four thick books on Sir James's life and was still none the wiser as to how he was connected to the little old lady.

"Morning, Jo." Alec gave her a fatherly pat on the shoulder as she passed his desk. "How are you?"

"Better, thanks."

"Sorted out the mess at home yet? Your friend that called me said your apartment was a car crash."

"Yup. They did an excellent job. I've got virtually nothing left."

"Ah, well. At least you weren't there when it happened, or walked in on them for that matter."

"Yes." She gave him a smile. "Thanks for being so good about it."

"S'all right. I know how frightening it can be."

Blimey, thought Joanna. *He's human after all.* "What do you have for me today?"

"Now then, I thought I'd let you back in gently. You can either have 'My Rottweiler is a kitty-cat really'—even though the dog took a chunk out of a senior citizen's leg in the park yesterday—or you can have a nice lunch with Marcus Harrison. He's starting up some memorial fund in remembrance of his granddad, old Sir James."

"I'll take Marcus," said Joanna.

"I was thinking you might." He wrote down the details and handed them to her with a sly grin.

"What?" Joanna asked, feeling her face color.

"Put it this way, from what I've heard on the grapevine, Marcus Harrison is more likely to chew you up and spit you out than the Rottweiler. Take good care, now." He waved to her as he briskly walked away.

Joanna went to her desk and dialed Marcus Harrison's number to arrange where they should meet, pleased at the coincidence. Given this whole thing had begun at James Harrison's memorial service, perhaps she might find out if his revered grandfather had known a little old lady called Rose.

Surprised by his low, friendly voice on the phone, she agreed to meet him for lunch in a smart restaurant in Notting Hill. Leaning back in her chair, she thought this might be one of the more enjoyable jobs she'd done since arriving on the news desk and wished she'd worn something a little more glamorous than jeans and a sweater.

Marcus ordered a good bottle of wine from the maître d'. Zoe had already said he could charge all expenses associated with the memorial fund to the trust, and had issued him with a float of £500. He sipped the crisp Burgundy, feeling pleasantly mellow. Things did seem on the up.

Every time he had called Zoe in Norfolk about his plans for the fund, she had been sweetness and light, never once alluding to his appalling behavior of the week before. Something was going on in her life, he just knew it. Whatever it was that had given her that sparkle in her eyes, Marcus was glad of it. It had made his own life so very much easier.

He lit a cigarette and watched the door for Joanna Haslam, the journalist, to arrive.

At three minutes past one, a young woman entered the restaurant.

She was wearing a pair of black jeans and a white sweater that clung to her breasts. She was tall and natural looking—hardly any makeup on her clear skin—very unlike the type he normally went for. Her thick, shiny brown hair hung heavy around her face, the curly ends falling beyond her shoulders. She followed the maître d' to Marcus's table and he stood up to greet her.

"Joanna Haslam?"

"Yes." She smiled, and he found himself arrested by expressive brown eyes and dimples in her cheeks. It took him a second to recover.

"I'm Marcus Harrison. Thanks for coming."

"Not at all." Joanna sat down opposite him.

He felt momentarily dumbstruck—Joanna Haslam was an absolute knockout. "A glass of Burgundy?"

"Thank you."

"Here's to you." He raised his glass.

"Thanks. Er, here's to the memorial fund," she countered.

"Of course." He laughed nervously. "Now, before we get down to business, why don't we order? Get it out of the way so we can chat."

"Absolutely."

From behind the safety of her menu, Joanna studied Marcus. Her stored mental picture had not been inaccurate. In fact, if anything, it had underplayed his attractiveness. Today, instead of the creased ensemble he'd worn to the memorial service, Marcus was wearing a soft wool royal-blue jacket and a black polo-neck sweater.

"I'll have the soup and the lamb. How about you?" he prompted.

"I'll have the same."

"No baby leaves arranged on a plate and fashionably called a radicchio salad, then? I thought that was all you girls ate these days."

"I hate to break it to you, but us 'girls' are not all the same. I was raised in Yorkshire. I'm a meat-and-two-veg woman through and through."

"Are you now?" He raised an eyebrow at her over his wineglass, enjoying the hint of a Yorkshire accent in her soft, melodic voice.

"I mean"—she blushed, realizing what she had just said—"I enjoy my food."

"I like that in a woman."

Joanna's stomach gave a twitch as she realized he was flirting with her. Trying to concentrate on the job at hand, she reached inside her rucksack and took out her tape recorder, notebook, and pen.

"Do you mind if I record the conversation?"

"Not at all."

"Right. We'll turn it off when we eat, otherwise you only pick up the crashing of cutlery." Joanna put the tape recorder near Marcus and switched it on. "So, you're launching a memorial fund in memory of your grandfather Sir James Harrison?"

"Yes." He leaned forward and stared at her intensely. "You know, Joanna, you have the most wonderful, unusual eyes. They're tawny colored, like an owl's."

"Thanks. So, tell me about the memorial fund."

"Sorry, your beauty is distracting me."

"Shall I put a napkin over my head for the duration of the interview?" Despite her ego's being boosted by his compliments, Joanna was getting frustrated.

"All right, I'll try to contain myself, but hold the napkin at the ready, won't you?" He grinned at her and took a sip of his wine. "Right, where should I start? Well, Grandpa, dear Sir Jim, or 'Siam,' as he was known to his friends in the theater business, left a large amount of money in trust to fund two scholarships a year for talented young actors and actresses without means. You know how few and far between government grants are these days. Even those who do receive a grant often have to work during their time at drama school to fund their living expenses."

As she tried to concentrate, Joanna could feel her body reacting instinctively to him. He really was incredibly attractive. She thanked God she'd taped the interview and could listen to it later—she'd hardly heard a word he'd said. She cleared her throat. "So, will you be accepting applications from any young actor or actress who has won a place at drama school?"

"Absolutely."

"Surely you'll be inundated?"

"I certainly hope so. We'll be auditioning in May, and the more candidates, the merrier."

"I see."

The pea and pancetta soup arrived and Joanna switched the tape recorder off.

"This smells good," said Marcus, taking a mouthful. "So, Joanna Haslam, tell me a little about you."

"But I'm the one doing the interview!"

"I'm sure you're much more interesting than I am," he encouraged.

"I doubt it. I'm just a straightforward Yorkshire girl. It was always my dream to be a respected journalist."

"Then what are you doing with the *Morning Mail*? From the sound of things, the broadsheets would be more your style."

"I'm earning my stripes and learning all I can. One day I'd love to move to a more upmarket newspaper." Joanna sipped her wine. "What I need is a great scoop to get me noticed."

"Oh dear." Marcus gave a mock sigh. "I don't think my memorial fund is going to do that."

"No, but I like the fact that, for a change, I'll be helping to publicize something worthwhile, that could really make a difference to someone."

"A hack with morals." Marcus's eyes twinkled. "That is unusual."

"Well, I've doorstepped and hassled celebrities with the rest of the mob, but I don't like the way British journalism is going these days. It's intrusive, cynical, and sometimes destructive. I'd welcome the new privacy laws if they were approved, which they won't be, of course. Too many editors are in bed with those that run the country. How can the public ever hope to receive neutral information and form their own opinions when everything in the media has a political or financial bias?"

"Not just a pretty face, are we, Miss Haslam?"

"Sorry, I'll get down from my high horse now," she said with a grin. "Actually, most of the time, I love my job."

Marcus raised his glass. "Well, here's to the new breed of young, ethical journalists."

As the soup dishes were removed and the lamb arrived, Joanna found her normally healthy appetite had deserted her. She picked at her food, while Marcus swept his plate clean.

"Do you mind if we continue?" Joanna asked, once the waiter had removed their dishes.

"Not at all."

"Right." Joanna pressed the record button on the tape recorder once more. "In his will, did Sir James specifically ask you to run the memorial fund?"

"It was left to the family—my father, my sister, and myself—to organize the trust. As Sir James's only grandson, I'm honored to have been handed the job."

"And of course your sister, Zoe, is so busy with her acting career these days. I was reading the other day she's playing Tess in a film remake. Are you and your sister close?"

"Yes. Our childhood was—how can I put this?—varied, so we've always clung to each other for security and support."

"And you were obviously close to Sir James?"

"Oh yes"—Marcus nodded without guile—"very."

"Do you think being part of such an illustrious family has helped or hindered you? I mean, did it put you under pressure to achieve?"

He paused. "On or off the record?"

"Off, if you'd prefer." Now that she'd drunk two glasses of wine, Joanna's resolution to keep the interview professional had crumbled somewhat. She paused her tape recorder.

"It's been a bloody burden, to be honest. I know how others might look at me and think, *What a lucky sod.* But in reality, having famous relatives is difficult. Currently, it's feeling pretty impossible to outstrip what my father does, let alone my grandfather."

Joanna noticed Marcus looked suddenly vulnerable, unsure of himself. "I can imagine," she said softly.

"Can you?" He met her gaze. "Then you'll be the first person to do so."

"I'm sure that's not true, Marcus."

"As a matter of fact, it is. I mean, on paper, I'm quite a catch, aren't I? Famous family, well connected, women presume I'm wealthy . . . It's entirely possible that no woman has ever really liked me for myself," he added. "I've not exactly had the most high-flying career, you know."

"What kind of things have you done in the past?"

"Well, production has always been my favorite aspect of the movie business—the behind-the-scenes machinations, working out how all the various parts fit together, that's what I'm really into. It's also something that no one in the family has touched before, a niche I can actually call my own . . . not that any of my films have done well." Marcus was surprised he was telling Joanna this, but her warmth elicited confessions.

"Would I have seen one of them?" she asked, intrigued.

"Erm." He colored slightly. "Remember *No Way Out*? I don't suppose you do, it went straight to VHS."

"Sorry, I haven't heard of it. What's it about?"

"We went to Bolivia, into the Amazon rain forest, to shoot it—the scariest and most amazing time of my life, actually." He brightened as he talked, his hands gesturing as he warmed to his subject. "It's a spectacular and untamed place. The film was about two non-indigenous guys from the US who get lost in the depths of the forest as they hunt for a suspected seam of gold. Nature slowly swallows them up as they try to find their way out and they both end up dead. Rather depressing, now that I think about it, but it had a strong moral message about Western greed."

"Right. So are you working on something now?"

"Yes, my production company, Marc One Films, is just trying to gather the funds for a fantastic new script." He smiled and Joanna could feel the excitement emanating from him. "It's the most incredible story. When I was traveling in the Amazon, I was lucky enough to meet some of the Yanomami—they're a tribe that didn't make contact with the Brazilian government until the forties. Can you imagine being cut off from modern civilization, and the shock of finding your world is so much bigger than you thought it was?"

"So a bit more extreme than coming to London from Yorkshire then?" Joanna said. She felt stupidly gratified that he laughed at her weak joke, and she kicked herself for being so keen.

"Rather more extreme, yes," he continued. "They were a very peaceful people—their culture was the ultimate democracy: they didn't even have chieftains, they made all their decisions by consensus, with everyone getting their say. The plot is about when the Brazilian government—without warning—drove bulldozers through their village to construct a major road."

"That's horrendous! Did they actually do it?"

"Yes!" Marcus threw his hands in the air. "It's just disgusting. The film's also about how, in the past few decades, a huge part of their population has been wiped out by diseases, and about the consequences of deforestation, murderous gold miners . . . It's also got a beautiful love story, with a tragic but moving end, of course, and . . ." He trailed off and looked at her sheepishly. "Sorry, I know I get really worked up. Zoe always gets bored when I talk to her about it."

"Not at all." Joanna had been so swept up listening to him that she had almost forgotten her brief. "It sounds like an amazing and worthwhile project. I really wish you luck with it. Now, I'd better get some statistics on the memorial fund, or my editor will have my head on a plate. Can you give me the date the applications have to be in by, the address to write to, and that sort of thing?"

Marcus talked for ten minutes, telling Joanna all she needed to know. She rather wished she could interview him about his film project instead, as the memorial material felt stale in comparison.

"Right. Thanks, Marcus, that was great," she said, gathering her notes. "Great. Oh, one last thing: we will be needing a photograph of you and Zoe together."

"Zoe's in Norfolk on location. She's there for ages." Marcus's eyes glinted. "I know I'm not as famous or pretty as my sister, but you'll just have to make do with me."

"That's fine," she said quickly. "If they want Zoe, they can always use a still from her file." She reached to turn the tape recorder off, but Marcus stopped her by putting his hand around her forearm. A burst of electricity shot across her skin at his touch. Marcus put his mouth close to the tiny microphone and whispered something into it.

He lifted his head and smiled at her. "You can turn it off now. Brandy for you maybe?"

Joanna glanced at her watch and shook her head. "I'd love to, but I'm afraid I have to get back to the office."

"Okay." Marcus looked deflated as he signaled for the bill.

"The picture desk will be in touch about the photographs, and really, thanks for lunch." Standing up, she stuck out her hand, expecting him to shake it. Instead, he gently lifted it to his mouth and pressed a kiss to her knuckles.

"Goodbye, Miss Haslam. It's been a pleasure."

"Bye." She left the restaurant on wobbly legs and returned to the office in a haze of wine and lust.

She sat down at her desk, rewound the tape recorder a little, then pressed play.

"Joanna Haslam. You are gorgeous. I want to take you out to dinner. Please ring me on 0171 932 4841 to arrange this as a matter of urgency."

She giggled. Alice, the reporter who sat at the next desk, glanced over at her.

"What?"

"Nothing."

"You went to lunch with old 'Hands-on Harrison,' didn't you?"

"Yes. So what?" Joanna knew she was blushing.

"Leave well alone, Jo. I had a friend who dated him for a bit. He's a total cad without an ounce of moral fiber in his body."

"But he's—"

"Handsome, charismatic . . . yeah, tell me about it." Alice took a bite of her egg sandwich. "My mate spent a year getting over him."

"I have no intention of getting involved with Marcus. I'll probably never see him again."

"Oh? So he didn't ask you out to dinner then? Or give you his telephone number?"

Despite herself, Joanna's blush became deeper.

"Of course he did!" Alice smirked. "Just watch yourself, Jo. You've had enough heartbreak recently."

"Thanks for reminding me. Excuse me, I've got to get this typed up." Irritated by both Alice's patronizing manner and her probably accurate assessment of Marcus—despite his ethical streak—she stuck on her headphones, plugged them into her tape recorder, and began the transcription of the interview.

Five minutes later, the color had drained from Joanna's face. She sat staring at the screen, her fingers pressing rewind on the tape recorder and returning repeatedly to the same words Marcus had spoken.

She'd been so busy drooling over him that she'd missed the moment he'd said it. *Siam* . . . Apparently it was Sir James Harrison's nickname. Joanna took off her hea

creased photocopy of the love letter

the name on the letter. Could it be

She needed a magnifying glass,

round the office in search of one.

from Archie, the sports reporter,

trained the glass on the first line.

My darling Sam . . .

She searched the space betwee

"S," and the left-hand corner of the "A." *Yes!* Joanna studied the dot again, aware it could be ink or a mark of some kind from the photo-copier. No. There was absolutely, definitely, a small dot between the "S" and the "A." Joanna took a pen and copied, as exactly as she could, the flowing writing of the word. And then she was sure: there was an unnecessary upward stroke after the capital "S" and before the "A." Putting a dot directly above the stroke, the word instantly changed: *Siam*.

Joanna gulped, a tingle of excitement running up her spine. She knew now who the love letter had been written to.

11

Joanna had decided to strike while the iron was hot and utilize Alec's sympathy and current good humor to her advantage. That afternoon, she went up to Alec's desk, which was piled high with every edition of their rival dailies—as well as not one but three overflowing ashtrays—perched atop stacks of copy. His shirtsleeves were rolled up, the perennial Rothmans hanging out of a corner of his mouth, sweat on his brow as he cursed the computer screen in front of him.

"Alec." She leaned over the desk and put on a winning smile.

"Not now, love. We're behind deadline and Sebastian hasn't rung in from New York with his report on the Redhead. I can't hold the front page for much longer. The ed's wetting himself as it is."

"Oh. How long before you're finished? I've got something I want to talk through with you."

"Midnight do, will it?" he said, not removing his eyes from the screen.

"I see."

Alec glanced up. "Is it important? Like world-threateningly, 'we're gonna sell another hundred thousand copies of the paper'–type thing?"

"It might be a previously uncovered sex scandal, yes." She knew these were the magic words.

Alec's expression changed. "Okay. If it's sex, you get ten minutes. Six o'clock in the local."

"Thanks."

Joanna went back to her desk and spent the next couple of hours dealing with the correspondence in her in-tray. At five to six, she walked round the corner to the pub, favored by journalists only because of its proximity to the office. It certainly had nothing else to its credit. She sat on a stained bar stool and ordered herself a gin and tonic, careful not to lean against the sticky bar top.

Alec strolled in at a quarter past seven, still in his shirtsleeves, even though the night was bitterly cold. "Hi, Phil. The usual," he called to the barman. "Okay, Jo, shoot."

So Joanna went right back to the beginning, to the day of the funeral. Alec drained his glass of Famous Grouse in one gulp and listened intently until she had finished.

"To be honest, I was going to give up on the whole episode. I was getting nowhere and then suddenly, today, out of sheer coincidence, I discovered who the letter was written to."

Alec ordered another whiskey. His tired, red eyes appraised her. "There might be something there. What interests me is that someone has obviously gone to great lengths to make your old dear disappear, along with her tea chests. That screams cover-up. Bodies don't just vanish into thin air." He lit another cigarette. "Joanna, just out of interest, did you have the letter on you that night your apartment was turned over?"

"Yes. It was in my rucksack."

"It hasn't struck you that it may not have been a chance burglary? From what your mate said, there was a high degree of needless destruction. They knifed your sofa and your bed, didn't they?"

"Yes, but—"

"Maybe someone was looking for something they thought you might have hidden?"

"Even the police seemed shocked at the devastation," Joanna murmured quietly. She looked up at Alec, realization dawning. "Oh God, you might be right."

"Christ, Jo, you've some way to go before you become a suspicious old cynic like me. In other words, a great newshound." He grinned, showing his nicotine-stained teeth, and patted her hand. "You'll learn. Where's the letter now?"

"Simon took it to work to have his forensic lab run some tests on it."

"Who's Simon? Is he a copper?"

"No, he's something in the civil service."

"Damn it, Jo! Grow up!" Alec slammed his glass onto the bar. "I'll bet a pound to a piece of pig shit you'll never see that letter again."

"You're wrong, Alec." Joanna's eyes flashed with anger. "I trust Simon implicitly. He's my oldest and best friend. He was only trying to help, and I know he'd never deceive me."

Alec shook his head condescendingly. "What am I always saying to you? Trust no bugger. Especially in this business." He ran a hand over his eyes and sighed. "All right, so the love letter's gone, but you say you have a photocopy?"

"Yes. And I made another one for you to keep." Joanna handed it over.

"Thanks." Alec unfolded it. "Let's have a look-see, then." He read it quickly, then studied the name at the top. "Could definitely be 'Siam.' Yep. The initial at the bottom is illegible. But it doesn't look like an 'R' to me."

"Maybe Rose changed her name, or maybe the letter isn't from her. There's definitely some kind of theater connection, but neither Rose nor Sir James is listed anywhere in that program."

Alec checked his watch and ordered another whiskey. "Five minutes and I'll have to scoot. Look, Jo, I honestly can't say whether you're onto something or not. When I've been in these situations, you know I've followed my gut. What is your gut telling you?"

"That this is big."

"And how do you intend to progress from here?"

"I need to speak to the Harrison family, learn what I can about Sir James's life. It may be as simple as James having an affair with Rose. But why would she send *me* that letter? I don't know." Joanna sighed.

"If my apartment was turned over because they thought I'd got it, then surely it's quite a big deal to someone."

"Yeah. Look, I can't give you company time to investigate this—"

"I could do a profile on a British theatrical dynasty," she cut in. "Starting with Sir James, and Charles, his son, then looking at Zoe and Marcus. I'd have the perfect excuse to get as much information out of them as possible."

"Bit light for the news desk, Jo."

"It wouldn't be if I discovered some kind of huge scandal. A few days, *please*, Alec," she begged. "I'll do any extra research in my own time, I swear."

"Go on then," Alec capitulated. "On one condition."

"What?"

"I want to be kept informed every step of the way. Not because I can't keep my big red nose out of it, but for your own protection." He looked at her hard. "You're young and inexperienced. I don't want you getting yourself in so deep you can't get out. No heroics, okay?"

"I promise. Thanks, Alec. I'm off then. See you tomorrow." Impulsively, Joanna kissed him on the cheek and left the bar.

Alec watched Joanna leave. Nine times out of ten when a cub reporter came to him with a "great" lead, he'd shoot it down in flames within a few seconds, send them away with their tail between their legs. But just now, his famous gut had twitched like billy-oh. She was onto something. Christ knew what, but it was something.

———

Even Marcus had been surprised at how quickly Joanna had called him after their lunch. She'd claimed her editor wanted some kind of feature on the entire Harrison family to back up the memorial fund piece, but he was hoping his charm had swayed her too. He had, of course, complied with her request to visit him at his apartment the following evening. In honor of her visit, he'd spent the day clearing the detritus of his disorganized, bachelor existence. He'd swept what lurked under his bed straight into a bin bag and even changed the sheets. Then he'd pulled his thickest books out from where they had been propping up a chair with a leg missing, and displayed them prominently on the coffee table. It was a long time since a woman's imminent presence had stirred something in him other than simple lust. Joanna had been one of the few people who had actually *listened* when he had talked about his film project, and now he was determined to convince her that there was more to him than most people gave him credit for.

The bell rang at half past seven. He opened the door and saw Joanna had made very little effort to dress up and was still in her work clothes of jeans and a sweater. He felt a twinge of disappointment.

He kissed her on both cheeks, deliberately lingering. "Joanna. Lovely to see you again. Come in."

She followed Marcus along the narrow corridor and into a small and basically furnished sitting room. She'd expected something much more luxurious.

"Wine?"

"Er, I'd prefer a cup of coffee, if you wouldn't mind," Joanna replied. She felt exhausted. She'd been up most of the previous night making notes on the biographies and a list of questions about Sir James.

"Spoilsport." Marcus grinned. "Well, I'm going to have a drink, anyway."

"Oh, all right then. Just a small glass."

Marcus came back into the sitting room with a whiskey for him and a full glass of wine for her, and sat down very close to her on the sofa. As she turned her head away, he gently tucked a curl of hair behind her ear. "Been a long day then, Jo?"

Joanna could feel the heat of his thigh next to hers, and edged away from him. She had to concentrate. "Yes, it has."

"Well, you just relax. Hungry? I have some pasta that I could knock together for us."

"No, please don't go to any trouble." She set up her tape recorder and placed it on the coffee table in front of them.

"It's no trouble at all, really."

"Could we get started and see how we go?"

"Of course, whatever you want."

She noticed the musky scent of his aftershave, the cute way his hair curled on his collar . . . *No, no, no, Joanna!*

"Right, as I told you on the phone, I'm going to be writing a big retrospective on Sir James and your family to back up the launch of the memorial fund."

"Wow. I'm truly grateful, Jo, I really am. The more publicity, the better."

"Absolutely, but I'm going to need your help. I want to discover what your grandfather was really like, where he came from and how his rise to fame affected and changed him."

"Blimey, Jo, surely you can go and get any one of the biographies on him, can't you?"

"Oh, I have those from the library already. I admit I've only leafed through them so far, but to be honest, anybody could do that." She looked at him earnestly. "I want to see him from the family's perspective, get to know the little details. For example, 'Siam,' that pet name you say his old acting friends used. Where did that come from?"

Marcus shrugged. "I've absolutely no idea."

"He had no connections with Southeast Asia, for example?"

"No, I don't think so." Marcus emptied his glass and poured himself another. "Come on, Jo. You've hardly touched your drink." He put his hand on her thigh. "You're awfully tense."

"Yes, I am, a bit." Joanna swiftly removed the hand, then picked up her wineglass to take a sip. "It's been a funny few weeks, one way and another."

"Tell me all about it."

The hand went back onto her thigh. She removed it again and turned to him, an eyebrow raised. "No. I have to get this article buttoned under by the middle of next week and you're not exactly helping, Marcus. It's in your interests, too, you know."

"Yes." Marcus hung his head like a chastened schoolboy. "I'm sorry, I just can't stop finding you attractive, Jo."

"Look, help me out, half an hour is all I'm asking for, okay?"

"I'll concentrate, I promise."

"Good. Now, what do you know about Sir James? Maybe start right from the beginning with his childhood?"

"Well . . ." Marcus had never really taken much interest in his grandfather's life, but he racked his brains to try to remember anything he could. "It's Zoe you need to speak to really. She knew him far better than I did, because she lived with him."

"Speaking to her would be great, but it's always interesting getting different perspectives on the same person. Did you, by any chance, ever hear your grandfather talk of someone called Rose?"

Marcus shook his head. "No. Why?"

"Oh, her name came up in one of the biographies I read, that's all," she replied casually.

"I'm sure James had lots of lady loves in his time."

"Did you know your grandmother? Her name was Grace, wasn't it?"

"I never met her. She died abroad before Zoe and I were born. My dad was only a few years old, if I remember rightly."

"Were they happily married?"

"Very, so legend has it."

"By any chance, did your grandfather keep his memorabilia? You know, old programs, newspaper cuttings, that kind of thing?"

"Did he ever!" Marcus chuckled. "There's an entire attic-full in his house in Dorset. They were all bequeathed to Zoe."

Joanna's ears pricked up. "Really? Wow, I'd love to look through that."

"Yeah. Zo's been saying for ages she's going to go down for the weekend and sort it all out. Most of it's probably rubbish, but there might be a few programs and photos that are quite valuable now. Sir James kept them all, he was a real hoarder." Marcus had a brain wave. "How about I give Zoe a call and organize for you to come to Dorset this weekend? Then we could have a look through what's up there. I'm sure she'd be grateful for any help sorting it out."

"Er . . . right." Joanna knew exactly why Marcus looked so thrilled with his idea and she only hoped the bedroom doors had secure locks. Yet the chance to get her hands on boxfuls of Sir James's past was too tempting, so she'd have to run the gauntlet.

"We could drive down on Saturday morning and spend the night there." Marcus looked like an eager little boy. "We'll need a good couple of days at it."

"Well, if you're sure," said Joanna uncertainly. "You'll ask Zoe then?"

"Of course I will. She's also short of cash to renovate the house Sir Jim left her. Maybe the sale of the stuff in the attic could raise some money to help her," Marcus improvised, knowing that Zoe would never sell anything of her beloved grandfather's for profit.

"Super. I really am grateful." Joanna packed her tape recorder into her rucksack and stood up.

"You're not going, are you? What about the food?"

"It's really sweet of you to offer," she said as she walked toward the door, "but really, if I don't get some sleep tonight, I'll be fit for nothing tomorrow."

"Okay," sighed Marcus. "Spurn me and my spaghetti. I don't care."

Joanna handed him a card. "There's my number at work. Would you call me tomorrow and let me know what Zoe said?" She pecked him on the cheek. "Thanks, Marcus. I appreciate it. Bye."

Marcus watched her as she left the apartment. There really was something about Joanna that set his heart pumping. And it *wasn't* just lust. He really *liked* her lack of guile, her openness and honesty, which were such refreshing traits after the pretty but self-obsessed actresses he usually went for.

As he went into the kitchen to cook some pasta for one, Marcus topped up his glass, put it to his lips, then paused. And with effort, threw the liquid down the sink.

"Enough," he said.

He wanted to be a better man for Joanna.

———

As Joanna walked through the frosty night toward Holland Park tube station, she finally accepted that, whatever reputation he may rightly have had, she was deeply attracted to Marcus. His flattery had boosted her flattened, bruised ego, and his obvious desire for her made her feel sexy again. It had been years since she'd even glanced at another man and the feelings Marcus had stirred in her were exciting yet troubling. She was determined not to be another notch on his bedpost. A quick fling might be physically satisfying, but wouldn't fill the emptiness that Matthew had left behind.

Despite this, a flush of pleasure went through her as she got onto the tube and thought about the weekend: being with Marcus and, at the same time, maybe—just maybe—discovering further clues to the mystery. And Alec—cynic that he was—thinking there might be something in it had given her the confidence to take this story seriously.

As she passed through the turnstile at Archway tube station, she pulled her scarf up against the draft that rushed through the station from the exit. As she emerged into the darkness of Highgate Hill, almost deserted this time of night, her boots echoed dully on the frozen pavement, and she looked forward to curling up in her makeshift bed at Simon's.

Perhaps it was the cold air inching steadily down her neck, but her steps slowed as she began to sense that someone was following her. Turning slightly, she tried to see if it was the shadow of a person or simply of the swaying tree branches that was playing off the ground. Finally, she came to a halt and listened.

In the distance, she heard shouts of laughter flying out into the night air from the pub down the road, the steady rumble of cars and buses shaking up the leaves and litter in whirls. Making up her mind, she dashed across the street and into a corner shop, where she bought a packet of chewing gum. Standing at the entrance, her head darted left and right, but the only figure she could see was a man in an overcoat at the bus stop opposite, smoking casually.

Walking along at a deliberately calm pace, she glanced behind at the bus stop. The man had disappeared, even though no bus had arrived. Her heart thumped against her chest, and on instinct, she flagged down a passing black cab and slipped inside, managing to gasp out Simon's address. The cabbie looked irritated as it was only a three-minute drive away.

Arriving at Simon's building, she pounded up the stairs as fast as she could. Wishing he was home, she bolted the door shut, before wedging a chair under the handle. Then she grabbed his cricket bat from the hallway cupboard and put that on the sofa bed.

Much later, she fell into a troubled sleep, her grasp barely loosening on the bat.

12

Zoe had spent most of her first week in Norfolk kicking her heels with too much time to think. A lot of the outside location filming had been curtailed by the presence of a thick blanket of snow. Although pretty and atmospheric, it made the film's continuity impossible. Instead, they'd done what they could in the old cottage the company had rented for the shoot. William Fielding, the actor playing Zoe's character's father, John Durbeyfield, was currently in a pantomime in Birmingham and would not join the set until next week. She'd contemplated going back to London, but given that Art had arranged for her to be picked up from here on the weekend anyway, it seemed a pointless journey.

On Friday morning, Zoe woke suddenly, dripping in sweat, with a gut-wrenching fear gnawing at her. Gone were the rose-colored glasses, the sense of wonder that fate, after all this time, had drawn the two of them back together. She only felt utter disbelief that she had even allowed herself to consider the possibility of a new liaison with him.

"Oh God," she muttered, panic gripping her. "What about Jamie?"

Zoe stumbled out of bed, pulled on her jeans and wellies, and went for a walk around the snow-covered village. She was so deep in her thoughts that its picturesque beauty was completely wasted on her. It was all very well declaring herself at last independent, free of the shackles that had previously bound her, but she *had* to be realistic. What she was about to do could affect the rest of Jamie's life. How could she keep the secret from Art? Surely, once they talked, got to know each other better, he'd realize—if he hadn't already. And then where would that leave the three of them?

"Damn! Damn!" Zoe kicked hard at some icy slush in frustration. She'd lived with the secret for so long; but it was going to be one hell of a shock for others . . .

If she and Art began a relationship again, and the truth about Jamie leaked out, could she *really* subject her precious child to the furor that would surround him?

No.

Never.

What on earth was I thinking?

That afternoon, Zoe packed her bags into her car and drove back to London. When she arrived home, she turned off her mobile and let the answering machine take all her calls, whether welcome or not. Then she uncharacteristically drank an entire bottle of wine and fell asleep on the sofa in front of a film that did not in any way match up to the drama of her own life.

———

Marcus had rented a Volkswagen Golf on his long-suffering credit card for the drive down to Dorset. Now, with Joanna beside him as he drove along the M3, he decided it was well worth the red statement in a month's time. She smelled divine, he thought, of freshly plucked apples. He only hoped the key to Haycroft House was where he remembered it had always been. He'd tried to reach Zoe several times yesterday to ask permission to stay at the house, leaving messages on both her mobile and her answering machine, but she hadn't got back to him. In the end, he'd decided that she couldn't say he hadn't tried, and had gone ahead with the weekend as planned.

Joanna sat next to him quietly. She'd been genuinely surprised when Marcus had called yesterday to say they were all set for the weekend. She'd been convinced Zoe would refuse point-blank to let a reporter sift through her grandfather's private life. She glanced at

Marcus's perfect profile and wondered whether Sir James had been as handsome when he was younger.

Eventually, he turned off the motorway and Joanna gazed out of the window at the wide-open fields that gently rose and fell into the distance. The countryside wasn't as dramatic as the Yorkshire moors, but she enjoyed not being hemmed in by tall buildings. The plants and animals were buried deep in their winter habitats, tucked beneath layers of snow that reflected the sunlight shining from a spectacular cloudless sky.

Marcus drove through a series of narrow country lanes with high snow-topped hedges. Finally, he turned the car into a gated drive and the house came into view. It was a large and obviously ancient thatched house, two stories high, built in pale gray brick. Moss grew on the thatch—a sharp green among the patches of white snow—and icicles dripped gently under the eaves around the small lead-paned windows, glistening in the sun.

"This is it," he said. "Haycroft House."

"It's beautiful," she breathed.

"Yes. Sir Jim bequeathed it to Zoe's son, Jamie. Lucky old him," Marcus added, rather bitterly, Joanna thought. "Stay there while I get the key." He jumped out of the car and headed for the water barrel that stood at the back of the house. Digging underneath the left side of the barrel, Marcus's fingers had to break through solid ice before he felt the large, old-fashioned key that would gain them access to the front door. "Thank God for that," he muttered, blowing on his numbed fingers and returning to the front of the house.

Joanna was already out of the car, peeping through the mullioned windows.

"Got it." He smiled as he put the key in the lock of the solid oak door and turned it.

They entered a dark, beamed hall that smelled of wood smoke. Marcus switched the light on and Joanna was startled by a fierce bear's head glaring down from above her on the wall.

"Sorry, I should have warned you about Mr. West," Marcus said, and reached up to pet the bear's straggly fur.

"Mr. West?" she repeated, shivering—the house was possibly colder inside than it was out.

"Yeah, Zo named him after one of her scary teachers at school. Don't worry, it wasn't shot locally," he teased her. "Come on, it's freezing. We'll light a fire in the sitting room. Could be a case of body heat to prevent hypothermia, you know," he quipped.

Purposely ignoring his comment, Joanna followed Marcus into a cozy sitting room, full of old sofas piled high with cushions. One wall was lined with shelves that held leather-bound books and family pictures. As Marcus searched for firelighters, Joanna studied the photographs more closely. She recognized Zoe Harrison as a little girl, beaming in the arms of Sir James Harrison. There were numerous shots of her at different ages, in her navy school uniform, or sitting on the back of a large chestnut horse, then others of her with Jamie, her son, grinning from ear to ear. Joanna searched for a picture of young Marcus, but found none. Before she could turn to ask, she heard him shout triumphantly.

"Let there be warmth!" he decreed as the firelighters he had thrown into the grate flared up, sending shadows dancing up the rough lath-and-plaster walls. He added some tinder, then placed a couple of logs on top. "Right, that'll soon warm the place up. Now for the heating."

Joanna followed Marcus through to a heavily beamed kitchen, complete with gray-flagged floors and an ancient range. Marcus opened one of the heavy iron doors and stuffed some newspaper inside, then threw in coal from the bucket and lit it.

"It may not look impressive and I can assure you it isn't." He grinned. "Oh, for good old gas central heating. Dad went on at Sir Jim for years to install a proper system, and he refused. I think he rather enjoyed freezing his nuts off. I'll just go and brave the cold once more and get the supplies from the car."

Joanna wandered around the kitchen, enjoying its original rustic charm. An old airer was suspended above the range and an herb rack hung from the ceiling, still full of dry, cracked bay leaves, rosemary, and lavender. The pitted oak table had clearly seen years of use, and the assorted open-fronted cupboards were crammed with a jumbled mix of tins, glass jars, and china.

Marcus arrived with a cardboard box full of food. Joanna noticed two bottles of champagne, and delicacies such as smoked salmon, which she loathed, and caviar, which she loathed even more, and wondered whether she'd either starve or freeze to death this weekend. From the amount of alcohol Marcus had brought, at least she could do it drunk. Joanna helped him unpack, then retreated to the relative warmth of the range.

"You're awfully quiet," he remarked, as he stowed the cold foods in the refrigerator. "Is there something I can do? I know it must be a bit odd, staying with a man you hardly know . . ."

"It's all right, Marcus, I've just had a lot on my mind. Work stuff," she clarified. "I really appreciate you taking the weekend to help me with my research."

"As much as I'd like to have you believe it, I'm not completely altruistic," he said. "I was hoping to have some fun with you this weekend."

She raised an eyebrow at him.

"Get your mind out of the gutter, Jo," he said, mock-shock on his face. "I meant sparkling conversation, and maybe a trip to the pub. Now, how about we go up to the attic and get out some of the boxes? The best thing is to bring them down and work through them in front of the fire."

She followed him up the creaking wooden stairs to the galleried landing. Marcus took an iron rod that was leaning against the wall and hooked it into a handle above him. A set of dusty metal steps appeared as he pulled on the rod. He climbed up and pulled a piece of string that immediately flooded the attic above them with light.

He offered her his hand. "Want to come and see just what we've decided to take on?"

She gripped his hand and climbed the steps behind him. Stepping out onto the hardboard floor of the attic, she gasped. The entire space, which must have run from one end of the house to the other, was filled with tea chests and cardboard boxes.

"Told you he was a hoarder," said Marcus. "There's enough stuff to fill an entire museum up here."

"Have you any idea if there's any chronological order to all this?"

"No, but I'd presume the stuff nearest us, the most accessible, is also the most recent."

"Well, I really need to start from the beginning, as far back as we can possibly find."

"Very good, milady." Marcus pretended to doff his cap. "You have a wander and point out the boxes you want taken down first."

Joanna picked her way through the boxes, choosing to start with one of the corners furthest away from the steps. Twenty minutes later, she had settled for three boxes whose cracked yellow newspaper cuttings suggested their age, as well as a battered suitcase.

Back downstairs, she sat on the hearth trying to grab what warmth there was. "I'm fre-freezing!" She laughed as she shivered uncontrollably.

"Shall we head to the pub first? I could murder a pint of foaming ale. We could warm up with some bowls of soup."

"No thanks." She headed for the old suitcase. "I want to get started."

"Right. If you don't mind, before my fingers drop off from frostbite, I'll pop off to the local. Sure you don't want to come?"

"Marcus, we haven't even started! I'll stay here," she said firmly.

"Okay. Well, don't secrete anything you find on your person, or I might have to find it later," he said as he left the sitting room. As he drove out of the gates, he noticed a gray car parked on the grass verge a few yards past the house. He glanced in and saw two men sitting inside, dressed in Barbours and ostentatiously poring over a walking map. Marcus wondered whether he should call the police. They might be casing the house for a robbery.

Joanna, in spite of the now-leaping flames of the fire, still felt chilled to the bone. She could not chance sitting too close because of the fragile paper she was handling. She had so far discovered absolutely nothing that she had not already gleaned from the four biographies.

She skimmed through the notes she'd been keeping as she'd read them. Born in 1900, Sir James had begun to make a name for himself as an actor in the late twenties, starring in a string of Noël Coward plays in the West End. In 1929, he'd married his wife, Grace, and become a widower in 1937 when she had died tragically abroad from pneumonia. According to the newspaper cuttings and interviews with friends in his various biographies, the death of Grace was something from which James had never fully recovered. She had been the love of his life and he'd never married again.

Joanna had also noted that there wasn't a single photograph of him as a child or a young man. The biographer had attributed this to a fire at James's parents' house—apparently somewhere near here—destroying everything they owned. The first photograph on record was of James and his young wife, Grace, on their wedding day in 1929. From what she could tell from the black-and-white photograph of the wedding party, Grace had been a slight woman, her new husband towering over her, and Joanna saw how tightly she gripped his arm.

After her death, James had been left to care for Charles, his five-year-old son. One biographer had noted that the child had been put in the care of a nanny, and then sent to boarding school at the age of seven. Father and son had apparently never been close, a fact that James had later blamed on his son's resemblance to his wife. "It pained me to even see Charles," he'd admitted. "I kept him at a distance. I know I was an absent father, and it's caused me great heartache in my later years."

In the thirties, James had made a number of successful films for J. Arthur Rank in England, and it was this that had really brought him to the public's attention. He'd had a brief fling with Hollywood, then, when war gripped Europe, James had gone abroad as part of ENSA, the entertainment branch of the British war movement, visiting British troops and boosting morale.

Once the war had ended, Sir James had worked at the Old Vic, taking on some of the big classic roles. His portrayal of Hamlet, followed two years later by Henry V, had moved him into the elite ranks of the great. It was then he'd bought the Dorset house, preferring to spend time alone there rather than circulate among the glitterati of the London theatrical scene.

In 1955, James had moved to Hollywood on a permanent basis. He'd spent fifteen years making some good and some—according to one reviewer—"frighteningly bad" pictures. Then he'd returned to the UK stage in 1970, and in 1976 had played King Lear with the RSC—his swan song, as he'd announced to the media. After that, he had devoted himself to his family, especially his granddaughter, Zoe, who had recently lost her mother. Perhaps, a biographer had suggested, he had been trying to pay penance for the earlier neglect of his own son.

Joanna sighed. Her lap and the floor were covered in aging newspaper, photographs, letters . . . none of which bore any further illuminating information. Although "Siam" was most definitely confirmed as Sir James's nickname, as it was used regularly throughout the mass of correspondence he had kept. Having read through every word of the letters at first, about people with nicknames like "Bunty" and "Boo," she had grown bored at the descriptions of the roles he was playing, general theater gossip, and the weather. Nothing incriminating there.

She glanced at her watch. It was ten to three already and she was only halfway through the suitcase.

"What am I really looking for?" she asked the dusty cold air.

Cursing the lack of time, she continued working her way through to the bottom of the suitcase and was just about to dump all the papers back in when she noticed a photograph sticking out of an old program. Pulling it out, she saw the familiar faces of Noël Coward and Gertrude Lawrence—the famous actress—and, standing next to them, a man she also recognized.

She rummaged through the pile for the photograph of James Harrison on his wedding day, and put it side by side with the one she'd just found. With his black hair and trademark moustache, James Harrison was instantly recognizable as he stood next to his bride. But surely the man standing next to Noël Coward, despite his blond hair and clean-shaven face, was also James Harrison? Joanna compared the nose, the mouth, the smile, and—yes!—it was the eyes that gave him away. She was sure it was him.

Perhaps, she mused, James had dyed his hair blond and removed his moustache for a role in one of Coward's plays?

She hastily put the photo to one side as she heard the key in the lock.

"Hello." Marcus entered the sitting room, bent down, and massaged her shoulders. "Find anything interesting for the article yet?"

"Lots, thanks. It's been absolutely fascinating."

"Good. Fancy some smoked salmon sandwiches? You must be starving, and beer always gives me an appetite." He wandered toward the door.

"No smoked salmon for me," she called after him. "Just some of that lovely bread you brought, and a nice hot cup of tea would be wonderful."

"I have caviar too. Want some of that?"

"No! Thanks, though."

Joanna went back to the piles of photographs and papers, then ten minutes later Marcus put down a tray with a plate of generously buttered bread and a pot of steaming tea onto the coffee table. He gave her a sweet smile.

"Can I help you?"

"Not really, no. I mean, thanks, but I know what I'm looking for."

"Okay." Marcus yawned and lay down on the sofa. "Wake me up when you're done, okay?"

Revived by the tea, Joanna continued sifting until the darkness had long since lengthened the shadows in the quiet room. She stretched her aching limbs and gave a groan. "Oh God, I need a nice hot bath," she murmured, shivering as she saw the fire had gone out.

Marcus's head popped up from the sofa and he stretched languidly. "Yep, the range may have roused itself to produce at least half a tub of lukewarm water. Come on, I'll show you the bathroom and where you're sleeping tonight."

Upstairs, Marcus took her into the large but rather shabby bedroom that would be hers for the night. A big brass bed smothered in an old patchwork quilt stood in the center of the low-ceilinged room, and an oriental rug covered the wood floor, which was liberally peppered with mouse-sized holes. Marcus dropped her holdall on the rickety chair next to the door, then tugged her along the corridor to another room. In it stood an impressive mahogany four-poster bed.

"James's room, where I shall be kipping. It's a very big bed . . . ," he whispered in her ear as he pulled her toward him.

"Marcus! Stop it," she said firmly as she wriggled out of his grasp.

He pushed a strand of her hair away from her face and sighed. "Jo, you have no idea how much I want you."

"You hardly know me. And besides, I'm not into one-night stands."

"Who says it would be? Christ, Jo, do you really think that's what I want?"

"I have no idea what you want, but I know what I *don't*."

"Okay," Marcus sighed, "I surrender. You may have noticed that patience has never been one of my virtues. I promise I won't touch you again."

"Good. Now, I'm going to have a bath, if you'll kindly show me where the bathroom is."

Ten minutes later, Joanna was lying in the claw-foot bath, feeling like a Victorian virgin contemplating her wedding night. She groaned, thinking of the self-control it had taken to pull herself out of his arms. Why was she being so old-fashioned?

Apart from the fact that sleeping around had never appealed to her, Joanna knew she was scared. If she gave Marcus what they both wanted, wouldn't he tire of her, as he had of all the other women? And then how stupid and used would she feel?

Well, there's no point overanalyzing it, she thought as she stepped out of the bath. Shivering her way back to the bedroom, she threw on her warmest sweater before pulling her jeans back on.

"Joanna!"

"Yes?" she shouted.

"I'm pouring the champagne! Come down."

"Coming." She padded downstairs to find him on the leather sofa in front of a newly restoked fire.

"Here." He handed her a glass as she sat down beside him. "Look, Jo, I just want to apologize for behaving like a lothario. If you don't want me in that way, it's absolutely fine. I'm sure I'm mature enough to enjoy your friendship, if that's all you want to offer me. What I'm saying is that you'll be perfectly safe tonight. I promise I will not creep into your bedroom and ravage you. Now, I hope we can relax and have a nice evening. I've booked a table at the pub in the village. They have nice plain English fare, none of this fancy sophisticated stuff that I'm already gathering you don't like. Anyway, cheers." He raised his glass and smiled at her.

"Cheers." She smiled back, feeling relieved yet disappointed at his fervent apology and acceptance of being "friends."

Half an hour later, they drove the bumpy mile down the pitch-black lanes to the local village. The ancient inn was low roofed and cozy with its dark wooden interior and huge fire. A cat dozed on the bar top as Marcus ordered a couple of gin and tonics and chatted to the barman before the two of them took their seats at a table in the dining room.

"By the way, this is my treat," said Joanna as they studied the menus, "to say thank you for arranging all this for me."

"My pleasure. And as it's your treat, I'm going to have the steak."

"Me too."

The young waitress came to take their order and Joanna chose a bottle of claret from the surprisingly extensive wine list.

"So, tell me about your idyllic childhood in Yorkshire," Marcus prompted.

As Joanna did so, Marcus listened with more than a little envy to her descriptions of family Christmases, riding horses on the moors, the tight-knit community that worked together to help their neighbors through the long, hard winters.

"The farm's been in my family for generations," she said. "My grandfather died about twenty years ago and Dora, my granny, handed the place over to my dad. But she still came and helped out at lambing time, right up until last year when her arthritis got the better of her."

"What will happen when your dad retires?"

"Oh, he knows I'm not interested in running the farm, so he'll keep the farmhouse and rent out the land to the neighboring farmers. He'd never sell. He keeps hoping I'll change my mind, which makes me feel guilty, but it's not for me. Maybe one day I'll have a son who has a thing for sheep, but . . ." She shrugged. "Dynasties have to end at some point."

"Yeah, well, I'm the next in line to the Harrison dynasty and I've made a rubbish job of it so far," Marcus said.

"Speaking of which"—Joanna cut into her steak—"any program I found I put in a pile. They really shouldn't be left up in the attic to rot. I'm sure the London Theatre Museum, for example, would be interested. Or I suppose you could hold an auction, raise money for the memorial fund, maybe?"

"That's a good idea. Mind you, whether Zoe would approve, I just don't know. Those boxes were willed to her, after all. But there's no harm in putting the idea to her, anyway."

"Excuse me for being blunt, but the way you describe her makes your sister sound like quite a tough cookie," commented Joanna.

"Zoe? No." Marcus shook his head. "I'm sorry if I gave you the wrong impression, but you know what siblings are like."

"I don't. I'm an only child. When I was younger, I always wanted a brother or sister to confide in."

"It's not all it's cracked up to be," Marcus said darkly. "I mean, I love Zoe, but we hardly had the ideal upbringing . . . I suppose from all the reading up on the family you've done, you know that our mum died when we were both young?"

"Yes," she said quietly, seeing his expression. "I'm sorry, that must have been awful for you."

"Yeah." He cleared his throat. "But you know, I coped. We both had to grow up pretty quickly. Especially Zoe, what with Jamie arriving when she was so young . . ."

"Do you know who the father is?"

"No. And even if I did, I'd never tell," he said abruptly.

"Of course not. And I promise I wasn't asking that with my journalist's hat on."

"Course not." His expression softened. "Besides, I like you whatever hat you're wearing. Anyway, Zoe's great, fiercely protective of those she loves and very insecure beneath that serene exterior."

"Aren't we all?" Joanna breathed.

"Yes. So, what's the score with your love life, Miss Haslam? I detect a deep distrust of the male species lurking somewhere in your psyche."

"I had a long relationship with someone, which ended just after Christmas. I thought it was for life, but it wasn't." Joanna sipped her wine. "I'm getting over it slowly, but these things take time."

"At the risk of getting my head bitten off for flirting, whoever that bloke is, he's an absolute idiot."

"Thanks. And the one good thing that's come out of it is that I've realized I'm just not willing to change who I am to suit someone else, if you know what I mean."

"I do," he said. "And you're right not to let that happen—you're lovely just as you are." As the words came out of his mouth, Marcus felt a peculiar tug at his heart. "Now, I fancy one of those enormous desserts with lashings of whipped cream, chocolate sauce, and glacé cherries that you'd never see gracing the tables of London's so-called fashionable restaurants. How about you?"

After coffee, Joanna paid the bill and they made their way back to Haycroft House. Marcus insisted Joanna sit by the fire while he went off to the kitchen. He arrived back a few minutes later clutching a furry hot-water bottle under each arm.

"There you go. If I can't keep you warm, then this will have to do instead."

"Thanks, Marcus. I'm going to go straight up, if you don't mind. I'm exhausted for some reason. Good night." She moved toward him and kissed him on the cheek. He returned the kiss, dropping it lightly on her lips.

"Night, Joanna," he murmured.

He watched her as she left the room, then sat down on the sofa and stared into the fire. There was just the tiniest chance, he admitted to himself, that he was actually falling in love with her.

———

Joanna closed the bedroom door behind her. She swallowed, trying to still her heartbeat. God, she'd wanted him just then . . .

No, this is a job, she told herself.

It was dangerous to become emotionally involved with Marcus. Apart from the fact that he might break her heart, it might cloud her judgment, complicate things.

Joanna took off her jeans and climbed into the big bed. And, tucking the hot-water bottle under her sweater, closed her eyes and tried to sleep.

13

On Saturday evening, Zoe was upstairs in her bedroom sorting out her laundry when she heard the doorbell ring. She decided to ignore it. Whoever it was, she couldn't face them tonight. Tweaking aside the net curtain that shielded her from the busy street beneath, she looked down.

"Oh God," she whispered when she saw the figure standing on the doorstep. She dropped the curtain back into place quickly, but not before he'd looked up and seen her.

The doorbell rang again.

Zoe looked down at her tracksuit trousers and ancient sweatshirt. Her hair was piled untidily on the top of her head and she wasn't wearing a stroke of makeup.

"Go away," she whispered, "please go away."

At the third ring Zoe leaned against the wall, her resolve crumbling, then went downstairs to open the door.

"Hello, Art."

"Can I come in?"

"Sure."

He stepped inside and closed the door behind him. Even dressed like a regular person in jeans and sweater, he was an arresting sight. Zoe couldn't bring herself to meet his gaze.

"What happened yesterday?" he asked. "Why did you leave Norfolk without telling me? My driver waited for you for over two hours."

"Art, I'm sorry, I . . ." She finally looked up into his warm green eyes. "I ran away. I was so . . . frightened."

"Oh, darling." He pulled her into his arms and held her close.

"Don't, *please*, it's wrong, *we're* wrong . . ." She tried to pull away, but he held her firmly.

"I nearly went mad when I couldn't get through to you, when I realized you were running away again. Zoe, my Zoe"—he smoothed away the blond hair from her face—"I've never stopped thinking about you, wanting you, wondering why—"

"Art . . ."

"Zoe, Jamie's mine, isn't he? Isn't he? However much you deny it, I've always known he was."

"No . . . no!"

"It didn't matter that you spun me some ridiculous story about another man. I didn't believe you then and I won't believe you now. After everything we shared together, even though we were so young, I knew you couldn't have done that to me. I knew you loved me too much to deceive me in that way."

"*Stop! Stop! Stop!*" She was crying now, still trying to break free of his grasp, but he held her tight.

"I have to know, Zoe. Is Jamie mine? Is he?!"

"*Yes! Jamie's yours!*" she screamed. All her energy spent, she sagged in his arms. "He's yours."

"God . . ."

They stood in the hallway, holding each other in mutual despair. Then he kissed her, first on the forehead, then on her cheeks, her nose, and eventually her mouth.

"Have you any idea how I've dreamed of this moment, longed for it, prayed for it . . . ?" He caressed her ears, her neck, then in one easy movement pulled her gently to the floor.

Afterward, as they lay in the hall in a tangle of discarded clothes, Art was the first to speak. "Zoe, forgive me. I . . ." His hands roamed the soft skin of her back, unable to stop touching her, confirming her physical presence next to him. "I love you. I always have and I always will. Listen, the car's waiting for me outside, but please, let me see you again. I understand how impossible this is for you, for both of us, but . . . *please*," he begged her again.

She offered him his boxer shorts and his socks, silently reveling in the intimacy of seeing him put on the mundane items.

When he was dressed, he stood up and pulled her to standing too. "There is a way, darling. For now, we just have to see each other in secret. I know it's not how it should be, but surely we owe it to ourselves to try it for a while?"

"I don't know." She leaned into his chest and sighed. "It's Jamie . . . I'm so scared for him. I don't want anything in his life to change. He mustn't be affected."

"He won't be, I promise. Jamie is our precious secret. And I am so very glad you told me, Zoe," he murmured. "I love you." He gave her a final smile, then headed for the door. With a kiss blown toward her, he opened it and was gone.

Zoe staggered to the sitting room and sank onto the sofa. She stared into space for a while, reliving every second of the past forty-five minutes. Then the demons began threatening to invade her mental tranquility, whispering their doubts and warnings about the ramifications of breaking the promise she'd vowed to keep forever.

No . . . Not tonight.

She wouldn't let the past *or* the present torture her. She would take this moment and wrap its pleasure and its peace around her for as long as she could.

———

Joanna woke at eight on Sunday morning, unaccustomed these days to the quiet of the countryside—no shouting from the street outside or car alarms, just silence. She allowed herself a delicious stretch in the comfortable old bed, before climbing out and dressing, then shivering her way down the stairs. She donned her coat, which hung over the banister at the bottom, and went to stir the glowing embers of yesterday's fire, adding firelighters, tinder, and logs to try to banish the god-awful cold.

There was so little time, she thought, staring at the boxes, and such an impossible mountain of documents still upstairs in the attic. At this rate, she'd need weeks to go through them carefully and systematically. Beginning again on the second box, she set to work.

At eleven o'clock, Marcus finally appeared, his face creased from sleep, an eiderdown wrapped round his shoulders. Yet somehow, he still managed to look attractive.

"Morning."

"Morning." Joanna smiled up at him.

"Been up long?"

"Since eight."

"Blimey, the middle of the night. Still at it, I see." He indicated the half-empty box next to her.

"Yep. I've just found some unused clothing coupons from 1943." She flapped the pieces of paper at him. "I wonder if Harvey Nicks would still accept them."

Marcus chuckled. "No, but they must be worth a few bob in their own right. I think Zoe and me'll have to seriously wade our own way through that stuff soon. Tea? Coffee?"

"I'd love a coffee."

"Right." Marcus shuffled out in the direction of the kitchen. Joanna, in need of a break, followed him and took a seat at the old oak table.

"I don't think your grandfather started collecting stuff until the mid-1930s, which is a real pain, because the biographies are all very vague about his childhood and early adulthood. Do you know anything about it?"

"Not really." Marcus lifted the range's hob cover and put the stovetop kettle on to boil. He sat down opposite her and lit a cigarette. "From what I know, he was born somewhere near here and ran away to London town to tread the boards at sixteen. At least that's the folklore, anyway."

"I'm surprised he didn't marry again after Grace died. Ninety-five years is a long time for just one marriage of eight years."

"Ah, well, that's what true love can do for you."

They sat in contemplative silence for a couple of minutes until the kettle whistled from the hob and Marcus stood up to take it off and pour the hot water into a mug. "There you go." He put a steaming coffee in front of her, and she held the mug to her chest.

"Your poor dad, losing his mother so young."

"Yeah. At least I had my mum around until I was fourteen. The women in our family seem to be accident prone, while the men thrive and live to grand old ages."

"Don't tell Zoe." She took a sip of the coffee.

"Or any future wife of mine, for that matter," Marcus added. "Anyway, are you going to take time out for a traditional Sunday roast, or do I have to go by myself?"

"Marcus, you've only just got up! How can you even *think* about beer and roast beef!"

"I was thinking of you, actually, and how hungry you must be."

"Really?" She raised an eyebrow. "That's very thoughtful of you. Okay then, I've got enough to write a half-decent article now anyway. I was wondering, though, whether you'd allow me to take one photo that I found with me to put in the article. It's of Sir James, with Noël Coward and Gertrude Lawrence—really atmospheric of the era. I thought the idea of having a photo of him as a young actor would mirror nicely the fact that the memorial fund is for the young actors of today. I'd send it straight back, of course."

"I don't see why not. I'll have to okay it with Zoe before you print it," Marcus replied.

"Thanks. Now"—Joanna stood up—"can you help me bring down another box?"

At one o'clock, Marcus pulled Joanna to her feet and bundled her into the car, ignoring her protests.

"How many words is this article going to be?" he asked her.

"You've got enough for a whole bloody book! Let's enjoy what's left of the weekend."

———

Joanna leaned back in her seat and gazed out the window, savoring the views of the glittering white countryside. They drove through the small town of Blandford Forum, its streets lined by tall Georgian houses, and Marcus, with a wry grin, pointed out all the pubs he had been kicked out of as a teenager. He pulled up outside a small red-brick pub with a cheerful green front door. "This place does the best Sunday roast for miles around—with the biggest Yorkshire puddings you've ever seen."

"That's a serious promise you're making to a Yorkshire girl," she giggled. "I hope you can keep it."

After a scrumptious lunch, complete with the crispy-yet-doughy Yorkshire puddings Marcus had promised plus lashings of gravy, Joanna dragged her companion to his feet.

"Right! I need to walk off that lunch," she said. "Any suggestions?"

"Yes, I'll take you up to Hambledon Hill. Climb in, milady." Marcus opened the passenger door of the car for her.

They stepped out a few miles later, and Joanna looked up at the gentle rise of a tall hill. It was now three in the afternoon and the sun was just beginning to set, sending golden rays skipping over the snow-covered slope. It reminded her so much of home on the Yorkshire moors that she felt a lump in her throat.

"I love this place," Marcus said, crooking his arm through hers. "I used to come up here a lot when I was staying with my grandfather during the holidays—I'd just sit on the top of the hill to have a think and get away from everything."

They walked upward, arm in arm, and Joanna reveled in how still and peaceful her mind felt here with Marcus, so far away from London. They stopped to sit down on a tree stump halfway up the hill, and admire the view.

"What did you think about when you came up here?" she asked him.

"Oh, you know ... boy stuff," he hedged.

"I don't know. Tell me," she encouraged him.

"I thought about what I was going to do when I was older," he said, looking into the distance. "My mum ... she really loved nature and was passionate about protecting it. She was what one might call an 'eco warrior' and used to go on Greenpeace marches and lobby Parliament. I just always wanted to do something that she'd be proud of, you know?" He turned and looked at her, and she found herself captivated by his gaze. "Something important, something that mattered, I—" He broke off, and kicked at the snow. "But since then, it's all gone wrong, so I think she'd be disappointed."

"I don't believe she would be," Joanna said eventually.

Marcus turned to her with a sad smile. "You don't?"

She shook her head. "No. Mums always love their kids, no matter what. And the main thing is, you've tried. And your new film project really sounds worthwhile."

"It is, *if* I can get the funding for it. To be honest, Jo, I really am crap with money. I've realized recently that I let my heart rule my head, jump in with both feet first because I'm excited by the idea, and never see the risks. I'm like that with relationships too ... all or nothing, that's me," he confessed. "Just like my mum was."

"There's nothing wrong with being passionate, Marcus."

"There is when you're using other people's money to fund it ... I've been thinking recently that if I get this new project off the ground, I'm going to shadow Ben MacIntyre, the director, as an assistant. Maybe I should concentrate on the 'vision' in future, rather than the finances."

"Maybe you should," Joanna agreed.

"Now, I'm freezing my knackers off, why don't we head home?"

"Soft southerners," she said in her broadest Yorkshire accent. "Can't 'ack the cold!"

They returned to the relative warmth of Haycroft House, and while Marcus heaved the boxes back into the attic, Joanna tidied the kitchen.

"All set?" Marcus stood in the hall as she arrived downstairs, having collected her holdall.

"Yes. Thanks for the weekend, Marcus. I've really enjoyed it. And I really don't want to go back to London."

Marcus returned the key to its hiding place before jumping behind the wheel next to her and starting the engine. Turning out of the drive, he caught a flash of the gray car he'd seen the day before, and Joanna followed his glance.

"Who's that? Nosy neighbors?" she said.

"Probably just some bird-watchers out to freeze their rocks off over some robins," he answered. "They were here yesterday too. Either that, or they're going to nick all the valuables in the place."

Joanna stiffened. "Don't you think you ought to let the police know?"

"Jo, I was joking!" he said as they passed the parked car.

Joanna was not calmed by his casual reply. The earlier peace she had felt evaporated, and for the rest of their drive to London, she surreptitiously kept an eye on the rearview mirror, tensing at every gray car they saw.

On Highgate Hill, Marcus parked the Golf in front of Simon's building.

"Thanks, Marcus. I can't tell you how grateful I am."

"Just make sure you get the family and me at least a double-page spread on the memorial fund in that rag of yours. Listen, Jo." He leaned over the gearstick and gripped her hand before she could escape. "Can I see you again? Maybe dinner on Thursday evening?"

"Yes," she said without hesitation. She leaned over and kissed him lightly on the lips. "I'll see you on Thursday. Bye, Marcus."

"Bye, Jo," he answered wistfully as she climbed out of the car and pulled her holdall out of the trunk.

"I'll miss you," he whispered as she gave him a wave and a smile and walked up to the front door.

As Joanna soldiered up the long flight of stairs, she decided that there was far more to Marcus Harrison than she had expected. But as she turned the key in the lock, the warmth in her belly was immediately replaced by the cold fear that she had been followed again. By whom? And what exactly could they want with her?

She took off her coat, with a renewed gratitude for the modern convenience of timed central heating, then placed the photograph she had acquired from Haycroft House on the coffee table. She went to the kitchen to put on the kettle for tea and make a sandwich, then settled down at the table. Collecting the pile of biographies, then pulling the music-hall program and the photocopy of the love letter Rose had given her out of her rucksack, she placed everything in front of her. She reread both Rose's note and the love letter, then flicked through the old program from the Hackney Empire, studying the photographs of the cast. Her heart began to pound as she finally recognized a face.

Mr. Michael O'Connell! Impersonator Extraordinaire! the program read beneath the photograph.

Joanna put the picture she had brought back from Dorset beside it and compared the faces of James Harrison and Michael O'Connell. Even though the picture in the program was old and grainy, there was little doubt. With his dark blond hair and devoid of a moustache, the young actor calling himself Michael O'Connell was a double for James Harrison. Unless they were twins, they had to be one and the same man.

But why? Why would Michael O'Connell alter his name? Yes, it was quite possible he would have decided to acquire a stage name that he felt suited him better, but surely he'd have done that right at the beginning of his career, not a few years later? By the time he'd married Grace in 1929, he'd apparently dyed his hair black and grown a moustache. And none of the biographies noted any change of name. The early details all related to the "Harrison" family.

Joanna shook her head. Maybe it was just coincidence that the two men looked so alike. And yet, it would finally explain the significance of the program, and the reason why Rose had sent it to her.

Had Sir James Harrison once been someone else? Someone with a past he wished others to forget?

STALEMATE

An impasse, wherein no
legal move is possible

14

Alec was not at his desk when she arrived in the office the following morning. When he did appear an hour later, she pounced on him immediately. "Alec, I've found something on—"

Alec held up a hand to stop her. "Deal's off, I'm afraid. You're being moved to Pets and Gardens."

Joanna stared at him. "What?"

Alec shrugged. "Nothing to do with me. The whole point in your first year here is that you work on every section of the paper. Your time on the news desk is over. You no longer belong to me. Sorry, Jo, but there it is."

"I . . . but I've only been on the section for a few weeks. Besides, I can't just let this story go. I . . ." Joanna was so shocked she couldn't take in what he was saying. "Pets and bloody Gardens?! Jesus! Why, Alec?"

"Look, don't ask me. I just work here. Go and see the ed if you want. He suggested a move round."

Joanna glanced down the corridor at the threadbare carpet in front of the glass-paneled office, worn down by nervous hacks facing a demolition job from their boss. She swallowed hard, not wanting to cry in front of Alec, or anyone else in the office for that matter.

"Did he say why?"

"Nope." Alec sat down behind his computer screen.

"Doesn't he like my work? Me? My perfume?! Everybody knows that 'dog poo and mulch' is the armpit of the newspaper. I'm literally being buried alive!"

"Jo, calm down. It'll probably only be for a few weeks. If it makes you feel any better, I did stand up for you, but it was a no-go, I'm afraid."

Joanna watched as Alec typed something on the screen. She leaned forward. "You don't think . . ."

He looked up at her. "No. I don't. Just type up that frigging piece about the memorial fund, then clear your desk. Mighty Mike is doing a direct swap with you."

"Mighty Mike? On news?!"

Mike O'Driscoll was the butt of many office jokes. He had the physique of an undernourished gnome and suffered from severe sincerity overkill. Alec only offered her another shrug. Joanna stomped back to her desk and sat down.

"Problem?" asked Alice.

"You could say that. I'm being swapped with Mighty Mike onto Pets and Gardens."

"Blimey, give the *Express* details of a scoop, did you?"

"I've done absolutely bugger-all," moaned Joanna, folding her arms and resting her head on them. "I just can't believe it."

"You think you've got problems—I've got Mighty Mike moving to the desk next to mine now," said Alice. "Oh well, no more freezing your tits off on someone's doorstep, just gentle little articles on canine psychology and what time of year to plant your begonias. I wouldn't mind a rest like that."

"Nor would I, when I'm sixty-five with a great career as a journalist behind me. Jesus!"

Joanna began to type aggressively, too upset to concentrate. Ten minutes later, there was a tap on her shoulder and a huge bouquet of red roses was pressed into her hand by Alec.

"These should cheer you up."

"Alec, I didn't know you cared," she quipped harshly as he returned to his desk.

"Blimey!" Alice looked at her with envy. "Who're they from?"

"A sympathizer, probably," Joanna muttered as she tore the small white envelope from the cellophane and opened it.

These are to say good morning. I'll call you later.
Yours ever, M x

Despite her bad mood, Joanna could not help but smile at Marcus's note.

"Come on then, spill the beans. Who is it?" Alice studied her. "It's not . . . is it?"

Joanna blushed.

"It bloody well is! You didn't, did you?"

"No, I didn't! Now, will you just shut the hell up!"

Joanna finished her particularly uninspired article on Marcus and the memorial fund, feeling guilty that she wasn't giving it everything, despite the flowers and how good he'd been to her. Then she cleared her desk and traipsed her belongings to the other side of the office.

Mighty Mike was virtually hopping up and down with excitement, which made the whole thing even worse. It transpired that it wasn't the news desk he was looking forward to, but the prospect of sitting next to Alice, whom he'd had a crush on for months.

At least that'll pay her back a little, thought Joanna bitchily as she sat down at Mighty Mike's recently vacated chair and studied the photos of cute pooches he'd pinned on the corkboard.

That night, the thought of going home alone to an empty apartment was just too much, so she went with Alice to the local to drown her sorrows in a few gin and tonics.

Forty-five minutes later, she saw Alec arrive. She left Alice and made a beeline for him. She perched on a bar stool next to him as he ordered his whiskey.

"Don't even start, Jo. It's been a hell of a day."

"Alec, answer me one question: am I a good reporter?"

"You were shaping up nicely, yes."

"Okay." Joanna nodded, trying to collect her thoughts and doing her best not to slur her words. "How long exactly does a junior usually stay on your section before being moved on?"

"Jo . . . ," he groaned.

"*Please*, Alec! I have to know."

"Okay, about three months minimum, unless I want to get rid of them faster."

"And I've only been here nine weeks. I counted. You just said I was shaping up very nicely, so you didn't want to get rid of me, did you?"

"No." Alec gulped down his whiskey.

"Therefore, I must deduce that my sudden demotion has nothing to do with my work, but with something else that I might have stumbled over. Yes?"

He sighed, then finally nodded. "Yup. I tell you, Haslam, if you ever say it was me who tipped you the wink, it won't be Pets and Gardens, it'll be the dole queue for you. Understand?"

"I swear, I won't." Joanna indicated both her empty glass and Alec's to the barman.

"If I were you, I'd keep your head down, your nose clean, and hopefully this whole thing'll soon be forgotten about," Alec said.

Joanna handed Alec his whiskey—anything to keep him there for a few more minutes. "The thing is, I discovered something more over the weekend. I wouldn't put it on state-secret level, but it is interesting."

"Look, Jo, I've been in this game a long time"—he lowered his voice—"and from the way those up there are acting, whatever you're onto might *well* be 'state-secret level.' I've not seen the ed so jumpy since Di's Gilbey tapes. I'm telling you, Jo, leave it be."

She sipped her gin and tonic and studied Alec—his greasy gray hair, which stuck up in tufts from constantly running his hands through it; the belly that strained over a worn leather belt; and a pair of whiskey-sodden eyes.

"Tell me something." She spoke quietly so Alec had to lean in to hear her. "If you were me, just at the start of your career, and you had stumbled onto something that was obviously so hot that even the editor of one of the bestselling dailies in the country had been warned off, would you 'leave it be'?"

He thought for a minute, then looked up and gave her a smile. "Course I wouldn't."

"Thought not." She patted his hand and hopped off the bar stool. "Thanks, Alec."

"Don't say I didn't bloody warn you. And trust no bugger!" he called as Joanna crossed the bar to retrieve her coat. She saw Alice was being chatted up by a photographer.

"You off?" Alice asked.

"Yes. I'd better go and do my homework on how best to prevent snails from eating one's pansies."

"Never mind, you've always got Marcus Harrison to console you."

"Yeah." Joanna nodded, too tired to argue. "Bye, Alice."

She hailed a taxi to take her to Simon's apartment, wishing she'd not had so many gin and tonics. On arrival she made a large mug of strong coffee, then checked the answering machine for messages.

"Hi, Jo, it's Simon. You weren't answering your mobile. I should be back by ten tonight, so don't lock the door from the inside. Hope all's well. Bye."

"Hi, Simon, Ian here. Thought you'd be home by now and can't get through on your mobile, but would you give me a call when you get in? Something's come up. Okay, bye."

Joanna wrote the message down on the pad, then saw the card lying there that Simon had given her with his friend's number on it.

IAN C. SIMPSON

Digging in her rucksack, she pulled out the pen she'd found after the break-in and studied the initials engraved on the side of it.

I. C. S.

"Bloody hell!" she said out loud to the empty room.

Trust no bugger . . .

Alec's words floated into her head. Was it the gin and the awful day she'd had that were making her paranoid? After all, there had to be a lot of people whose initials were I. C. S. On the other hand, how many robbers carried an initialed gold fountain pen when they were trashing a home?

And the love letter . . .

She'd never even paused to consider whether Simon's offer might be anything other than genuine. Yet he'd been so insistent he take it, now that she thought about it. And what exactly did he *do* as a "civil servant"? This was a man who'd got a first at Cambridge, with a big brain that was hardly likely to be utilized processing parking tickets. And he was a man with convenient "mates" in a forensics lab . . .

"Damn!"

Joanna heard the sound of footsteps up the stairs. She stuffed the card and the pen into her rucksack and jumped onto the sofa.

"Hi, how are you?" Simon came in, put down his holdall, and walked over to kiss the top of her head.

"Fine, yes, fine." She feigned a yawn and uncurled her legs from under her. "I must have dozed off. I had a few drinks at the pub after work."

"It was that good a day?"

"Yeah. That good. How was your trip?"

"A lot of boring presentations to sit through." Simon went into the kitchen and switched on the kettle. "Want a cuppa?"

"Go on then. Oh, by the way," Joanna added casually, "there was a message from someone called Ian for you on the answering machine when I got home. He wants you to ring him back."

"Sure." Simon made two cups of tea, then sat down next to her. "So, how've you been?"

"Okay. My apartment's almost back to normal and I've filled in all the insurance forms and everything's being processed. My new bed is arriving tomorrow and the computer guy is coming to set everything up. So I'll ship out of here now that you're back."

"Take your time. There's no rush."

"I know, but I think I'd like to get home."

"Of course." Simon took a sip of his tea. "So, any more progress on strange little old ladies and their correspondence?"

"No. I told you I wasn't going to pursue it, unless your forensic friend came up with anything." She glanced at him. "Did he?"

"Nothing, I'm afraid. I popped into the office on the way home and there was a note on my desk from my mate. Apparently the paper was too delicate to be properly analyzed."

"Oh well," she said as casually as she could. "Do you have the letter? I'd like to keep it anyway."

"I'm afraid I don't. It disintegrated during the chemical process. My mate did say he thought it was over seventy years old. Sorry about that, Jo."

"Never mind. It was probably of no importance anyway. Thanks for trying, Simon."

Joanna was proud of her control, when all she really wanted to do was to rugby-tackle him to the ground and punch his lights out for his betrayal.

"That's okay." He was staring at her, his surprise at her calm exterior obvious on his face.

"Besides, now it seems like I have more pressing problems of my own to attend to, rather than flying off on some wild goose chase. My beloved editor has decided—for reasons best known to himself—to transfer me from the news desk onto Pets and Gardens. So, I have to focus on how to make my stay there as short as possible."

"I'm sorry to hear that. Didn't he give you a reason?"

"Nope. Anyway, at least I don't have to doorstep anymore, just wander round the Chelsea Flower Show in a floaty dress and a pair of white gloves." She gave him a sad shrug.

"You seem to be taking it very well. I would have thought you'd be fuming."

"What's the point? And as I said, tonight I've had a few gins to take away the pain. You should have heard me in the pub earlier. Anyway, if you don't mind, I'll take a shower and then hit the sack. The shock's worn me out."

"You poor old thing, you. Don't worry, one day you'll be the ed and can get your own back," Simon said, trying to comfort her.

"Maybe." Joanna stood up to head for the bathroom. "I'll see you tomorrow."

"Yes, night, Jo." Simon kissed her on the cheek, then once he heard the shower turn on, he went into his bedroom and shut the door. He took out his mobile phone and dialed a number.

"Simon here, Ian. Thought I told you not to leave messages on my home phone—Haslam's staying here."

"Sorry, forgot. How was the training?"

"Tough, but it'll pay off. What's up?"

"Phone Jenkins at home. He'll tell you."

"Okay. See you tomorrow."

"Night."

Simon dialed the number from memory.

"Sir, it's Warburton."

"Thank you for calling. Did you tell her the letter had disintegrated as planned?"

"Yes."

"Did she take the news well?"

"Surprisingly so."

"Good. You're to report straight to me at nine tomorrow morning. I have a special assignment for you."

"Right, sir. Good night."

Simon clicked off the phone and sat down on his bed, giving his tired muscles a rest. It had been a grueling week at the agency's base in the Scottish Highlands, running drills for counterterrorism training. On top of that, tonight he felt he was being forced to step into murky waters, as if his personal and work lives were colliding. And at all costs, he was desperate to keep them separate.

The following morning at a quarter to eight, Simon tiptoed through the darkened sitting room to reach the shower and realized Joanna had already left. He picked up the note she had propped on the kitchen table.

Went home to get some clean clothes before work.
Thanks for having me. See you soon. x

There was nothing wrong with the note, but knowing her so well, he had the distinct feeling something was up. Last night, she'd been far too calm about the letter's disappearing.

Simon would have bet his life that she was still on the trail of her little old lady.

15

As filming in Norfolk continued, Zoe completely immersed herself in the character of Tess, the woman who had become an outcast in her village for having an illegitimate child. Zoe could not help but draw parallels between their lives. And only hoped she wouldn't come to the same tragic end.

"Keep it up, Zoe, and you'll be heading for a BAFTA," said Mike, the director, as he drove her back to the hotel after watching the rushes. "You're positively glowing for the camera. Bed early for you tonight, darling. We have a long day tomorrow."

"Of course. Thanks, Mike. Good night."

They collected their keys from reception, and Zoe walked up the steep, creaking stairs to her room. Her mobile rang from inside her handbag as she opened her door. Fumbling among the mints, lipsticks, and other detritus, she finally found it and closed the door behind her before answering.

"It's me."

"Hello 'me.' How are you?" she whispered with a secret smile.

"Oh, hectic as usual. And missing you."

Zoe sank onto the bed, cradling the phone to her ear as she drank in his voice. "I miss you too."

"Can you make it to Sandringham this weekend?"

"I think so. Mike says he wants to do some early morning mist shots, but I should be free by lunchtime. I'll probably fall asleep by seven, though. I'll have been up since four."

"As long as it's in my arms, I don't care." There was a pause on the line. Then, "God, Zoe, just now I wish I was anyone else."

"I don't. I'm glad you're you," she said soothingly. "Only a couple more days and we'll be together. Are you sure it's safe?"

"Absolutely. Those who have to know are aware of the delicacy of the situation. And remember, discretion *is* their job. Don't worry, darling, please."

"It's not me, Art, it's Jamie I'm concerned for."

"Of course, but trust me, will you? I'll have my driver wait for you outside the hotel from one onward on Friday. I've got York Cottage in the grounds for the weekend, told the rest of the family I want some privacy. They understand. They won't disturb us."

"Okay."

"I'm counting the hours, darling. Good night."

"Night."

Zoe clicked the phone off and lay on the bed staring at the cracked ceiling of her hotel bedroom, a smile drifting across her face. A whole weekend with Art was more than she'd ever enjoyed before.

And even for Jamie's sake, she could not refuse.

Having taken a hot bath, Zoe went downstairs for supper. Most of the cast and crew had driven to the nearby town of Holt to try an apparently excellent Indian restaurant, so the small dining room, with its dark wooden cottage-style tables and chairs, was blissfully empty. She sat down in the corner near the fire and ordered the local pork casserole from the young waitress, realizing she was starving.

Just as her food arrived, William Fielding, the old actor playing her father, appeared, swaying slightly, at the entrance to the restaurant.

"Hello, m'dear. All alone?" He smiled, his gentle eyes creasing at the corners.

"Yes." Then, a trifle reluctantly, Zoe said, "Why don't you join me?"

"I'd like that very much indeed." William shuffled toward her, pulled out a chair, and eased himself into it. "This darned arthritis is eating away at my bones. And the cold here isn't helping." He leaned in so near that Zoe could smell the alcohol on his breath. "Still, should be happy I'm working, and playing a man a good few years younger than myself. I feel like your grandfather, not your dad, m'dear."

"Nonsense. Age is how you feel inside, and you skipped up those stairs during filming today like a spring chicken," Zoe said, trying to comfort him.

"Yes, and it nearly bloody well killed me," he chuckled. "Still, can't let our revered director think I'm past it."

The waitress was hovering by the table with a menu.

"Thank you, m'dear." William put on his glasses and perused it. "Now, what do we have here? I'll have the soup, the roast of the day, and a double whiskey on the rocks to wash it down."

"Yes, sir."

"Would have a nice glass of claret, but the stuff they serve here is no better than vinegar," William remarked as he removed his glasses. "Enjoying the lunches, though. Location catering is always one of the treats of filming, don't you think?"

"Absolutely. I've put on almost four pounds since the beginning of the shoot," Zoe admitted.

"Looks like you could do with it, too, if you don't mind me saying. Suppose you're still getting over the death of dear Sir James."

"Actually, I don't think I'll ever really get over it. He was more of a father to me than my real dad. I miss him every day, and the pain doesn't seem to get any less," Zoe admitted.

"It will, m'dear. I can say that because I'm old and I know. Ah, thank you." William took the whiskey from the waitress and drank a large gulp. "I lost my wife ten years ago to cancer. Didn't think I could live without her. But I'm still here, surviving. I miss her, but at least I've accepted that she's gone now. Lonely old life, though. Don't know what I'd do if I didn't have the work."

"A lot of actors seem to live to grand old ages. I've often wondered if that's because they never really retire, just carry on until they—"

"Drop down dead. Quite." He drained his whiskey and signaled for another. "Your grandfather lived until ninety-five, didn't he? A good innings if I may say so. It inspires me to think I could have another thirteen years or so still to go."

"Are you really eighty-two?" she said with genuine surprise.

"To you, my dear, this very year. To the rest of the business, I hover around sixty-seven." William put a finger to his lips. "I only ever remembered precisely how old I was because I knew Sir James was exactly thirteen years older, to the day. We shared a birth date. Once celebrated it with him, many, many years ago. Aha! Soup, and it smells delicious. Excuse me while I plunder my bowl."

"Not at all." Zoe watched as William rather messily slurped the soup into his mouth with a shaking hand.

"So, did you know my grandfather well?" she asked when William had pushed the bowl away and ordered another whiskey.

"Yes, many, many years ago, before he became—and I mean quite literally—James Harrison."

"What do you mean, 'quite literally'?"

"Well, as I'm sure you know, 'James Harrison' was his stage name. When I met him, he was as 'Oirish' as they come. Hailed from West Cork somewhere—called Michael O'Connell when I first knew him."

Zoe regarded him in astonishment. "Are you sure you're thinking of the same actor? I know he was fond of Ireland, talked about it being a beautiful place, especially toward the end of his life, but I had no idea he actually *was* Irish. And it's never mentioned in any of his biographies. I thought he was born in Dorset, and I certainly never heard a hint of an Irish accent in his voice."

"Aha! Well, there you are. Just shows what a talented actor he was. He had the most brilliant gift for mimicry—could do any accent or voice one suggested. In fact, that's how he began his career—as an impersonator in music halls. Surprised you didn't know, being so close to him, but without a doubt, you're descended from Irish blood."

"Goodness! So, tell me, where did you first meet my grandfather?"

"At the Hackney Empire. I was only nine at the time. Michael was twenty-two and in his first professional job."

"You were nine?" marveled Zoe.

"For my sins, yes. Born in a prop basket, that's me," William said with a smile. "My mama was in variety, too, and seemed to have mislaid my papa. So she took me to the theater when she worked, and I'd sleep in a drawer in her dressing room. When I got bigger, I used to do odd jobs for the performers—bring in food, take messages, and fetch and carry for a few bob. That's how I met Michael, except, like everyone else, I used to call him 'Siam.' His first job was playing the genie of the lamp in the Empire pantomime. He'd shaved his head and darkened his skin, and he looked just like some pictures I'd seen of the king of Siam, with his pantaloons and headdress. The nickname stuck, as I'm sure you know."

"Yes." Zoe nodded, her supper forgotten as she listened to him.

"Of course, he was desperate to get into proper theater, but we all have to start somewhere. Even in those days he had charisma. All the young dancing girls used to queue up to go out with him. Must have been that Irish charm, even if by then he spoke with a plum in his mouth. One had to, in those days, you see, although he used to entertain us all with his Irish ballads." William chuckled.

Zoe watched William carefully as he drained another glass. He'd had three double whiskies since he joined her. And he was recalling seventy-year-old memories. There was every chance he had James confused with someone else. She picked at her cooling casserole as his roast beef arrived.

"Are you saying he was a ladies' man?"

"Indeed he was. But he always dumped them with such charm that they ended up loving him anyway. Then one day, halfway through the season, he suddenly up and left. After two or three days, when he hadn't appeared for the performance, I was sent round to his lodgings to find out if he was ill, or had simply imbibed too much juice. All his belongings were still there, but, m'dear, your grandfather was not."

"Really? Did he ever come back?"

"Yes, but it was over six months later. I popped round quite a bit to his lodgings to see if he'd returned. He'd always been generous with sweets and the odd few coppers if I ran errands for him. Then one day, my knock was answered. He opened the door with a smart new haircut and an expensive suit to boot. I remember him telling me it was from Savile Row. He looked like a real gentleman. Always was a handsome sod." William chuckled again.

"Wow. This is some story. I had no idea. He never mentioned anything to me. Did you ask him where he'd been?"

"Of course I did. I was fascinated. Your grandfather told me he'd been doing some lucrative acting work and that's all he'd say. He told me he was coming back to the Empire to continue his act, that it had all been arranged. And when he did, the management didn't bat an eyelid. It was like he'd never been away."

"Have you ever told anyone else about this?" she asked.

"Absolutely not, m'dear. He warned me not to. Michael was my friend. He trusted me when I was a young'un and I trusted him. Anyway, I haven't got to the most interesting bit yet." William's rheumy eyes were alight with the thrill of entertaining his captive audience. "Shall we order coffee and wander through to the bar and the comfy seats? My backside has gone positively numb on these hard chairs."

The two of them found a comfortable banquette in the corner of the bar. William heaved a contented sigh and lit up an untipped cigarette.

"Anyway," he continued, "one day, a couple of weeks after he'd come back, he called me into his dressing room. He handed me two shillings and a letter and asked me if I'd run an errand for him. He sent me off to stand in front of Swan and Edgar—the department store by Piccadilly Circus, don't you know? And he told me to wait there until a young woman dressed in pink came along and asked me if I had the time."

"And did you?"

"Of course I did! In those days, for two shillings, I'd have gone to the moon!"

"And the woman came?"

"Oh yes. In her lovely clothes, with her clipped vowels. I knew immediately she was a lady. And I mean a *real* lady."

"Was it just the once?"

"No. Over those few months, I met her ten, maybe fifteen times. I'd hand her an envelope."

"And did she give you anything?"

"Square packages, wrapped in brown paper."

"Really? What do you think was inside them?"

"I have no idea. Not that I didn't try to guess." William flicked his ash into the ashtray and flashed her a smile, his eyes disappearing further into his pouchy face.

Zoe bit her lip. "Do you think he was involved in something illegal?"

"Could have been, but Michael never struck me as the kind of man to be mixed up in anything criminal. He was such a gentle man."

"So what do you think it was all about?"

"I suppose . . . well, I always thought it was some kind of a secret love affair."

"Between who? Michael and the woman you met?"

"Perhaps. But I think she was an emissary, just as I was."

"You didn't look inside the packages?"

"No, although I could have done. I was always a loyal bod, and your grandfather was so generous to me, I couldn't betray his trust."

Zoe sipped her coffee, feeling weary but fascinated, whether or not the tale was truth, fiction, or a little of both embellished by the passage of time.

"Then the next thing that happens is Michael calls me round to his lodgings and says he's got to go away again. He gives me enough money to make sure I'll eat well for a good year and suggests that I forget what's taken place in the past few months, for my own sake.

If anyone was to ask me, especially those in authority, I was to say I didn't know him. Or at least, only in passing." William stubbed out his cigarette. "And then it's bon voyage, Michael O'Connell. Literally, my darling, he disappeared off the face of the earth."

"You have no idea where he went?"

"None. Then blow me down, the next time I see Michael O'Connell is a good eighteen months later, and his picture is staring down at me from a theater on Shaftesbury Avenue under the name 'James Harrison.' He'd dyed his hair black, and was sporting a moustache, but I'd have known those blue eyes anywhere."

Zoe looked at him in amazement. "So, you're saying he disappeared *again*, then resurfaced with dark hair, a moustache, and another name? William, I have to tell you, I'm finding all this hard to believe."

"Well." He belched loudly. "I swear it's all true, m'dear. Of course, having seen his picture outside the theater and knowing it was him, even with an assumed name, I went to the stage door and asked for him. When he saw it was me, he swiped me into his dressing room and closed the door. He told me it would be much, much better for my general well-being if I stayed away from him, that he was someone else now, and that it was dangerous for me to know him from before. So"—William shrugged—"I took him at his word."

"Did you ever see him again?"

"Only from the stalls, m'dear. I wrote to him a couple of times but the letters were never answered. Got an envelope sent to me every birthday, mind you, with a wad of cash inside it. No note, but I knew it was from him. So, there you are. The strange tale of your beloved grandfather in his early years, never before repeated by these lips. Now that he's no longer with us, I hardly think it matters anymore. And you may well be able to investigate further, if it pleases you to do so." William scratched his ear. "I'm trying to remember the name of the young lady I met all those times in front of Swan and Edgar. She told me once. Daisy . . . ? No. Violet . . . I'm sure it was a flower . . ."

"Lily? Rose?" suggested Zoe.

A smile crossed his face. "By golly, you're right! It was Rose!"

"And you have absolutely no idea who she was?"

"Can't betray all his secrets, y'know." William tapped his nose. "I had an idea all right, but perhaps it's best that remains in the grave with him."

"I'm going to have to go up to the attic in his house in Dorset where he kept all his memorabilia, and sift through it. See if I can find anything relating to what you've told me."

"I doubt you will, m'dear. If it's been covered up for this long, strikes me we'll never know the truth. Still, makes for an interesting story over supper." He smiled at her.

"Yes." Zoe stifled a yawn and looked at her watch. "William, I think I must go to bed. I've an early call tomorrow. Thank you so much for telling me all this. I'll let you know if I turn anything up."

"You do that, Zoe." William watched her as she stood. He caught her hand and squeezed it. "You're so like him when he was young, m'dear. I was watching you this afternoon and you have the same gift. You're going to be very famous one day, and make your grandfather proud."

Tears came to Zoe's eyes. "Thanks, William," she murmured, and walked out of the bar.

16

Joanna had spent a miserable three days on Pets and Gardens, and an uncomfortable two nights sleeping in a makeshift pile of blankets and cushions on the floor of her bedroom, because the delivery of the new bed had not yet materialized. Tonight, she was meeting Marcus for dinner, and just the thought of having a soft, comfortable bed beneath her might actually have been enough to tempt her into staying with him for the night. She pulled on her well-worn and only LBD and teamed it with a fitted cardigan and slip-on shoes. Then she added some mascara to her lashes, a little blusher, and some lipstick. And, with her long hair still damp from the shower, set off for the bus stop.

As she walked, she tried to keep her gait natural, and resisted the urge to constantly look behind her. She kept her bundle of keys in her fist, the sharp edges poking out from between her knuckles, just in case of an attack.

As the bus trundled along Shaftesbury Avenue toward Soho, Joanna mused on the evening ahead. And hated herself for being so excited at the prospect of seeing Marcus again. She'd also spent the last few days pondering whether she should take Marcus into her confidence and tell him what she had discovered about his grandfather. She'd had to make the painful decision not to trust Simon, and had done her best to assign him to the "enemy camp"—even though she didn't know who this "enemy" actually was. Given her demotion, she'd had to take Alec out of the equation too. As the bus pulled to a stop near Lexington Street, Joanna alighted, deciding she could really do with an ally. Marcus was waiting for her in Andrew Edmunds—a rustic but charming candlelit restaurant.

"How are you?" He kissed her warmly on the lips.

"Fine, I'm fine." She slid into the chair opposite him.

"You look fabulous, Jo. Love the dress." Marcus's eyes traveled up and down her body. "Glass of champagne?"

"Go on then, you've forced me into it. Is it a special occasion?"

"Of course. We're having dinner together. That's special enough for me. Good week?"

"Terrible, actually. Apart from the fact I've been demoted at work, my new bed still hasn't arrived."

"Poor you. I thought you were staying with a friend until it did."

"I was, but it got a bit . . . crowded. Simon came back and the apartment's too small for both of us."

"Try and jump you, did he?"

"God, no!" Joanna pushed down a smidgen of guilt. "He's my oldest friend. We've known each other for years. Anyway"—she took a deep breath—"it's a long story, vaguely connected with your family, actually. I'll tell you over supper."

Once they had ordered food and wine, Marcus looked at her quizzically across the table.

"Go on then."

"Go on what?"

"Tell me all about it."

Joanna looked at him, suddenly uncertain. "I don't know whether I should."

"That big a deal?"

"That's the thing, I don't know. It may be something or nothing."

He reached across the table and took hold of her hand. "Joanna, I swear it won't go further than me. Strikes me that you need to talk to someone about it."

"You're right. I do. But I'm warning you, it's bizarre and complicated. Okay." She took a slurp of the very good red wine to give her confidence. "It all started when I turned up at your grandfather's memorial service . . ."

It took the starter, the main course, and most of the dessert before Joanna had brought Marcus up to date on "Little Old Lady–Gate," as she had nicknamed the situation. She decided not to tell him about the anonymous men on her trail, somehow afraid to voice the full reality of what she thought was happening.

At the end of her story, he lit a cigarette and slowly blew out the smoke, gazing at her steadily. "So that whole piece about me and the memorial fund was a cover-up so you could procure information about my grandfather and his dodgy past?"

"Originally, yes," Joanna admitted. "Sorry, Marcus. Although of course the article is going to be printed in the paper."

"I admit to feeling just a little used, Jo. Tell me honestly, are you having dinner with me tonight to see what else you can extract, or did you actually want to see me?"

"I wanted to see you, promise."

"Really?"

"Really."

"So, apart from the other thing, you do like me?" he probed.

"Yes, Marcus, of course I do."

"Okay." His expression cleared with what even Joanna believed was genuine relief. "Let's go over the facts again: strange old lady at Sir Jim's funeral, letter, program, your apartment gets trashed, you give said letter to so-called friend to have it analyzed, who then tells you it's disintegrated in the process—"

"And you know what?" Joanna butted in. "I can't believe it did. I mean, think of letters from hundreds of years ago that are still in existence, but would have been chemically processed to determine their age." She shook her head in frustration. "The question is, why did Simon lie to me? He really is my best friend."

"Sorry, Jo, but I think you're right to be suspicious of him. So,"

Marcus continued, "then you mention it to your boss, who tells you to follow it up, but does a quick U-turn a few days later and has you moved to a useless section of the paper where you can cause no harm." Marcus rubbed his chin. "Whatever it is you're onto, it's something. The question is, what do you do now?"

Joanna rifled through her rucksack for the envelope. "This is the photo I borrowed from the house in Dorset to dress up the article. And this is the theater program the little old lady gave me." She laid them side by side. "See? It's him, isn't it?"

Marcus studied both pictures. "It certainly looks like him, yes. If anyone would know more about this, it's my sister, Zoe. Except she's filming in Norfolk at the moment."

"I'd love to speak to Zoe, although I have to be very careful from now on, look as though I've dropped the whole thing. Could you arrange it?"

"Maybe, but it'll cost you."

"What?"

He grinned. "A brandy back at my place."

———

Joanna sat in Marcus's living room watching the flames leap in the gas fire. She felt calm, a little drowsy, and comforted that she had shared her secret with someone else.

"There you are." Marcus handed her a brandy glass and sat down next to her. "So, Miss Haslam, where do we go from here?"

"Well, you try and arrange for me to see Zoe and—"

He put a finger to her lips. "No, I wasn't talking about that. I was talking about us." He ran his finger up her cheek and caught a lock of her hair. "You see, I really don't want to just play Watson to your Holmes." He took the glass away from her before she had even taken a sip, then leaned toward her. "Let me kiss you, Joanna, please. You can tell me to stop at any time if you want to, and I promise I will."

Her stomach coiled in anticipation as Marcus put his lips to hers. She closed her eyes as she felt his tender kiss become more passionate, his tongue gently caressing hers. His arms closed around her shoulders and she relaxed into him as sense and right and wrong vanished in a haze of longing. Then he abruptly pulled away.

"What?" she murmured.

"Just making sure you don't want me to stop."

"No, I don't."

"Thank God for that," he whispered, and pulled her back toward him. "Oh, Joanna, God, you're gorgeous . . ."

An hour later, she saw his face next to hers, his expression full of wonder. And gave him a contented smile.

"Joanna, I think I love you . . ."

His arms wrapped around her shoulders and she drank in the smell of his fresh, clean hair and the faint musky aftershave on his neck.

"You okay?" he whispered.

"Yes."

He rolled away from her and propped himself up on his elbow.

"I meant what I said, you know. I think I'm falling in love with you."

"Bet you say that to all the girls," Joanna replied briskly.

"Before maybe, but never afterward." He sat up and reached for his trousers to dig in his pocket for his cigarettes. "Want one?"

"Go on then."

Marcus lit up two cigarettes and they sat on the floor cross-legged, smoking.

"That was really enjoyable." Joanna smiled at him.

"The sex?"

"No, the ciggie." Joanna stubbed hers out in an ashtray.

"You old romantic, you. Come here." Marcus reached for her again and kissed her. "You know, ever since that first lunch I've thought about you constantly. I mean, could we put this on a more permanent basis?"

"Are you asking me out?" she teased him.

"I suppose I am, though after the past hour, I'm quite happy to stay in as much as possible."

"Oh, Marcus, I don't know," Joanna sighed. "I told you before I had a long-term relationship with an awful ending. I'm still very vulnerable. Besides, your reputation goes before you, and—"

"What do you mean?"

"Come off it. Everyone I know in London has told me what a player you've been."

"Okay, okay, I admit I've been out with a few women, but I swear I've never felt like this before." Marcus stroked her hair. "I promise I'd never do anything to hurt you. Please give me a chance, Jo. We can take it as slowly as you like."

"Marcus, that was not very slow."

"Why are you so flippant every time I try and talk to you seriously?"

"Because"—Joanna rubbed her eyes, weary now—"I'm really scared."

"All I want is to be a part of your life. Give me a chance and I swear I won't let you down."

"Okay, I'll think about it." Joanna yawned. "I'm exhausted."

"You can stay tonight, seeing as you haven't a bed of your own to go to." He smiled at her.

"I've been perfectly okay on the floor for the past few days."

"Joanna, don't be so defensive. I was joking. There is nothing I would like more than to wake up next to you in the morning."

"Really?"

"Yes, really."

"Okay. Thanks."

He stood and offered her his hand to pull her to standing. He led her out of the sitting room and into the bedroom, then threw back the duvet.

"Ahh, a bed. Heaven." Joanna climbed in and snuggled down contentedly as Marcus slid in beside her and turned off the light.

"Jo?"

"Yes?"

"Do we really have to go to sleep straightaway?"

———

The following morning, Joanna was awoken by Marcus nuzzling her neck. Still half asleep, she came to as Marcus gently caressed her, then slowly made love to her again.

"Oh my God! Look at the time. It's twenty past nine! I'm going to be horrifically late!" Joanna sprang from the bed, and ran into the sitting room to search for her clothes. Marcus followed her.

"Don't go, Jo. Stay here with me. We could spend the day in bed."

"I wish. I'm holding on to my job by a whisker as it is," she said as she hopped around the room trying to put her tights on.

"Come back tonight, then?"

"No, they have absolutely promised delivery of my new bed and I have to go straight home to meet them at five thirty." Joanna threw her dress over her head.

"I could come and help you make up the bed," he said hopefully.

"Tell you what, I'll give you a ring from work." Joanna put on her jacket and picked up her rucksack. She kissed him. "Thanks for last night."

"And this morning," he reminded her, as he opened the front door.

"Yes. By the way, would you call Zoe for me?"

He kissed her on the nose. "Leave it with me, ma'am."

Marcus watched her leave, then stretched, his muscles feeling deliciously sore from last night. Crawling back into bed, he fell asleep again within minutes.

The telephone woke him at one o'clock. He ran for it, hoping it was Joanna.

"Marcus Harrison?" a male voice inquired.

"Yes?"

"You may not remember me, but I was five years above you at Wellington College. My name's Ian, Ian Simpson."

"Yeah... actually, I think I do remember you—you were head boy, weren't you? How're you doing?"

"Fine, just fine. Listen, how do you fancy getting together for a drink? Discuss old times, you know."

"Er... When were you thinking of?"

"Tonight actually. Why don't you meet me at St. James's Club?"

"Can't, I'm afraid. I'm already booked." Marcus wondered why on earth Ian Simpson would want an urgent drink with him out of the blue. He couldn't remember a single conversation they had ever conducted—at school, Marcus had always steered clear of him and his renowned sadistic tendencies toward the younger boys.

"Could you cancel, by any chance? There's something we should talk about, which might be to your financial benefit."

"Really? Well, I suppose I could make it around seven."

"Perfect, as long as you don't mind me shooting off. Look forward to it."

"Yeah, bye." Marcus put the telephone down and shrugged in puzzlement. Later on, just before he was leaving, he dialed Joanna.

"Hello, sweetheart, did your bed arrive?"

"Yes, thank God. The woman upstairs only just caught them as they were about to leave. I *told* the delivery people to ring the upstairs bell if I wasn't at home. Oh well, at least it's here now."

"Want me to help test out the new bed later on? I'm highly qualified, I can assure you," he said with a smirk to himself.

"I'm sure you are," Joanna drawled sarcastically. "How about we take it slow and watch a film instead? I've got the new telly all set up," she added. "You could bring *No Way Out*."

"Really, Jo? Didn't I mention how depressing that film is? And I should know, I produced it," Marcus said.

"Really." She gave an inward smile at his embarrassment. "I want to see what you helped create. I'll get the popcorn. Deal?"

"Deal, but I get to say 'I told you so' when you end up hating it."

"We'll see. Bye, Marcus."

"Bye, darling."

————

As he walked into the bar at St. James's Club, Marcus recognized Ian Simpson instantly, although his round face and angular chin had already begun to soften into fleshy pouches. *A drinker*, Marcus thought as Ian walked toward him, his burly frame reminding him that Ian had been the captain of the first XV rugby team. He'd led the team to victory, and had taken no prisoners while doing so.

"Marcus, good to see you, old chap." Ian shook his hand brusquely. "Do sit down. Drink?"

"A beer would be great, thanks." Marcus eyed the whiskey that sat in front of Ian, but remembered his promise to himself and resisted.

"Super." Ian signaled for a waiter and ordered a pint and another whiskey. He leaned forward, his elbows resting on his knees, his hands clasped together. "So, how've you been?"

"Er, since leaving school? Fine. Been a while, hasn't it? I left over seventeen years ago."

"And what line of work are you in?" Ian said, ignoring his remark.

"I have my own film production company."

"How glamorous. I'm a poor old civil-service bod, earning just enough to bake my daily bread. But then, I suppose with your background, there was a natural progression."

"Sort of, although one could say my family's been a hindrance, in fact."

"Really? You surprise me."

"Yes, it surprises most people," Marcus agreed morosely. "At the moment I'm starting up a fund in memory of my grandfather, Sir James Harrison."

"Really?" Ian said yet again. "Well now, what a coincidence, as that's just what I wanted to talk to you about. Thank you." The waiter put their drinks on the table.

Marcus eyed Ian suspiciously, and wondered if there'd ever be a time when someone was interested in meeting him for himself, rather than his family.

"Cheers."

"Yes, cheers." Marcus took a healthy slug of his beer, watching Ian as he drained his first whiskey, then picked up his second. "Now, what's this about?"

"It's all a bit hush-hush and you have to understand that we're really taking you into our confidence by telling you. You see, the situation is this: apparently your granddad was a bit of a lad, had a ding-dong with a certain lady who was very much in the public eye. She wrote him some rather steamy letters. Your granddad returned all of them years ago, apart from one. We thought we'd retrieved it—he always promised to will the last and most, shall we say, compromising one to this lady's family on his death." Ian picked up his glass and sipped from it. "It seems the letter was the wrong one."

The letter Joanna was sent by the old lady, deduced Marcus.

"Can't say I remember anything of that nature being in the will," murmured Marcus innocently.

"No. Subsequently, the . . . family concerned have contacted us to see if we can retrieve this last letter. It could all be very embarrassing if it fell into the wrong hands."

"I see. Is there any point in asking who the family might be?"

"No, but I can tell you they're rich enough to offer a substantial reward to anyone who might come across it. And I mean substantial."

Marcus lit up a cigarette and studied Ian. "And how far have you got with your inquiries?"

"Not far enough. We hear tell that you're friendly with a young journalist."

"Joanna Haslam?"

"Yes. Have you any idea how much she knows?"

"Not really. We haven't discussed it much, although I did know she'd been sent a letter, presumably the one that found its way to you."

"Quite. Er, look, Marcus, to put it bluntly, you don't by any chance think that Miss Haslam is encouraging your friendship because she thinks you might lead her to further information, do you?"

Marcus sighed. "I suppose it is a possibility, especially after what I've just heard."

"Forewarned is forearmed, as they say. And obviously this conversation is completely between us. The British government is relying on your discretion in this matter."

Marcus had had enough of Ian's cloak-and-dagger behavior. "Listen, cut the crap, Ian, and tell me exactly what you want."

"You have access to your grandfather's houses, both in London and in Dorset. Perhaps what we need is in one of them."

Maybe that's what Joanna was looking for, Marcus thought with a jolt.

"It might be, yes. Certainly the attic at Haycroft House is chock-full of boxes containing my grandfather's memorabilia."

"Then perhaps it would be a good idea if you took another trip down there and looked through the boxes again?"

"Hold on, how do you know that I've already looked?" Marcus demanded. "Have you been spying on me and Joanna?!"

"Marcus, old chap, like I said, the British government is just trying to resolve the matter as quickly and quietly as possible. For everyone concerned."

"Jesus!" Marcus wasn't reassured by Ian's tone. "Is this letter going to start World War Three or what?"

"Hardly." Ian's features softened into a smile. "Simply an . . . indiscretion on the part of a certain young lady way back when, which the family would prefer to keep quiet. Now, there may be other places we are unaware of, trusted friends of your grandfather who might have been given the letter for safekeeping. The situation is so delicate that we have to keep the net tight. What I've told you tonight is on a need-to-know basis only. So any pillow talk with Joanna will veto our agreement and put you both in a . . . vulnerable position. We've chosen you because we know you are a man of discretion, with perfect and innocent access to places and people we cannot touch without arousing suspicion. And as I stressed before, you'll be well rewarded for your troubles."

"Even if I don't find it?"

Ian reached in his pocket and pulled out an envelope. He put it on the table. "There's a small retainer to cover any expenses. Why not take the lovely Joanna off for a weekend away, wine her and dine her and find out how far she's got in her search? Slowly, slowly, catchee monkey, as the saying goes."

"Yes, I get your drift, Ian," Marcus murmured, wanting to punch Ian on his patronizing and oft-broken nose.

"Good. And if you discover the golden ticket, what's in that envelope will seem like small change. Now, I've got to head off, I'm afraid. My card's in there too. Call me any time of the day or night if you have news." He stood up and held out his hand. "Oh, and by the way, not wishing to be overdramatic, but I should warn you, the stakes are high. Any leaks down the wrong drain and you could find yourself next to it in the gutter. Good night."

Marcus watched Ian leave the room. He sat down abruptly, somewhat shaken by Ian's final riposte. He gave in and ordered a whiskey, feeling decidedly nervous, but as he took a large gulp, he comforted himself that at school Ian had always used fear tactics with the younger boys to subjugate them to his will. Yet, the teachers had seen him as a charming and caring individual. It was obvious that Ian hadn't changed, but Marcus was now a grown man and would take his threats with a pinch of salt.

His fingers were itching to find out exactly how much was in the envelope. What if he *could* find that letter, then pass it into the right hands? From what Ian had hinted, he could virtually name his price. It might give him enough money to turn his film into reality, and actually make a difference to the world . . .

He then wondered whether, despite what Ian had said about

"leaks down the wrong drain," he should come clean with Joanna and tell her about the past half hour's conversation. Then they could work together—no secrets from the start. But what if Ian found out? He didn't want to put Joanna at risk . . . Perhaps he'd leave telling her for now, see how things developed, and then make a decision.

What she doesn't know can't hurt her, he decided as he drained his glass. It seemed Ian had already paid the bill, so he picked up the envelope and went downstairs to the gents' toilet. Locking himself in a cubicle, he counted the thick wad of notes in the envelope, his pulse racing. Five thousand pounds in twenties and fifties.

Of course, the next step was to see Zoe and find out what she knew about this letter—no longer just to please Joanna, but for his film project too . . .

———

Arriving by taxi half an hour later at Joanna's apartment, he could feel the envelope full of cash burning guiltily in his jacket pocket. He shrugged it off quickly and let her lead him into a cozy sitting room, where a gas fire had already been turned on and a large bowl of popcorn sat on the coffee table.

"I've missed you today," Marcus said, then leaned down to give her a deep kiss.

"You only just saw me this morning," Joanna said, as she reluctantly broke her lips away from his.

"May as well have been eons ago," he murmured, dipping down for another kiss, but she ducked out of his reach.

"Marcus, the film!"

He pulled out the old VHS tape that he had dug out of a drawer in his apartment. "Let me say again, this is not a movie that sets the mood for romance."

Joanna popped it into the VCR, then turned her TV on, and they settled down on the new sofa together, Joanna nestling her head against the crook of his shoulder.

Marcus barely noticed the first half hour of the film, so intent was he on looking down at Joanna's face, seeing her attention completely focused on what he had produced. He felt a knot of anxiety settle in his stomach. What if she thought it was rubbish? What if she thought *he* was rubbish? What if . . .

Finally, when the credits rolled up on the screen, Joanna turned to him, her eyes shining.

"Marcus, that was amazing," she murmured.

"Did you . . . what did you think?" he asked.

"I thought it was brilliant," she said. "It's one of those films that really stays with you, you know? The cinematography was just gorgeous and so atmospheric, it really took you into the rain forest—"

Before she could say more, Marcus kissed her. Her mouth tasted salty-sweet from the popcorn as she kissed him back. The credits continued rolling on the TV screen, but the two paid no attention to them.

17

On Friday afternoon, Zoe arrived back at the hotel from the shoot and ran up to her room to collect her holdall. Heart banging against her chest, she delivered her keys to reception.

"Your driver's waiting in the bar for you, Miss Harrison."

"Thanks." Zoe walked through to the main body of the pub full of locals. Before her eyes had time to scan the room, a man was by her side.

"Miss Harrison?"

"Yes." She had to crane her neck upward to look at him. He was tall, well built, with sandy hair and very blue eyes. He looked completely out of place in his immaculate gray suit, shirt, and tie. "Hello."

"Can I take your bag?" His face crinkled into a warm smile.

"Thank you."

Zoe followed him outside to the car park, where a black Jaguar with dark tinted windows was waiting. He opened one of the back doors.

"There you are. Climb in."

Zoe did so. He stowed her bag in the boot, then got in behind the wheel.

"Were you waiting long?" she asked.

"No, only about twenty minutes." He started the engine and reversed out of the car park.

She settled back onto the soft fawn-colored leather as the Jaguar purred along the country roads.

"How far is it?"

"Half an hour or so, Miss Harrison," the chauffeur replied.

Zoe felt suddenly uncomfortable, embarrassed in front of this polite, handsome man. He must have known he was driving her to an assignation with his employer. She couldn't help but wonder how many times he'd done this kind of thing for Art before.

"Have you been working for, er, Prince Arthur for long?" she asked into the silence.

"No, this is a new duty for me. You'll have to give me marks out of ten." She caught his smile in the rearview mirror.

"Oh no, I couldn't . . . I mean, this is my first time too . . . er . . . I mean, going to Sandringham."

"Well then, we're both beginners in the royal enclave."

"Yes."

"I'm not even sure whether I should be speaking to you. I suppose I'm lucky they let me keep my tongue and my nu— Yes, well, you know what I mean."

Zoe giggled as the back of his neck turned slightly pink. "I won't tell if you won't," she added, feeling much more comfortable.

Soon, her chauffeur picked up a mobile and dialed a number. "Arriving at York Cottage in five with HRH's package." He signaled left and drove through a pair of heavy wrought-iron gates. Zoe looked back as they closed silently behind the car.

"Almost there," he said as he drove along a wide, smooth road. Swaths of late-afternoon mist covered the open parkland, making it impossible to see much. The car turned right and down a narrow lane lined with bushes on either side, then came to a stop.

"Here we are, Miss Harrison." The chauffeur stepped out of the car and opened the door for her.

Zoe barely had time to take in the elegant Victorian building nestling among tall trees before Art emerged from the front door. "Zoe! How lovely to see you." He kissed her warmly but slightly formally on both cheeks.

"Shall I take Miss Harrison's luggage inside?" the chauffeur asked.

"No, I'll take it, thank you," said Art.

The chauffeur watched as the prince put a protective arm around Zoe Harrison's shoulders and led her inside. He'd rather been expecting an arrogant, vain celebrity with delusions of grandeur. What he'd found instead was a very beautiful, sweet, and nervous young woman. He walked back to the car, climbed inside, then dialed a number.

"Package delivered to York Cottage."

"Okay. He's insisting on privacy, wants the area kept clear. We'll cover from here. Report at twelve hundred hours tomorrow. Night, Warburton."

"Night, sir."

Forty-eight blissful hours later, they were standing in the entrance hall of York Cottage, with Zoe ready to leave for London.

"Zoe, it's been wonderful." Art kissed her gently on the lips. "It's gone so quickly. When are you back in Norfolk?"

"I'll be back on Tuesday. I'm in London until then."

"I'll call you, but I might be able to pop round to see you before then. I'm going back to town later tonight."

"Okay. And thank you for a really lovely time."

They walked out to the waiting Jaguar together. The chauffeur had already stowed her holdall in the boot, and he opened the door for her.

"Take care." Art waved as the chauffeur started the engine. Zoe watched as he receded through the trees and the car eventually passed through the gates of the estate.

"I'm taking you to Welbeck Street. Is that correct, Miss Harrison?"

"Yes, thank you."

Zoe stared unseeingly out of the window. The past forty-eight hours had left her emotionally and physically drained. The intensity of Art's presence for so long had exhausted her. She closed her eyes and tried to doze. Thank God she had a couple of days off to recover, to *think*. Art had mentioned plots and plans he'd dreamed up to let them spend time together alone. He wanted to tell his family of their love, and then, perhaps, the country . . .

Zoe sighed heavily. Fine thoughts, but how could there ever be a future? The effect of the attention Jamie would have to deal with could be catastrophic.

What have I started?

"Are you too warm, Miss Harrison? Let me know and I'll turn the heating down."

"No, I'm fine, thank you," she answered. "Did you have a nice weekend?"

"Yes, it was pleasant enough, thank you. Yourself?"

"Pleasant, yes." She nodded in the gloom of the car.

The chauffeur remained silent for the rest of the journey. She was grateful that he'd sensed she was not in the mood for small talk.

They arrived in Welbeck Street at just after three o'clock. The chauffeur carried her holdall to the front door as she unlocked it.

"Thank you. What's your name, by the way?"

"I'm Simon, Simon Warburton."

"Night then, Simon, and thank you."

"Night, Miss Harrison."

Simon got back into the car and watched as Zoe shut the front door behind her. He radioed in that she had been delivered safely and headed back to the car pool to hand in the Jag and pick up his own car.

To say he had lied to Zoe when she'd asked him if he'd had a good weekend was an understatement. When he'd arrived back at his apartment from Norfolk on Friday afternoon, he'd spotted the letter from New Zealand immediately. As he'd read it, Simon had realized that somewhere deep inside he'd never really expected Sarah to come back to him. But the actuality of her telling him she wasn't was no less devastating. She'd met someone else, she'd explained. She loved this new man—*and* New Zealand—was engaged to marry him and would stay there. She was sorry, of course, guilty . . . the usual platitudes, which read hollow to Simon's devastated heart.

Simon had cried very few times in his life. Friday night had been one of them. After waiting for her all this time, stalwartly resisting other offers, the bitterness he felt that she should leave it until just before she was due to return ate into him.

The one person he wanted to comfort him—his oldest friend— was either out or ignoring his calls. And to cap it all, he'd had to spend his Sunday chauffeuring a lovesick film star back to London.

What on earth was he doing anyway, being a bloody chauffeur, after all his years of special training? When they'd briefed him last week at Thames House for his "special assignment," he had been told he was "helping out" as the Royalty Protection Branch were under-staffed, but it really hadn't washed with him. If he was minding one of the royals, that would have been different, but to draft him in just to chauffeur the mistress of the prince third in line to the throne seemed ridiculous. And the protocols on how to address the royals seemed endless, as if they weren't simply human like everyone else, but an entirely different species.

Simon handed over the Jaguar, the driving of which had been the one pleasure of the past three days, and climbed back into his own car. He only hoped that he was now "relieved" of his special duty and could get back to the real meat of his job.

He drove up to North London, wishing fervently he was not arriving home to an empty apartment. On impulse, he hung a right at the crossing and drove past Joanna's apartment. Seeing the lights were on, he parked his car outside, got out, and went to ring the bell.

He saw Joanna peer out of the window, and then open the front door.

"Hello," she said.

He could sense she wasn't pleased to see him. "Have I called at a bad time?"

"A bit, yes. I'm just writing up an article for tomorrow." She hung about in the doorway, obviously reluctant to invite him in.

"Okay. I was only passing."

"You look tired," said Joanna, torn between asking him why he looked so miserable, and not wanting to let him in.

"I am. I've had a busy weekend."

"Join the club. Everything okay?"

He nodded, not quite meeting her eye. "Yes, everything's fine. Give me a ring and come round to supper sometime. We've got things to catch up on."

"Yes." Joanna regarded him, knowing something was wrong and feeling horribly guilty at her refusal to invite him in. But she just couldn't trust him any longer. "I will."

"Bye then." Simon stuffed his hands into his pockets and walked back down the path.

———

Zoe was just relaxing in a hot bath when she heard the doorbell ring.

"Damn." She lay there hoping the caller would go away. It couldn't be Art—he was still traveling back from Sandringham—and she'd spoken to Jamie at school earlier.

The doorbell rang again. Giving up, she grabbed a towel and dripped down the stairs.

"Who is it?" she called through the door.

"Your darling brother, sweetheart."

"Come in! I'm going to get my robe, then I'll be down." Opening the door, she flew back up the stairs, returning five minutes later to the sitting room. "You look well, Marcus. Plus, you haven't made yourself a drink yet, and you've been here all of five minutes."

"The love of a good woman, that's what it is."

"I see, who is she?"

"Tell you in a bit. How's filming going?" he asked.

"Well. I'm enjoying it."

"You look radiant, Zo."

"Do I?"

"The love of a good man, maybe?" Marcus fished.

"Ha! You know me, wedded to my art and my child." Zoe smiled at him innocently. "Tell me, who is this woman who has put you on the path to sobriety?"

"I wouldn't go that far, but yes, I really think she might be the 'one.' How do you fancy meeting her over dinner tomorrow night at the bistro round the corner from me? My treat. Then you can take a look at her. You know I've always trusted your opinion."

"Have you?" She frowned. "I don't think so, but yes, of course I'll come and meet her."

The sound of a mobile emanated from somewhere in the room. Zoe stood up and began searching for her handbag. She located it by the doorway and pulled the phone out. "Hello?"

Marcus watched her face soften into a smile.

"Yes, I did, thanks. Did you? Me too. My brother's here, speak later? Okay, bye."

"And who was that?" Marcus raised an eyebrow. "Father Christmas?"

"Just a friend."

"Yeah, sure." He studied her as she tried to tuck away her dreamy expression with her mobile phone. "Come on, Zo, you've met someone, haven't you?"

"No . . . yes . . . oh God! Sort of."

"Who is he? Do I know him? Do you want to bring him along to supper tomorrow night?"

"I wish," she muttered. "It's all a bit complicated."

"Married, is he?"

"Yes, I suppose you could say that. Look, Marcus, I really can't say any more. I'll see you tomorrow night, at about eight, if that's okay."

"Sure." Marcus stood up. "Her name's Joanna by the way." He walked to the front door. "Be nice to her, won't you, sis?"

"Of course I will." She kissed him. "Night night."

———

Marcus returned home that evening, having stopped off to buy some cleaning supplies, determined to tackle the last of the bachelor grime for when Joanna came round next. Whistling as he went up the stairs to his apartment, he stopped in surprise as he realized his door was open. Before he could confront the would-be burglar, a man dressed in builder's dungarees poked his head out of the door.

"Are you the tenant?"

"Yes. Who on earth are you? And who let you in?"

"Your landlord—he's a mate of mine. Just here to check on that damp for him."

"What damp?" Confused, Marcus pushed past the builder and went into his apartment.

"'Ere, guv." The builder indicated a stretch of wall running just above the architrave, covered in fresh plaster. "Your neighbors reported it on their side. It's in your walls, I'm afraid."

"It's Sunday night! And my landlord didn't say you were coming."

"Sorry 'bout that. 'E must have forgot. Anyway, all sorted now."

"Er, good. Thanks," he said as he watched the builder pack his tools into a kit box.

"I'll be off then."

"Right. Thanks."

"Night, guv."

Marcus watched, bemused, as the man walked past him, then left the apartment.

18

On Monday night, wearing her favorite dark green blouse over jeans, having trimmed the loose threads off it hastily before leaving the apartment, Joanna sat fidgeting next to Marcus in the low-lit bistro. And feeling more than a little apprehensive about meeting Zoe Harrison.

"For God's sake, Jo, it'll be fine! Just don't ask who Jamie's father is. She's paranoid about it and when she hears you're a journalist, she'll be uneasy anyway." Marcus ordered a bottle of wine and lit a cigarette.

"She might calm down when I tell her I'm only interested in what type of begonias she plants in her garden," said Joanna morosely. "Really, I don't know how much longer I can stand it at work."

Marcus wrapped an arm around Joanna's shoulders. "You'll be back in pole position sooner than you know it, especially if you uncover the great mystery of Sir Jim."

"I doubt it. My editor wouldn't print it anyway."

"Ah, but there'll always be some scandal rag that will, darling." He kissed her. "Here's Zoe."

Joanna recognized the woman walking toward them, and was relieved that she, too, was dressed casually, in a pair of jeans and a cashmere sweater that matched her eyes. Her blond hair was coiled in a topknot and her face was devoid of makeup—far from the glamorous star Joanna had expected.

"Joanna, I'm Zoe Harrison." She smiled as Joanna stood up. "It's lovely to meet you."

The two women shook hands. Joanna, always aware of her height, realized she towered over the dainty Zoe.

"Red or white, Zo?" Marcus asked as the waiter opened the wine.

"Whichever you're both having." Zoe sat down opposite them. "So, where did you meet my brother?"

"Er . . . I . . ."

"Joanna is a journalist for the *Morning Mail*. She interviewed me about the memorial fund. By the way, when is that piece going in, darling?"

"Oh, any time in the next week or so." Joanna was watching Zoe's face. A flicker of anxiety had just passed across it.

Marcus handed Zoe and Joanna a glass of white wine each.

"Cheers. Here's to having the two most beautiful ladies in London all to myself."

"You're such a smoothie, brother dear." Zoe raised an eyebrow at Joanna, then took a sip of her wine. "What kind of stuff do you write about, Joanna?"

"I'm on Pets and Gardens at the moment." She noted Zoe's relief at this.

"But not for long," Marcus cut in. "I'm hoping this woman will become successful enough to keep me in my old age."

"She'll need to," drawled Zoe. "Not exactly a candidate for the governor of the Bank of England are we, Marcus?"

"Don't mind my sister," he said to Joanna, shooting Zoe a warning glance. "We spend most of our lives bickering."

"We certainly do," said Zoe. "But it's best you see Marcus as he really is, Joanna. We don't want any shocks or surprises along the way, do we now?"

"No, sis, we certainly don't. Now, why don't you shut up and we can all choose our food?"

Joanna saw Zoe grinning at her from across the table and knew she was enjoying teasing her brother. She smiled back.

After the waiter had taken their order, Marcus excused himself to run to the shop next door for a packet of cigarettes.

"I hear you're up in Norfolk shooting *Tess*?" said Joanna.

"Yes."

"Are you enjoying it?"

"Very much. It's a wonderful role." Zoe's face lit up. "I just hope I can do it justice."

"I'm sure you will. It's great to see an English actress in the role," Joanna said. "I've always loved Hardy's books, especially *Far from the Madding Crowd*. I studied it for O level and they made us watch the video of the film every time it was too wet to play netball. Don't they say that every man is either a Gabriel Oak or a Sergeant Troy? I wanted to be Julie Christie desperately, so I could kiss Terence Stamp in his soldier's uniform!"

"So did I!" Zoe giggled. "There's something about a man in uniform, isn't there?"

"Maybe it was all those shiny buttons."

"No, it was definitely the sideburns that nailed me," said Zoe with a grin. "God, you think back to some of the people you fancied then and shudder. Simon Le Bon was another one I used to dream of at night."

"At least he was good-looking. No, mine was much worse."

"Who?" Zoe asked. "Go on."

"Boy George from Culture Club." Joanna blushed and looked down.

"But he's—"

"I *know*!"

When Marcus came back in with his cigarettes, the two women were giggling together.

"Was my sister telling you some hilarious tidbit from my infancy?"

"Why is it that men immediately presume we are talking about them?" Zoe shot back.

"Because they have an inflated sense of their own importance."

"Don't they just?"

Both women rolled their eyes and laughed.

"Could you both control yourselves enough to begin the starter?" Marcus said sulkily as the waiter arrived at their table.

Two bottles of wine later, Marcus was feeling like the odd one out. Although it pleased him to see that Zoe and Joanna had hit it off, he felt like he was gate-crashing a girls' night out as they shared stories from their teenage pasts that he really didn't think were that funny. Besides, it wasn't getting them anywhere in terms of what he needed to know. Zoe was in full flight about a prank at boarding school, involving a hated teacher and a Durex full of water.

"Thanks, Marcus," Joanna said as he poured more wine into her glass.

"That's okay, ma'am. I aim to please," he muttered.

"Marcus, stop sulking!" Zoe tapped her nose as she leaned across the table to Joanna. "A tip from one who knows: if his lips pucker and he goes slightly cross-eyed, it's a sign he's throwing a moody."

Joanna winked. "Message received and understood."

"So, brother of mine, how's the memorial fund going?" Zoe asked him.

"Oh, you know, plodding along. I'm arranging the launch in the foyer of the National Theatre in a couple of weeks' time and getting an audition panel together at the moment. I thought it should consist of one head of a drama school, one director, one well-known actor, and one actress. I was wondering if you wanted to be the actress, Zo, seeing as it's Sir Jim's fund."

"I'd definitely like that. Lots of gorgeous eighteen-year-old males who I'll have to wine and dine to make sure they're of the right caliber . . ."

"Can I have the ones you don't want?"

"Joanna!" cried Marcus.

"A sort of alternative Miss World," added Zoe.

"You should have them audition in their swimming trunks," Joanna hooted.

"While reciting a speech from *Henry V* . . ."

Marcus shook his head in despair as the two women giggled hysterically.

"Sorry, Marcus," Zoe said as she wiped her eyes on her napkin. "Seriously, I'd be honored to be on the panel. Oh, speaking of actors, I had a fascinating conversation with William Fielding, who's playing my father in *Tess*. Apparently he knew James way back when."

"Really?" Marcus replied casually, his ears pricking up.

"Yes." Zoe took a gulp of her wine. "He told me some outrageous yarn about James not being 'James' at all when he first met him. Apparently he was Irish, from Cork, and called Michael . . . O'Connell, I think the surname was. He was doing some music-hall show at the Hackney Empire and suddenly disappeared out of the blue. Oh, and William also mentioned something about letters that were written, some kind of tryst James was having with a woman."

Joanna listened in amazement. Here was absolute confirmation of her theory on the two men being one and the same. Excitement crackled up her spine.

"How would he know about the letters?" asked Marcus as calmly as he could.

"Because he was Michael O'Connell's messenger. He had to stand in front of Swan and Edgar waiting for someone called Rose." Zoe rolled her eyes. "I ask you, William's a dear old boy, but it all sounds rather far-fetched to me."

Joanna's heart was starting to thump against her chest but she kept silent, praying Marcus would ask the right questions.

"It might be true, Zo."

"Some of it, maybe. William obviously did know him years ago, but I think the passage of time has clouded his memory and maybe he's got James confused with someone else. Although, admittedly, he seemed very definite about the details."

"You've never heard anything from your grandfather about this?" said Joanna, unable to stop herself from asking.

"Never." Zoe shook her head. "And to be honest, if there was a story to tell, I'm sure James would have told me before he died. We kept few secrets from each other. Granted, toward the end when the morphine was addling his brain, he did mutter on about Ireland, something about a house in a place . . ." Zoe searched her memory. "I can't remember the name exactly but I think it began with an 'R.'"

"I've read some of your grandfather's biographies. I'm surprised nothing was mentioned in there," Joanna remarked.

"I know. That's why I find it all so hard to believe. William said that James eventually told him it was better if they went their separate ways and broke off contact."

"Wow. Surely it would be worth investigating?" said Marcus.

"Oh, I will, when I have time. That attic at Haycroft House needs sorting out anyway. When I've finished filming, I'll go and spend a weekend there and see what I turn up."

"Unless you want me to do it, Zo."

"Marcus"—Zoe raised an eyebrow at him—"I can hardly see you trawling through boxes of dusty old letters and newspaper cuttings. You'd get fed up after the first one and dump the lot on a bonfire."

"You're right there." Joanna rolled her eyes. "He went to the pub and left me to it. I reckon you'd need a good week or more to go through everything. I managed a couple of boxes."

"You were looking through James's stuff? What were you hoping to find, exactly?" Zoe asked with a worried frown.

"Oh, just a couple of photos of Sir James as a young actor to go with the memorial fund article," Joanna answered hastily, realizing in that moment that Zoe hadn't given Marcus express permission for the recent treasure hunt.

"Listen, girls, I had an idea the other day," Marcus piped up, clearly wanting to move the conversation along.

"What?" Zoe asked suspiciously.

"Well, to be truthful, it was Joanna's," Marcus corrected himself. "When we were down there a couple of weeks ago, Joanna came up with the idea of either auctioning some of the stuff to raise funds for the memorial scholarship, or handing it over to the Theatre Museum. But that means the whole lot will have to be sifted through and cataloged."

Zoe hesitated. "I'm not sure whether I want to let it go."

"It's all rotting away up there, Zoe, and if you don't do something with it soon, there'll be nothing worth holding on to anyway."

"I'll think about it. So, you didn't discover anything significant while you were looking through the stuff?"

"Sadly, no. The most I did was expose the secrets of Dorset pond life," Joanna muttered.

"So, the actor you were talking about was William Fielding?" confirmed Marcus.

"And the lady whom he met was definitely called Rose?" added Joanna quickly.

"Yes and yes." Zoe looked at her watch. "Sorry to spoil the party, chaps, but I need my beauty sleep. I'm back off to Norfolk tomorrow." She stood up. "The food was fab, and the company even better."

"Do you fancy coming along with me to the National Theatre tomorrow?" Marcus asked her. "I'm meeting the events organizer to discuss the details of the launch at two thirty."

"I'd love to, but I'll be in Norfolk filming by then. Sorry, Marcus," Zoe replied, then turned to Joanna. "You and I must set a shopping date. I'll take you to that little boutique I mentioned."

"I'd love it, thanks."

"Great." Zoe picked up her jacket from the chair and put it on. "How about next Saturday? Oh, except Jamie's home for an exeat weekend. I tell you what, why don't you and Marcus come to my house on Saturday morning? Marcus can babysit while you and I go out."

"Hold on a minute . . . I—"

"You owe me, Marcus." Zoe kissed him on the cheek. "Night, Joanna." She waved and disappeared out of the bistro.

"Well, you certainly scored a hit with my sis. I've rarely seen her so relaxed," Marcus said, taking Joanna's hand. "Come on, let's go back to my place. We can have a brandy and discuss what Zoe said."

They left the bistro and walked the five minutes back to Marcus's apartment. He lit a posh candle he'd splurged on and ushered Joanna to sit on the sofa. She was still shell-shocked from what Zoe had said, and let Marcus pour her a brandy before he settled down next to her.

"So, it seems you were right about Michael O'Connell and Sir Jim being the same person," Marcus mused.

"Yes."

"William Fielding knew James all those years ago, under a different name, leading a different life, and, up until his death, never said a word. That's loyalty for you."

"It might also have been fear," added Joanna. "If he was delivering and receiving letters for James, and those letters contained sensitive information, it was surely imperative he keep his mouth shut? He may well have been paid to keep quiet. Or blackmailed, maybe."

Joanna yawned. "God, Marcus, I'm so tired of trying to understand what any of it means."

"Then let's leave it now and think some more in the morning. Come to bed?"

"Yes."

He kissed her, then pulled her up to embrace her.

"Thanks for supper," she said. "I thought Zoe was lovely, by the way."

"Mmm. We weren't trying a bit *too* hard for our own selfish reasons, were we? It'd be very convenient for your investigation to get pally with Zoe."

"How dare you!" Furious, Joanna disentangled herself from his grasp. "Christ! I make an effort to get on with your sister for *your* sake, find I genuinely like her, and you accuse me of that! Jesus! You really don't know me very well, do you?"

"Simmer down, Jo." He was taken aback by her sudden anger. "I was joking. It was great to see the two of you getting on. Zoe could do with a female friend. She never opens up to anyone."

"I hope you mean that."

"I do, I do. And let's face it, you didn't exactly have to torture her to spill any beans. She did it without any prompting whatsoever."

"Yes." Joanna walked toward the hall. Marcus followed her.

"Where are you going?"

"Home. I'm too cross to stay."

"Joanna, please don't go. I've said I'm sorry. I . . ."

She opened the door and sighed. "Look, I just think we're going too fast, Marcus. I need some breathing space. Thanks for dinner. Night."

Marcus closed the door behind her miserably, pondering the complexity of women, then sat down to work out how he could interrogate William Fielding further without arousing his sister's suspicion.

19

William Fielding sat beside his old gas fire in his favorite armchair. His bones ached and he felt weary. He knew his days as a working actor were numbered, before he had to give in and turn himself over to some ghastly home for the ancient and bewildered. And once he stopped working, he doubted he'd last too long.

Talking to Zoe Harrison had been one of the pleasures of making *Tess*. And it had sent his brain skittering rather unwillingly back into the past.

William looked down at the thick gold signet ring clasped in his gnarled hand. Even now his stomach turned to think of it. After all the kindness Michael had shown him, he'd been low enough to steal from him. Just the once, when he and his mama had been desperate. She had said it was a bad stomach bug that had rendered her unable to work. But in retrospect, William rather suspected an assignation with a back-street butcher and a knitting needle to remove an unwanted tiny human.

And it had just happened that Michael O'Connell had sent him to his lodgings to pick up a change of clothes. William had let himself in, and there, sitting on the washbasin, had been the ring. He'd taken it straight to the pawnbroker's and got enough to keep himself and his mum out of penury for a good three months. Tragically, she'd died of septicemia only a couple of weeks later. The odd thing was that Michael had never questioned him about the missing ring, even though he was the obvious candidate to have stolen it. A few months later, having saved hard, William had gone to the pawnbroker's and bought it back. But by then, Michael had vanished again.

He had decided he was going to give the ring to Zoe when he saw her down in Norfolk. He knew she thought him an old codger and a storyteller, and who could blame her? But it felt right that she should have it. As William lay in bed that night, the ring on his own finger so he would not forget it in the morning, he pondered whether he should also tell her the secret he'd kept to himself for seventy years. He'd absolutely believed James Harrison's warnings of danger, because eventually, he had discovered who "Rose" had actually been . . .

———

"Hi, Simon, having a good week?" Ian clapped him on the shoulder.

For want of anything better to do, Simon had joined the boys in the pub down the road from Thames House.

"Honestly? Not great. I got dumped by my girlfriend and I'm still on standby at the palace as an upmarket taxi driver," he replied.

"My commiserations on the woman, but you know better than to question the workings of them upstairs. Drink?"

"Go on then. I'll have a pint."

"You should buy me one, actually. It's my birthday. I'm bloody forty today and I intend to get absolutely hammered," said Ian, as he tried and failed to gain the barman's attention.

By the looks of Ian, Simon reckoned he'd already achieved his objective. His skin looked gray and sweaty, and his eyes were bloodshot and unfocused.

"So, in search of new totty then?" Ian sat down opposite him.

"I think I'll let the dust settle before I walk back into the lion's den." Simon took a gulp of his pint. "Anyway, I'll get over it, I'm sure."

"That's the spirit." Ian burped. "I hope it's taught you a lesson." He wagged his finger at Simon. "My motto is, don't get under the thumb, get your leg over."

"Not really my style, sorry, Ian."

"Speaking of womanizers, I met someone the other night. Now, he could teach us all a thing or two. What a prat! He has girl after girl falling at his feet."

"Do I hear the ring of jealousy?"

"Jealous of Marcus Harrison? Jesus, no! Never done a decent day's work in his life. Just as I said to Jenkins when he asked me to get Harrison's help with an inquiry, offer him a few pound notes and he's yours for the taking. Of course, I was right. We've paid the sod to spy on his girlfriend. And from the gist of the conversation he had with her last night, he's not even realized his apartment has been bugged."

"Ian, you're talking too much." Simon shot him a warning glance.

"Virtually every single person in this boozer is from our place and I'm hardly giving away state secrets, am I? Stop being so tight-arsed and buy your mate a birthday pint."

Simon wandered to the bar, thinking it wasn't the first time he'd seen Ian like this. Whether it was his birthday or not, Ian had been hitting the bottle hard for the past few months. He doubted it would be long before a warning shot was passed across his bow. It was drummed into you time and time again during training. Just one slip of the tongue—a single careless comment—could spell disaster.

Simon paid for the two beers and took them back to the table.

"Happy birthday, mate."

"Thanks. Will you come on with us? We're going for a curry, then to some club in Soho that Jack says does a great line in busty teenagers. Could be just what you need, Si."

"I think I'll pass, but thanks anyway."

"Look, I'm sorry if I'm out of it tonight, but I had a particularly nasty job to organize this morning." Ian swept a hand through his hair. "Poor old bloke. He actually pissed his pants, he was so terrified. God, they don't pay us enough for this shit."

"Ian, I don't want to hear this."

"No, I'm sure you don't. It's just . . . jeez, Si, I've been doing this for nearly twenty years now. You just wait; you're fresh at the moment, but the strain'll get to you. Being unable to share details of your daily existence with your family and friends . . ."

"Sure, it gets to me sometimes, but I'm coping okay just now. Why don't you go and talk to someone about it? Maybe you need a break, a holiday."

"You know as well as I do that if you show any signs of cracking, bingo! You're out on your arse pen-pushing for the local council. No." Ian drained his pint. "I'll be fine. I've got something else in the works—that'll pay off well soon. It's all about contacts, isn't it?" Ian tapped his nose conspiratorially. "It was just one hell of a way to spend a birthday."

Simon clapped Ian on the shoulder as he stood up. "Don't let it get to you. Have a good night."

"Yeah, sure." Ian forced a smile and waved as Simon left the pub.

The telephone rang at seven the following morning, just as Zoe was packing her case for the journey to Norfolk.

"Zoe? It's Mike here."

"Hi, Mike." Zoe smiled into the receiver at the deep tones of the director. "How's things up in Norfolk?"

"Not good, I'm afraid. William Fielding was brutally attacked in his home yesterday morning by a gang of thugs. He's on the critical list and they're not sure if he's going to make it."

"Oh God, no! How awful."

"I know. You really do start to wonder what the world is coming to. Apparently they burst into his house in London, stole God knows what paltry possessions he owned, and left him for dead."

"Oh God." Zoe choked back a sob. "The poor, poor man."

"And—sorry to be practical—but as you can imagine, it's messed up our filming schedule for this week. By the sound of things, even if he does make it, he'll be in no fit state to continue with the film. We're looking through the rushes now to see what we have and haven't got. With some careful editing, we reckon we're just about there. Anyway, until we've sorted that out, filming's on hold. So no need to come to Norfolk today."

"Of course." Zoe bit her lip. "Listen, Mike, do you happen to know which hospital William's in? If I'm going to be in London for the next few days, I'd like to go and see him."

"That's sweet of you, Zoe. He's in St. Thomas'. Don't know whether you'll find him compos mentis or not. If he is, send our love from everyone on the set."

"Of course. Okay, Mike, thanks for calling."

Zoe put the telephone down, berating herself for making derogatory comments about William to Joanna and Marcus on Monday night. Unable to settle to anything at home and surprised at just how upset she was about his assault, Zoe set off after lunch for St. Thomas'.

With her unimaginative bunch of flowers, grapes, and fruit juice, Zoe was directed to intensive care. "I'm here to see William Fielding," she informed a burly nurse.

"He's too ill to see any visitors other than close family. Are you close family?"

"Er, yes, his daughter, actually." *On celluloid, anyway*, Zoe thought.

The nurse took Zoe to a room in the corner of the ward and there was William, his head swathed in bandages, his face covered in lurid blue and purple bruises. He was hooked up to various machines that bleeped intermittently around him.

Tears sprang to Zoe's eyes. "How is he?"

"Very poorly, I'm afraid. He's slipping in and out of consciousness," said the nurse. "Now you've turned up, I'll get the doctor along to talk to you about his condition and take some details. We weren't aware he had any children. I'll leave you alone with him for a while."

Zoe nodded silently, then, when the nurse left, sat down and took William's hand in hers. "William, can you hear me? It's Zoe, Zoe Harrison."

There was no response. William's eyes remained closed, his hand limp in hers. Zoe stroked his hand gently. "All the cast and film crew in Norfolk send their love. They hope to see you back soon," she whispered. "Oh, William, what a terrible thing to happen. I'm so sorry, I really am."

The scenario was so reminiscent of sitting by James's bedside and watching him slip away that further tears fell down Zoe's cheeks. "I'm sorry we didn't have a chance to talk more about when you knew my grandfather. It was fascinating, it really was. Some of the things you were telling me . . . well, he must have really trusted you all those years ago."

Zoe felt one of William's fingers twitch inside her palm and his eyelids flickered.

"William, can you hear me?" One of his fingers was wiggling so strongly that Zoe had to let go of his hand. His index finger lay on the sheet, enclosed by a large signet ring, twitching violently.

"What is it? Is the ring hurting you?" Zoe noticed William's fingers did look swollen. "Do you want me to take it off?"

The finger waggled again.

"Okay." Zoe struggled to remove the ring, which seemed far too tight a fit.

"I'll put it in your locker for safekeeping."

Then she noticed his head was shaking slowly from side to side. "No?"

His index finger was pointing at her.

"You want me to look after it for you?"

He managed a pathetic thumbs-up.

"Okay, of course I will." Zoe stowed the ring away in her pocket. "William, do you know who did this to you?"

He nodded, slowly but definitely.

"Can you tell me?"

Again, a nod.

Zoe put her ear close to his lips as he struggled to form a word. The first attempt came out as a hoarse, unrecognizable whisper.

"William, can you try again?" she urged him.

"Ask . . . Rose."

"You said 'Rose,' is that right?"

He squeezed her fingers, then spoke again.

"Lady in . . ."

"Lady in where?" urged Zoe, hearing William's breathing becoming more ragged.

"Wait . . ."

"I'm here, William, I'm not going anywhere."

". . . Wait . . ."

"I will wait, I promise."

William sighed, his strength gone, then his eyes closed and he slipped away into unconsciousness. Zoe sat there for a while stroking his hand, hoping he'd return to her, but he didn't. Eventually, Zoe stood up and walked out of the ward, passing quickly by the nurses' station before anyone accosted her and asked for the personal details on William she could not give.

She stood outside the hospital, staring blankly at the traffic. Deciding she really didn't want to go home, she rang Marcus.

"Hi, are you still at the National?"

"Yeah, I am. Just finished the meeting," Marcus replied. "Are you all right? You sound a bit off."

"Can I come and meet you? Oh, Marcus, it's just terrible. I'm at St. Thomas'—"

"Jesus, are you hurt?"

"No, don't worry. It's a friend . . ."

"How about you come down to the Royal Festival Hall? It's closer to you," he suggested. "I'll see you in the café there in ten."

Zoe crossed the road, then walked along the South Bank, the wind biting at her face and drying the last of her tears. Marcus was standing outside the Festival Hall, concern on his face, and she let him sweep her into a hug, then steer her inside.

They settled themselves at a table in the café and ordered two steaming cups of tea.

"So, what's wrong? What happened?" Marcus asked her.

"You remember I was telling you about that actor, William Fielding?"

"Yes?"

"He was brutally attacked yesterday. I've just been to see him in hospital and it looks pretty unlikely that he'll make it through the night." Zoe slumped down in her seat, and tears came to her eyes again. "It's just upset me so much."

Not half as much as it's upset me, thought Marcus with a grimace. He reached out and took her hand. "Come on, sweetheart, he wasn't family, was he?"

"I know, but he's such a sweet old chap."

"Was he able to talk?"

"No, not really. When I asked him if he knew who had done this, he whispered something about Rose, and a lady in somewhere who was waiting for him." Zoe blew her nose. "I think he was rambling. And there was me telling you about him only last night."

Only last night . . . Is it a coincidence? But how could they have known? Unless . . . Marcus swallowed hard as his blood ran cold. "Did you write down what he said?"

"No. Should I have done?"

"Yes. It might help the police with their inquiries." He fumbled in his jacket pocket for a pen and an old receipt. "Write down exactly what he said."

"Should I take it to the police?" she asked as she finished scribbling.

"Tell you what, seeing as you're so upset, I'll do it for you."

"Okay, Marcus. Thanks." Zoe nodded gratefully and handed the paper to him. Her mobile rang, the noise startling them both. "Hello? Yes, Michelle, Mike called me this morning. I know, wasn't it? I went to see him in hospital and . . ."

When Zoe had finished talking, she put her mobile down on the table, then drained her cup of tea.

"Marcus, thanks so much for listening to me. I've got to head off."

"No problem, sis. Call me anytime," he said as she bent down to kiss him. Then he sat back and gazed out at the tourist boats and barges chugging along the silver River Thames.

It had dawned on him that perhaps his apartment had been bugged. That builder who had turned up . . . When he'd called his landlord, he'd known nothing about it . . . If so, they had heard him and Joanna talking about William Fielding.

If they were paying him to find out what he could, then surely they'd want to make sure they would be the first to know? It was the only way he could think of that others could have known about William Fielding and his association with James Harrison so quickly.

The sound of a mobile ringing shook him out of his thoughts. Puzzled, as it was not the sound of his own phone, he realized it was Zoe's mobile lying on the table. He picked it up and clicked it on.

"Zoe? It's me." The voice sounded very familiar.

"Er, Zoe's not here. Can I take a message?"

The line went dead at the other end, but not before Marcus had recognized the voice of the caller from Zoe's film premiere . . .

CASTLING

A defensive maneuver by the rook to defend the king. It is the only time that two pieces may be moved at once.

20

"Come in, Simpson, and take a seat."

Ian's head throbbed. He only hoped he wouldn't throw up all over his boss's expensive leather-topped desk.

"Can you explain to me why the job was not completed?"

"I'm sorry?"

Jenkins leaned forward. "The old bugger's still hanging on. He's likely to die soon, but Zoe Harrison already managed to get into the hospital to see him. God only knows what he told her. Bloody hell, Simpson! You've messed up good and proper on this one."

"Sorry, sir. I took his pulse and I was convinced he was dead."

Jenkins drummed his fingers on the desk. "I'm warning you, one more slip-up like that and you're out. Do you understand me?"

"Yes, sir." Ian's woolly head was spinning. He wondered if he might pass out.

"Send Warburton in. And damn well get your act together, do you hear?"

"Yes, sir. Sorry again, sir." Ian stood up and walked as carefully as he could to the door.

"You all right, mate? You look green!" Simon was sitting in a chair outside.

"I feel it. I have to dash. You're in."

As he watched Ian run for the toilets, Simon stood up and knocked on the door.

"Come."

Jenkins smiled at Simon. "Sit down, will you, Warburton?"

"Thank you, sir."

"Firstly, I want to ask you, without compromising any loyalty and friendship you may have struck up, whether you think Simpson is feeling the pressure, whether he could do with a . . . break."

"It was his fortieth birthday yesterday, sir."

"Hardly an excuse, but still . . . I've told him to shape up. Keep an eye out, will you? He's a good member of the team, but I've seen others go in a similar direction. Anyway, enough of Simpson. You're due upstairs in ten minutes for a meeting."

"Really, sir? Why?" Simon knew that "upstairs" in Thames House was reserved for the highest ranks.

"I have personally recommended you for the assignment. It's of the utmost delicacy, Warburton. Don't let me down, will you?"

"I'll do my best not to, sir."

"Good." Jenkins nodded. "That's all."

Having left the office, Simon took the elevator up and was then ushered along the thickly carpeted corridor of the upper floor, where an elderly receptionist sat in state alone at the end of it.

"Mr. Warburton?" she asked.

"Yes."

The woman pressed a button on her desk, then stood up. "Follow me."

She led him along another corridor and finally tapped on a thick oak-paneled door.

"Come!" barked a voice from inside. She pushed the door open.

"Warburton to see you, sir."

"Thank you."

Simon walked toward the desk, noting the huge chandelier that lit the vast room, the heavy velvet curtains that hung at either side of the tall windows. The grand setting was in stark contrast to the diminutive, ancient figure sitting behind the desk in a wheelchair. Yet his presence dominated the space.

"Sit down, Warburton."

Simon did so, in a high-backed leather chair.

The piercing eyes surveyed him. "Jenkins tells me good things about you."

"That's gratifying to hear, sir."

"I've read your file and I was impressed. Like to sit where I'm sitting one day, Warburton?"

Simon presumed he meant this in the context of the room, rather than in the wheelchair. "I would, sir, of course."

"Do a good job for me and I can guarantee immediate promotion. We're putting you on the Royalty Protection Branch permanently from tomorrow."

Simon's heart sank in disappointment. He'd been imagining a much more challenging assignment. "May I ask why, sir?"

"We think you are the most suited for the task. I believe you've already met Zoe Harrison. As I'm sure you have gathered, she and His Royal Highness are 'involved.' You will be assigned to her as her full-time personal security officer. You will be briefed by one of their officers this afternoon."

"I see. Sir, may I ask why you feel it necessary to place an MI5 agent such as myself as a bodyguard? Not wishing to sound churlish, but the position is hardly what I've been trained for."

A glimmer of a smile hovered on his lips. "As it happens, I rather think it is." He pushed a file toward Simon. "I must leave for a meeting now. You will stay here, read this dossier, and have it memorized by the time I return. You will be locked in while you read it."

"Right, sir."

"Once you have read it, you will understand exactly why I want you to be close to Miss Harrison. The situation suits our purposes well."

"Yes, sir." Simon took the thick file.

"Do not make any written notes. You will be searched on the way out." The old man wheeled himself round his desk and across the carpet. "We can discuss things further when you've absorbed the information."

Simon stood up, walked to the door, and opened it to allow the wheelchair to pass through. The door closed behind him and he heard the key turn in the lock on the outside. He went back to sit in a chair and studied the file. The red stamp on the front told him he was about to read the highest category of classified information. Few pairs of eyes would have glanced at it previously. He opened the dossier and began to read.

An hour later, the door was unlocked and opened.

"Have you read and understood, Warburton?"

"Yes, sir." Simon was still reeling from shock.

"Are you aware of why we think you would be suitable to act as Zoe Harrison's bodyguard for the foreseeable future?"

"I believe so, sir."

"I've chosen you because your discretion and capabilities are highly regarded by Jenkins and your colleagues. You are a personable young man who is quite capable of befriending a female such as Miss Harrison. She will be informed by the palace that you are to move into her house from the weekend and accompany her wherever she goes."

"Yes, sir."

"This should give you ample opportunity to discover what she knows. Her phone lines in Dorset and London have already been tapped. You will also be given the appropriate hardware to place around the house. You will understand now it is of the utmost urgency that we find the letter we need. Sadly, it seems Sir James has decided to play games with us from beyond the grave. The letter you brought to us was a decoy. Your directive is to find and retrieve the letter."

"Yes, sir."

"Warburton, I need hardly tell you that what I have entrusted you with is of the utmost delicacy. Others, such as Simpson, have been briefed on a need-to-know basis only. The subject matter must not under *any* circumstances be discussed outside this room. If there are leaks, it will be you whom I will blame. However, if the situation is brought to a satisfying conclusion, I can guarantee you'll be very well rewarded."

"Thank you, sir."

"When you leave here, you will be issued with a mobile phone which contains one telephone number. You will use it only to report directly to me at four o'clock each afternoon. Otherwise, in your role as personal security officer to Miss Harrison, you will report to the palace security office." He gestured to an envelope on the table, which Simon picked up. "Your orders are in there. HRH wishes to see you in his rooms at the palace in one hour. I'm relying on you, Warburton. Good luck."

Simon stood up, shook the proffered hand, and walked toward the door. Then he turned in afterthought. "Just one thing, sir. Haslam told me that the name of the old lady who sent her the letter was 'Rose.' "

The man in the wheelchair gave a cold smile and his eyes glinted. "As you know, that situation has been dealt with. Suffice to say, 'Rose' was not quite who she seemed."

"Right, sir. Goodbye."

———

Zoe gazed out of the window, admiring the Queen Victoria Memorial, which stood in front of the palace, from a different and very privileged angle.

"Come away, darling. You never know who's hovering up a tree with a telephoto lens these days." Art closed the thick damask curtain tightly and led her back to the sofa.

They were in Art's sitting room, and adjoining this were his bedroom, bathroom, and study. Zoe snuggled into Art's arms and he handed her a glass of wine.

"Here's to us, darling," he toasted.

"Yes." She raised her glass to his.

"By the way, did you find your mobile phone?"

"Yes. Marcus called to say I'd left it on the table when I had a cup of tea with him earlier. Why? Did you speak to him?"

"No. As soon as I realized, I hung up. I was only calling to ask you to bring a nice snapshot of yourself, so I could put it in a frame and admire you when you're not here."

"Christ, I hope Marcus didn't recognize your voice," Zoe breathed, panic suffusing her.

"I doubt it. I only said three words."

"Well, he didn't mention you'd called me. Hopefully he's forgotten all about it."

"Zoe, we need to talk. You do realize, if we continue to see each other, it would be naive to assume that close family won't put two and two together about Jamie?"

"Don't say it, Art, please! Think of the scandal if anyone found out the truth and the effect it would have on him!" Zoe broke away from his grasp and paced the room in agitation. "Maybe we should just forget it. Maybe I—"

"No." He caught her hand as she passed him. "We've already wasted so much time. Please. I swear I will do everything I can to make sure we remain a secret, even though it kills me to do so. I want you with me everywhere. I'd marry you tomorrow if I could."

"Oh, Art, I hardly think a single mother is an acceptable consort—let alone a wife—for a prince of England now, any more than she was ten years ago." Zoe gave a harsh chuckle at his naivety.

"If you're referring to the little meeting you had with the suits that took place while I was suddenly whisked off on a tour of Canada ten years ago, before returning to find your 'Dear John' letter, I know all about that."

"Do you?" Zoe was amazed.

"I always suspected you were put under pressure to write it, to tell me it was over. I had a showdown yesterday morning with my parents' senior advisers. They finally admitted that they'd called you in and told you the relationship had to end."

"Yes, they did." Zoe put her head in her hands. "I can hardly bear to think about it, even after all this time."

"Well, I didn't help matters by telling the family I'd met the girl I wanted to marry. At twenty-one, just finishing at university, and you being only eighteen, I insisted I wanted our engagement announced as soon as possible." Art shook his head. "I was so stupid—I panicked them into taking action, just like any ordinary parent would. Except, of course, my situation was magnified tenfold."

"I had no idea you'd told them that," Zoe said, stunned at his revelation.

"I've regretted what I did every day since. I feel completely responsible for what subsequently happened. If I hadn't rushed in like a bull at a gate, but instead calmly courted you for another few years, things could have been very different. And it put you through hell."

"Yes, it did," Zoe agreed, remembering the pain of writing the letter, then refusing to acknowledge Art's frantic letters and telephone calls in return. "Of course, I didn't tell them about the baby. But even if I had, I knew they'd suggest I got rid of it. I've often wondered whether they heard about Jamie's birth. I was scared every day that they might come and steal him away. I never left him alone for a second when he was tiny." Zoe let out a breath, remembering her terror and how she'd clung to Haycroft House and anonymity for the sake of her baby.

"When I came back from Canada, I was sent abroad on my naval training and didn't know anything that was happening at home for months. If only I *had* known at the time."

"It wouldn't have made any difference, would it? They'd never have let us marry."

"No. But that's all in the past. We're grown-up now, not children anymore. My parents know how I feel about you; they could hardly discard the feelings of a thirty-two-year-old man the way they did a twenty-one-year-old, and they're aware that my intentions are serious."

"Christ," Zoe groaned. "And what did they say? Are they going to sling me back into the gutter from whence I crawled?"

"No. I told them that if they weren't prepared to accept you, I was equally prepared to abdicate my right to the throne." Art smiled wryly. "I mean, it's hardly a big deal, is it? I'm the second spare, hardly likely to get a crack of the whip anyway."

Zoe gazed at Art in amazement. "You'd do that for me?" she whispered.

"Absolutely, yes. My life is a sham. I have no particular role to play, and as I said to my parents, the public have been up in arms about the cushy number the junior royals have got. Of course, they don't reckon that serving in the navy for ten years was anything like hard work. They're convinced I got special feather-filled pillows on my bunk and a down duvet with a crest on it, while everyone else was sleeping on rocks under a hair blanket . . . Good God, I probably had it harder than anyone else." He sighed. "The point is, they can't have it both ways. If I'm to fulfill the public's wish for me to be a 'normal' person, then equally they must respect the fact that I have fallen in love with a woman who already has a child. Which, in the times we live in, is hardly something unusual."

"It sounds great in practice, Art, but I just can't see it happening. How did the meeting end?"

"Well, I think the palace attitude has softened in the past few years, what with all the divorces in the family. We finally agreed that, for now, you and I would continue to see each other as discreetly as possible whenever we wanted. That you could come here to me, and stay as often as you liked. That within the family and among its advisers, you would be an open secret."

"And if the secret got out?"

Art shrugged. "Nobody quite knows how the public will react. We all suspect a mixture: some saying how outrageous our liaison is, others agreeing with the more modern approach to a royal relationship. And I accept it would have ramifications on Jamie, especially if they found out that I'm his father."

"There'd be a witch hunt," Zoe said with a shudder. "Art, we *have* to keep this a secret. Swear to me no one on the inside will tell. If there's a whisper, I'm gone with Jamie. I'll move to LA. I—"

"Zoe." He came toward her and held her hands. "I really do understand. What can I say? Trust me. I'll do all I can to protect you and Jamie. And that leads me on to one more thing we need to discuss."

"What's that?"

"I'm afraid the one thing the powers that be—and myself to be honest—must insist on is that we install a personal security officer with you at home. Just in case."

"In case of what?" Zoe was outraged. "In my house?"

"Darling, calm down. You're the one who says you want this to remain our secret for as long as possible. A personal protection officer—a bodyguard to all intents and purposes—is also responsible for being your forward defense. He can be useful in making sure that there's no one lurking outside, bugging your house or listening to your calls. You know all too well that the minute you become entangled with a member of the Firm, you become a target."

"Oh my God, this gets worse . . . What on earth do I tell Jamie? Don't you think he might find it odd when he comes home from school to find a strange man sleeping in the spare room?"

"If you're not ready to tell him about us yet, then I'm sure we can concoct some story for him. But at some point, he will need to know."

"That you're his father? Or that we're an item? Do you know what really upsets me about all this?" Zoe wrung her hands in despair. "That if you were anyone else, it would be the most natural and beautiful thing in the world for us all to be together as a family."

"Don't I know it." Art sighed, looking so miserable that Zoe immediately felt guilty. After all, this was not his fault, just an accident of birth. And he was doing all he could to be with her.

"Sorry," she whispered. "It's just all so complicated, when it should be so simple."

"But not hopeless?" He looked at her with desperation in his eyes.

"No, not hopeless," she said.

"You've already met the man we've chosen: Simon Warburton, the driver who took you to and collected you from Sandringham. I've spoken to him at length this morning, and he's a nice chap, very highly trained. Please, Zoe, let's at least try it. Take one day at a time. And I promise, I'll completely understand if you find it all too much and make the decision to end it."

Zoe leaned on his shoulder as he stroked her hair.

"I know what you're thinking," Art said. "*Is he really worth it?*"

"I guess I am."

"And am I?"

"God help me," Zoe groaned. "I know you are."

21

Joanna stared at her computer screen, then flicked through her thesaurus to try to find new and inspiring ways of describing the bliss on a particular spaniel's face as he noisily ate his way through the bowl of dog food he was testing. She also had a toothache. After her lunch break, it had become grim enough for her to ask Alice for the number of a dentist where she could get an emergency appointment.

Her extension rang and she picked up the phone. "Joanna Haslam."

"It's me, darling."

"Oh, hi," she said to Marcus, lowering her voice so nobody could hear her.

"Are you ready to forgive me yet? I'm virtually bankrupting myself with all these flowers I've sent you."

Joanna glanced at the three vases full of roses that had arrived over the past couple of days and suppressed a smile. The truth was, she'd missed him. In fact, more than missed him . . . "I might be, yes."

"Good, because I have some information for you, something that Zoe told me."

"What is it?"

"Tell me your fax number. Given the circumstances, I can't email or say what it is on the phone. I want to see if you come to the same conclusion I did."

"Okay." Joanna gave him the number. "Send it now and I'll go and stand by the machine."

"Call me straight back when you've read it. We need to arrange a time to talk."

"Okay, I'll call you when it's through. Bye." Joanna put down the receiver and hurried across to the fax machine before someone else in the office could nab it. Waiting for the message to come through, she pondered yet again her feelings for Marcus. He was so very different from the serious and measured Matthew. And perhaps, with all his faults, was actually just what she needed. Last night, as she'd lain alone in her new bed, missing his arms around her, she had decided to trust him, take him on face value when he said he loved her, and sod the consequences. Protecting herself and her heart from further upsets was safe, but was that really living?

The fax machine rang and Marcus's message started to come through.

Hi, darling. I miss you. Now, below is . . .

"How's the toothache?"

She jumped and saw Alice behind her, trying to read the fax. Joanna pulled the message out of the machine and folded it.

"Dreadful." Joanna walked back to her desk, eager to lose Alice and read the fax.

Alice propped herself on Joanna's desk and folded her arms. "Miss Haslam, I see danger ahead."

"Alice, we face danger every time we eat raw eggs or step into a car. I'll just have to take my chances."

"True. Bring back the days when women married their neighbors' sons and were barefoot and pregnant in the kitchen! At least we didn't have to worry about waging psychological warfare with men. They courted us and then they had to marry us if they wanted a shag."

"Oh please!" Joanna rolled her eyes. "I for one am glad the suffragettes chained themselves to the railings."

"Yup, it's allowed you to spend your days becoming a dog-food expert and your nights either alone or in bed with someone you're not sure will still be there the following night."

"Wow, Alice." Joanna eyed her fellow reporter. "I didn't know you were such an old-fashioned girl."

"Maybe I am, but how many of your single girlfriends over the age of twenty-five are actually happy?"

"Lots, I'm sure."

"Okay, but when are they *most* happy? Or *you* for that matter?"

"When they've had a good day at work, or met a ma—" Joanna stopped herself.

"See?" Alice grinned in triumph. "I rest my case."

"At least we have the freedom of choice."

"Too much freedom, if you ask me. We're all too fussy. If we don't like his brand of aftershave, or his oh-so-irritating habit of channel hopping when we're trying to watch the latest BBC costume drama, we toss him aside and go off in search of fresh meat. We believe we must seek perfection, and of course, it doesn't exist."

"Then surely I should stick to the man who's currently interested, even if he isn't perfect?" countered Joanna.

"Touché," Alice agreed as she slid off Joanna's desk. "And if Marcus Harrison gets down on one knee, don't question it, grab him with both arms. If he messes you around afterward, at least you'll have half of whatever he does to fall back on, which is more than you get when you break up with some rat with whom you've had a 'modern,' noncommittal relationship. Okay, back to work. Hope my dentist sorts you out." She waved and walked off across the office.

Joanna sighed and wondered which "rat" had just dumped Alice. She unfolded the fax from Marcus and read it.

Ask Rose. Lady in . . . wait.

A thought dawned on her. Perhaps Rose had actually been a lady-in-waiting? She dialed Marcus's number.

"Did you work it out?" he asked her.

"I think so."

"Let's meet up tonight to discuss it."

"I'd love to, but I can't. I've got an awful toothache and I need to go to the dentist."

"Afterward, then? There's something else I really need to tell you and not over the telephone."

"Okay, though I might not be able to talk. Come to mine."

"Great. Do you miss me? Just a little?"

"Yes. I do." Joanna smiled. "See you later."

Tucking the fax into her jeans pocket, she switched off her computer, grabbed her coat, and headed for the door. Alec was crouching at his desk, hiding from her as usual. She made a U-turn and went to stand behind him.

"When's my piece about Marcus Harrison and his memorial fund going in? He keeps asking me and it's getting very embarrassing."

"Ask Features. It's their shout," he muttered.

"Okay, I . . ." Joanna glanced at Alec's screen and recognized the name at the top. "William Fielding. Why are you writing about him?"

"Because he's dead. Any more questions?"

Joanna gulped. Maybe that was what Marcus had wanted to tell her. "Where? When? How?"

"Got beaten up a couple of days ago and died in hospital this afternoon. The ed's launching a campaign on the strength of it, trying to pressure the government into providing free security equipment for the old and infirm, and tougher penalties for the yobs that perpetrate the crimes."

Joanna sat down abruptly in the seat next to Alec.

"What's up? You all right?"

"Oh God, Alec. Oh God."

He looked nervously in the direction of the ed's office. "What, Jo?"

She tried to clear her thoughts. "He . . . William knew things about Sir James Harrison. This wasn't an accident! It was planned, it must have been, just like Rose's death."

"Jo, you're talking crap," Alec snarled. "They've arrested a man for it."

"Well, I tell you now, he didn't do it."

"You can't know that, Jo."

"I can, Alec. Listen, do you want to hear or not?"

He hesitated. "Okay. But make it fast."

When Jo had finished expounding her theory, Alec folded his arms, thinking. "Okay, so let's say you're right and his death *was* arranged. How did they find out so quickly?"

"I don't know. Unless . . . unless Marcus's apartment is bugged. He faxed me a few minutes ago, then hinted it wasn't safe to speak on the phone." Joanna pulled the fax out of her pocket and laid it on his desk. "He said William had spoken these words to Zoe. Maybe she went to the hospital to see him before he died."

He read the fax, then looked at Joanna. "You've worked it out, I presume?"

"Yes. William was trying to say Rose was a lady-in-waiting. Alec"—Joanna wrung her hands—"this is getting too intense. I'm scared, I really am."

"First rule until we know what you're dealing with: be careful what you say at home. I've dealt with situations like this before, back when I was reporting on the IRA—bugs are bloody tricky to find, but I'd have a good look for them in your apartment if I were you. Worst-case scenario is that they were placed when your apartment was ransacked. Maybe even inside the walls."

"And probably at Marcus's too," she sighed.

"For Christ's sake, Jo, I think you should just leave well alone."

"I've been trying to, but it seems to keep following me around." She ran a hand through her hair in frustration. "I don't know what to do, really. Sorry, Alec. I know you don't want to hear." She stood up and walked toward the door. "Oh, by the way, you were right. I never did get that letter back. Night."

Alec lit up another Rothmans and stared at the screen. He had less than two years before he collected his pension and ended a fine career. He shouldn't do anything to rock the boat. But then again, he knew he'd regret it every day for the rest of his life if he let this story go.

Finally, he stood up and took the elevator down to the archives to gather as many cuttings as he could on Sir James Harrison, and to try to dig something up on a lady-in-waiting called Rose.

––––––

Joanna emerged from the Harley Street dentist two hours later, with her head throbbing from the drill and half her mouth numb from novocaine. She walked slowly down the steps and along the street, feeling decidedly woozy. A woman brushed past behind her and Joanna jumped, her heart beating far too hard against her chest.

Had they been listening that night at Marcus's apartment? Were they watching her again now? Joanna broke out in a sweat and purple patches appeared before her eyes. She dropped onto her haunches in front of a neighboring building, putting her head down between her legs, and tried to take long, deep breaths to slow her breathing. Then she leaned back against the railings that flanked the building and looked up at the clear night sky.

"Damn it," she groaned quietly, wishing a taxi would arrive inches away from her and carry her off home. Staggering upright, Joanna decided buses and tubes were a nonstarter tonight. She set off along the street once more, hoping she'd find a taxi in the maze of roads behind Oxford Street. She walked along Harley Street, constantly sticking out her arm to full taxis; turned the corner; and found herself in Welbeck Street. This was where Zoe lived—number ten—she remembered. Zoe had written the address down for her after they'd had supper.

Joanna paused on the street, seeing she was standing almost directly opposite number ten. Another wave of faintness overtook her and she wondered if it would seem intrusive to knock on Zoe's door and ask for a cup of hot sweet tea to help her on her way. She could see the lights were on inside the house and decided she'd go and knock on the front door.

Just as she was trying to stagger to her feet, she saw Zoe's front door open. From Joanna's perfect vantage point, she saw Zoe peep from behind the door, then another figure leapt out of a car in front of the house and ran up the short path toward her. The two of them disappeared inside the house and the door shut behind them.

Joanna knew she was gawping like an idiot. But she was absolutely positive she had just seen Arthur James Henry, Duke of York—commonly known to his family and the media as "Art"—royal prince and third in line to the throne, walk into Zoe Harrison's house.

Forty-five minutes later, having eventually managed to find a taxi, Joanna lay back on her new and very comfortable beige-colored sofa, and took a sip of the brandy she'd poured to help with her toothache. She stared up at the cracked magnolia ceiling for inspiration. Forget letters from strange little old ladies, deaths of aging actors, plots and conspiracies . . . Unless she was imagining things, she had just witnessed some kind of tryst between one of the world's most eligible—and newsworthy—bachelors, and a young and very beautiful actress.

Who had a child.

A tremble of excitement traveled up Joanna's spine. If she had caught that moment on camera, by now she could have probably netted £100,000 from whichever British newspaper took her fancy.

"Zoe Harrison and Prince Arthur, Duke of York. What a story!" she breathed.

Tomorrow she'd have to do some research, find out whether the two of them had any past, or whether she should write off what she'd seen as a meeting of two "old friends." She was seeing Zoe on Saturday. It might be possible to extract some information subtly.

There was no doubt that a scoop like this would have her off Pets and Gardens faster than you could say "manure."

Then Joanna groaned, horrified by her treacherous thoughts. How could she even *think* of blowing the whistle? She was going out with Zoe's brother—whom she might, just might, be in love with—and she and Zoe had got on well enough for her to think there could be the basis for a strong future friendship. She also remembered somberly what she had said to Marcus at their first meeting about welcoming the privacy laws.

The sad thing was that if the prince and Zoe *were* having a relationship, whether she spilled the beans or not, the story would be broken in the very near future. The newshounds could sniff out a scandal before the two people concerned had shared a first kiss.

There was a knock on the front door, and Joanna reluctantly got off the sofa to open it. Marcus grinned at her, proffering half a bottle of brandy.

"Hi, sweetheart, how's the toothache?" he murmured as he went in for a kiss.

"Better after a brandy, thanks. I've just run out, so this is perfect. You mentioned earlier on the phone that we had to talk . . ." She trailed off as Marcus held a finger to his lips. Then he took out a piece of notepaper and handed it to her.

William Fielding attacked. Think our apartments have been bugged, the note read. *Had weird builder arrive to repair damp. Need to do a search before we can talk. Put some loud music on.*

Joanna nodded, her suspicions confirmed. She turned up the CD player to full volume and they proceeded to conduct a thorough sweep of the apartment, feeling for new grooves in the wall, along the floorboards, underneath lampshades, and in the backs of cupboards.

"This is ridiculous!" Joanna sighed, forty minutes into their fruitless search. She slumped down onto the new sofa, and Marcus joined her. "We've been through everything with a fine-tooth comb, unless they've hidden something inside the walls," she whispered in his ear, trying to make herself heard by him over the music that was pounding out of the stereo.

"Have a think—who's been in your house since this whole thing started?" he whispered back.

"Me, Simon, you, at least four different police officers, three deliverymen . . . ," she whispered, counting them off on her fingers, then paused.

Without further word, she leapt off the sofa to the landline telephone sitting on a side table in a corner of the room. She inspected the wire and felt along its length to where it led into the wall. Pointing at it, she looked at Marcus, her eyes wide. She put a cautious finger to her lips, then pulled him into the hall, grabbed their coats, and ushered him out of the apartment.

They walked down the quiet lamp-lit street, and Joanna could feel herself trembling. Marcus wrapped his arm around her tightly.

"Oh God, Marcus . . . my phone . . . I was surprised at the time when the telephone engineer turned up without notice after I'd been burgled!"

"It's okay, darling, it'll all be okay."

"It's been there since January! All the things they must have heard! Alec warned me about this. What do we do? Do we pull out the line? How do we get rid of it?"

He paused, then shook his head. "No, or they'll know we're onto them. And just come back and replace it."

"I can't bear the thought of them in my apartment again! Jesus!"

"Listen, Jo, we're in a good position. We're one step ahead of them, finally—"

"How can you say that? We don't know where the bugs are or how many there are."

"We'll just have to be careful with what we say," he said slowly. "And where we say it. We don't know if they can just transmit your phone conversations or are able to transmit all the sound in your apartment. But we can't let them know that we know. We'll also have to be careful using our mobile phones—they might be tapping those too."

She nodded, then bit her lip. "William Fielding's murder wasn't a coincidence," she said eventually. "I think that's a certainty now."

"Wait, Fielding is dead? I thought . . ."

She nodded grimly. "My editor was writing up the article when I left the office. Apparently he died in hospital late this afternoon. This is getting dangerous . . . Shouldn't we stop investigating? Just leave it be?"

Marcus stopped walking, and pulled her to him in a fierce hug. "No. We'll sort this out together. Now, let's go bug hunting again." He kissed her, and they returned to the apartment.

Even more determined now, Joanna tried to think of all the areas of her apartment that had remained untouched in the chaos of the burglary. She and Marcus felt along all the skirting boards and the architraves, until eventually, her fingers connected with a small rubber button, perched on the top of her sitting-room door frame. She carefully unstuck it and held it up into the light as Marcus came over to inspect it with her.

He tapped his nose, then replaced it where she had found it. Then he went outside to ring the bell and for the next thirty minutes, proceeded to come into the apartment and out again as various outrageous characters, with a wide range of accents. Joanna had to conduct imaginary conversations with a Jamaican importer of rum, a Russian descendant of the tsar, and a South African game shooter. Finally, it was Joanna who had to step outside to try to control her—by that time—hysterical laughter. She decided that Marcus had missed his calling—he was a wonderful actor and mimic. When the game was finally over, Joanna removed the bug, wrapped it in layers of cotton wool, and stuck it unceremoniously into a box of Tampax.

It had been a long time since she'd laughed so much—and when they finally climbed into bed, Marcus made love to her so tenderly, it brought tears to her eyes for the second time that night.

I feel . . . happy, she thought.

"I love you," he murmured just before his eyes closed.

As Marcus lay fast asleep beside her, Joanna couldn't help but feel contented and protected, even given the tension of "Little Old Lady–Gate" and their discovery tonight. Snuggling up to his warm body, she dozed off, trying to banish the nightmarish thought of ears in the walls by thinking about how she might love him too.

Simon knocked on the front door of number ten Welbeck Street at ten o'clock the following morning.

Zoe opened it. "Hi."

"Hello, Miss Harrison."

"I suppose you'd better come in." Reluctantly, Zoe stood aside so he could enter.

"Thank you."

She shut the door behind Simon and they stood in the hall.

"I've given you a room at the top of the house. It's not very big, but it has its own shower and toilet," she said.

"Thank you. I shall do my best not to intrude. Sorry and all that."

Zoe saw Simon was as uncomfortable about the situation as she was and her antipathy softened somewhat. Neither of them had any choice in the matter, after all. "Look, why don't you go and put your stuff upstairs, then come down for a coffee? It's the door on the left, right at the top of the stairs."

"Okay, thanks." He gave her a grateful smile. She watched him mount the stairs with his holdall, then went into the kitchen to put on the kettle.

"Black or white? Sugar?" she asked as he wandered into the kitchen ten minutes later.

"Black, one sugar, please."

She put the mug in front of him.

"This is a lovely old house, Miss Harrison."

"Thank you. And please, if we're to live together—I mean, under the same roof," she added hastily, "I think you'd better call me Zoe."

"Okay. And I'm Simon. I understand that having me here is the last thing you want. I promise I'll be as unobtrusive as possible. I'm sure you've already been warned that I'll have to accompany you on all your journeys, either behind you while you drive your car yourself, or, if you'd prefer, I'll chauffeur you."

"No, I wasn't told." Zoe sighed. "I have to go and pick up my son, Jamie, from school this afternoon. Surely you don't need to come with me to do that?"

"I'm afraid I do, Miss Ha— Zoe."

"Christ!" Zoe's hard-won calm was in danger of collapsing and turning to all-out panic. "I really haven't thought this through at all. Who am I meant to say you are?"

"Perhaps it's best to say that I'm an old friend of the family, a distant relative, who's over in London from abroad, and I'm staying with you for a while until I find a place of my own."

"You must understand that Jamie's very bright. He'll quiz you on exactly which side of the family you're from and want to know the details." Zoe thought for a while. "You'd better say you're a great-nephew of Grace, who was my grandfather's dead wife."

"Fine. Then it might be easier if I drive you to the school this afternoon. I think your son might think it strange if he notices me tailing you."

"Okay." Zoe bit her lip. "And the other thing is, I don't want any members of my family to know either. It's not that I don't trust them, but—"

"You don't trust them," he finished for her, and they shared a smile.

"Exactly. Goodness, this is going to be so difficult. I mean, my friend and I are going shopping tomorrow. Do you have to come along with us too?"

"I'm afraid so, but at a discreet distance, I promise."

Zoe sipped her coffee. "I've actually started to have much more sympathy for the royal family and those connected with them. It must be a ghastly feeling, having no privacy in your own home and out of it."

"They've grown up with it, accepted it as part of their lives."

"It can't be much fun for you, either. I mean, what about your home life? Do you have a wife, a family who misses you when you're away?"

"No. A lot of the chaps in this job tend to be single."

"I'm sorry you've got such a boring posting. I can hardly see international security agencies having my name on their hit list. I mean, nobody even knows about Art and me."

"*Yet.*"

"Yes, well, it'll stay that way for as long as I can make it," she said firmly, then stood up. "If you'll excuse me, I need to go and do some stuff before I—*we*—pick up Jamie."

22

Marcus spent Friday afternoon turning his own apartment upside down. He'd looked at the area of wall in the sitting room where he'd remembered the "builder" packing up his tools on Sunday evening, and it was indeed right next to his landline cable.

Eventually, he too found a small, black button-shaped device, hidden in the underside lip of the coffee table. He removed it carefully, marveling at the minuscule electronics within.

Joanna arrived after work and Marcus put his finger to his lips and showed her a jar of instant coffee, then gingerly picked out the bug he'd buried in the dark brown granules.

"Now, darling, why don't you take a shower before we go out to dinner?" he said loudly. "And when we get back, I'm going to paint you from head to toe in chocolate sauce and lick it off."

She grabbed a pen and a sheet of paper from her rucksack and wrote in bold letters, *Can't wait*. Then with a raise of an eyebrow, she placed the pen and the note on the side table in full view of Marcus, before heading to the bathroom.

———

The following morning, after a quick coffee and toast that Marcus had brought on a tray into bed, they dressed and walked along the road to catch a bus to Welbeck Street. When they'd found seats, Marcus turned to her with a serious expression.

"I know we've had some laughs with this bugging business, but it makes me feel sick that they've been listening to every word we've said."

"I know. Surely it's illegal to tap phone lines and place bugs? Could we call the authorities and tell them?"

"Hardly! The 'authorities' *are* those that placed the equipment there in the first place."

"Oh, Marcus, I should never have dragged you into this. It's all my fault."

"No it isn't, darling." Marcus felt a pang of guilt surge through him. He looked down at Joanna's head resting against his shoulder and wondered whether he should just tell her about his meeting with Ian, and the money he'd been given.

No. He'd left it too late already. She'd only be furious with him—might end the relationship . . .

And Marcus simply couldn't bear the thought of that.

————

"Hi, you two, come in." Zoe led them inside the house. "Shall we go straight off? I'm tingling to get to the shops."

"Absolutely," Joanna replied as Zoe ushered them both through to the kitchen.

"Jamie is upstairs in his room, playing on his computer. Should keep him happy for ages. I'll just nip upstairs to say goodbye and get my coat, then we'll be off." As Marcus lit up a cigarette, Zoe frowned. "And please don't smoke around Jamie."

"Christ! I'm doing *you* the favor," Marcus said tetchily. "Don't be too long, Jo. I can think of better ways to spend a Saturday than babysitting my nephew." He winked at her.

"And I can't think of a better way to spend my Saturday than shopping!" Joanna gave Marcus an affectionate kiss.

"You owe me for this."

"Zoe, I . . ."

Joanna heard a familiar voice behind her. She turned round and saw Simon staring at her from the kitchen door, the shock in his eyes mirroring her own.

Zoe stood behind him in her coat.

"Did I mention Simon was coming to stay, Marcus?"

"Simon who?" Marcus asked.

"Warburton. He's a distant cousin of ours from Auckland in New Zealand, on Grandmother Grace's side. He wrote and said he was coming to the UK and could he stay with us for a while. So," said Zoe, "here he is."

Marcus frowned. "I didn't know we had any distant cousins."

"Nor did I until James's memorial service," Zoe improvised hastily.

Joanna was speechless as she watched Marcus shake hands with Simon.

"Good to meet you, Simon. So, we're distantly related?"

"Yes, it seems that way." Simon had recovered his cool.

"Here for long?"

"A while, yes."

"Good. Well, we must meet up for a boys' night out at some point. I'll show you the best places in town."

"I look forward to it."

"Come on then, Jo, let's hit the road. Jo?" Zoe said.

Joanna was still staring at Simon. Zoe watched her nervously.

"Yes, I'm coming. Right. Bye, Simon. Bye, Marcus." Joanna turned and followed Zoe out of the front door.

Simon shrugged on the jacket he'd been holding. "I'm off too. I thought I might take in some sights. Good to meet you, Marcus."

Zoe and Joanna spent a delightful morning on the King's Road, then caught a bus to Knightsbridge. They wandered round Harvey Nichols until their feet ached, then took refuge in the café on the top floor.

"It's on me, by the way," said Zoe, as she grabbed a menu from the bar. "Any woman who is prepared to take on my brother deserves at least one free lunch!"

"Thanks, I think," Joanna said with a grin, as Zoe ordered two glasses of champagne.

"You know, I think you're really good for Marcus. He needs a steadying influence and he's really fallen for you. If he asks you to marry him, please say yes, and then we can do this kind of thing regularly."

Joanna was touched by how eager Zoe was to make friends, and once again felt horribly guilty for any duplicitous thoughts she'd had of shopping Zoe to her newspaper. When their lunch arrived, Joanna tucked into her delicious open-faced sandwich, topped with Parma ham and peppery rocket. She noticed that Zoe only picked at hers.

"Wasn't it tragic about William Fielding?" Joanna mentioned as she sipped her champagne.

"Dreadful. I went to visit him in hospital, you know, the day before he died."

"Yes, Marcus mentioned it."

"He was in a terrible state. It really upset me, especially as we'd had that chat about my grandfather only a few days before. He gave me a beautiful signet ring for safekeeping. Here, I'll show you." Zoe fumbled in the zip pocket of her handbag, produced the ring, and handed it to Joanna.

"Wow, it's so heavy." Joanna turned the ring round in the palm of her hand and looked at the insignia. "What are you going to do with it?"

"Take it to his funeral next week and see if any of William's relatives turn up, I suppose." Zoe tucked the ring safely back in her handbag.

"What about your film? Are they continuing with it?"

"They reckon they've got just about enough in the can to work around William's . . . absence. I'm heading back to Norfolk on Wednesday."

"And how long is your, er, friend Simon staying for?" Joanna asked lightly.

"I'm not sure. He's in London for a while and I've said he can stay as long as he wants. The house is so big, there's ample room for the two of us."

"Right." Joanna didn't know what else to say.

"I watched your face when you saw him at the house. You almost looked as though you recognized him. Do you know him?"

"I . . ." Joanna blushed, unable to lie. "Yes."

Zoe visibly crumpled. "I knew you did. Where from?"

"I've known Simon for most of my life. We virtually grew up together in Yorkshire. Not Auckland, I might add!"

"Then I suppose you know that he isn't in any way related to me?" Zoe said slowly.

"Yes. Or if he is, he's never mentioned it."

Zoe looked at Joanna uncertainly. "Are you aware of what he does for a living?"

"He's always said he was a pen-pusher for the civil service, which I suppose I never quite believed. He got a first from Cambridge and is very, very bright. Really, Zoe, you don't have to explain. It's obvious you have your reasons for making up Simon's past for me and Marcus. I suppose it was just sod's law that I happened to know him. I won't say anything, I promise."

"Oh, Joanna"—Zoe fiddled with her napkin—"I'm so scared to trust anyone at the moment. And you less than most, being a journalist. Sorry," she added quickly. "Yet I feel I want to tell you. If I don't talk to someone about all this, I think I shall go mad."

"If it's any help, I think I know," Joanna said quietly.

"You do? How? Nobody knows." Zoe looked horrified. "Has it leaked to the press already?"

"No, don't worry," Joanna was quick to reassure her. "Again, it was pure coincidence. I saw a . . . a man go into your house on Thursday evening."

"How come? Were you spying on me?"

"No." Joanna shook her head firmly. "I went to the dentist in Harley Street, felt faint afterward, and found myself in Welbeck Street while I was looking for a taxi. I was just about to knock and ask for a cup of sugary tea and a sit-down, when your front door opened."

Zoe frowned. "Please don't lie to me, Joanna, I couldn't take it. Are you sure someone at your newspaper hadn't tipped you off?"

"No! If there was a tip-off, they wouldn't give it to a junior reporter on Pets and Gardens like me."

"True. Oh Christ, Jo." Zoe looked straight at her. "Did you see who the man was?"

"Yes."

"Then I suppose you can guess why Simon is living in my house?"

"Some kind of protection, I presume?"

"Yes. They—*he*—insisted on it."

"Well, you couldn't ask for anyone better to look after you. Simon is quite the nicest man I know."

A glimmer of a smile crossed Zoe's face. "Like that, is it? Should I tell Marcus he has a rival?"

"God, no. We're more like brother and sister. We really are just good friends."

"Speaking of Marcus, you haven't said anything to him about what you saw on Thursday night, have you?" Zoe asked anxiously.

"No. I'm actually very good at keeping secrets. Tell me if you don't want to talk about it, but are the two of you . . . I mean, is it serious?"

Zoe's blue eyes filled with tears. "Very. Unfortunately."

"Why 'unfortunately'?"

"Because I want Art to be an accountant in Guildford—a married man even—but not . . . well, who he is."

"I understand completely, but you can't help who you fall in love with, Zoe."

"No, but can you imagine how it'll affect Jamie if the story gets out? I'm terrified."

"Yes. I was only thinking the other night that it will leak at some point, especially if you're both serious about each other."

"I can hardly bear to think about it. The worst thing is, I just can't seem to stop myself, however much I know I should for Jamie's sake. Art and I . . . well, it's always been this way."

"You've known each other for a long time?"

"Yes. Years. I swear, Joanna, if I ever read about this conversation in your newspaper, I couldn't be held responsible for my actions," Zoe said fiercely.

"Zoe, I admit I would *love* to be the person to hand this scoop to my editor, but I'm a Yorkshire girl, and up there a person's word is her bond. I won't, okay?"

"Okay. God, I need another drink." Zoe signaled to the waiter and asked for two more glasses of champagne. "Well, as you seem to know most of it now anyway, and as I'm desperate to talk to someone, I might as well tell you the whole story . . ."

From his vantage point at a table behind a convenient pillar, Simon saw the two women were deep in conversation. He took the opportunity to go to the men's room, and closing the toilet door, he dialed a number on his mobile.

"It's Warburton, sir."

"Yes."

"A problem this morning. I'm afraid Haslam arrived unexpectedly at Miss Harrison's house. Obviously, she recognized me. If she questions me, what do I tell her?"

"That you are working for the Royalty Protection Branch. Which, to all intents and purposes, you are. Did you place the bugs on arrival?"

"Yes, sir."

"Good. Any other news?"

"Nothing, sir."

"All right, Warburton. Good luck."

Marcus was watching a Wales-versus-Ireland rugby match on the television and working his way through Zoe's supply of beer. It was a quarter past four and still the girls were not back. Thankfully, Jamie was ensconced in his room, playing some complicated computer game. Marcus had gone in briefly, but after Jamie had begun to explain about "magic coins" he'd ducked out again. It wasn't like he'd never made an effort over the years, he thought to himself. Chocolates, zoo trips . . . nothing seemed to have made an impression on Jamie, and eventually Marcus had given up. It was as if all his nephew's love had been focused on Great-James, and his mother, and there wasn't any room for him.

"Hi, Uncle Marcus." Jamie poked his head around the door. "Can I come in?"

"Of course. It's your house." Marcus managed a smile.

Jamie walked into the room, and stood with his hands in his pockets facing the television. "Who's winning?"

"Ireland. Wales are getting hammered."

"Great-James once told me a story about Ireland."

"Did he?"

"Yes. He said he'd been to stay there once, in a place by the sea."

"Yeah, well, a lot of Ireland's by the sea."

Jamie went to the window and tweaked the net curtains to see if there was any sign of his mother returning. "He told me where he went, showed me on the big atlas. It was a huge house, he said, surrounded by water, like it was sitting in the middle of the sea. And then he told me a story about how a young man fell in love with a beautiful Irish girl. I remember the story had a sad ending. I said to Great-James it sounded as if it would make a good film."

Marcus's ears pricked up. He watched Jamie, who was still looking out of the window. "When did he tell you this?"

"Just before he died."

Marcus stood up and went to the bookcase. His eyes ran along the titles until he found the old atlas. Turning the pages to Ireland, he laid the book on the coffee table. He beckoned Jamie to him.

"Where did Great-James say this place was?"

Jamie's finger went immediately to the bottom of the map and pinpointed a location halfway along the southern Atlantic coast.

"There. The house is in the bay. He said I would like it, that it was an enchanted place."

"Mmm." Marcus closed the atlas and looked at Jamie. "Want something to eat?"

"No, Mumma said she'd cook me something when she got back. She's been a long time."

"Yes, hasn't she? Women, eh?" Marcus rolled his eyes conspiratorially.

"Mumma said the lady she's gone with is your girlfriend."

"She is."

"Will you marry her?"

"Maybe I will." Marcus smiled. "I really like her."

"Then I'll have an aunt. That'll be fun. Well, I'll go back to my room now."

"Sure."

When Jamie had gone, Marcus took out a piece of paper and wrote down the name of the town Jamie had pointed to.

———

Zoe and Joanna rolled in at half past five with numerous shopping bags.

"Had a good couple of hours, ladies?" Marcus asked, irony soaking his voice, as he met them in the hallway.

"Great, thanks," said Zoe.

"So great we thought we'd do it again tomorrow. We didn't quite finish everything we wanted to do," Joanna said with a grin.

"It's Sunday tomorrow, Jo!" Marcus looked aghast.

"Yes, and these days all the shops are open, sweetheart."

"We're joking, brother dear," said Zoe. "Besides, I'll have to give my credit card a two-week rest at a health spa after the abuse it's taken today."

The door opened again and there was Simon. "Hi, chaps."

"Hello. See the sights?" asked Marcus.

"Yes."

"Which sights were those, Simon?" Joanna could not resist.

"Oh, you know, the Tower, St. Paul's, Big Ben." Simon looked squarely back at her. "I'll see you later." He nodded at them, then went up the stairs.

"Where's Jamie?" asked Zoe.

"In his room."

"Marcus, you've not let him sit on that computer all day, have you?" Zoe frowned.

"Sorry. I did my best, but he's not exactly social, is he? Come on, Jo, don't bother taking your coat off. Let's scoot."

Zoe kissed Joanna, then Marcus. "See you guys soon. And thanks for a fun day, Jo."

"Not at all. I'll ring you during the week," she replied.

They exchanged a small, conspiratorial smile as Marcus ushered Joanna out of the door.

Zoe went upstairs to see Jamie and discover whether supper should be sausages and mash or cottage pie. Jamie went for the former and followed his mother downstairs to chat to her while she cooked.

"You know, I don't think Uncle Marcus likes me all that much," he said.

"Jamie, of course he does! He's just not used to children, that's all. Did he say anything to you today when he was here, darling?"

"No, nothing. He just drank a lot of beer. Maybe his new girl-friend will make him feel better. He said he might like to marry her."

"Really? That would be wonderful. Jo is lovely."

"Have you got a boyfriend, Mumma?"

"I . . . there's a man I really like, yes."

"Is it Simon?"

"Lord, no!"

"I like Simon. He seems nice. He came and played on my computer game with me for a bit last night. Is he coming down for supper?"

"Actually, I thought you and I could have supper together and a nice chat."

"It's a bit awful not to ask him, isn't it? I mean, he is our guest."

"Go on then," Zoe said, weakening, "see if he wants to join us."

Five minutes later, Simon, looking vaguely embarrassed, walked into the kitchen.

"Are you sure it's okay, Zoe? I can easily get a pizza."

"My son insists on your presence," said Zoe with a smile, "so sit yourself down."

Throughout supper, she did her best to keep a straight face as Simon regaled Jamie with stories of the New Zealand sheep farm he lived on back home.

"Mumma, one day, can we go and visit Simon in Auckland? It sounds cool!"

"I should think so, yes."

"Simon, do you want to come and see the new computer game Mumma got me today? It's fantastic, but much better when there's someone else to play against."

"Jamie, poor Simon," Zoe sighed.

"It's fine. I'd love to play," Simon offered.

"Come on then." Jamie stood up and indicated that Simon should do the same. With a shrug and a smile at Zoe, Simon followed Jamie out of the kitchen and upstairs.

An hour later, she went upstairs to the sound of excited screams emanating from both her son and Simon.

"You've not come up to tell me it's time for bed? It's Saturday and we've nearly got to level three and *I'm* winning," said Jamie, not taking his eyes from the screen.

"Then you can win again tomorrow. It's gone half past nine, Jamie."

"Mumma, please!"

"Sorry, Jamie. Your mum's right. We'll play again tomorrow, I promise. Night night." Simon put his controller down and gave Jamie a pat on the shoulder.

"Night, Simon," Jamie called as he left the room.

Zoe tidied up Jamie's room while she waited for him to come back from the bathroom, then she tucked him in. "Anything you'd like to do tomorrow?"

"Finish the game."

"Apart from that?"

"No, not really. Stay in bed late, watch loads of TV, drink loads of Coke, all the things I can't do at school." He grinned up at her.

"Okay, deal, apart from the Coke." Zoe kissed him. "Night."

"Night, Mumma."

Simon was pouring himself a glass of water from the kitchen tap when Zoe arrived downstairs.

"Sorry. All that excitement made me thirsty. I'll clear out of your way."

"I think you deserve a proper nightcap after that masterpiece of imagination at the supper table. Are you sure you didn't train as an actor?" she said with mock suspicion.

"As it happens, I do feel I know New Zealand rather well. My girl— I mean, my *ex*-girlfriend, has spent the past year out there."

"Ex?"

"Yeah. She loves it so much she's decided to stay and marry a local."

"I'm sorry. Would you like a brandy? Or a whiskey?"

"I . . . As long as I'm not in your way."

"No. You-know-who is off elsewhere on official business, so I'm by myself all weekend. The drinks cabinet's in the sitting room. Let's go in there and I'll put the fire on. It's turned nippy."

Simon sat in an armchair with his brandy while Zoe stretched out on the sofa.

"You've certainly made a hit with my son."

"He's a bright kid. You must be proud of him."

"I am. Marcus is always saying that I mollycoddle him too much."

"I think he's an extremely well-adjusted and normal young man."

"I try my best, but it's never easy bringing up a child by yourself, although at least he had my grandfather here. Changing the subject, Joanna sent you a message. She said she wants you to ring her." Zoe studied Simon's expression. "She told me she's known you for years and she promised she won't let on about knowing who you really are to Marcus. Will she?"

"Absolutely not. I trust Jo implicitly. She knows most of my secrets."

"Except for one. Until today anyway," Zoe countered. "I also told her about Art. What with you being here and something else she'd seen, she'd virtually guessed anyway. You really think that even though she's a journalist, she wouldn't spill the beans?"

"Never."

"Well, I do hope she and Marcus stay together. She's a good influence on him."

Simon nodded silently as he took a sip of his brandy. "I bet you miss your grandfather."

"I do, very much."

"Were you close?"

"Extremely. I know Jamie misses him as well, although he doesn't say much. He was the man of the house, his father figure. Mind you, there's lots of things I'm discovering that I didn't know about him."

"Really? Like what? His life seems to have been pretty well documented."

"William Fielding was telling me only last week before he died that my grandfather originally hailed from Ireland. In fact, he told me all sorts of things about him. Whether they were true or not, who knows? Fact gets mixed with fiction when you go back seventy-odd years."

"Yes," Simon remarked as casually as he could. "Did Sir James tell you stories of the old days? I'll bet he knew the great and the good."

"He did, yes. His letters are all festering away in the attic in the house in Dorset. When filming is finished I'm going to go down there and sort them out." Zoe stifled a yawn.

"You're tired, I'll leave you alone." Simon drained his brandy glass and stood up. "Thanks for the drink."

"No problem. Thanks for amusing my son. Night."

"Night, Zoe."

As Simon went up the stairs to his room, he was as convinced as he'd ever been that Zoe Harrison had no idea about her grandfather's past. He hoped, for both their sakes, it stayed that way.

———

Despite both of their apartments feeling unsafe, Marcus and Joanna had no choice but to opt for Crouch End that night—as Marcus pointed out, she at least had new locks on her door.

"How do you fancy spending the weekend after next in a lovely country hotel in Ireland?" Marcus asked her in bed, after he'd pulled a duvet over them to muffle their voices.

"What? Why?" Joanna asked.

"Because I think I've pinpointed the place where dear old Sir Jim may have originally hailed from."

"Really?"

"Yes. Jamie and I had a chat. He told me how Sir Jim had spun him some tale about this magical place in Ireland where a man and a woman had fallen in love. He showed me the place on the map."

"Where was it?"

"According to Jamie, it was a small village in West Cork, called Rosscarbery. Apparently this house stands alone, right out in the bay. I'll make some calls on Monday, get the travel agent to recommend a good hotel. Even if it turns out to be a red herring, it's a great excuse for a holiday—and for getting away from our bugged apartments. It'd be even better if you could take an extra day off, then it wouldn't be such a rush to get there and back."

"I'll try," she said, "but my boss isn't exactly in a generous mood with me."

"Just tell him you're uncovering an IRA plot."

"Yeah, garden plots maybe," Joanna said with a snort of derision.

23

"I've had a call from the palace. I'm picking His Royal Highness up at eight tonight."

"Yes." Zoe nodded distractedly to Simon as he pulled the car out of the drive, her gaze still fixed on the receding figure of Jamie standing on the steps of his school. She sat in the front of the Jaguar, formality dispensed with. It felt better like this.

"You know, I think Jamie was more sorry to say goodbye to you than he was to me," said Zoe.

"That's not true at all, but we did have fun together. There are some bright spots to this job after all." Simon headed onto the motorway in the direction of London. "Zoe?"

"Yes?"

"Far be it from me to comment, but do you not think it might be safer for you to go and see His Royal Highness at the palace rather than him coming to Welbeck Street? It's so much more secure."

"I know. But I feel so tense there. I always think there might be someone listening at the door."

"Okay. I'll make myself scarce tonight, obviously."

"Thanks. Er, Simon, when I go to Norfolk this week to start filming again, how will you explain your presence there?"

"Oh, I'll check in, hang out in the bar, be a groupie on the film set . . ." He shot her a grin. "I can be pretty inconspicuous when I want to."

"I'll take your word for it," Zoe replied grimly.

Outside number ten Welbeck Street, the photographer waited patiently.

––––––

Having deposited Zoe home earlier, Simon pulled the car to a halt outside Welbeck Street for a second time that day. The prince had been a more irritating passenger, compared to Zoe's calming presence. Simon clenched his teeth as he sensed him shuffling impatiently in the backseat and tapping away at his mobile phone.

"Don't bother opening the door. I'll hop straight out," the prince barked as Simon made to get out of the car.

"All right, sir."

Simon watched as he made his way up the steps, neither of them noticing an infrared light flash on the other side of the road. He sighed and looked at his watch. The two of them could be hours and he really didn't want to contemplate how they were spending their time. He took a thriller out of the glove box, switched on the spotlight above him, and began to read.

His mobile rang at ten to eleven.

"I'm coming out in five minutes."

"Right. I'm outside and ready to go, sir."

Simon put his book away and turned the engine on. Exactly five minutes later, the front door opened. Zoe appeared, looked both ways, then beckoned to her companion. In the hallway he gave her a quick peck on the cheek and ran out to the car.

The infrared light flashed again.

"Okay, Warburton, back home, please."

"Yes, sir."

––––––

There was a somber mood the first morning back in Norfolk on the film set of *Tess*. Everyone was shocked by William's death and it had broken the jovial atmosphere.

"Thank God it's only one more month," said Miranda, the actress playing Tess's mother. "It feels like a grave here too. That your new boyfriend?" she asked in the same breath as she studied Simon, who was drinking a glass of Coke at the bar.

"No, he's a journalist who's been sent up here to cover me for a week. They're doing an interview to coincide with the release of the film." Zoe repeated the story the two of them had concocted together.

Despite his protestations that he would fade into the background, Simon's presence had drawn some attention in the past two days. He was far too attractive to be "inconspicuous," as he'd suggested, and everyone had noticed him as he hung around the edges of the film set, scribbling pretend notes onto a pad. Zoe had found Simon's presence unsettling, but at least in the evenings, due to the heavy workload, she was crawling upstairs to bed soon after she returned from the set, and could avoid him.

On Thursday morning, as she was studying the script for that day's shoot, her mobile phone rang.

"Hi, sis, it's me. How're you getting on?"

"Fine, Marcus."

"Are you coming home at the weekend? Only you mentioned going to Dorset and making a start on the attic."

"I can't, I'm afraid. I'm going away actually."

"I see. Anywhere nice?"

"Just a house party with some friends."

"What 'friends'?"

"Marcus! Just tell me what you want," Zoe snapped.

"Well, would you mind if Jo and I went down to Dorset and had another go at the boxes in the attic?"

"I don't see why not. But don't throw anything away until I've seen it. Okay?"

"Sure. I'll divide it into 'worth it' and 'worthless' piles."

"Okay." Zoe had no time to argue. "I'll speak to you soon. Love to Jo. Bye." As she made her way downstairs, Zoe briefly wondered whether it was sensible to let her brother loose in Dorset, but then pushed the thought aside. She was looking forward to a quiet weekend spent in Art's arms.

———

Marcus put down the receiver, and stepped out of the phone box, looking around him to see if anyone was watching. Ian still hadn't been in touch, but Marcus was certain it was him that had been behind the bugs.

He picked up coffees and bacon rolls from the bakery and went up the stairs to his apartment, where Joanna was just stepping out of the shower, her wet hair sleek over one shoulder.

"I called Zoe," he said. "She's given the okay to go down to Dorset and have another rifle through all that stuff in the attic. Do you want to come?"

"Oh, Marcus, I can't this weekend. I'm on shift at the office." She began to dry her hair with the towel.

"They work weekends on Pets and Gardens?"

"Yes! Lots of country stuff happens on weekends, like dog shows, winter poppy sales, and snowdrops coming out."

"Wow, I'm riveted."

"Well, some of us really do have work to do, Marcus. I'd have no apartment and nothing to eat if I lost my job."

"Sorry, Jo." Marcus could see he'd upset her. "Do you mind if I go down to Dorset?"

"Why would I mind? I'm not your keeper."

"No, but I want you to be." He walked over and held her in his arms. "Don't be cross. I've said I'm sorry."

"I know, I just . . ."

"I understand." He pulled her towel off and kissed her, and Joanna forgot everything else.

———

When the car reached the front entrance of the grand Georgian house, Simon helped Zoe and the prince out, then removed their luggage from the boot.

"Thanks, Warburton. Why don't you take the weekend off? My man is here. Any problem and we'll call you."

"Thank you, sir."

"See you on Sunday evening, Simon." Zoe smiled sweetly over her shoulder as the prince led her inside.

Two hours later, Simon arrived back at his apartment in Highgate with a sigh of relief. It was over a week since he'd been home and had some time to himself. He listened to his messages; four of them were from Ian, sounding drunker and less intelligible each time, cackling about a great "number" he'd pulled on "them upstairs." Simon had no idea what the hell he was talking about and wondered whether he should have a quiet word in the right ear about Ian's drinking and erratic behavior.

He dialed Joanna's number and left a message suggesting she come round for supper tomorrow night so they could have a chat. *Probably in Marcus Harrison's bed*, thought Simon, as he put the receiver down. He showered, prepared himself a Spanish omelet and salad, then sat down to watch a film. The telephone rang a few minutes later.

"Simon? You're home." It was Joanna.

"I am."

"I thought you might be off back to Auckland for some sheep-shearing."

"Very funny. I called to see if you were free for supper tomorrow night."

"No."

"A hot date with Marcus?"

"No, a hot date at some agricultural event in Rotherham. A new form of revolutionary weed killer is being premiered. As you can imagine, it's hugely exciting. I'm not going to be back until late tomorrow, but I can do Sunday lunchtime."

"Fine, although I'm working in the afternoon, so come early and I'll make brunch."

"Okay. Yours at elevenish then?"

"Great. See you then."

Simon put the receiver down, thinking how sad it was that there was a cool breeze blowing through their relationship. Ever since, he admitted to himself, he'd failed to return the letter to her. There was no doubt that Joanna was suspicious of him, especially now she knew he wasn't a simple civil-service bod. And that it was his fault. He'd compromised both her trust and their friendship for the sake of his job. Simon stood up, removed a beer from the fridge, and took a large gulp, wanting to knock off the edges of his betrayal . . .

Like Ian.

He had not yet killed a man—or a woman—but he wondered how he would feel after he had. Surely, once he'd done that, taken another human's life, all bets were off? Beyond that, nothing felt morally relevant.

Is it worth it . . . ?

Simon walked to the sink and poured the rest of the beer down the drain, telling himself it hadn't happened yet. He loved his job, his life, but the situation with Joanna had brought things into sharp focus.

And he knew that one day, he would have to choose.

The front doorbell rang. Simon groaned, then went to the intercom. "Hello?"

"It's me."

Speak of the devil . . .

"Hi, Ian. I was just hitting the sack."

"Can I come up? Please?"

Reluctantly, Simon pressed the buzzer. He studied Ian as he stumbled through the door. He looked ghastly. His face was red and bloated, his eyes bloodshot pinpricks. Always known for his collection of Paul Smith and Armani suits, tonight Ian resembled a vagrant with his dirty mac and plastic carrier bag, from which he retrieved a half-empty bottle of whiskey.

"'Lo, Simon." He slumped in a chair.

"What's up?"

"The bastards have put me on *compassionate* leave. For a month. I have to go and see the quack twice a week, like I'm some kind of loony basket case . . ."

"What happened?" Simon perched on the edge of the sofa.

"Oh, I blew a job last week. Went to the pub for a few jars, lost track of time, lost the target."

"I see."

"You know, it's not exactly a fun job, this, is it? Why do I always have to do the nasty stuff?"

"Because they trust you."

"*Did* trust me." Ian burped, then swallowed more whiskey straight from the bottle.

"Sounds like you've got a paid holiday. I'd enjoy it if I were you."

"You think I'll be allowed back? No way. It's over, Simon, all those years, all that work . . ." And then he began to cry.

"Buck up, Ian, you don't know that. They won't want to lose you. You've always been one of the best. If you get your act together, prove that this was a blip, I'm sure you'll get another chance."

Ian hung his head. "No, Si. It's parking tickets for me, if I'm lucky. I'm scared, I really am. I'm a risk, aren't I? Drunk in charge of all those secrets. What if they . . . ?" Ian's voice trailed off and fear filled his eyes.

"Course they won't." Simon hoped he sounded convincing. "They'll look after you. Help you get better."

"Bullshit. You really think there's a special rest home for burned-out intelligence officers?" Ian started to laugh. "It was James Bond that made me want to go into the service in the first place. I used to look at those gorgeous women and think, *If they're a free perk, then that's the job for me.*"

Simon remained silent, knowing there was little he could say.

"This is it," Ian sighed, "the end. And what do I have to show for my years of faithful service? A bedsit in Clapham and a clapped-out liver." He smirked at his own sad summary.

"Come on, mate. I know things look bleak now, but I'm sure if you stay off the juice for a while, things'll get better."

"The booze is the only way I can make it through. Anyway"—Ian's eyes lit up suddenly, whether with anger or remorse Simon couldn't tell—"at least I've got some money saved. And the last little 'sideline' has netted me a serious windfall. You know"—Ian swayed as he walked toward Simon—"I was actually feeling a bit guilty about it. You said she's a nice person, apparently, and it was a shit thing to do to someone nice." He hiccupped. "Now, I'm glad I did it."

"Who are you talking about, Ian?"

"Nothing. Nothing . . ." Ian stood up. "Sorry to disturb you. Got to go. I wouldn't want to see you tainted by association." He staggered toward the door, then wagged his finger at Simon. "You're going to go far, old chap. But just watch your back, and tell that journo girlie of yours to get the hell out of Marcus Harrison's bed. It's dangerous, and besides, from what I've heard through the headphones, he's a crap lover." Ian managed a ghost of a smile, then disappeared out of the front door.

———

On Sunday morning, after a quiet Saturday watching the rugby and reading, Simon woke from his first restful sleep in days. He saw that his clock read eight thirty-two—far past his usual infallible seven a.m. inner alarm clock. Switching on Radio Four and leaving the coffee to brew, he was just about to go downstairs to collect his usual heap of Sunday papers when the telephone rang.

"Yes?"

"There's trouble. You're to report immediately to Welbeck Street. We'll be calling you with further instructions."

"I see. Why the change?"

"Read the *Morning Mail*. You'll find out. Goodbye."

Swearing, he ran downstairs to the main entrance of the building and picked up the *Morning Mail* from the pile on the mat. Reading the headline, he groaned.

"Jesus! Poor Zoe." Anger and worry twisting in his stomach, he raced back upstairs and hastily pulled on his suit. *Bloody Joanna*, he thought, *this is how she gets back at me, betraying Zoe to make a quick buck* . . .

He was just about to leave when his doorbell rang. He realized he'd invited Joanna round for brunch. Trying to control his anger, Simon pressed the button that would allow her entry. *Everyone is innocent until proven guilty*, he reminded himself as he donned his jacket.

"Hello," she said breezily as she walked in, kissed him on the cheek, and handed him a pint of milk. "I know you're always out of milk, just thought I'd—"

He handed the paper to her. "Seen this?"

"No, I knew you'd have the Sundays, so I didn't bother buying them. I . . ." Joanna's eyes fell on the headline. "Oh, damn. Poor Zoe."

"Yes, poor Zoe," he mimicked.

Joanna studied the photograph of the Duke of York, his arm looped around Zoe's shoulders, and another of him kissing her on top of her head. They could have been any pair of attractive young lovers taking a stroll in the countryside.

"'Prince Arthur and his new love, Zoe Harrison, enjoying a weekend together at the house of the Hon. Richard Bartlett and his wife, Cliona,'" Joanna read out. "Didn't you drive them down there?"

"Yes. I dropped them off on Friday. And I have to go now."

"Oh, so brunch is off?"

"Yes, it's off." He glared at her. "Joanna?"

"Yes?"

"Have you seen which newspaper is covering the story?"

"Of course I have. It's ours."

"Yes, *yours*."

The penny dropped as she studied Simon's angry expression.

"I hope you're not thinking what I *think* you're thinking."

"There's every chance I am, yes."

Joanna blushed, not from guilt, but from indignation. "God, Simon! How could you even suggest it? Who the hell do you think I am?"

"An ambitious journalist, who saw the opportunity for the scoop of the year dangled before her."

"How dare you! Zoe's my friend. Besides, you're presuming she's told me."

"Zoe said she had spoken about it to you. I've been with her almost twenty-four hours a day and I just can't see how anyone else could have found out. Perhaps you didn't mean to, but in the end you just couldn't resist and—"

"Don't you dare patronize me, Simon! I'm extremely fond of Zoe. Okay, I admit I thought about it—"

"See!"

"But of course I could never betray a friend!" she shot back.

"It's *your* paper, Jo! Zoe asked me whether she should trust you and I gave your discretion top marks! I wish to God I hadn't now."

"Simon, *please*, I swear I didn't leak the story."

"That poor woman. She's got a son she's trying to protect, who's now going to be hounded. She's going to be in bits and—"

"Jesus, Simon." Joanna shook her head in astonishment and hurt. "Are you in love with her or what? You're just her bodyguard. It's the prince's job to comfort her, not yours."

"Don't be ridiculous! And you're one to talk. Hanging around with that prick Marcus, just to get more information about that love letter, thinking you're some kind of vigilante modern-day Sherlock Holmes—"

"Enough, Simon! As a matter of fact, I really like Marcus. In fact, I might even be in love with him, not that it's any of your business who I spend my time with and—"

"How could you have deceived her so cold-heartedly?"

"I bloody didn't, Simon! And if you don't know me well enough to realize I could never betray my friend like that, then I wonder what all *our* years of friendship have been about. And you're not so lily-white! You lied to me about the letter I trusted you with. 'Disintegrated,' you said. I bloody well know you used me to retrieve it for your lot at MI5!"

Simon stood there, speechless.

"You did, didn't you?" she continued, knowing she'd hit home.

"I'm leaving." Shaking with fury, he picked up his holdall and walked to the door, then paused and turned back. "And I suppose it's my duty to warn you that Marcus Harrison is being paid by 'my lot' to sleep with you. Ask Ian Simpson. Let yourself out, Joanna." The door slammed behind him.

Joanna stood there in stunned silence. She could hardly believe what had happened in the past few minutes. In all the years they'd known each other, she could barely remember a cross word being exchanged between them. If that was Simon's reaction—a man who had known her for all these years—then she held out no hope for Zoe's believing her. And what was all that rubbish Simon had spouted about Marcus's being "paid" to sleep with her? Surely not? Marcus had known nothing about "Little Old Lady–Gate" when she'd originally told him.

Joanna let out a small shriek of frustration, feeling like the fabric of her world was slowly disintegrating. She rifled in her rucksack and drew out her wallet. Pulling out Ian Simpson's card, she thought for a moment, then went to Simon's telephone and picked up the receiver. Not quite sure what she would say, but knowing she had to speak to him, she dialed the number.

It rang for ages before it was finally picked up.

"'Lo, Simon," a sleepy voice answered.

"Is that Ian Simpson?"

"Who wants to know?"

"This is Joanna Haslam, a friend of Simon Warburton. Look, I know this may sound ridiculous, and I don't want to drop Simon in it or anything, but he mentioned that apparently my, er, boyfriend, Marcus Harrison, might . . . um . . . be in the employ of someone you work for?"

There was silence on the other end of the line.

"Maybe you could just continue to say nothing if the answer is yes."

There was a long pause, then she heard a click on the line as he hung up.

Joanna put the receiver down, knowing Simon had told the truth. Thoughts raced through her mind as she tried to remember every conversation she'd ever had with Marcus. She took a deep, shuddering breath of anger and hurt, then sat down to plan her next move.

———

Simon had driven off at top speed, then, realizing he was far too upset to drive without being a hazard, he pulled over and switched the engine off while he calmed down.

"Damn it!" He banged the steering wheel with the palms of his hands. It was the first time in his adult life he could ever remember completely losing control. Joanna was his oldest friend. He'd not even given her a chance to explain—he'd condemned her before she'd even opened her mouth.

The question was, why?

Had Ian Simpson's visit unsettled him? Or was it—as Joanna had suggested—because he was becoming far fonder of Zoe Harrison than he should be? "Damn," he breathed, trying to analyze his feelings. Surely it wasn't love? How could it be? He'd only known her for a couple of weeks, and most of that time he'd spent at a distance. Yet there was something about her that touched him, a vulnerability that made him want to protect her. And not, he finally admitted to himself, in a purely professional sense.

He realized this would explain his irrational dislike of her royal lover. The man was decent enough, had always been polite to him, yet he felt animosity toward him. He was surprised that the intelligent and warm Zoe could find herself in love with him. However . . . he was a "prince." Simon supposed that made up for rather a lot.

He groaned as he remembered his final words to Joanna. He'd completely breached the rules when he'd told her about Marcus's being paid to find out what she knew.

She's a nice person . . .

Ian's drunken words from Friday night suddenly came floating back to him.

What if . . . ?

"Oh shit!" Simon slammed his fist down on the steering wheel as the whole scenario came into sharp focus. He'd presumed Ian had been talking about Joanna when he'd mentioned a "she." But he himself had tapped the phone and placed bugs around the house in Welbeck Street. He'd *known* they were listening in . . .

What if it had been Zoe Ian had been talking about? He'd alluded to making some income on the side recently, and Joanna certainly wasn't a press target—someone newspapers would spend a fortune to get the gossip on.

But Zoe *was* . . .

As Simon started the engine, he realized he'd got it completely wrong.

He arrived at Welbeck Street to find a posse of photographers, camera crews, and journalists camped outside on the doorstep. Fighting his way through them and ignoring their shouts and questions, he let himself inside. Slamming the door, he fastened every lock and bolt it had to offer.

"Zoe? Zoe?" he called.

There was no reply. Maybe she hadn't made it back yet from Hampshire, although he'd been told she had when he'd called in en route. Checking the sitting room, he saw the long lens of a camera through a crack in the old damask curtains and ran to pull them tighter. He walked into the dining room, the study, and then the kitchen, calling her name. Upstairs, he checked the main bedroom, Jamie's room, the guest room, and the bathroom.

"Zoe? It's Simon! Where are you?" he called again, now with a mounting sense of urgency.

He ran up the stairs to the two small attic rooms and saw his own was empty. He pushed open the door to the room across the narrow landing. It was filled with discarded furniture and some of Jamie's baby toys. And there, huddled on the floor in a corner, between an old wardrobe and an armchair, and hugging an ancient teddy bear to her, was Zoe, her face raw with tears, hair swept back harshly in a ponytail. Wearing an ancient sweatshirt and jogging bottoms, she looked not much older than her son.

"Oh, Simon! Thank God you're here, thank God." She reached out to him and Simon knelt down next to her. She laid her head against his chest and sobbed.

There was little he could do but close his arms around her, willing himself to ignore how wonderful it felt to hold her.

Eventually, she looked up at him, her blue eyes wide with fear. "Are they still outside?"

"I'm afraid they are."

"When I got here, one of them had a ladder. He was look . . . looking into Jamie's room, trying to take a photograph. I . . . Oh God, what have I done?!"

"Nothing, Zoe, just fallen in love with a famous man. Here." Simon offered her his hanky and watched as she dried her tears.

"I'm so sorry for being pathetic. It was all such a shock."

"Nothing to apologize for. Where's His Royal Highness?"

"Back at the palace, I suppose. They woke us up in Hampshire at five o'clock, said we had to leave. Art went off in one car and I came here in the other. I arrived back at eight and the media were already camped outside. I thought you'd never come."

"Zoe, I'm sorry. They didn't call me until half past ten this morning. Have you heard from His Royal Highness since you arrived back?"

"Not a word, but besides that, I'm so worried about Jamie. What if the press have gone to his school like they've come here, to get a picture of him? He knows nothing . . . Oh God, Simon, I've been so selfish! I should never have begun this again and risked his safety. I—"

"Try to keep calm. I'm certain the prince will call you, and the palace will make sure both you and Jamie are safe and looked after."

"You think so?"

"Of course. They won't just leave you stranded here. Listen, why don't I go and call in now?"

"Okay. And can you ask whoever you speak to to get Art to ring me? There was no time to discuss anything this morning."

"If you want to come downstairs, I've shut all the curtains. No-body will see you."

Zoe shook her head. "Not just yet, thanks. I'll calm down a little first."

"Then I'll bring you some tea. Milky, no sugar, isn't it?"

"Yes." There was a glimmer of a smile on her lips. "Thanks, Simon."

He went downstairs to the kitchen, switched on the kettle, and felt like the shit he was for comforting a woman who had almost certainly been shopped by a mole—listening in to bugs *he'd* placed—from his own organization. An organization that was meant not only to uphold the security of Great Britain, but also to protect those who needed it. He called in to the palace security office. "It's Warburton. I'm at Welbeck Street and the place is besieged. What is the directive?"

"At present, none. Stay where you are."

"Really? Understandably, Miss Harrison's very distressed. Is there a more secure address being arranged for her?"

"Not that I know of."

"It might be better if she was at the palace."

"That's not possible."

"I see. What about her son? She's obviously very concerned about the effect this will have on him. He's at boarding school in Berkshire."

"Then she'd better talk to the headmaster, see what he can arrange in terms of extra security. Is that all?"

Simon took a breath, trying to control his anger. "Yes, thanks." He then made a call to Jamie's school, and mounted the stairs with two mugs of tea and a plate of cookies.

"Did you speak to them?" she asked, her eyes hopeful.

"Yes." Simon handed Zoe a mug, then knelt down next to her. "Shortbread?"

"Thanks. What did they say?"

"That we're to hold tight here. They're arranging something at the moment. Oh, and the prince sends his love," he lied. "He'll call you later."

Zoe's face lit up with relief. "And Jamie?"

"I've spoken to the headmaster and they're aware of the situation. The media isn't down there yet, but they'll take extra precautions as necessary. The headmaster said Jamie's fine. Apparently, they don't have that 'rag,' as he put it, in the school anyway."

"Thank goodness." She took a tiny bite of the cookie. "What on earth am I going to say to him? How do I explain all this?"

"Give Jamie a little more credit, Zoe. He's a bright boy and remember, he's grown up in the spotlight, what with your grandfather and you. He'll cope."

"Yes, I suppose you're right. Was it Joanna who leaked the story, do you think?" she asked slowly.

"No, I'm pretty sure she didn't, though when I first saw the news, she happened to be at my apartment, and I . . . jumped to conclusions too fast."

"It is a coincidence."

"Yes, but I don't believe it was her. And nor should you," Simon said firmly. "I've known her forever, and she's a loyal friend. Really, Zoe."

"She was the only one that knew, Simon. Who else could it have been?"

"I have no idea," Simon lied again. "Sadly, with this kind of thing, walls tend to have ears." *Literally*, he thought.

"So we're stuck here until they tell us what to do."

"Looks like it, yes."

She sipped her tea, then looked up at him and smiled. "Simon?"

"Yes, Zoe?"

"I'm awfully glad you're here."

24

As dusk fell on Welbeck Street, there was still no word for either of them from the prince or the palace. When Marcus finally called, Zoe had calmed down marginally. As he was at Haycroft House, sorting through the boxes in the attic, he hadn't heard the news until he'd gone to the pub and been accosted by the locals wanting to know details.

"Nicely done, netting a royal, Zo," he'd said, trying to cheer her up. "I'll be on my way back to London later tonight, so if you need me, you know where I am. Stay cool, and ignore what the tossers in the media say, it'll blow over. Love you, sis."

"Thanks, Marcus."

Zoe had hung up, feeling comforted by Marcus's support. She decided to come out of hiding in the attic and went downstairs to the shrouded drawing room, still holding on to Jamie's teddy.

Simon prowled around the house for want of anything better to do, methodically checking for cracks in the curtains and signs of chisels under sash windows. He also surreptitiously removed the bugs he'd placed and stuffed them in a tissue box in his bedroom. He didn't want anyone at HQ getting off on Zoe's distress. He simply wished that they'd hurry up and decide what they were going to do with Zoe, as the two of them were currently marooned in the house until they did. He crept down the hall, hearing the voices buzzing beyond the front door. Venturing into the drawing room, he saw Zoe was still sitting paralyzed on the sofa.

"Cup of tea? Coffee? Something stronger?" he suggested.

Zoe looked up and shook her head. "Thanks, but I'm feeling a bit queasy. What time is it?"

"Ten to five."

"I must go and call Jamie. I always do at tea time on a Sunday." She bit her lip. "What on earth do I say?"

"Speak to the headmaster first, take his advice. If Jamie knows nothing at the moment, then maybe it's best it stays that way."

"Yes, you're right. Thanks, Simon." She picked her mobile off the floor and dialed the school's number.

Simon went to the kitchen to make himself his umpteenth cup of tea, pondering why the prince had still not rung Zoe. If he professed to love her, then surely a brief but reassuring chat would be uppermost in his mind? Surely it wasn't possible that he and the palace would not come to Zoe's rescue, simply leave her here to face the music alone?

"He sounds fine. He obviously knows nothing." Zoe's relieved voice broke into his thoughts.

Simon turned and smiled at her. "Good."

"The headmaster said there are a couple of journalists hanging about outside the school gates, but he's informed the local constabulary and they're keeping an eye out. Jamie wanted to know what sort of a week I'd had and I said it had just been normal." Zoe gave a weak laugh. "Of course, I'm not stupid enough to think it'll be long before he does hear about it . . . You really think it best not to say anything?"

"For now, yes. Ignorance is bliss, especially when you're ten. He's safe there and maybe if there's no further ammunition, the whole thing will blow over."

Zoe sat down at the kitchen table and rested her head on her arms. "Ring, Art, please ring."

Simon patted her shoulder gently. "He will, Zoe, you'll see."

At eight o'clock that evening, Simon set up the portable TV from Jamie's room in Zoe's bedroom. He'd tried to tempt her to eat something, but she'd refused. She sat, slumped on the bed, her face as pale as the moonlight shining through the bay window. He drew the curtains just in case someone below had a ladder.

"Look, why don't you call Art? You have his mobile number, don't you?"

"Don't you think I already *have*?" Zoe rounded on him. "Like, a hundred times so far today? It goes straight to voicemail."

"Okay, sorry."

"So am I. None of this is your fault and I don't want to take it out on you."

"You're not," said Simon. "And if you did, it's understandable."

Zoe stood up and began to pace the room, while Simon plugged the aerial socket in, then switched the television on. The screen flickered into life, and sound blared out.

"*. . . that Prince Arthur, Duke of York and third in line to the throne, has a new lady love. Zoe Harrison, actress and granddaughter of the late Sir James Harrison, was seen walking with the prince in the grounds of a friend's stately home in Hampshire.*"

Zoe and Simon looked on in silence as the ITV reporter spoke from in front of her Welbeck Street house. Behind him, they could see a horde of photographers overflowing onto the pavement and all the way to the other side of the street. Police were ushering cars through the bottleneck and trying to control the crowd.

"*Miss Harrison arrived at her house in London early this morning and has so far avoided speaking to the media camped on her doorstep. If Miss Harrison is romantically involved with the duke, it would cause a dilemma for the palace. Miss Harrison is an unmarried mother, with a young son of ten. She has never revealed who the father is. Whether the palace will give its blessing to such a controversial relationship remains to be seen. A spokesman for Buckingham Palace issued a short statement this morning, confirming the duke and Miss Harrison were together in Hampshire attending a house party, but that their relationship was no more than that of good friends.*"

Simon scanned Zoe's face for a reaction. There was none. Zoe's eyes were glassy.

"Zoe, I . . ."

"I should have known how it would be," she said faintly as she walked to the bedroom door. "I've been there before."

————

The following morning, having still had no instructions, Simon called in yet again to the security office.

"Any directive?"

"None at present. Stay where you are."

"Miss Harrison has to go out today, to a studio in London to do some post-syncing. How exactly do I extricate her without causing a riot in a central London street?"

There was a pause on the other end of the line. "Use the years of training that the British government paid for. Goodbye, Warburton."

"Damn you!" Simon swore into the receiver, knowing it was now patently obvious that the palace had no intention of supporting Zoe.

"Who was that?" Zoe stood at the kitchen door.

"My boss."

"What did he say?"

Simon took a deep breath. It was pointless lying to her. "Nothing. We're to stay where we are."

"I see. So, we're on our own?"

"Yes, I'm afraid so."

"Fine." She turned in the doorway. "I'm going to write a letter to Art." Zoe walked into the study and pulled open one of the small drawers of her grandfather's fine antique desk, searching for his beautiful ink pen. Finding it, she pulled off the top and scrawled on an old electricity bill to test it. The pen was empty. She rifled through the drawers looking for a cartridge, pulling bills out and dropping them onto the floor as she did so. After finally finding a cartridge, she knelt down to gather up the bills and stuff them back into the drawer. And then caught the name of the company on the top of one of them.

Regan Private Investigation Services Ltd.
Final Payment Due.
Total = £8,600

James had scrawled *Paid* across it, and the date *10/19/95* underneath it. Zoe chewed her lip, wondering why on earth her grandfather would have needed to hire the services of a private detective agency, especially so near to the end of his life. From the amount he'd paid, they'd done some kind of major investigating.

"You okay?"

She jumped at the sound of Simon's voice. He stood in the doorway, concern on his face.

"Yes, fine." She stuffed the bill back into the drawer and closed it.

"What time do you need to be at the studio?"

"Two o'clock."

"Right. Then we should leave around one. I'm going to go out now. I want to move the car, position it better for a hasty getaway."

"Am I going to have to face that barrage out there?"

"Not if you're prepared to wear a silly hat and do some breaking and entering." He grinned at her. "I'll see you in a few minutes."

Zoe returned her thoughts to her letter, trying to push aside her fear and anger.

Dearest Art, she wrote. *Firstly, I just want to say that I understand the dreadful position this whole situation has put you in. I feel—*

Zoe's mobile rang, breaking her flow.

"Yes? Oh, hello, Michelle." She listened while her agent spoke. "No, I don't want to go on *GMTV*, or give an interview to the *Mail*, the *Express*, the *Times*, or the bloody *Toytown Gazette*! I'm sorry they're hassling you . . . What can I say apart from the fact I have *nothing* to say? No comment . . . All right. I will. Bye." Zoe ground her teeth. The mobile rang again. "What?!" she barked.

"It's me."

"Art!" She gave a small sob of relief. "Oh God, I thought you'd never call!"

"I'm sorry, darling. All hell's let loose here, as you can imagine."

"It's not exactly comfortable at this end either."

"No. I'm so sorry, Zoe. Look, we need to talk."

"Where?"

"Where indeed. Is Warburton there with you?"

"Yes, I mean, not at this minute. He's gone out to move the car. It's like some kind of siege here. I feel like a caged animal." She willed herself not to cry down the line to him.

"It must be ghastly for you, darling. Really, I completely understand. What about your grandfather's house in Dorset? Could you slip out and get there by tonight?"

"Probably. Could you?"

"I can certainly do my best. I'll try and be there around eight."

"Please, please try."

"Of course. And just try to remember I love you."

"I love you too."

"I have to go. I'll see you later. Bye, darling."

"Bye."

Zoe felt all her tension and recent resolve to end the relationship flood away. Just hearing his voice had given her courage. She looked at the letter she had begun and tore it up. He still *loved* her . . . Maybe there *was* a way . . .

The front door opened and Zoe heard a barrage of voices hurling questions at Simon. The clamor receded as he slammed the door behind him, and she poked her head out into the hall.

"They're like a pack of baying wolves. No doubt I'll now end up on the front page of some rag, being suggested as Jamie's father . . . ," he said.

Zoe's face darkened. "I hope not."

"Sorry, Zoe, that was insensitive of me."

"But accurate," she said wryly.

"You look better," said Simon as he studied her. "Get some things off your chest?"

"Art rang. He suggested I go down to my grandfather's house in Dorset tonight. He's going to try and join me there later. So we absolutely have to get out of this house with no one spotting us. I'm going to go upstairs and take a shower."

"Fine. But travel light. And don't worry, I've cased the joint and have a cunning plan." Simon smiled and tapped his nose.

"Okay." She gave a weak laugh and walked up the stairs. When Simon heard the bathroom door lock, he went into the study and opened the drawer he'd seen Zoe close earlier. He sifted through its contents as quickly as he could. Finding the invoice that Zoe had been so engrossed in, he folded it up and stuck it in his suit pocket. Sliding the drawer shut, Simon left the room and headed up the stairs.

They met in the tiny rear courtyard ten minutes later. Simon suppressed a smile at the outfit Zoe had chosen: black jeans, black turtleneck sweater, and a bucket hat pulled down low over her blond head.

"Okay. I'm going to give you a leg up over that wall," he said. "There's a ledge about four feet down on the other side that you can step onto. Then we go over the next wall, and then the next. The antique furniture shop four doors down has a back door. We break in if we have to, find our way onto the shop floor, and walk out the other side as if we're customers."

"Won't the back door be alarmed?"

"Bound to be, but we'll cross that bridge when we come to it. Right. Let's go."

Slowly, they made their way over the walls separating the back of each building along the street. Simon was glad that Zoe was young and fit, and with his help, they made short work of the six-foot walls.

Finally, they stood in front of a grilled rear door. A small red light was flashing above it.

"Damn." Simon inspected the door. "It's deadlocked from the inside." He walked to the small window next to it, which also had a grille over it. Taking a pair of wire cutters from his pocket, Simon worked away until the bottom part of the grille broke free, revealing an old sash window. There was a gap of half an inch between the window and the frame.

"I don't know whether this window is alarmed, so get ready to leg it back over the wall if I set it off," he warned her.

Zoe stood in an agony of suspense as Simon turned red from exertion. Finally, the window gave a small groan of assent and slid up. The alarm did not go off.

Simon tutted and beckoned her over. "People really should be more careful. No wonder there are so many burglaries. Hop in." He indicated Zoe should squeeze through the one-and-a-half-foot gap and open it wider from the inside to let him through. Sixty seconds later, both she and Simon were standing on the other side in a store-room full of old, elegant chairs and mahogany tables.

"Sunglasses on," he ordered.

Zoe pulled a pair of huge black sunglasses out of her pocket and put them on.

"How do I look?" she asked with a grin.

"Like an adorable ninja ant," he whispered. "Now, follow me."

He led her through the storeroom and quietly opened the door at the other end. Checking beyond it, he beckoned her to him and indicated a flight of stairs beyond the door.

"Okay, this must take us up into the showroom," he whispered. "Nearly there now."

Simon mounted the stairs with Zoe behind him. He turned the handle of the door at the top and peeped inside. He nodded to her, opened it further, and crept through it, signaling for Zoe to do the same. Once inside, Simon headed for a long, ornate chaise longue in the deserted showroom and Zoe followed him. Eventually, an aging man appeared from another door around the corner.

"My apologies, sir, I didn't hear the front bell ring."

"Not to worry. Er, my wife and I were interested in this. Can you tell me a little bit about it?"

Five minutes later, after promising to come back with their sitting-room measurements, Zoe and Simon stepped into the bright sunshine of an unusually springlike February day.

"Don't look behind you, Zoe, just keep walking," Simon muttered as he marched swiftly toward his car, parked a few yards up the street.

Once inside the Jaguar, Simon signaled into the flow of traffic, heading toward Soho and the recording studio. Zoe turned back and saw the media huddle still outside her front door less than fifty yards away. Just as they turned the corner, she gave them the finger.

"Do you know, I really enjoyed that," she giggled. "And the thought that all those vultures are now waiting outside a deserted house has cheered me up no end." She reached for his hand, resting on the gearstick, and squeezed it. "Thanks, Simon."

Zoe's light touch played havoc with his concentration. "We aim to please, madam. But don't be lulled into a false sense of security. Sooner or later, someone'll twig you're no longer at home."

"I know, but let's just hope it's not before tonight."

Simon dropped her off on Dean Street in front of the recording studio, then phoned in on his mobile.

"Sorry to ring earlier than usual, sir, but it might be hard to do so later."

"Understood."

"I've found something. It may be nothing, but ..." He read out the details on the invoice he had retrieved from the drawer in the desk.

"I'll get onto it, Warburton. I hear you're having a busy time."

"Yes. I'm driving Miss Harrison down to Dorset tonight."

"Keep talking to her, Warburton. Sooner or later, something will slip out."

"I'm really not convinced she knows anything, but I will, sir. Goodbye."

Simon hung up, drove off, and managed to find a space in the multistory car park in Brewer Street then texted Zoe to tell her to call him when she was finished, and he'd pick her up outside the recording studio. Feeling suddenly hungry, he took himself off for a McDonald's. He eyed the pub across the road, longing for a pint, but the image of Ian, disgustingly drunk and tearful, made him think better of it. He chomped his way through the tasteless hamburger and fries and tried to concentrate on his book, but visions of Zoe kept filling his brain as he recalled the touch of her hand on his.

Get a grip, Warburton, he lectured himself. *First rule of operation: never become emotionally involved.* Yet, as he waited eagerly for her call, he knew he'd already passed the point of no return. There was nothing he could do save execute a damage-limitation program and expect to suffer horribly when his services were no longer needed and they went their separate ways.

When Zoe jumped back into the car two hours later, Simon noticed she'd added makeup to her face. He rather preferred her without, thought she was so beautiful that she didn't need it . . .

Stop it, Warburton!

He started the engine and headed toward the M3 to Dorset.

"Had a good post-thingy?" he asked her casually.

"Fine. Of course, everyone was far more interested in my relationship with Art than anything else." Zoe swept a hand through her long blond hair. "Mike, the director, was very sweet, mind you. He told me he has an apartment in the south of France and he said I could use it any time I wanted."

"I hate to say it, but I suppose he's also thinking how having the new girlfriend of a prince of England starring in his film might boost worldwide ticket sales."

"That's awfully cynical, but you're probably right." Zoe sighed as she looked out at the River Thames running underneath Chiswick Bridge.

"Anyway, you seem much happier."

"Of course I am." She turned to him, her eyes full of warmth. "I'm seeing Art in a couple of hours' time."

Simon pulled into the drive of Haycroft House at just after six p.m. Inside, as always, it was freezing. And spread all over the sitting room were the higgledy-piggledy contents of a dozen boxes from the attic.

"Damn you, Marcus!" Zoe cried as Simon attempted to light the fire and she began to heap the piles of old paper back into the crates. "I *knew* he'd get bored halfway through and give up. Now it's even more of a mess than it was before."

"Oh well, if you're stuck down here for a while, I suppose it'll give you something to do."

"I'm hoping Art might have other plans arranged. Maybe he'll suggest we go abroad for a while, but then what about Jamie? Oh God, I don't know, Simon. I'll just have to wait till he gets here. For now, can you help me stack all these boxes in a corner?"

Eventually, with the sitting room tidied, the fire lit, and the kitchen range coaxed into action, Zoe set about storing the food Simon had purchased earlier that she had hidden in the car.

"Thank God I have some clothes still in my wardrobe here," she said distractedly. "I should go and change. Will he have eaten, do you think? Should I make something? Maybe put a casserole in the range so it won't matter what time he arrives?"

Simon fielded her questions as best he could, sensing her tension. While she went upstairs to change, Simon walked outside with his binoculars to survey the lay of the land. His heart sank as he saw two cars parked beyond the gate, then a ladder being lengthened and balanced precariously against the hedge surrounding the house. *How do these people do it?* he wondered, as he garnered the courage to go inside to inform Zoe.

"Oh God, no!" She stood in the kitchen, a look of desolation on her face.

"Zoe, I'm afraid I have to warn security the media are down here."

"Why can't they leave us alone?! Why? Why? Why?!" She thumped the table, harder each time.

"I'm sorry, but I need to call now."

"Yes. Whatever." She slumped into a chair.

Simon left the room and duly delivered the message. He went back into the kitchen, where Zoe was sitting smoking a cigarette.

"Didn't know you smoked," he commented.

"Marcus must have left the packet here, and if there was Prozac, Ecstasy, or even heroin in the house, I'd take it tonight." Her eyes were rimmed red with exhaustion. "He won't come now, will he?"

"No. Look, why don't I knock up a little something for supper? I haven't seen you eat a thing since I arrived at Welbeck Street yesterday morning."

"That's kind of you, but I just couldn't force it down."

"Fine. Then I'll cook it for me."

Zoe shrugged, then stood up. "There should be enough hot water for a bath by now. I'm going to take one."

When she'd left the kitchen, Simon set about gathering ingredients together and began to chop vegetables, whistling to himself just to break the deathly silence of the ancient walls around him.

Zoe arrived back downstairs an hour later in her grandfather's old paisley robe, and smelled something enticing wafting from the kitchen.

"What is it?" She peered over Simon's shoulder at the pot he was stirring.

"Does it matter? You don't want any, remember?" He indicated an open bottle of red wine on the table. "Help yourself. I opened it for culinary purposes only, of course."

"Of course." Zoe smiled, then poured herself a glass, sat down, and watched Simon at work.

"Is this part of your training?"

"No. I just love cooking. Sure you don't want some?"

"Go on then, as you've worked so hard."

Simon filled two plates and put one in front of Zoe. "It's spicy beef with lentils. I should have marinated the meat for a few hours first, of course, but it should be edible." He sat down opposite her.

Zoe forked up a mouthful. "This is really good, Simon."

"Don't sound so surprised," he laughed.

"You're wasting your talents. You should open a restaurant."

"That's what Joanna always says."

"She's right." Zoe continued to eat. "Were you and Joanna ever . . . you know?"

"Lovers? No, never. I always thought of her as my sister. Somehow it would have seemed . . . incestuous. Although . . ."

"Yes?"

"Oh, it was nothing really. A few weeks ago, she was staying with me and we kissed." Simon felt his face redden. "Her boyfriend had just dumped her, but I still thought my relationship with my ex-girlfriend was intact. So I stopped it." Simon paused with a forkful of food halfway between his mouth and his plate. "If I'd known then that my ex was about to dump me, I wonder if I'd have reacted differently."

"Well, you'll never know now." Zoe shrugged.

"Would you like some more? There's plenty." Simon studied her empty plate.

"I'd *love* some more, thanks, it's delicious! Will you do this forever?" she asked as he put a second helping in front of her.

"What's that?"

"Be a bodyguard. Subjugate your own life for the safety of others."

"Who knows?"

"I just think you're wasted. It's a bit of a dead-end job, isn't it?"

"Wow, thanks," he laughed.

"I didn't mean it like that." She blushed.

"It's okay. You're right, I don't want to be doing it forever."

"Well." Zoe raised her glass. "To both of us finding our true paths."

"To us." Simon raised his glass of water.

At that moment, Zoe's mobile rang.

"Excuse me." She left the kitchen to take the call.

Simon duly cleared the plates away and made coffee. Ten minutes later, Zoe was back in the kitchen, a smile lighting up her face. "Oh, Simon! It's all going to be okay."

"Is it? Good."

"That was Art. He's arranged for us to go abroad. An industrialist friend of his has offered us his private jet and his summer house in Spain. Apparently it has the most sophisticated security, so we can relax and talk about the future in complete peace, without a prying eye in sight."

"Right, er, great. When do you leave?"

"Tomorrow morning. Art said they will be calling you, but I have to be at Heathrow for nine o'clock. We're meeting in the VIP suite at Terminal Four. And then, you'll be glad to hear, you'll be free of me. Art's taking his own people to look after us while we're there."

"Okay. Coffee?"

"I'd love some. Let's drink it by the fire," she said as she led him into the sitting room with the coffee. "It'll be so fabulous not to have anyone spying on us. We so desperately need time to talk." Zoe settled herself down cross-legged by the fire, and cradled the mug between her hands.

Simon sat down on the sofa and took a sip of his coffee. "So, if he asks, will you marry him?"

"Do you think he'll ask? Could he, with this situation?"

"Okay, let me put it another way: do you *want* to spend the rest of your life with him?"

Zoe's eyes shone. "Oh God, yes! I've wanted it every single day for more than ten years."

"*Ten* years? Blimey, then I was wrong. The story did take a long time to leak," he teased her gently.

"No." She paused, picking at a loose thread on the rug. "I first met him over ten years ago. I was so young . . . just eighteen. I'm not so naive as to think it'll all be plain sailing this time. His family may veto me, just like they did back then. I may be flying to Spain for Art to tell me as nicely as he can that it's a no-go."

Simon did not mention the discussion he'd heard on Radio 5 Live as to whether the royal family was ready for an unmarried mother to join the clan. The opinion polls rather suggested not.

"There is one thing I was going to ask you." She glanced up at him.

"Fire away."

"Well, I'm not sure how long I'll be away. I was wondering . . . well . . ."

"Spit it out, Zoe."

"If you'd go and visit Jamie for me at school this weekend? I promised to go down, and obviously I'm not going to make it. He seemed so fond of you and—"

"Of course I will. Consider it done."

"I'll let the school know where I'll be. Maybe I'll tell them to tell Jamie I'm shooting a . . . a commercial or something in Spain. I don't want to lie to him, but I also think it's vital that Art and I have time together to talk."

"Yes," Simon agreed absently, thinking how exquisite she looked in the firelight. He stood up, not wishing to prolong the agony any further. "I'm going to turn in, Zoe. We have an early start and I may have to do some extravagant driving to lose those rats outside."

"Of course." Zoe stood up and walked toward him, stood on tiptoe, and planted a kiss on his cheek. "Thank you, Simon. I'll never forget what you've done for me in the past two days. You've kept me sane."

"Thanks." His heart contracted. "Night then," he muttered, and left the room.

―――――

"Art!" Zoe left Simon's side and ran into the prince's arms at Heathrow the next morning.

"Hello, Zoe." Art kissed her on the top of her head. "Right, we'll be off. Thanks, Warburton, for all your help." He nodded at Simon perfunctorily.

"Yes, bye, Simon." Zoe waved at him as Art led her into the VIP room. A small posse of security men followed after the couple.

Simon made his way back through the maze of airport corridors that took him landside again. His mobile phone rang.

"Warburton."

"Yes, sir?"

"You're relieved of security duty until Miss Harrison returns. Stand by for further instructions."

"Right. Thank you, sir."

Simon drove the Jaguar back to the car pool and handed over the keys. He then headed for the pub, where he treated himself to a perfect foaming pint of Tetley's bitter, in which he intended to knowingly and wholeheartedly drown his sorrows.

THE ISOLATED PAWN

A pawn that has no friendly pawn
adjacent to it. It may be either
seen as a weakness, or used as an
opportunity for counterplay.

25

Joanna sat at her desk, dejectedly typing an article about the top ten plants that could kill your pet. She felt numb, empty, used, and confused, and on the verge of giving it all up and returning to Yorkshire to count sheep for the rest of her days.

Marcus had called her on her mobile and even a number of times on the tapped landline at her apartment last night. Joanna had not returned his calls. In reality, she was "out" to Marcus for the rest of her life, after the way he had betrayed her. She shuddered at the thought that during all those beautiful times they had spent together, he had simply been using her for anything she knew.

She was counting the minutes until it was half past five and time to switch off her screen. Though why she wanted to go home to an empty apartment with no boyfriend and no best friend, she didn't know. It didn't help that the whole office was buzzing with the news of Zoe Harrison and the prince. Or that this morning Marian, the female features editor, had called her into her domain.

"You wrote the piece on Marcus Harrison, Zoe's brother."

"Yes," Joanna had replied sullenly.

"And word has it that you're screwing him." Marian never minced her words.

"I was, but I'm not now."

"As of when?"

"As of yesterday."

"What a shame. I was going to suggest sending you to try and get an interview from her, seeing as you're almost family."

"Impossible, I'm afraid."

"Pity. It could have got you off Pets and Gardens." Marian chewed her pen as she studied Joanna. "Okay, Jo, it's your call. If you won't do it, then someone else will. You trying to protect her?"

"No."

"Fine. Because if you are, the best thing you could do is to get her to agree to talk to you. At least that way she'll get a sympathetic hearing."

Marian had waved her out dismissively and Joanna had slunk back to her desk.

At long last, it was twenty-nine minutes and fifty-five seconds past five. With a groan of relief, Joanna switched off her computer and headed for the door. She was waiting for the elevator when Alec came up to her.

"Hi, Jo. You okay?"

"No, Alec, I'm not."

"Right, well, I want a word, but not here. I'll meet you in the French House in an hour. Looks like you were right." Without giving her a chance to say no, Alec turned on his heel and went back into the office.

Given she felt she now had nothing to lose, Joanna spent an hour wandering aimlessly around Leicester Square and the Trocadero, increasingly annoyed with the tourists getting in her way. Alec was already on a stool when she arrived in the crowded bar.

"Glass of wine?"

"Yup." She nodded, pulling up the bar stool next to him.

"Hear it's not been a good day."

"Nope."

"Marian told me that you refused to try and get an interview with Zoe Harrison. You could have used it as leverage to come back to me."

"It would have been a pointless exercise, Alec. Zoe probably thinks I was the one who spilled the beans in the first place and would prefer to pose semi-naked for the *News of the Screws* rather than talk to me."

"Shit!" Alec's mouth dropped open. "You knew about her and the prince?"

"Yes. She'd told me all about it. Thanks." Joanna took a slug of her wine. "In quite some detail, I might add."

"Jesus," Alec groaned. "So, you could have broken the story?"

"Oh yes. And now I wish I bloody well had, as I seem to have got the blame."

"Christ, Jo! You're going to have to toughen up. Breaking a story like that could have given your career a lifetime boost."

"Do you think I don't know that?! I spent most of last night thinking that maybe this game isn't for me, because I don't have the necessary lack of moral fiber. I seem to have this awful, unjournalistic quality of being able to keep a secret." She finished off her glass of wine. "Can I have another?"

"Well, at least you're beginning to drink like a hack." Alec signaled to the barman. "C'mon, you'll cheer up after the news I've got for you."

"Am I being reinstated?"

"No."

Joanna slumped forward and rested her head on her arms. "Then nothing you say can cheer me up."

"Even if I was to tell you I've found out some juicy info on your little old lady?" Alec lit up a Rothmans.

"Nope. I've given up on that one. That letter's ruined my entire life. I've had enough."

"Fine." He took a drag of his cigarette. "Then I won't tell you I'm pretty sure I know who she was. That, just before she arrived in England, she'd been living in France for the past sixty years."

"I still don't want to know."

"Or that James Harrison managed to purchase his house in Welbeck Street outright in 1928. It was owned by a senior politician who had been in Lloyd George's cabinet prior to that. Seems strange a penniless actor could afford a grand house like that, doesn't it? Unless, of course, he'd just come into a large sum of money."

"Sorry, Alec, I'm still not there."

"So finally, I won't tell you that there was a Rose Alice Fitzgerald working as a lady-in-waiting in a certain royal household in the 1920s."

Joanna gaped at him. "Sod it! Let's get a bottle."

The two of them adjourned to a corner table, and Alec told her what he had discovered.

"So what you're saying is that my little old lady, Rose, and James Harrison, a.k.a. Michael O'Connell, were in cahoots, blackmailing someone in the royal household?" she said.

"It's what I've surmised, yes. And I think the letter that she sent you was actually a love letter from Rose herself to James, a.k.a. Michael—or, in the letter, 'Siam'—which had nothing whatsoever to do with the real plot."

"So why does Rose talk about not being able to see James in the letter?"

"Because the Honorable Rose Fitzgerald was a lady-in-waiting. She came from an upper-crust Scottish family. I hardly think a penniless Irish actor would have made a good match for her. I'm sure they had to keep their liaison secret."

"Christ! Why have I had so much to drink? My head's foggy. I can't think straight."

"Then I'll think for you. Put simply, I reckon Rose and Sir James—"

"Michael O'Connell, in those days," Joanna butted in.

"Michael and Rose were lovers. Rose had discovered something juicy while going about her duty in the royal household, told Michael, a.k.a. James, who then blackmailed the person concerned. The parcels you say William Fielding used to collect for Michael/James, well, I reckon they contained money. Then Michael does a disappearing act, possibly flees the country, dumping poor old Rose along the way. A few months later, he arrives back; adopts a new persona; buys his pile in Welbeck Street with the cash he's gathered; marries his wife, Grace; and all is tickety-boo."

"Okay. Let's work on your premise," said Joanna. "I might as well face it, it's as good as any I've come up with so far and it does all seem to fit. Why the sudden mass panic when James Harrison dies?"

"Well now, let's try some lateral thinking. We know for certain that Rose arrived back in the country just after Sir James popped his clogs, having been abroad for many years. Is it possible that Rose planned to reveal all after Sir James's death? Maybe blacken his name, pay him back for dumping her all those years ago?"

"Then why hadn't she done it before?"

"Perhaps she was frightened. Maybe James had something on her, had threatened her. And then, when she knew she was ill and time was running out, she decided she had nothing to lose? I dunno, Jo, I'm guessing here." Alec ground out a cigarette in the ashtray and lit another.

"But would that panic the establishment? MI5 is involved, Alec. All I know is it's something very, very big," breathed Joanna. "Big enough for the high-ups to persuade Marcus Harrison to wine, dine, and bed me to see what I knew."

"Who told you that?"

"My friend Simon."

"You sure about that?"

"Oh yes."

Alec swore under his breath. "Blimey, Jo, what is all this?"

"If we follow your idea, then obviously whatever it was Rose and Michael had discovered was major." She lowered her voice further. "Christ, Alec, two people have already died in odd circumstances . . . I don't want to be the third."

They sat in silence, Joanna desperately trying to clear her fuzzy mind. Alec's old words rang through her: *Trust no bugger* . . .

"Alec, why this sudden interest after freezing me out?"

He barked out a laugh. "If you think I'm being paid to spy on you, don't worry, sweetheart. Strikes me you need some help. Because this just won't go away, will it? Everyone else seems to have screwed you over. I may be an unlikely knight in shining armor, but I'll have to do."

"*If* I decide to continue investigating."

"Yeah. So, what next?"

"Marcus and I were going on a trip to Ireland next weekend before I found out the truth of why he was seeing me. William Fielding had indicated an Irish connection and Marcus seems to have managed to pinpoint where, if anywhere, Michael O'Connell might have originally hailed from."

"How?"

"He said that Zoe's son mentioned a place in Ireland that his grandfather had talked about before he died. He might have got it wrong, but . . ."

"Never dismiss child-talk, Jo. I've coerced some of my best scoops out of nippers."

"Then you are quite without scruples, Alec."

"That's what makes a good journalist." He checked his watch. "I gotta go. We never had this conversation, of course. And I shall not advise you to go to Ireland and sit in the local bar, where any amount of gossip can be overheard, nor shall I suggest you do it quickly before Marcus—or perhaps someone else—gets there before you. And I shall certainly not mention that you do not look well tonight and there's every possibility that over the next couple of days it will develop into flu and you'll be too sick to make it into work." Alec stuffed his cigarettes into his pocket. "Night, Jo. Call me if there's trouble."

"Night, Alec."

She watched him leave the bar, and despite herself, she smiled. If nothing else, Alec, or the wine, or a mixture of both, had managed to lift her spirits. Hailing a taxi, she decided to sleep on it, digest the information before making a plan.

There were eight new messages from Marcus on her answering machine when she got home. That was in addition to the seven on her mobile, plus numerous calls she had asked the receptionist to bar at work.

"They must have paid you one hell of a lot of money, you slimy, double-crossing, rancid, decomposed little toad," she growled to the machine as she headed for the bathroom and a shower.

The doorbell was ringing when she emerged, dripping, wrapped in a towel. Peeping through the curtains, Joanna saw that the decomposed little toad was standing on her doorstep.

"Oh *Christ*!" she cried, then switched the TV on, prepared to ignore him for as long as it took.

"Joanna," he was shouting through the letter box. "It's me, Marcus. I know you're in. I saw you behind the curtains. Let me in! What have I done wrong? *Joanna!*"

"Damn! Damn! Damn!" Joanna growled as she put on her robe and stomped to the door. Marcus was going to wake up half the neighborhood if she didn't allow him entry. She saw his eyes peering through the letter box at her.

"Hi. Let me in, Jo."

"Piss off!"

"Charmed, I'm sure. Can you let me know exactly what I'm supposed to have done?"

"If you don't know, then I'm not bloody telling you. Just get out of my life and stay out, forever."

"Joanna, I love you." His voice broke. "If you don't let me in to discuss whatever crime it is I'm meant to have committed, then I shall have to stay out here all night and . . . *sing* my love to you."

"Marcus, if you don't get off my doorstep in the next five seconds, I'm calling the police. They'll arrest you for harassment."

"Okay. I don't mind. Of course, we'll probably make the front page of tomorrow's newspaper, with my newfound status as brother of Prince Arthur's new love, but I'm sure that won't worry you . . . I—"

Marcus almost toppled through the front door as Joanna opened it.

"Okay. You win." She was quivering with anger. Marcus went to touch her. She flinched and backed away. "Don't come near me. I mean it."

"Okay, okay. Tell me then, what is it I've done?"

Joanna crossed her arms. "I have to say, I thought it was odd that you were so caring, so overblown in your affections. I mean, I'd already been told what a rotten, stinking rat you were. And silly me, I decided to take you at face value, thought that maybe you felt differently about me than the rest of the female population of London."

"I do, really, Jo. I—"

"Shut up, Marcus. I'm talking. Then, I discover that your feelings for me didn't even come into it. It was your wallet that was enjoying my company."

"I—"

"I was told a couple of days ago that you were being paid to woo me and bed me." Joanna saw the hectic red blush rise up into his cheeks. And had an urge to slap him very hard.

"No, Joanna, whoever said that has got it totally wrong. I mean, I was given some money, but not to get information from *you*. It was to try to find the missing letter. I swear I didn't know anything about Rose when you told me, or on the first night we went to bed. It happened a couple of days later. I thought of telling you that I'd been approached to help, but I thought you'd get frightened off. And now you don't believe me, and—"

"Would *you* believe you?!"

"No, of course I wouldn't. But . . ." Marcus looked as if he was about to burst into tears. "Please, you have to believe that I've never felt like this before, never. It had nothing to do with money, apart from the fact I thought that if we pooled our resources and our knowledge, we might find the answers, and . . . I . . . dammit!" Marcus raked his fingers roughly over his eyelids.

Joanna was genuinely surprised by his reaction. She'd expected him to tough it out, deny it, or callously confirm it when he knew he'd lost. Instead, she seemed to be witnessing genuine confusion and grief. But after Matthew, Simon, and now Marcus, she'd had enough of being betrayed.

"You took that money, Marcus, and kept it a secret from me. I should have believed everyone who told me how selfish you are. And your sister? I bet you were the one who told the *Mail* about her and the prince, weren't you? You knew everyone would blame me, but all you cared about was making some fast cash!"

"No!" Marcus said vehemently. "I would never sell out Zoe like that!"

"But you sold *me* out! So, how could I ever believe you?" She was breathless with anger now.

"I don't know what to say to make you believe me!"

"There's nothing left to say. Your five minutes are up. I want you to leave."

"I just wanted to protect you . . . I know that doesn't make much sense, but . . . can you give me one last chance?" he begged her.

"Absolutely not. Even if you're telling the truth now, you still lied to me. For money. You're a coward, Marcus."

"You're right. I didn't tell you because I thought I might lose you. I'm not lying when I say I love you, Joanna, and I'm going to regret this for the rest of my life."

"Goodbye." She closed the door without another word, before he could see the tears in her own eyes. It was tiredness, emotion, and tension, that was all, she reassured herself as she headed for bed. Marcus was a newly acquired habit she could easily break. She lay there, desperate for sleep, turning to what Alec had said earlier to stop her thoughts of Marcus. Her brain was like a newborn hare, springing from one fresh fact to the next, and eventually she gave up, climbed out of bed, and switched on the kettle. After making herself a hot, strong cup of tea, then sitting on the bed cross-legged, Joanna took her "Rose" information folder from her rucksack. She studied the facts, then drew a precise diagram that collated all the information she had gathered so far.

Should she give it one more try? Ireland was meant to be extremely beautiful and the flights and accommodation had all been booked. At the very least, she could use the trip as a much-needed break from London and all that had happened since Christmas.

"Sod it!" she breathed. She owed it to herself to take one step further down the line. Otherwise she'd spend the rest of her life wondering. And she really had nothing left to lose . . .

"Except my life," she muttered darkly.

———

Three days later, having checked in for the flight to Cork, Joanna took out her mobile as she walked toward the departure gate.

"Hello?"

"Alec?"

"Yeah?"

"It's me. Can you tell the ed I've got the most dreadful flu? So bad, in fact, I might not be feeling better until the middle of next week."

"Bye, Jo. Good luck. And watch your back. You know where I am."

"Thanks, Alec. Bye."

It was only once she was up in the air and on the way to her destination across the Irish Sea that she gave a sigh of relief.

26

As Joanna was touching down at Cork Airport, Marcus lay in bed. It was already midday, but he couldn't see much point in getting up. This had been pretty much the pattern since he'd been booted out of Joanna's apartment. He was utterly devastated, by both the loss of her and the fact that he had no one to blame but himself.

He hauled himself out of bed and wandered into the sitting room, deciding to put his feelings for her down on paper. Picking up an unfamiliar gold pen from the side table, his heart twisting as he realized it must be Joanna's, he then began to write her a letter. As he closed his eyes, he saw her appear in front of him, as she had a hundred times since he'd woken up that morning. He'd fallen in love properly for the first time in his life. It wasn't lust, or obsession, or any of the peripheral feelings he'd had for women before. This went way deeper, down into his gut. His head and heart ached for her like he had an illness—he could think of nothing else. He even hated his precious film project—the reason he had taken the money from that idiot Ian in the first place . . .

Later that evening, he took a bus up to Crouch End and walked to Joanna's apartment. Seeing it was in darkness, he posted the letter to Joanna through the letter box, praying that she would read it and contact him. Then he went home and back to bed, cradling a bottle of whiskey.

Just before midnight, the doorbell rang.

Marcus jumped out of bed, like a rabbit free of a trap, his hopes high that Joanna had responded to his heartfelt letter. He opened the door expecting to see her. Instead, he recognized the tall, burly frame of Ian Simpson.

"What do you want this time of night?" Marcus asked him.

Ian stepped inside without asking. "Where's Joanna Haslam?" he demanded, his eyes darting around the living room.

"Not here, that's for sure."

"Then where?" Ian walked toward him, his height imposing.

"I really don't know. I only wish I did."

Ian stood so close to him that Marcus could hear his uneven breathing and smell the alcohol fumes coming off him. Or perhaps it was his own stench of whiskey, he thought, pushing down an urge to be sick.

"We were paying you to keep tabs on her, remember? Then her mate Simon tipped her off."

"Si . . . what . . . ?"

"Simon, you idiot! Your sister's bodyguard."

Marcus took a step back and passed a hand over his bleary eyes. "Look, I did my best to find you that letter, but Joanna's left me high and dry, and—"

Ian grabbed Marcus by the collar of his shirt. "You know where she is, don't you, you lying shit!"

"I really don't. I . . ." Close up, Marcus could see that Ian's eyes were bloodshot. The man was off his head with anger and booze. "C-can you let me go and we can talk about this rationally?"

A punch in the stomach sent Marcus reeling toward the sofa. His head hit the wall and he saw stars.

"Steady on, mate! We're on the same side, remember?"

Ian laughed. "I hardly think so."

Marcus struggled upright and watched as Ian paced around the room.

"She's gone somewhere, hasn't she?" Ian demanded. "She's on the trail."

"What trail? I—"

Ian advanced toward him and landed a kick in Marcus's groin, which sent him rolling around on the floor, howling in pain.

"It would be a good idea if you told me. I know you're covering up for her, protecting her."

"No! Really. I—"

A kick in the kidneys produced further yells of pain and Marcus vomited copiously.

"What were the two of you planning? Tell me."

"Nothing. I . . ." Marcus could take no more and he searched his mind desperately for something to tell Ian in order to get rid of him and put him off the scent. Then he had a brain wave. "We were going to Ireland this weekend. I told her that's where I thought Sir James originally came from."

"Where in Ireland?"

"County Cork . . ."

"What part?"

Ian crouched down and peered into his face, his fist at the ready. "Just tell me, mate, because I can do a lot worse."

"I . . ." Marcus struggled to remember the name of the place. "Rosscarbery."

"I'll make some calls. If I find out you're lying, I'll be back, do you understand?"

"Yes," Marcus gasped.

Ian made a snorting sound that could have been laughter, pity, or a mixture of both. "You were always a coward at school. You haven't changed, Marcus, have you?" Ian aimed the tip of his toe at Marcus's nose. Marcus cringed as the toe swung wide and hit a cheek. "Be seeing you."

Marcus listened for the door closing behind Ian, then rolled onto his knees, moving his jaw from side to side and cursing with the pain. He managed to heave himself upright and sat slumped against the sofa staring into space, his face, his groin, and his stomach throbbing.

"Jesus!"

Thank God he'd managed to come up with the Ireland line. Of course, Ian would be back when he discovered Joanna wasn't there—it was the last place on earth she'd go if she thought there was any chance of *his* being there—but at least he'd be prepared. Maybe he should go and stay with Zoe for a while until this blew over . . .

Then a sudden surge of fear settled on Marcus's already painful chest. What if she *did* go . . . ? No . . . After all, why would she? On the other hand, Ian had said she was still on the trail . . .

"Christ!"

Had he just unwittingly thrown Joanna to a mentally unstable and drunken lion? Marcus dashed to the kitchen, and rifled through the pile of papers to find the telephone number for the hotel he'd booked them into, then picked up the receiver.

———

Simon whistled along to Ella Fitzgerald as he drove down the motorway toward Berkshire and Jamie's school. The few days he'd had of waiting for instructions had been long overdue. He felt rested and calmer than he had done for a while, even if the spare time had given him the opportunity to think about Zoe. On the upside, he knew that the specter of Sarah had been washed away. On the downside, he knew those feelings had been transferred and magnified a thousandfold. Even the fact that he was seeing Zoe's son in half an hour's time filled him with illicit pleasure, because it was contact by proxy with her.

Having made sure to locate a restaurant that purported to serve excellent Sunday lunches, Simon drove Jamie toward it, along the narrow country lanes. Confused at having been taken out to lunch by Simon, Jamie was quieter than he had been at home in London.

"I'll have the beef, I think." Simon perused the menu and looked at Jamie. "You?"

"The chicken, thanks."

Simon ordered the food, a pint for himself, and a Coke for Jamie.

"So, how's your week been?" He couldn't help noticing how similar Jamie was to his mother. The same startling blue eyes, thick blond hair, and delicate features.

"Fine," Jamie said uncertainly. "How long is Mumma away for?"

"I don't know exactly. I think she'll probably be back sometime next week."

"Oh. What kind of work is it?"

"Some TV commercial, I think. I'm not sure."

Jamie took a sip of his Coke. "Are you staying at the house in London?"

"Actually, tomorrow, I've decided to go do a bit of touring. Scotland, maybe Ireland. How's school?" Simon moved the subject on.

"Okay. You know, the same."

"Right."

Simon was grateful when their food arrived. Jamie picked at his chicken, answering most attempts at conversation in monosyllables. He refused dessert, even though there was homemade apple pie with ice cream on the menu.

"I remember always yumming everything up when my parents came to take me out for lunch from school. You sure you're okay, old chap?"

"Yes. Do they have boarding schools in New Zealand?"

"I . . . yes, of course they do. If you're miles away from anything, on a sheep farm, you have to board in the city," Simon invented. "Sure I can't tempt you to a pudding?"

"Positive."

Simon was relieved when it was time to take the boy back to school. Jamie sat in the car staring out of the window, humming to himself.

"What's that you're humming?"

"A nursery rhyme, 'Ring a Ring o' Roses.' Great-James used to sing it to me all the time. When I got older, he told me it was all about people dying of the Black Death."

"Do you miss him, Jamie?"

"Yes. But I know he's still looking after me from heaven."

"I'm sure he is."

"And I still have his roses to remind me of him on earth."

"Roses?"

"Yeah. Great-James loved roses. He has them on his grave now."

Simon brought the car to a halt in front of the school and Jamie opened the door to climb out. "Thanks for lunch, Simon. Safe journey back to London."

"Anytime. Bye, Jamie."

Simon watched as Jamie raced up the steps and inside the school. Sighing, he drove the car back along the gravel drive and out of the school. When he arrived back at his apartment an hour later, there was a message on his answering machine.

"*Report to me at zero eight hundred hours tomorrow morning.*"

Knowing his short break was well and truly at its end, Simon made himself a Caesar salad, then showered and took himself off to bed, trying not to imagine Zoe together with her prince in Spain.

27

On arrival at Cork Airport, Joanna went to the car-rental desk and rented a Fiesta. Having furnished herself with a map and some Irish pounds, she followed the signs to the N71 and was surprised that the main road from the airport resembled a byroad from her native Yorkshire. The late-February day was sunny and she took in the fast-burgeoning green of the rolling fields on either side of her.

An hour later, Joanna found herself driving down a steep hill into Rosscarbery village. To her left, a deep estuary bordered by a low wall stretched into the sea far away. Houses, cottages, and bungalows were dotted on either side of it. When she reached the bottom of the hill, Joanna stopped the car to take a better look. The tide was out and all manner of bird life was swooping down onto the sand, and a bevy of swans were floating gracefully on a large pool of water left behind by the tide.

After getting out of the car, Joanna leaned against the low wall, breathing in deeply. The air smelled so different from that of London: clean, fresh, with a hint of salt that indicated that the Atlantic was less than a mile away. It was then that she saw the house. It stuck right out into the estuary at the end of a narrow causeway, built on a bed of rock with water surrounding it on three sides. It was large, covered in gray slate, a weathervane on the chimney spinning slightly in the breeze. From the description Marcus had given her of a big house out in the bay, surely this had to be it?

A cloud swept over the sun, casting a shadow across the bay and onto the house. Joanna shuddered suddenly, then walked back to her car, started the engine, and drove off.

That evening, Joanna sat in the cozy bar of the hotel she had checked into and sipped a hot port by the fire. She felt more relaxed than she'd felt for weeks, and even though thoughts of Marcus—under whose name the reservation had been made—filled her head, she had fallen asleep that afternoon on the big old double bed in her room. She'd only lain down on it to study the map of Rosscarbery, and the next thing she knew, it was seven o'clock and the room was in darkness.

It's because I feel safe here, she thought.

"Will ye be wanting to take your supper in the dining room or here by the fire?"

It was Margaret, wife of Willie, the jovial owner and landlord.

"Here will do just fine, thanks."

Joanna sat eating her bacon, cabbage, and potatoes and watched as a trail of locals came through the door. Young and old, they all knew one another and seemed to be on intimate terms with the minutiae of one another's lives. Feeling sated after her supper, she sauntered toward the bar and ordered a final pre-bedtime hot port.

"You here for a holiday, so?" a middle-aged man in overalls and wellingtons asked her from his perch by the bar.

"Partly," she replied. "I'm also searching for a relative of mine."

"Sure, there's always people coming over here looking for a relative. It might be said our blessed country managed to germinate half the Western Hemisphere."

This elicited chuckles from the other drinkers in the bar.

"So, what would your relative be called then?" asked the man.

"Michael O'Connell. I'd reckon he was born here around the turn of the century."

The man rubbed his chin. "There's bound to be a few of those, being as it is such a common name hereabouts."

"Have you any idea where I could check?"

"The register of births and deaths, next door to the chemist in the square. And the churches, of course. Or you could go into Clonakilty, where your man has started up a business tracing Irish heritage." He drained his pint of stout. "He's bound to find an O'Connell that's related to you on his computer, long as you've paid him his fee." The man winked at his neighbor on the bar stool next to him. "Strange really, how times change. Sixty years ago we were bogmen who'd crawled out from under a stone. Nobody wanted to exchange the time of day with us. Now, even the president of the United States wants to be related to us."

"True, true," his neighbor said, nodding.

"Do you by any chance know who owns the house sticking out into the estuary? The gray stone one, with the weathervane?" Joanna asked tentatively.

An old woman dressed in an ancient anorak, a woolen hat covering her hair, studied Joanna from her seat in the corner with sudden interest.

"Ah, jaysus, that old wreck?" said the man. "It's been empty as long as I've been living here. You'd have to be asking Fergal Mulcahy, the local historian, maybe. I think it was owned by the British once, long ago. They used it as a coastguard's outpost, but since then . . . I'd say there's a lot of property lying about these parts without an owner to tend to it."

"Thanks anyway." Joanna took the hot port from the bar. "Good night."

"Night, missus. Hope you find yer roots."

The old woman in the corner stood up soon after Joanna left and headed for the door.

The man at the bar nudged his neighbor at the woman's departure. "Should have sent her down to mad Ciara Deasy. She'd be sure to spin her a tale or two of the O'Connells of Rosscarbery."

Both men chuckled and ordered another round of Murphy's on the strength of the joke.

The next morning, after a big Irish breakfast, Joanna prepared to go out. The weather was filthy, the spring promise of yesterday forestalled by a grim, gray rain that shrouded the bay below her in mist.

She spent the morning wandering around the fine Protestant cathedral and spoke to the friendly dean, who let her look through the records of baptisms and marriages. "It's more likely you'll find your fella registered in St. Mary's, the Catholic church down the road. Us Protestants always have been a minority around here." He smiled ruefully.

At St. Mary's, the priest finished hearing confession, then unlocked the cupboard where the register books were kept. "If he was born in Ross, he'll be in the records. There wasn't a baby round these parts that wasn't baptized here in those days. Now, it's 1900 we're after, is it?"

"Yes."

Joanna spent the next half an hour looking through the names of those baptized. There was not a single baby O'Connell in that year. Or the years before or after.

"Are you sure you have the right name? I mean, if it was O'Connor, then we'd be in business," the priest said.

Joanna wasn't sure about anything. She was over here on the apparent words of an old man, and the throwaway comment of a young boy. Chilled to the bone now, Joanna left the church and wandered across the square and back to her hotel for a bowl of soup to warm her up.

"Any luck?" asked Margaret.

"Nothing."

"You should ask some of the old ones in town. They might remember the name. Or Fergal Mulcahy, as your man at the bar suggested last night. He teaches history up at the boys' school."

Joanna thanked her and that afternoon was annoyed to discover that the Registry of Births, Marriages, and Deaths was closed. Seeing the rain had stopped and needing some fresh air and exercise, she borrowed a bicycle from Margaret's daughter. She set off from the village and toward the estuary, the wind stinging her face as the bicycle juddered along with its sticky gears. The narrow causeway wound round for a good half a mile before the coastguard's house came into view. When she drew near it, she propped up her bicycle by the wall. Even from here, she could see there were holes in the slate roof, and the windowpanes were cracked or boarded up.

Joanna took a step toward the rusting gate. It creaked open. She climbed the steps up to the front door and tentatively grasped the handle. The old lock may have been rusty, but it still knew how to keep out uninvited visitors. She wiped some grime away from the window on the left of it with her sleeve. Peering in, she could see nothing but blackness.

Stepping back from the house, she considered other means of entry. She noticed a broken windowpane overlooking the estuary at the back. The only way to get to it was to walk down into the estuary itself and climb up the high, sloping seawall behind the house. Luckily the tide was out, so Joanna walked down the steps, slippery and green from seaweed, and onto the wet sand. She reckoned the wall stood about ten feet high, protecting the house from the water around it.

Managing to get a foothold in the crumbling brick, she clambered laboriously up the wall, and onto a ledge of about two feet wide. Just above her was the broken window. Pulling herself to standing, she peered inside. Even though there was little wind outside the house, she could hear the soft cry of it inside. The room through the window must have been the kitchen; there was still an old black range—rusty with neglect—along one wall and a sink with an old-fashioned water pump over it along the other. Joanna looked down and saw a dead rat in the middle of the gray slate floor.

A door banged suddenly from somewhere inside the house. Joanna jumped in fright and almost fell backward off the ledge. Turning round, she sat and dangled her legs off the edge to ease herself down before she jumped, landing in the soft, wet sand below. Dusting the sand from her jeans, she hurried back to her bicycle, climbed on, and pedaled as fast as she could away from the house.

Ciara Deasy watched Joanna from the window of her cottage. She'd always known that one day, someone would come and she'd be able to tell her story at last.

———

"This is your man, Fergal Mulcahy," announced Margaret, guiding Joanna over to the bar the next day.

"Hello." Joanna smiled, trying to keep the surprise out of her voice. She'd expected Fergal Mulcahy to be a fusty professor-type person with a thick gray beard. In fact, Fergal was probably not much older than her and was dressed very pleasantly in a pair of jeans and a fisherman's sweater. He had thick black hair and blue eyes, and reminded Joanna painfully of Marcus. Then he stood up and she saw he was much taller than her ex-boyfriend, with a far leaner frame.

"Good to be meeting you, Joanna. I hear you've lost a relative." His eyes crinkled kindly as he smiled.

"Yes."

Fergal tapped the bar stool next to him. "Take a seat, we'll have a glass and you can tell me all about it. A glass and a pint, Margaret, please."

Joanna, who had never tasted stout in her life, found the creamy, iron taste of the Murphy's very palatable indeed.

"Now then, what's the name of this relative of yours?"

"Michael O'Connell."

"You've tried the churches, I suppose?"

"Yes. He wasn't on any of the christening entries. Or the marriages. I would have tried the registrar's office but—"

"It's closed on the weekends, I know. Well, I can sort that. The registrar just happens to be my father." Fergal dangled a key in front of her. "And he lives above the shop."

"Thanks."

"And I hear you're interested in the coastguard's house?"

"Yes, although I'm not sure it has anything to do with my missing relative."

"A grand old house it was once. My dad's got photos of it somewhere. Sad it's been left to rack and ruin, but of course none in the village would touch it."

"Why's that?"

Fergal sipped at his fresh pint. "Maybe you know how it is in small places. Myths and legends grow out of a small grain of truth and some mighty gossip. And being empty so long, that house has had its fair share of stories. I'd reckon it'll be some rich American who'll come along and steal the place for nothing."

"What were the stories, Mr. Mulcahy?"

"Come now, call me Fergal." He smiled at her. "I'm a historian. I deal with facts, not fantasy, so I've never believed a word of it." His eyes twinkled. "Except you wouldn't find me down there around midnight on the eve of a full moon."

"Really? Why?"

"It is said around these parts that about seventy years ago or so, a young woman from the village, Niamh Deasy, got herself in trouble with a man who was staying at the coastguard's house. The man left to return to his homeland in England, leaving the girl with child. She went stone mad with grief, so they say, gave birth to a dead baby in the house before dying soon after herself. There are those in the village who believe the house is still haunted by her, that Niamh's cries of pain and fear can still be heard echoing from the house on a stormy night. Some have even spoken of seeing her face at the window, her hands covered with her blood."

Joanna's own blood ran cold. She took a nervous sip of the Murphy's and almost choked on it.

"'Tis only a story." Fergal looked at her with concern. "I didn't mean to upset you."

"No . . . You haven't, really. It's fascinating. Seventy years ago, you say? There must have been people around at the time who are still living today."

"There are indeed. The girl's younger sister, Ciara, still lives in the family homestead. Don't try talking to her, mind. She's never been the full shilling, since she was a child. She believes every word of the story, and adds her own finishing touches to it, I can tell you."

"So the baby died?"

"That's the story, although some say that Niamh's father murdered it. I've even heard tell that the baby was taken off by the leprechauns . . ." He smiled and shook his head. "Try and envisage a time, not so long ago, without electricity, when the only form of sport was to gather together to drink, play music, and swap stories, true or otherwise. News has always been like Chinese whispers in Ireland, each man vying with the other to make his story bigger and better. In this case, mind, 'tis true the girl died. But in that house, mad from thwarted love?" Fergal shrugged. "I doubt it."

"Where does this Ciara live?"

"Down in the pink cottage overlooking the bay, opposite the coastguard's house. A chilling view for her, you might say. Well now, would you like to pop along the road and have a look through the records my father has?"

"Yes, if it's convenient for you?"

"'Tis fine. No rush." Fergal indicated Joanna's stout. "We'll go when you're ready."

The small office that had recorded every birth and death in the village of Rosscarbery for the past 150 years did not seem to have changed much in that time, apart from the harsh strip light illuminating the bog-oak desk.

Fergal busied himself in the back room, searching for the records from the turn of the century. "Right now, you take the births, I'll take the deaths."

"Okay."

They sat on each side of the desk, silently going through each entry. Joanna found a Fionnuala and a Kathleen O'Connell, but not a single boy born of that surname between 1897 and 1905.

"Anything?" she asked.

"No, not a thing. I have found Niamh Deasy—the girl that died—though. She was registered as dead on the second of January 1927. But there's no note that her baby died with her, so let's see if someone else registered the baby's birth."

Fergal went to fetch another ancient, leather-bound book and they both pored over the yellowing pages of births together.

"Nothing." Fergal shut the book and a fug of dust flew into the air, making Joanna sneeze violently. "Maybe the baby was a myth after all. Are you sure now that Michael O'Connell was born here in Rosscarbery? Each townland or district kept their own records, you see. He could have been born a few miles up the road, in Clonakilty for example, or Skibbereen, and his birth would be registered there."

Joanna rubbed her forehead. "To be honest, Fergal, I know nothing."

"Well now, it might be worth checking the records in both those towns. I'll just close up here, then I'll walk you back to the hotel."

The bar was fuller than it had been the previous night. Another Murphy's arrived in front of Joanna and she was drawn into a group that Fergal was talking to.

"Go and see Ciara Deasy, just for the craic!" laughed a young woman with dancing eyes and a mane of red hair, upon hearing of Joanna's fascination with the coastguard's house. "She terrified all of us kids with her talk. I'd say she was a witch."

"Stop that now, Eileen. We're no longer peasants believing in such fantasy," admonished Fergal.

"Doesn't every land have its fables?" Eileen asked, fluttering her eyelashes at Fergal. "And its eccentrics? Even the EU can't ban those, you know."

There then ensued a heated debate between the pro- and anti-EU supporters.

Joanna yawned surreptitiously. "It's great to meet you all and thanks for your help. I'm going to go to bed now."

"A young London thing like you? I thought 'twas dawn before you all crawled to your beds," said one of the men.

"It's all your clean fresh air. My lungs can't get over the shock. Night, everyone." She headed off in the direction of the stairs but was halted by a tap on the shoulder.

"I'm free tomorrow morning until twelve," said Fergal. "I could take you to the public records office in Clonakilty. It's larger than the one here and they'll probably have a record of who owns the coastguard's house. We could pop in to the church as well, see if that throws anything up. I'll come by at nine tomorrow."

Joanna smiled at him. "Yes, thank you. That would be great. Night."

—

At nine the next morning, Fergal was waiting for her in the deserted bar. Twenty minutes later, they were in a large, newly built council office. Fergal seemed to know the woman behind the counter and he indicated to Joanna that she should follow him and the woman into a storeroom.

"Right, that's all the Rosscarbery plans over there." The woman pointed to a shelf loaded with files. She walked to the door. "If you need anything else, Fergal, just you call me, okay?"

"Sure, Ginny. Thanks."

As Joanna followed Fergal over to the shelf, she got the feeling that this young man was the stuff of every local girl's dreams.

"Right. You take that pile, I'll take this. The house is bound to be here somewhere."

For an hour they went through pages of yellowing, dusty files, until at last Fergal gave a whoop of triumph. "Got the bugger! Come here and look."

Inside the file was the plan of the coastguard's house in Rosscarbery.

"Drawn for a Mr. H. O. Bentinck, Drumnogue House, Rosscarbery, 1869," Fergal read out. "That was a local Englishman living here at the time. He left during the Troubles. A lot of the English did."

"But surely that doesn't mean he still owns it? I mean, it's over one hundred and twenty years ago."

"Well, his great-great-granddaughter, Emily Bentinck, still lives at Ardfield, along between here and Ross. She's turned the estate into a business venture and trains racehorses there. Go and ask her if she knows any more, so you should." Fergal was looking at his watch. "I'll have to go in half an hour. Let's get these plans photocopied and run to the church, okay?"

Once Fergal had greeted the priest and done some fast talking, the old records of baptism were unlocked from their cupboard and opened for them.

Joanna scanned her finger quickly down the register. "Look here!" Her eyes lit up with excitement. "Michael James O'Connell. Baptized the tenth of April 1900. It has to be him!"

"There you go now, Joanna," said Fergal with a broad smile. He looked at his watch. "I'll have to go back to Ross now. I can't be late for my class. I'll write you down some directions to the Bentinck estate on the way."

———

"So, where do you go from here, now you've found your man?" he asked as Joanna drove out of Clonakilty toward Rosscarbery.

"I don't know. But at least I feel I haven't been on a completely wild goose chase."

Having dropped Fergal at his school, Joanna followed his directions to Ardfield, and after a frustrating twenty minutes of narrow country roads, turned in to the gate of Drumnogue House. As she bumped along the potholed drive, a large white house appeared in front of her. She parked next to a muddy Land Rover and got out of the car. The house had a stunning view of the Atlantic, stretching out into the distance beyond it.

Joanna began to hunt for signs of life, but there were none behind the tall Georgian windows. Ionic columns framed the front door, and as she approached, she could see it was slightly ajar. Knocking and receiving no reply, she pushed it gently. "Hello?" she called, her voice echoing in the cavernous hallway. Not feeling she should go any further, Joanna retreated and walked around to the back, where she saw a stable block. A woman in an ancient anorak and a pair of jodhpurs was grooming a horse.

"Hello, sorry to bother you, but I'm looking for Emily Bentinck."

"You found her," the woman said in a clipped English accent. "Can I help you?"

"Yes. My name's Joanna Haslam. I'm over here doing some research on my family. I was wondering whether you could tell me if your family still owns the coastguard's house down in Rosscarbery?"

"Interested in buying it, are you?"

"No, sadly I couldn't afford it," Joanna said with a smile. "I'm more interested in the history of it."

"I see." Emily continued to brush down the horse with firm strokes. "Don't really know that much about it, apart from the fact my great-great-grandfather commissioned its construction in the late nineteen hundreds on behalf of the British government. They wanted an outpost in the bay to try and stem the smuggling that was going on down there. I don't believe our family ever actually owned it."

"I see. Do you know how I might be able to find out who did?"

"There you go, Sergeant, good boy." Emily patted the horse on its rump and led it back into one of the stables. She came out and looked at her watch. "Come inside and have a cup of tea. I was just going to brew up anyway."

Joanna sat in the huge, untidy kitchen as Emily put a kettle on the range to boil. Every available wall was covered with hundreds of rosettes won in competitions both in Ireland and abroad.

"Must admit I've been a little tardy in tracing the family history. So damned busy with the nags outside and putting this place back on its feet." Emily poured Joanna a cup of tea from a large stainless-steel pot. "Granny lived here until her death, using just two rooms downstairs. The place was going to rack and ruin when I came here ten years ago. Sadly, some things are lost forever. The dampness in the air rots everything it gets into."

"It's a beautiful old house, though."

"Oh yes. In its heyday it was extremely well regarded. The balls, parties, and hunts were legendary. My great-grandfather entertained the great and the good from all over Europe, including English royalty. Apparently we even had the Prince of Wales here for a tryst with his mistress. It was a perfect hideaway, you see. The cotton boats used to sail regularly from England to Clonakilty and you could pop on a boat from there and sail round the coast without anyone knowing of your arrival."

"Are you restoring it?"

"I'm certainly trying to. Need the horses to come back with a few wins at Cheltenham next week and that'll help us on our way. The house is too big for just me. When more of it's habitable I intend to make it pay its own way and open it to tourists as an upmarket B & B. Could be way past the millennium before that happens, mind you. So"—Emily's bright eyes studied Joanna—"what do you do?"

"I'm a journalist, actually, but I'm not here on official business. I'm looking for a relative. Before he died, he mentioned Rosscarbery, and a house that stuck out into the bay."

"Was he Irish?"

"Yes. I found a record of his baptism in the church at Clonakilty."

"What was his name?"

"Michael O'Connell."

"Right. Where are you staying?"

"The Ross Hotel."

"Well, I'll have a hunt through the old deeds and documents in the library later today and see if I can dig anything up for you on the place. Now, I'm afraid I need to get back to the stables."

"Thank you, Emily." Joanna drained her teacup, stood up, and they walked out of the kitchen together.

"Do you ride?"

"Oh yes. I was brought up in Yorkshire, and I had four legs under me for most of my childhood."

"If you want a mount while you're staying here, you're welcome to one. Bye now." Emily waved her off.

———

Later that evening, Joanna was sitting in her usual place in the bar by the fire when the landlord called to her.

"Telephone for you, Joanna. It's Emily from up at Drumnogue."

"Thanks." She stood up and walked round the bar to take the receiver.

"Hello?"

"Emily here, Joanna. I dug up some interesting stuff while I was in the process of looking for your information. Seems our neighbor has managed to siphon off at least ten acres and fence them with trees while dear old Granny wasn't looking."

"I'm sorry. Can you get them back?"

"No. Round here, after seven years of fencing off land, if no one has claimed it back, it's yours. Explains why our next-door neighbor runs away in fright every time I approach him. Never mind, got a few hundred acres left, but I should think about fencing them off in the near future."

"Oh dear. Did you manage to find any documents relating to the coastguard's house?"

"I'm afraid not. I found a couple of title deeds to hovels that probably are no more than ruins now, but none relating to the coastguard's house. You should look up the title deeds at the Land Registry office in Dublin."

"How long does that take?"

"Oh, a week, two weeks maybe."

"Could I do it myself?"

"I suppose so, yes, as long as you took the planning map with you. It's a bit of a hack to Dublin, though; a good four hours by car. Take the express train from Cork, it's faster."

"Then I might go tomorrow. I've never been to Dublin and I'd like to see it. Thanks for your help anyway, Emily. I do appreciate it."

"Hold your horses, Joanna. I said I didn't find any title deeds, but I did find a couple of other things you might be interested in. Firstly, and it might be coincidence, I found an old ledger used to keep a record of staff wages in 1919. A man by the name of Michael O'Connell is listed on it."

"I see. So he may have worked up at your house many years ago?"

"Yes, it would seem so."

"Doing what?"

"The ledger doesn't say, I'm afraid. But in 1922, his name vanishes from the list, so I presume he must have left."

"Thank you, Emily. That's really helpful."

"Secondly, I found a letter. It was written to my great-grandfather in 1925. Do you want to pop over tomorrow and see it?"

"Could you read it to me now? I'll just get a pen and paper out to make notes." Joanna signaled to Margaret for some paper and a pen.

"Righto, here goes. It's dated the eleventh of November 1925. *'Dear Stanley'*—that's my great-grandfather—*'I hope this letter finds you well. I am asked by Lord Ashley to write to inform you of the arrival to your shores of a gentleman, guest of HM Government. He will be staying for the present at the coastguard's house and will be taking up residence on the second of January 1926. If possible, we would like you to meet him off the boat, which will dock in Clonakilty harbor at approximately zero one hundred hours, then see him safely to his new lodgings. Would you please arrange for a woman to come in from the village and clean the house up before his arrival? Such a woman might wish to work for the gentleman on a regular basis, keeping house and cooking for him.*

"'The situation with this gentleman is highly delicate. We would prefer his presence at the coastguard's house to be kept quiet. Lord Ashley

has indicated that he will be in touch with further details regarding this. All expenses taken care of by HM Government, of course. Do invoice me with the bills. Lastly, love to Amelia and the children. I am yours very faithfully, Lt. John Moore.'

"There you go, dear," said Emily. "Did you get the gist of all that?"

"Yep." Joanna skimmed the shorthand notes she had taken. "I suppose you didn't find any correspondence indicating who this gentleman might actually be?"

"None, I'm afraid. Anyway, hope it helps you on your way. Good luck in Dublin. Night, Joanna."

28

Zoe opened the shutters and walked out onto the wide terrace. The Mediterranean Sea sparkled beneath her. The sky was a cloudless blue, the sun already beating down. It could have been a July day in England; even the maid had commented how unusually hot it was for late February in Menorca.

The villa she and Art were staying in was simply beautiful. Owned by one of the king of Spain's brothers, its whitewashed, turreted outer shell was nestled in forty acres of lush grounds. Inside the villa, the warm breeze blew in gently through the floor-to-ceiling windows, and the vast tiled floors were kept sparkling by invisible hands. It was built high up, overlooking the sea, so unless the paparazzi were prepared to scale sixty feet of rock face, or dodge the Rottweilers that patrolled the high walls topped by lethal electrified wire, Zoe and Art had the comfort of knowing they could enjoy each other's company undisturbed.

Zoe sat down on a lounger and gazed into the distance. Art was still asleep inside and she had no wish to wake him. To all intents and purposes, the past week had been blissful. For the first time, there was nothing and no one to drag them apart. The world was going on somewhere else, managing to turn without either of them.

Night and day, Art had sworn undying love to her, promised that he'd let nothing stand in his way. He loved her, he wanted to be with her, and if others wouldn't accept it, then he was prepared to take drastic action.

It was a scenario she'd dreamed of for years. And Zoe could not understand why she didn't feel ecstatic with happiness.

Maybe it was simply the stress of the past few weeks catching up with her; people often said that their honeymoons were less than perfect—the reality being less than the expectation. Or maybe Zoe had come to realize that she and Art hardly knew each other on a day-to-day basis. Their brief affair years ago had been as immature and vulnerable human beings, blindly seeking their way toward adulthood. And, in the past few weeks, they'd spent no more than three or four days together, and still fewer nights.

"Snatched moments . . . ," Zoe muttered to herself. Yet here they were, and rather than feeling relaxed, she was undeniably tense. Yesterday evening, the chef had cooked them a wonderful paella. When it was served, Art had pouted and suggested that next time the chef consult him on the menu before he presented it to them. Apparently, he loathed shellfish of any kind. Zoe had tucked in to the paella with gusto and praised the chef fulsomely on the recipe, which had sent Art into a sulk. He'd also accused her of being "too friendly" with the staff.

There had been numerous other small things over the past few days that had irritated rather than angered Zoe. It seemed they always did what *he* wanted. Not that he wouldn't ask her opinion first, but then he would talk her out of her ideas and she'd end up agreeing to his plans for the sake of a quiet life. She'd also discovered that they had very little in common, which was not surprising, given that their worlds had been so vastly different. For all Art's fine private school and university education, his broad cultural knowledge and his grasp of politics, he had little idea of the kind of routine staples that filled the average person's day. Like cooking, watching soaps on TV, shopping . . . just normal, pleasurable activities. She'd realized how difficult he found it to relax, how he was full of nervous energy. And even if he *had* agreed to watch a film with her, she doubted they'd have been able to reach a consensus on which one to choose.

Zoe sighed. She was sure most of these differences were discovered by every couple who suddenly began living together twenty-four hours a day. It would work itself out, she assured herself, and their magical romance of the past could be sparked into life once more.

The problem was exacerbated, of course, by the fact that they were held captive in the most luxurious prison imaginable. Zoe looked beneath her and thought how much she'd like to leave the house and go for a long walk on the beach alone. But that would mean alerting Dennis, the bodyguard, who would then tail her in the car, so that the whole point of being solitary was lost. Yet for some reason, she thought, she hadn't objected to Simon's being around her. She'd found his presence and his company calming.

Zoe stood up and rested her elbows on the balcony railing, remembering the twenty-four hours she and Simon had spent together at Welbeck Street. The way he'd cooked for her, soothed her when she was in such distress. She'd felt like herself then, like Zoe. Comfortable to be who she was.

Was she herself with Art?

She didn't know.

"Morning, darling." His voice called her from the bed as she tiptoed across the room to the bathroom.

"Morning," Zoe replied brightly.

"Come here." Art's arms stretched toward her.

She walked toward the bed and let Art embrace her. His kiss was long, sensuous, and she lost herself in it.

"Another day in paradise," he murmured. "I'm famished. Have you ordered breakfast?"

"No, not yet."

"Why don't you go and see Maria and have her bring us some fresh orange juice, croissants, and some kippers? She said she could have them flown in yesterday and my taste buds are tingling for them." He gave her a fond pat on the bottom. "While you do that I'll take a shower. I'll see you on the terrace downstairs."

"Oh, but, Art, I was going to take a show—"

"What, darling?"

"Nothing," she sighed. "I'll see you downstairs."

They spent the rest of the morning sunbathing by the pool, Zoe reading a novel, Art scanning the English newspapers.

"Listen to this, darling. Headline: 'Should the son of a monarch be allowed to marry a single mother?'"

"Really, Art, I don't want to know."

"Yes, you *do*. The newspaper had a phone poll, and twenty-five thousand of their readers called to register their opinion. Eighteen thousand of them said yes. That's over two-thirds. I wonder if Mater and Pater have read it."

"Would it make any difference if they had?"

"Of course. They're terribly sensitive to public opinion, especially at the moment. Look, there's even a Protestant bishop interviewed in the *Times* who's come out in support of us. He's saying single mothers are part of modern society and that if the monarchy is going to last into the new millennium, it has to throw off its shackles and show it can adapt too."

"And I'll bet there's some whinging moralist in the *Telegraph* who's saying it's the duty of public figures to set an example, not use the sloppy sexual behavior of the general public as a get-out," Zoe muttered darkly.

"Of course there is. But look, darling." Art got up from his chair and sat on her sunbed. He took her hand in his and kissed it. "I love you. Jamie is my flesh and blood anyway. From whichever moral standpoint you look at it, our marriage is the right thing to happen."

"But no one can ever know that, can they? That's the point." Zoe got off the lounger and began to pace. "I just don't know how I'm ever going to tell Jamie about us."

"Darling, you've given up over ten years of your life for Jamie. He was a mistake that—"

Zoe swung round, her eyes blazing. "Don't you *dare* call Jamie a mistake!"

"I didn't mean it like that, darling, really. All I'm saying is that he's growing up now, forging a life of his own. Surely this is about you and me, and our chance for happiness before it's too late?"

"We're not talking about an adult here, Art! Nowhere near. Jamie's a ten-year-old boy. And you make it sound like a sacrifice that I brought Jamie up. It wasn't like that at all. He's the center of my world. I'd do it all over again."

"I know, I know. I'm sorry. Gosh, I seem to be getting it all wrong this morning," Art muttered. "Anyway, I've got some good news. I've arranged for a boat to come and collect us this afternoon. We're going to cruise over to Mallorca and pick up my friend Prince Antonio and his wife, Mariella, in the harbor. Then we're going to sail the high seas for a couple of days. You'll love them, and they're very sympathetic to our predicament." He reached out an arm to her and stroked her hair. "Come on, darling, do cheer up."

Just after lunch, as the maid was packing Zoe's clothes to take on the boat, her mobile rang. She saw it was Jamie's headmaster and answered it immediately.

"Hello?"

"Miss Harrison? It's Dr. West here."

"Hello, Dr. West. Is everything all right?"

"I'm afraid not. Jamie has gone missing. He disappeared this morning, just after breakfast. We've searched the school and grounds thoroughly and there's no sign of him so far."

"Oh God!" Zoe could *hear* the blood pumping round her body. She sat down on the bed before she crumpled to the floor. "I . . . has he taken anything? Clothes? Money?"

"No clothes, although it was pocket-money day yesterday, so he might well have that. Miss Harrison, I don't wish to panic you, and I'm sure he's fine, but the truth is that I'm concerned that, under the circumstances, there's a very small chance that Jamie may have been abducted."

Zoe put her hand to her mouth. "Oh my God, oh God! Have you called the police?"

"That's obviously why I'm calling you. I wanted to ask your permission to do so."

"Yes, oh yes! Do it immediately. I'll make arrangements to fly home as soon as possible. Please, Dr. West, ring me the instant you have any news."

"Of course. Try to keep calm, Miss Harrison. I'm only erring on the side of caution. This kind of thing is relatively common: a spat with a friend, a telling-off from a master . . . The boy is usually back within a few hours. And it may just be that simple. I'm going to interview all the boys in his class now, see if they can shed any light on his disappearance."

"Yes, thank you. G-goodbye, Dr. West."

Zoe stood up from the bed, her entire body shaking, trying to garner her courage. "P-please, G-God . . . anything, I'll give anything, just let him be okay, let him be okay!"

"Señora? Are you all right?"

Maria received no response.

"I go get 'is Royal 'ighness, okay?"

Art entered the room a few minutes later. "Darling, whatever is it?"

"It's Jamie!" She looked at him with agonized eyes. "He's gone missing from school. His headmaster thinks he might have been abducted!" Zoe palmed the tears from her eyes. "If anything has happened to him because of my selfishness, I—"

"Hold on now, Zoe. I want you to listen to me. All boys run away from school. Even I did once, sent my detectives into a spin, and—"

"Yes, but you *had* detectives, didn't you?! I asked you if Jamie was going to get some protection but you said it wasn't necessary, and now look what's happened!"

"There is absolutely no reason to suspect foul play. I'm sure Jamie is fine and will arrive back at the school as right as rain in time for supper, so—"

"If there was no reason to suspect foul play, then why on earth did you give *me* a bodyguard and not your own *son*? Your own son, who is far more vulnerable than I am! Oh God! Oh God!"

"*Zoe!* Will you calm down. You're blowing this out of proportion."

"What?! My son goes missing and you accuse me of being over-dramatic! Get me on a plane home, *now*!" Zoe began throwing things on top of the half-packed suitcase.

"Now you really are being silly. Certainly, if he hasn't turned up by tomorrow morning, then we'll get you home, but for tonight, come on the boat and enjoy supper with Antonio and Mariella. They're so looking forward to meeting you. It'll help take your mind off it."

Zoe threw a shoe at him in frustration. "Take my mind off it! Jesus Christ! It's my son we're talking about, not some family pet that's gone off for a wander! Jamie is missing! I can't float round the Med enjoying myself while my child, my baby"—Zoe gave a huge sob—"might be in danger."

"You're going completely over the top." Art's lips pursed together in irritation. "Besides, I doubt we can get you home tonight. You'll have to fly out in the morning."

"No, you *can* get me home tonight, Art. You're a prince, remember? Your wish is everyone else's command. Get a plane here *now* to take me back, or I'll find one myself!" She was shouting now, past caring what he thought of her.

"Okay, okay." He put his hands out as he backed away toward the door. "I'll see what I can do."

Three hours later, Zoe was standing in the small VIP room at Mahon Airport. She was traveling on a private plane to Barcelona, and then from there on a late British Airways flight to Heathrow.

Art had not accompanied her to the airport, boarding the boat to Mallorca instead. They had said a terse goodbye as Zoe had climbed into the car, kissing each other politely on the cheek.

She fumbled in her handbag for her mobile. It would be midnight before she stepped onto British soil to search for her son. And in the meantime, there was only one person she could trust completely to help her find him.

Zoe dialed his number, praying he'd answer. He did.

"Hello?"

"Simon? It's Zoe Harrison."

29

Joanna sat on the Cork–Dublin express staring at the rivulets of water streaming down the other side of the glass. It had not stopped raining since last night. The pitter-patter of the raindrops had kept her awake, and—like some kind of hypnotic torture—the faint noise had grown inside her head to become pounding hailstones. Not that she'd been able to sleep anyway. She'd been far too tense, spending most of the night staring at the cracks in the ceiling, trying to work out where the new information would lead her.

The situation with this gentleman is highly delicate . . .

What did that mean? What does anything mean at the moment? Joanna thought wearily. She crossed her arms and closed her eyes to try to doze away the remaining hours.

"Is this seat taken?"

The voice was male and American. She opened her eyes to see a tall, muscular man dressed in a checked shirt and jeans.

"No."

"Great. It's so unusual to find a smoking carriage on a train. We don't have those anymore back home."

Joanna was faintly surprised that she *had* sat in a smokers' carriage. She wouldn't have done normally. But then normally she wasn't this tired or confused.

The man sat down across the table from her and lit up a cigarette. "Want one?"

"No thanks, I don't smoke," she replied, praying this man was not going to smoke endlessly and keep her talking for the next two and a half hours.

"Want me to stub it out?"

"No, you're fine."

He took another drag as he studied her. "You English?"

"Yes."

"I was there myself before I came over here. I stayed in London. I loved it."

"Good," she said abruptly.

"But I just love Ireland. You on vacation here?"

"I suppose so. A working holiday."

"You a travel writer or something?"

"No, a journalist, actually."

The man studied the Ordnance Survey map of Rosscarbery on the table in front of her. "Thinkin' of buying some property?"

It was asked in a casual drawl, but Joanna stiffened and regarded the man carefully. "No. I'm just investigating the history of a house I'm interested in."

"Family connections?"

"Yes."

The tea trolley came by next to them.

"Jeez, I'm starving. Must be all this good ol' fresh air. I'll take a coffee, and one of those pastries, ma'am, and a packet of tuna sandwiches. Want anything . . . er . . . ?"

"Lucy," she lied swiftly. "I'll have a coffee, please," she said to the young woman in charge of the trolley. She reached into her rucksack to take out her purse, but the man waved it away.

"Hey, I can just about run to a cup of coffee." He presented it to her and smiled. "Kurt Brosnan. No relation to Pierce, ma'am, before you ask."

"Thanks for the coffee, Kurt." She folded up the Ordnance Survey map, but he appeared to have lost interest anyway as he unwrapped the plastic from his tuna sandwich and took a large bite.

"You're welcome," he said. "So, you think you got some heritage over here in Ireland?"

"Possibly, yes." Joanna resigned herself to giving up her nap for as long as this Kurt was on the train. Now that he was munching away on his sandwich and spraying crumbs over the table, she kicked herself for her earlier paranoia. *Not everyone is out to get you*, she reminded herself. And he was American after all, nothing to do with any of it.

"Me too. Down in a li'l ol' village on the coast in West Cork. It seems my great-great-grandfather hailed from Clonakilty."

"That's the next town to where I've been based, in Rosscarbery."

"Really?" Kurt's face lit up like a child's, happy with the small coincidence. "I was only there the day before yesterday, in that great cathedral. I had the best pint of stout I've had so far afterward, in that hotel in town—"

"The Ross? That's where I'm staying."

"You don't say! So, you off to Dublin?"

"Yes."

"Been before?"

"No. I have some business to do, then I thought I'd take a potter around the city. Have you?"

"No, ma'am, my first time too. Maybe we should join forces."

"I've got to go to the Land Registry. It might take hours to find out what I need to know."

"Is that where they keep title deeds to homesteads?" inquired Kurt, tucking in to a pastry now.

"Yes."

"You tryin' to find out whether you have an inheritance?"

"Sort of. There's a house in Rosscarbery. No one seems to know who owns it."

"It is a bit more casual here than at home. I mean"—Kurt rolled his eyes—"no one has alarms on their cars, or locks their front doors. I was in a restaurant in town yesterday when the owner said she had to leave for a while and would I put my plate in the sink and shut the door behind me! It sure is a different way of life. So"—Kurt indicated the map—"show me the house."

Despite her initial misgivings, the journey to Dublin passed pleasantly enough. Kurt was good company and entertained her with stories about his native Memphis. As the train pulled into Heuston Station, Kurt pulled out a small notebook and a gold pen from his pocket.

"Give me your number in Rosscarbery. When you get back there, maybe we could get together for a drink."

Joanna wrote down her mobile number on a slip of paper and passed it to him. He tucked it into his jacket pocket with a pleased grin.

"Well, it sure has whiled away a journey talkin' to you, Lucy. When do you travel back to West Cork?"

"Oh, I'm not sure. I'm leaving it flexible." She stood up as the train came to a halt. "Good to meet you, Kurt."

"And you, Lucy. Maybe see you again soon."

"Maybe. Goodbye." She smiled at him, then followed the other passengers out of the carriage.

Joanna took a taxi to the Land Registry office near the river by the Four Courts building. After endless form-filling, she queued at the counter and was eventually handed a file.

"There's a free desk over there if you want to study the deeds," said the young woman.

"Thanks." Joanna made her way toward the desk and sat down. Disappointment filled her when she saw that the coastguard's house had been handed over from HM Government on June 27, 1928, to become the property of "the Free State of Ireland." After taking a photocopy of the deeds and the plans, she handed the file back, thanked the woman, and left the office.

Outside it was still pouring with rain. Opening up her puny London umbrella, she walked until she reached Grafton Street, and the myriad of small lanes off it, filled with enticing-looking pubs. She dashed into the closest one, and ordered a glass of Guinness. She took off her jacket, which, although labeled "waterproof," had belied its description, and brushed a hand through her damp hair.

"Fine, soft day out, isn't it?" said the barman.

"Does it ever stop raining here?"

"Not often, no," said the barman without irony. "And they all wonder why so many of us end up raving alcoholics."

Joanna was just about to order a cheese sandwich, when a figure she recognized came through the door.

He saw her, then waved at her in delight. "Lucy! Hi there."

Kurt came to sit next to her at the bar, the water on his jacket making a puddle on the floor below him. "I'll have a Guinness, please, and another for the lady," he said to the barman.

"I . . . I've already got one, thanks," she said, attempting to hide her disbelief at the coincidence.

He seemed to catch her tone. "Hey, it's not really so weird. You are in one of the most famous pubs in Dublin. The Bailey is on every tourist's 'must go' list—James Joyce himself used to drink here."

"Really? I didn't notice the name. I ran in here to get out of the wet."

"So, how did your research go?"

"Nowhere." She reached for her Guinness.

"Yeah, well, I've had a morning pretty like that. It's so darned wet out there you need a set of windscreen wipers to see anything. I've decided to give up, spend the evening drinking and the night in the lap of luxury. I booked myself a room at the Shelbourne, supposedly the best hotel in town."

"Right. I'll have a cheese bap, please," Joanna said to the barman.

"Say, why don't you come have dinner with me tonight at the hotel? My treat, to cheer you up."

"Thanks for the offer, but—"

Kurt held up his hands. "Ma'am, I swear, no funny business. Just strikes me you're alone, I'm alone, and maybe we'd enjoy the night better if we kept each other company."

"No thanks." Joanna stood up, seriously rattled now. Kurt's face appeared earnest enough, but Joanna was still shaken by his sudden appearance.

"Okay." Kurt looked very put out. "So when do you head back to West Cork?"

"I . . . er . . . don't know yet."

"Well, maybe I'll see you when I'm back that way."

"Maybe you will. Bye now, Kurt."

———

"Sign there," Margaret said to the young man standing in front of her reception desk.

"Thanks." He looked up at her. "By any chance, has a young Englishwoman called Joanna Haslam crossed your path in the last few days?"

"And who'd be wanting to know?"

"I'm her boyfriend," he said with a warm smile.

"Well, yes, there has been a girl by that name staying here. She's gone up-country today, though. Back tonight or tomorrow," she said.

"Great. I don't want her to know I'm here. It's her . . . birthday tomorrow and I thought I'd surprise her." He put a finger to his lips. "Mum's the word, eh?"

"Sure, Mum's the word, so."

Margaret handed the man his key and watched as he went upstairs. *Oh, to be young again*, she thought fondly, before going to the cellar to change the barrel.

CAPTURE

Eliminating an opponent's
piece from the board

30

The following morning, Simon sat in the chair in front of the leather-topped desk.

"Simpson has gone AWOL," said the old man opposite him.

"I see."

"And so has your friend Miss Haslam."

Simon wanted to quip that maybe they'd eloped, but thought it unwise.

"Could it be a coincidence, sir?"

"I somehow doubt it under the circumstances. We've just had the evaluation of Simpson's psychological report. The psychologist was concerned enough to recommend he receives urgent and immediate treatment." He wheeled his chair around the desk. "He knows too much, Warburton. I want you to find him, and fast. My instincts tell me he may have gone after Haslam."

"I thought her apartment was bugged. And Marcus Harrison's. Did the listeners not give you an indication of where she might be?"

"No. We think they've discovered the bugs as nothing of interest has been heard in the past few days. In fact, the device at Harrison's apartment has not been transmitting correctly, but our men are preparing a replacement. In Miss Haslam's case, nothing has been heard at all, apart from irate calls on her landline from Marcus Harrison, wanting to know where she is."

"And no one has any idea where either of them might have gone?"

"You've read the file, Warburton," he replied irritably. "If you were Haslam, wishing to ferret out further information about our man, where would you go?"

"Dorset perhaps? To continue searching through the attic? I took a look in the attic last time I was there and there are endless boxes of material, sir."

"Don't you think we know that?! I've had a dozen men working night and day up there since Zoe Harrison left with HRH for Spain. They've found nothing." He wheeled himself back behind his desk. "Harrison is still in residence at his London apartment. Maybe you should have a word with him."

"Yes, sir. I'll pay him a visit."

"Report back to me when you have. And we'll take it from there."

"I will, sir."

"I hear you went to visit young Jamie Harrison yesterday?"

"Yes, sir, I did."

"Business or pleasure?"

"I did it as a favor for Zoe Harrison, sir."

"Watch it, Warburton. You know the rules."

"Of course, sir."

"Righto. Let me know when there's news."

"I will."

Simon rose from his chair and left the room, praying that the old man hadn't seen the blush heating his face. Even if his mind and his body could be trained and disciplined, it was obvious his heart could not.

Having found no one at home at Marcus's apartment, Simon had gone back to the office and called Joanna's parents, who hadn't heard from her either. He was convinced she was still on the trail. *France, maybe?* he'd thought, then spent a fruitless couple of hours going through passenger lists of all planes and ferries that had departed in the past few days. Her name was on none of them.

So, where else was connected with the mystery they were both desperate to uncover . . . ?

Simon thought back to the day he'd memorized the file. No written notes had been allowed. There was somewhere else, he was sure of it . . .

Then, finally, it came to him.

Forty-five minutes later, he'd found Joanna's name on a flight to Cork three days ago, and immediately booked himself on the late-afternoon flight that day. He was just on his way to Heathrow through a logjammed Hammersmith when his mobile rang.

"Hello, Zoe." Simon was so startled by her voice that he had to pull over and park, which proved a tricky operation in the heavy traffic. "Where are you?"

"At Mahon Airport in Menorca. Oh, Simon."

He heard her choke back a sob.

"What is it? What's the matter?"

"It's Jamie. He's gone missing. His headmaster thinks he might have been kidnapped or abducted. God, Simon, he might be dead. I—"

"Hold on a minute, Zoe. Tell me calmly and carefully what's happened."

She did her best to do so.

"Has the headmaster called the police?"

"Yes, but Art wants it to be as low-key as possible. He says he doesn't want the media involved unless absolutely necessary, because of—"

"Putting him, you, and Jamie back in the spotlight," Simon finished for her. "Well, he might have to suffer it. At the end of the day, it's more important that Jamie is found. It's always more helpful if members of the public are alerted to a missing child."

"How did Jamie seem when you went to see him?"

"A little quiet, admittedly, but okay."

"He didn't say he was worried about anything, did he?"

"No, but I got the feeling that maybe he was, which also tells me

Jamie is probably all right. Maybe he just needed some time alone. He's a sensible kid, Zoe. Try and keep calm."

"I'm not going to be back in London for hours. Would you do me a favor?"

"Sure."

"Would you go to the house in London? You still have the key, don't you? If he's not there, try Dorset. The key's under the water barrel round the back to the left side."

"Surely the police—"

"Simon, he knows you. He trusts you. *Please.* I—" Zoe's voice disappeared.

"Zoe? Zoe? Are you there?

"Damn!" He slammed his hands on the steering wheel. He should go to Ireland immediately, help someone else who didn't realize she was vulnerable, someone who needed him too.

So . . . where did his loyalty lie?

Logically, there was no contest. It lay with his oldest friend, and his allegiance to the government he served. But his treacherous heart lay with a woman and a child whom he'd known for no more than a few weeks. He agonized for a minute, then indicated out into the flow of traffic. As soon as he could safely do so, Simon swung the car into a U-turn and headed back for central London.

The Welbeck Street house was in darkness, and there seemed to be no sign of anyone outside. Simon had half expected the media still to be there, waiting for a specter that had long since vanished. He turned the key in the lock, then switched on the light. He checked all the rooms downstairs, knowing from his highly trained instincts that the search was fruitless. The house *felt* empty.

Still, he checked in Zoe's room, then Jamie's. He sat down on Jamie's bed, looking round the room, its mixture of teddies and remote-control cars a testament to the betwixt-and-between age Jamie was at. His walls were covered with a variety of nursery prints; on the back of the door hung a Power Rangers poster.

"Where are you, old chap?" he asked the air, staring blankly at a small but intricate tapestry sampler that hung above Jamie's bed. Receiving no reply, Simon went up again to investigate the top floor of the house.

Returning downstairs, he wandered into the drawing room and saw a panda car halt in front of the house. A police officer climbed out and headed for the front door. He'd opened it before the man had time to press the bell.

"Hi."

"Hello, sir, are you a resident of this establishment?" inquired the detective.

"No." Simon wearily produced his identification.

"Right, Mr. Warburton. I presume you're looking for the young man who's done a bunk, are you?"

"Yes."

"All got to be kept hush-hush for now, apparently. Them up high don't want his disappearance getting to the newspapers, because of his mum and her . . . boyfriend."

"Quite. Well, I've checked the house and he's not here. Are you going to stay, just in case he should make an appearance?"

"No, I've been asked to check the place over, that's all. I can organize someone here, if your lot request it."

"I think it would be advisable. It's likely, if he's free to do so, that the young man in question will head for home," Simon said. "I have to leave now, but make sure someone is stationed outside, will you?"

"Righto, sir, I will."

A little more than two hours later, Simon pulled his car to a halt in front of Haycroft House. He checked his watch and saw it was just after ten o'clock. He retrieved his flashlight from the glove box, climbed out of the car, and set off in search of the water barrel and its hidden key. He found it with a shiver of disappointment; Jamie had obviously not got there before him. He trudged round to the front of the house and opened the heavy front door.

Switching on the lights, Simon went from room to room, seeing the pans still on the drainer from the supper he'd cooked Zoe, her bed upstairs still unmade from the morning they'd left so early.

Nothing. The house was empty.

He returned downstairs and called the sergeant now stationed at Welbeck Street to find out if Jamie had returned. He hadn't. Informing him that there was no sign of Jamie here either, Simon went into the kitchen to make himself a cup of black coffee, before he contemplated the drive back to London. He sat down at the table and rubbed his hands harshly through his hair, trying to think. If Jamie hadn't made an appearance by tomorrow morning, then the palace be damned. They'd have to go public on this. He stood up and spooned some instant coffee into a mug and added boiling water, playing over and over in his head the last conversation he'd had with the boy.

After his third mug of coffee, which made him feel liverish and sick, Simon stood up and prowled round the house one last time. He turned on the floodlights outside and opened the kitchen door to the back garden. The garden was large and obviously well stocked, although its current seasonal condition was that of a sketch waiting to be painted. Simon shone his flashlight into the hedge that fringed the garden. In one corner of the garden, presumably positioned to catch the best of the sun, was a small pergola. Beneath it, a bench made of stone. Simon walked over to it and sat down. The pergola was covered in some kind of creeping plant—Simon put a hand up to touch it and gave an "Ouch!" when a vicious thorn pricked his finger.

Roses, he thought. *How beautiful this would look in the height of summer.*

Roses . . .

Great-James loved roses. He has them on his grave now . . .

Simon jumped up immediately and ran to the back door to make a phone call.

The cemetery was only a quarter of a mile down the road from the house, behind the church. Simon parked his car outside the iron gate. Discovering it was padlocked, he swung himself over the top of it and began to walk through the graves, shining a light on each name. Despite himself, Simon shuddered. A half-moon appeared from behind a cloud, bathing the cemetery in a ghostly light. The church clock struck midnight, the bell clanging slowly and mournfully, as if in remembrance of the dead souls that lay at his feet.

Finally, Simon reached the 1970s and then the 1980s. Right at the back of the cemetery, Simon espied a gravestone that had 1991 chiseled into it. Slowly, as he walked past, the dates on the headstones became more and more recent. He was almost at the edge of the cemetery now, with one last grave remaining, set alone, with a small bush planted below the headstone.

SIR JAMES HARRISON

ACTOR

1900–1995

"Good night, sweet prince,
and flights of angels sing
thee to thy rest."

And there, lying huddled on top of the grave, was Jamie.

Simon approached the boy silently. He could tell from the way Jamie was breathing that he was fast asleep. He knelt down next to him and angled the flashlight so he could see the boy's face, yet at the same time not disturb him. Simon felt for his pulse, which was steady, then his hand. It was cold, but not dangerously so. Simon breathed a sigh of relief and stroked his blond hair gently.

"Mumma?" Jamie stirred.

"No, it's Simon, and you're perfectly safe, old chap."

Jamie shot up from his prone position, his eyes wide and terrified.

"What . . . ? Where am I?" He looked around him, then began to shiver.

"Jamie, you're fine. Simon's here." Instinctively Simon pulled the boy to him. "Now, I'm going to pick you up, put you in my car, and drive you down the road to home. We're going to make a big fire in the sitting room, and over a hot cup of tea, you can tell me what happened. Okay?"

Jamie looked up at him; his eyes, at first fearful, were now trusting. "Okay."

When they reached the house, Simon took the eiderdown from Zoe's bed and tucked it around the shivering boy on the sofa. He lit a fire as Jamie stared silently into the distance. Having made a cup of tea for both of them and alerted the London sergeant and Zoe's mobile to Jamie's safe return, Simon sat down at the other end of the sofa.

"Drink it, Jamie. It'll warm you up."

The boy sipped at the hot liquid, his small hands clasped round the mug. "Are you cross with me?"

"No, of course not. We were all worried, yes, but not cross."

"Mumma will be furious when she finds out."

"She already knows you'd disappeared from school. She's on her way home from Spain and should have already landed. I'm sure she'll call the moment she can. You can speak to her and let her know you're safe."

Jamie sipped some more tea. "She wasn't filming in Spain, was she?" he said slowly. "She was with him, wasn't she?"

"Him?"

"Her boyfriend, the prince. Prince Arthur."

"Yes." Simon studied the boy. "How did you know?"

"One of the older boys put a page from a newspaper in my locker."

"I see."

"Then Dickie Sisman, who's always hated me because I made the under-tens' rugby A team and he didn't, kept calling Mu-Mumma a prince's wh-whore."

Simon winced, but said nothing.

"Then he asked who my father w-was. I said Great-James, and

Dickie and the others laughed at me, said he couldn't be my dad because he was my great-grandfather and I was stupid. I knew that he wasn't my father really, b-bu-but he *was*, Simon. Great-James was my dad and now he's g-gone."

Simon watched Jamie's shoulders heave with sobs.

"He said he'd never leave me, that he'd always be there when I needed him, that all I had to do was call and he'd answer . . . But he didn't! Be-because he's dead!"

Simon gently took the tea mug from him, sat down, and pulled Jamie into his arms.

"I didn't think he'd gone, not really," Jamie continued. "I me-mean, I knew he wasn't there in person—he'd said he wouldn't be— but that he'd always be somewhere, but when I needed him he was nowhere!" More sobs shook from Jamie's chest. "And then Mumma was gone too. And there was nobody. I couldn't stand it at school anymore. I had to just get out, so I w-went to Great-James."

"I understand," said Simon quietly.

"Wo-worst of all, Mumma lied to me!"

"Not on purpose, Jamie. She did it to protect you."

"She's always told me everything before. We didn't have secrets. If I'd have known, then I could have defended myself when the boys were so awful to me."

"Well, sometimes adults misjudge situations. I think that's what has happened with your mother."

"No." He shook his head wearily. "It's because I'm not number one anymore. Prince Arthur is. She loves him more than she loves me."

"Oh, Jamie. That could not be further from the truth. Your mother adores you. Believe me, she was frantic when she heard the news. She moved heaven and earth to get on a plane and come back home to find you."

"Did she?" Jamie wiped his nose morosely. "Simon?"

"Yes?"

"Will I have to move into one of their houses?"

"I don't know, Jamie. I think that kind of decision is a long way off."

"I heard one of the masters laughing in his study with the PE teacher. He said that it wouldn't be the first time a bastard has moved into a p-palace."

Simon cursed the cruelty of human nature under his breath. "Jamie, your mum is going to be home very soon. I want you to promise me you'll tell her everything you've told me, so there'll be no misunderstandings in future."

Jamie looked up at him. "Have you met *him*?"

"Yes."

"What's he like?"

"Nice. He's a nice man. You'll like him, I'm sure."

"I don't think I will. Do princes play football?"

Simon laughed. "Yes."

"And eat pizza and baked beans?"

"I'm sure they do."

"Will Mumma marry him, Simon?"

"I think that's something only your mother can tell you." His mobile rang in his pocket. "Hello? Zoe? Did you get my message? Yes, Jamie's safe and absolutely fine. We're down in Dorset. Want a word with him?" Simon passed the phone to Jamie and stood up to leave the room and give him some privacy. When he returned once the call was finished, he saw a little color was returning to Jamie's cheeks.

"Will she be very angry with me?"

"Did she sound angry?"

"No," Jamie admitted. "She sounded very happy. She's coming straight here to see me."

"There you go then."

Simon sat next to him and Jamie snuggled down on his knee, yawning. "Wish you were the prince, Simon," he said drowsily.

So do I, he thought.

Jamie lifted his head and smiled at Simon. "Thanks for knowing where to look."

"Anytime, old chap, anytime."

————

At past three a.m., Zoe paid the taxi driver and opened the front door to Haycroft House. Everything was silent. She went first to the kitchen, then into the sitting room. Jamie was curled up on Simon's knee, fast asleep. Simon's head was resting against the back of the sofa, his eyes closed too. Tears came to her eyes at the sight of her son. And Simon, who had so generously helped them both when it seemed no one else would.

Simon opened his eyes as she walked toward them. Very carefully, he extricated himself from beneath Jamie, substituting a cushion for his lap and indicating they should leave the room.

They walked silently into the kitchen. Simon closed the door behind him.

"Is he okay? Really?"

"He is absolutely fine, promise."

Zoe sat down in a chair and put her head in her hands. "Thank God. You can't imagine what was going through my mind on that interminable flight."

"No." Simon walked to the kettle. "Tea?"

"I'd love some chamomile tea. There's some in the cupboard over there. Where did you find him?"

"Asleep on your grandfather's grave."

"Oh, Simon! I . . ." Zoe clapped a hand to her mouth in horror.

"Don't blame yourself, Zoe, really. I think what happened to Jamie was an unfortunate combination of some unkind but natural teasing at school, delayed grief, and . . ."

"The fact that I wasn't there either."

"Yes. There you go." He put the tea in front of her.

"So he knows about Art from the other boys?"

"I'm afraid so."

"Damn it! I should have told him."

"We all make mistakes, I did too, remember? I advised you not to tell him. But thankfully this situation is something that can easily be rectified."

"I knew he was too calm after James died." Zoe took a sip of her tea. "I should have seen this coming."

"I think when he was in trouble, it hit Jamie for the first time that the man he adored—his father figure—really had gone for good. Especially when others were maliciously suggesting a substitute. But he's a good kid, he'll cope. Look, now that you're here, I'm afraid I have to leave."

Zoe was startled. "To go where?"

"Duty calls." Simon tiptoed back into the sitting room to collect his jacket from the chair and then met Zoe in the hall. "Jamie's still sleeping soundly. I think a dollop of TLC from his mum is the only medicine he needs."

"Yes. And boy, have we got some talking to do." She followed him to the front door. "Simon, how can I ever thank you?"

"Really, don't think about it. Take care of both of you, and send my love to Jamie. Tell him I'm sorry I had to leave before I said good-bye."

"Of course." Zoe nodded wistfully. "Simon?"

He turned and looked at her. "Yes?"

She paused, then shook her head. "Nothing."

"Bye, Zoe." Simon gave her a small, tight smile, opened the door, and left.

31

Joanna pulled her rented Fiesta alongside the curb in front of the Ross Hotel and switched off the engine gratefully. She was exhausted from another sleepless night in a cheap B & B in Dublin, jumping every time she heard a creak. Kurt's turning up at the pub had really unsettled her. The question was, had he been tailing her or was she just totally paranoid?

She sat there for a few moments, gazing out at the rain still pelting down on the picturesque square.

"That bloody old lady," Joanna muttered to herself. If only she had never met her . . . where would she be now? At home in London, still working the news desk, not sitting in the rain in a godforsaken Irish town.

Enough was enough. She had decided she was going home to England as soon as she could, and would consign the last few weeks to the past and do her best to forget all about it. She would post all the information she had gathered to Simon and he could do what he liked with it. She reckoned he'd been planted in Zoe Harrison's house to discover what she knew and what secrets the house held. Well, he could have everything she had. And that was an end to it.

Joanna opened the door to the car, retrieved her holdall from the boot, and walked into the front entrance of the hotel.

"Hello there. Did you have a good trip?" inquired Margaret, appearing behind the bar.

"Yes. It was . . . fine, thanks."

"Grand."

"I'm going to check out now, Margaret, and fly home. If I can get a seat on a flight this evening from Cork."

"Right then." One of Margaret's eyebrows raised slightly. "Someone left an envelope for you while you were away." She turned and grabbed it from Joanna's pigeonhole. "There."

"Thanks."

"'Twill be a birthday card, no doubt?"

"No, my birthday's not until August. Thanks anyway."

Margaret watched her mount the stairs. She thought for a moment, then placed a call to Sean, her nephew, at the local garda station. "You know you were after asking me about that young man, the one who checked in yesterday, Sean? Well, maybe he's not who he seems after all. He's gone out, said he'd be away until sixish . . . I think you'd better, so."

Joanna unlocked the door to her room, put down her holdall, and tore open the letter. Skimming the lines, she sank onto the bed. It took her a while to decipher the erratically spelled scrawl.

Deer miss,

I hurd in the bar you talk of costgard house. I no bout it. you come talk to me un you will see the troot. pink cottige oposit costgard house is wear I will be.

miss ciara deasy

Ciara . . . The name rang a bell. Joanna searched her memory to find who it was that had spoken the name. It had been Fergal Mulcahy, the historian. He'd said Ciara was mad.

Was there any point in going to see her? Surely, it would only lead to another wild goose chase—half-remembered stories that had little bearing on a long-ago situation she wanted nothing more to do with.

Look at the trouble half-crazy little old ladies have got me into already, she told herself firmly.

Joanna screwed the letter up into a ball and tossed it into the wastepaper basket. She picked up the telephone, dialed nine for an outside line, and spoke to Aer Lingus reservations. They could get her a seat on the 6:40 flight out of Cork. She paid for the flight on her long-suffering credit card and began to pack her things into her rucksack. Then she picked up the telephone again and dialed Alec at the newspaper.

"It's me."

"Christ, Joanna! I thought you might have called me before now."

"Sorry. Time disappears here without you realizing it."

"Yeah, well, the ed's haunted me every day, wanting to know where the doctor's certificate has got to. He sent someone round to your apartment and they know you've not been there either. I did my best, but the upshot is, I'm afraid you're fired."

Joanna sank onto the bed, a lump in her throat. "Oh God, Alec!"

"Sorry, sweetheart. I don't know whether he's being leaned on, but that's how it is."

Joanna sat there silently, willing herself not to cry.

"Jo, you still there?"

"I'd just decided to give up on the whole bloody mess! I'm flying back to London tonight. If I come and see the ed tomorrow, prostrate myself at his feet, apologize profusely, and offer to make the tea until he forgives me, do you think I stand a chance?"

"Nope."

"I didn't think so." Joanna stared miserably at the flowered wallpaper. The faded roses danced in front of her eyes.

"So, from what you're saying, you've found out nothing?"

"Virtually nothing. Only that a Michael James O'Connell was born a few miles down the coast from here, and possibly spent his early years working in a big house for the great-grandfather of someone I spoke to. Oh, and there's an old letter from a British official—it says that a gentleman was shipped over to stay at the house as a guest of His Majesty's Government. In 1926."

"Who was it?"

"Dunno."

"Don't you think you should find out?"

"No, I don't. I'm in over my head. I want . . ." Joanna bit her lip. "I want to come home and have my life back like it was before."

"Well, seeing as that's impossible, have you anything to lose by investigating further?"

"I can't hack it, Alec, I really can't."

"Come on, Jo. As I see it, the only way you can relaunch your career is by getting a cracking story and flogging it to the highest bidder. You now have no allegiance to this newspaper. And if others won't publish it here, they'll publish abroad. I have a feeling you're very close to some answers. For Christ's sake, don't fall at the final hurdle, Jo."

"What 'answers'? None of it makes sense anyway."

"Someone will know. They always do. But watch your back. It won't be long before they track you down."

"I'm going, Alec. I'll call you when I get back to London."

"Okay, Jo. Make sure you do. Take care now."

For several minutes, Joanna sat paralyzed on the bed, thinking that so far this year, she'd lost her boyfriend, most of her possessions, her best friend, and now her job. Contrary to what Alec thought, she still had a lot more left to lose.

"Like my life," she muttered to herself.

Five minutes later, she had picked up her holdall, locked the door behind her, and was walking downstairs.

"You off, so?" chirped Margaret from behind reception.

"Yes." Joanna handed Margaret her credit card. "Thanks for making my stay so pleasant."

"Not at all. Hope you'll be back to see us again soon."

Joanna signed the credit-card slip Margaret handed her.

"There you go. Bye, Margaret, and thanks." She picked up her holdall and walked to the door.

"Joanna, you weren't expecting anyone to come visit you here, were you?"

"Why? Did somebody call me?"

"No." Margaret shook her head. "Safe journey home, and mind yourself."

"I will."

Joanna stowed the holdall in the boot of the Fiesta, then drove out of the square and down toward the estuary. As she indicated left and waited for a car to pass, she noticed a small, single-story pink cottage, standing solitary on the opposite side of the estuary from the coastguard's house. The two dwellings were no more than fifty yards apart across the sandbanks. Joanna hesitated for a moment, shook her head in resignation, then indicated right. If she was fast, she could still make her flight. She didn't notice the car behind her also change direction and follow some distance behind as the Fiesta drove down the narrow road.

"Come in," said a voice from inside, when she knocked on the front door. She did as she'd been bid. The small front room she'd stepped into was rustic, reminiscent of another era. A healthy fire burned in the large grate, a black kettle hung above it on a chain. The sparse wooden furniture was shabby, and the only adornments on the walls were a large crucifix and a yellowing print of the Madonna and Child.

Ciara Deasy was sitting on a high-backed wooden chair on one side of the fire. Her face had settled into soft wrinkles, indicating that she was somewhere between seventy and eighty. Her white hair was cut into a savage short back and sides, and as she stood to greet Joanna, her legs did not betray a whisper of unsteadiness.

"The lady from the hotel?" Ciara shook Joanna's hand firmly.

"Joanna Haslam," she confirmed.

"Sit down," Ciara said, indicating a chair on the other side of the fireplace. "Now, tell me, why would ye be wanting to know about the coastguard's house?"

"Miss Deasy, it's a long story."

"They're my favorite kind. And call me Ciara, now, will you? 'Miss Deasy' makes me sound like an old maid. Which I am, there's no denying it," she cackled.

"Well, I'm a journalist and I'm here investigating someone called Michael O'Connell. It just might be that when he returned to England, he was known as someone completely different."

Ciara's eyes sharpened. "I'd be knowing he went by the name of Michael, but I never knew his second name. And yer not wrong about him changing his name."

"You knew he used a different identity?"

"Joanna, I've known since I was eight years old. Nigh on seventy years is a long time to be called a liar, an inventor of fairy stories. The village has thought I've lost my wits since, but of course I haven't. I'm as sane as you."

"And do you by any chance know if 'Michael' has any association with the coastguard's house?"

"He stayed there while he was sick. They wanted him hidden away till he was better."

"You met him?"

"I wouldn't say I was formally introduced, no, but I went there to the house sometimes with Niamh, God rest her soul." The old woman crossed herself.

"Niamh?"

"My older sister. Beautiful, she was, so beautiful, with her long dark hair and blue eyes . . ." Ciara gazed into the fire. "Any man would have fallen for her, and he did."

"Michael?"

"That's the name he used, yes, but we know different, don't we?"

"Ciara, why don't you tell me the story from the very beginning?"

"I'll try, so I will, but 'tis a long time since I've spoken these words." Ciara took a deep breath. "It was Stanley Bentinck who suggested it; he lived up in the grand house in Ardfield. He told her there was an important visitor coming over and Niamh was a maid in the household at the time. So Mr. Bentinck had her look after the visitor in the coastguard's house, as she only lived a stone's throw away. She'd come back from there with her blue eyes shining, so she would, and a secret smile. She told me the gentleman was English, but she'd never say any more.

"Of course, I was only a girleen at the time, not old enough to understand what was happening between them. I went across to help with the cleaning sometimes, and I caught them once, in the kitchen, embracing. But I knew nothing of love, or physical matters, at that age. Then he went, disappeared that night out to sea, before they came to get him—"

"They?" interrupted Joanna.

"Those as was after him. She'd warned him, see, even though she knew she'd lose him, that he'd have to go for the sake of his life. But she was convinced he'd send for her when he got back to London. Looking back now, there was no hope, but she didn't know that."

"Who was it that was after him, Ciara?"

"I'll be telling you when I've finished. After he'd gone, Niamh and my daddy had a fierce fight. She was screaming mad, he was shouting back at her. Then, the next morning, she disappeared too."

"I see. Do you know where she went?"

"I don't. Not for the next few months, anyway. Some from the village said they'd seen her with the Gypsies up at the Ballybunion fair, others that she'd been spotted in Bandon."

"Why did she leave?"

"Now, Joanna, you'll stop asking questions and you'll hear the answers. About six months after she disappeared, Mammy and Daddy went to mass with my sisters, but I stayed home, having a bad cold. Mammy didn't want me to cough all through the preaching. 'Twas as I lay in bed I heard the noise. A terrible noise it was, like an animal in its final death throes. I went to that front door"—Ciara indicated it with her hand—"in my nightgown, and listened. And I knew it was coming from the coastguard's house. So I walked across to it with that awful sound ringing in my ears."

"Weren't you frightened?"

"Terrified altogether, but it was as if I was drawn to it, like my body was not my own." Ciara looked across the bay. "The front door was open. I went inside and found her upstairs, lying on *his* bed, her legs covered with blood . . ." She shielded her face with her small hands. "I can still see her face now, clear as day. The agony on it has haunted me for the whole of my life."

Cold fingers crawled up Joanna's spine. "It was your sister Niamh?"

"Yes. And lying between her legs, still attached to her, was a new-born babe."

Joanna swallowed and stared at Ciara silently while she composed herself.

"I . . . I thought the baby was dead when I saw it, for it was blue and it didn't cry. I picked it up and used my teeth to cut the cord, like I'd seen Daddy do with the cows he kept. I wrapped it in my arms, trying to give it warmth, but nothing would stir it."

"Oh God." There were tears in Joanna's eyes.

"So I moved up to Niamh, who had stopped screaming by now. She was lying still, her eyes closed, and I could see the blood still seeping out of her. I tried to stir her, to hand her baby to her, to see if she could help it, but she didn't move." Ciara's eyes were wide and haunted, her mind having crossed back over the years, reliving the dreadful scene again.

"So I sat on the bed, nursing the lifeless babe, trying to wake my sister. Finally, her eyes did open. I said to her, 'Niamh, you have a babe. Will you hold it?' She beckoned me to come close to her, put my ear to her mouth so she could whisper."

"What did she say?"

"That there was a letter, in her skirt pocket, for the baby's daddy in London. That the baby should go to him. Then she raised her head, kissed the babe on its brow, gave a sigh, and spoke no more."

Ciara pressed her eyes shut, yet the tears still escaped from them, and the two women sat together in silence.

"How terrible for you to witness that so young," Joanna whispered eventually. "What did you do?"

"I wrapped the babe in a covering from the bed. 'Twas wet from all the blood but better than nothing. Then I reached in Niamh's pocket and took out the letter. I knew I must run for the doctor with the babe, and not having a pocket in my nightshirt and in fear of losing it, I took up a floorboard and stowed the letter away beneath it to collect later. I stood up and crossed Niamh's hands over her breast, like I'd seen the undertaker doing for my granny. Then I gathered up the babe and ran for help."

"What happened to the baby?" asked Joanna slowly.

"Well now, this is where I become confused. I'm told they found me, standing in the middle of the estuary, screaming that Niamh was dead in the house. Joanna, I was a sick girl after that for many months. Stanley Bentinck paid to have me taken above to hospital in Cork. I had pneumonia and they said my mind was wandering so much with stories that they put me in the madhouse once I was well. My mammy and daddy came to see me there. They told me all I'd seen had been a dream, brought on by the fever. Niamh had not come back. There'd been no baby. It was all my imagination." Ciara grimaced. "I tried for weeks telling them that she was still dead in the house and asking after the babe, but the more I talked about it, the more they shook their heads and left me longer in that godforsaken place."

"How could they?" Joanna shuddered. "Someone must have taken the baby out of your arms!"

"Yes. And I knew what I'd seen was real, but I was beginning to know that if I continued to say so, I'd be spending the rest of my life with the other mad people. So, eventually, I told the doctors I'd seen nothing and the next time my daddy came up to see me, I pretended to him too I was out of my fit, that I'd never seen anything, that the fever had made me hallucinate." Ciara gave a wry smile. "He was after bringing me back home that very day. Of course, from that moment on, everyone in town saw me as stone mad. The other children would laugh at me, call me names . . . I got used to it, played their game and frightened them with strange talk to get my own back," she cackled.

"And what you saw was never mentioned again by your parents?"

"Never. You know what I did, though, Joanna, don't you?"

"You went back to the house to check whether the letter was still there?"

"I did, I did. I had to know I was right and they were wrong."

"And was it there?"

"Yes."

"Did you read the letter?"

"Not then. I couldn't, I didn't know how. But later, when I'd learned, I did, most definitely."

Joanna took a deep breath. "Ciara, what did the letter say?"

Ciara regarded her thoughtfully. "I might be telling you that in a while. Listen to me, I haven't finished."

Is she telling the truth? Joanna wondered. Or was she, as the other inhabitants of the town seemed to think, simply deluded?

"'Twas a good few years until it all made sense. I was eighteen when I discovered why. Why they'd kept it quiet, why 'twas something so important they'd been prepared to lock their daughter away and call her mad for saying what she'd seen . . .'"

"Go on," urged Joanna.

"I was in Cork city, buying some linen for new sheets with Mammy. And I saw a newspaper, the *Irish Times*. There was a face on the front I knew. 'Twas the man I'd seen at the coastguard's house."

"Who was he?"

Ciara Deasy told her.

32

He sauntered up the stairs to his hotel room, and discovered the room was unlocked. Shrugging at the slapdash behavior of the chambermaid, who must have forgotten to lock it after cleaning it, he pushed it ajar.

Two uniformed officers were standing in his bedroom.

"Hi. Can I help you?"

"Would you be Ian C. Simpson, by any chance?"

"No, I would not," he answered.

"Then would you be telling us why you have a pen with his initials on it by your bed?" asked another, older officer.

"Of course. There's a simple explanation."

"Grand. Ye be telling us then. Down at the station might be more comfortable."

"What? Why? I'm not Ian Simpson and I've done nothing wrong!"

"Grand, sir. Then if you'll accompany us, I'm sure we can sort this out."

"I will not! This is ridiculous! I'm a guest in your country. Excuse me, but I'm leaving." He turned and headed for the door. The officers made a grab for him and held him tightly by his arms as he struggled.

"Let me go! What the hell is going on here? Look in my wallet, I can prove that I'm not Ian Simpson!"

"All in good time, sir. Now, would you be coming quietly? We don't want to upset Margaret and her regulars downstairs."

He sighed and surrendered himself to the officers' viselike grip. They marched him off down the corridor. "I'll be contacting the British embassy about this. You can't just break into someone's bedroom, accuse them of being someone they're not, and cart them off to jail! I want a lawyer!"

The crowd at the bar watched with interest as the officers escorted the man outside and into the waiting car.

———

Simon arrived at Cork Airport at ten past four that afternoon. He'd been on the wrong end of a bollocking from Thames House, for failing to get on the flight last night or the early one this morning. The truth was, he'd pulled into a service station on the way back from Dorset, realizing he was falling asleep at the wheel, and had passed out for the next four hours. When he woke, it was past nine, and he'd had to catch the one o'clock flight, which had been delayed by two hours.

Emerging from arrivals, Simon made a phone call.

"Glad you've made it, at long last," Jenkins said sarcastically.

"Yes. Any news?"

"The Irish police think they've located Simpson. He was holed up at the same hotel as Haslam. They've taken him to the local station as we requested and are waiting for you to arrive to give a positive identification."

"Good."

"He was apparently unarmed and they didn't find a weapon in his room, but I think we should send a couple of our people over to help you escort him back."

"Sure. And . . . Haslam?"

"Our Irish colleagues tell us she's just checked out. Seems she's headed back to London. Her name's on the passenger list for the six forty flight out of Cork. As Simpson is under lock and key for the present, I want you to wait at the airport for her arrival. Find out what she's discovered, if anything. Call me for further instructions later."

"Right, sir." Simon sighed heavily, not relishing another two-hour stint at an airport or the ensuing conversation with Joanna. He walked over to the newsagent's, bought a paper, and settled down on a seat that gave him a clear view of the entrances to the departure hall.

At six thirty, the final call for Heathrow was being broadcast over the loudspeaker. Having already confirmed with the check-in desk that Ms. J. Haslam was a no-show and then gone airside to scour the departure lounge thoroughly, Simon was certain she wasn't here. He watched the final passenger run through the boarding gate and down the stairs to the waiting plane.

"That's it, sir. We're closing the flight," said the young Irish woman on the desk.

Simon strode to the large window and watched the stairs slide silently away from the plane and the door shut. He sighed in resignation, thinking it had all seemed too easy.

Twenty minutes later, Simon was in a rented car, haring down the N71 toward Rosscarbery.

———

The sitting room was lit by the flames from the fire, casting ghostly, flickering shadows on the walls. The two women sat in silence, hardly noticing the night that had descended on them, too lost in their own thoughts.

"You believe me, don't you?"

After all of these years of being labeled mad, it was hardly surprising Ciara Deasy needed reassurance, Joanna supposed.

"Yes." Joanna put her fingers to her temples. "I just . . . can't think straight at the moment. There are so many things I want to ask you."

"There's time, Joanna, maybe tomorrow, so, we can speak. Ye have a rest, collect your thoughts, then come back and see me."

"Ciara, have you kept the letter?"

"No."

Joanna slumped in disappointment. "Then there's no way of proving what you've told me."

"The house has."

"Sorry?"

"I left it in there under the floorboards. I'd a feeling 'twas the safest thing."

"Would the damp not have got to it by now?"

"No. That house might be old, but it's dry. It was built to withstand the worst of weather. Besides"—Ciara's eyes glinted—"I put it inside a tin box under the window in the bedroom where she died. The one that you can see this very cottage from."

"Then . . . should I go and get it? If I'm going to prove that neither of us are mad, I need it."

"Be careful, Joanna. That house, it holds bad spirits, so it does. I still hear her crying, sometimes, from across the estuary . . ."

"I will." Joanna refused to be spooked. "How about I get it tomorrow morning when it's light?"

Ciara glanced out of the window, lost in her own thoughts. "There's a storm brewing. The estuary'll be swollen by the morning . . ."

"Okay." Joanna stood up, the darkness and talk of storms and ghosts galvanizing her into action. "Thank you, Ciara, for telling me all you know."

"You take care now." She squeezed Joanna's hand. "Don't be trusting anyone, will ye?"

"No. Hopefully, I'll be back here tomorrow with the letter."

Outside, the wind was now howling across the estuary, the rain scudding at an angle. Joanna shivered uncontrollably as she saw the black mass of the coastguard's house outlined against the sky. Struggling in the darkness to unlock her car, she climbed inside with relief and slammed the door shut against the gale. She switched the engine on to stem the noise outside, and drove off up toward the village. A hot port and the warmth of the fire would comfort her frayed nerves, she told herself, give her a chance to sort out her thoughts.

She was just switching off the engine, ready to go back into the hotel and tell Margaret she was staying for an extra night, when a familiar figure emerged from the front door of the hotel a few yards away from her. She instinctively ducked down as he stepped out onto the pavement.

Please God, don't let him see me . . .

The blood pumped in her ears as headlights bathed the car in bright light for a few agonizing seconds, then there was darkness once more. She sat up, leaned her head back, and breathed again. They were obviously onto her, which meant she had very little time left and couldn't wait until the morning. She had to go to the coastguard's house now and retrieve the letter before someone else did.

There was a tap on her rear window and Joanna nearly jumped out of her skin. She turned round and saw another familiar face smiling at her through the glass. She rolled down her window reluctantly as he walked round the car toward her.

"Hi, Lucy."

"Hi, Kurt," she said carefully. "How are you?"

"Fine."

"Right."

"I thought I'd missed you. I dropped by the hotel and they said you'd gone. I was just on my way back to my hotel in Clonakilty when I saw you out here in the car." He studied her. "You look awful pale. Anything wrong?"

"I'm fine."

"You going somewhere?"

"I . . . no. I just got back. It's bed for me now."

"Sure. You positive you're okay?"

"I'm fine. Bye, Kurt."

"Yeah, bye." He gave her a cheery wave as she rolled the window back up, waited until she saw him walking away, then legged it through the rain to the entrance of the hotel. Peering out of the window, she waited until Kurt's car had driven off out of sight, then ran back to her car and started the engine.

She drove back along the causeway toward the house, her eyes continually darting to the rearview mirror, but no other car appeared behind her.

———

Simon drove through the lashing rain toward the garda station at the other end of Rosscarbery village. He'd stopped off at the hotel to quickly check out the room Ian had been staying in, before going to identify him. Margaret, the woman in charge, had told him that the room had already been cleared by the guards and all Ian's possessions taken down to the station half an hour ago. As for Joanna, Margaret had not seen her since she'd checked out and left for the airport at four o'clock that afternoon.

He pulled up in front of a small white terraced house, its lit Garda sign outside the one indication that this was a police station. The reception was deserted. He rang a bell and eventually a young man came through a door.

"Good evening to you, sir. Terrible weather we're cursed with, isn't it? How can I be helping ye?"

"My name's Simon Warburton. I've come to identify Ian Simpson." Simon flashed his identification card.

"I'm Sean Ryan and I'm glad to be seeing you. Your man's given us trouble ever since he arrived. He's not happy to be here. Not that any of them are, to be fair."

"Is he sober?"

"I'd say that he was, yes. We gave him a breath test and he was under the limit."

That makes a change, Simon thought. "Right, let's go and take a look at him then."

He followed Sean down a short, narrow corridor. "I had to lock him in the back office, Simon, he was acting up so. Watch yourself, won't you?"

"Yes," Simon replied as Sean unlocked the door, then stepped aside to let Simon enter first. A man was slumped over the desk, his head resting on his arms, a Marlboro Light burning to its filter in the ashtray. The man looked up at Simon and let out a sigh of relief.

"Thank God! Maybe you can tell this ignorant bunch of Paddies that I'm not Ian bloody Simpson!"

Simon's heart sank. "Hello, Marcus."

———

Joanna parked the car on a grass verge just opposite the coastguard's house, turned off the engine, and reached for her flashlight, galvanizing what was left of her shredded nerves to get out of the car and cross the causeway to the house.

She opened the door and switched on the flashlight, her legs feeling weak beneath her. She shone the flashlight beam onto the sandbanks and saw the tide had begun to come in, filling the estuary with water. She knew the only way to get inside the house was to wade through it, climb up the wall, and slip in through the kitchen window.

As she made her way down the steps and into the sea, she gritted her teeth against the shock of the freezing water that reached up to just below her knees, the pelting rain soaking the top half of her body. Wading across to the steeply sloping back wall, she shone the flashlight upward to locate the kitchen window. A few more feet and she was just beneath it. She reached up to grab the top of the wall with her fingertips, then pulled her body upward, her muscles straining with the effort as she struggled to find a foothold. She cried out in pain as she lost her grip and nearly toppled over backward into the water. Another three tries and her foot managed to find an indent in the brick so she could haul herself up.

Panting hard, she lay on top of the wall. Standing up carefully on the slippery ledge, Joanna shone the flashlight and located the broken windowpane. Realizing the width was too small to shimmy through, she pulled down the sleeve of her jacket and, covering her hand with it, punched at the bottom corner of the remaining glass, which splintered, then eventually fell away, until there was enough room to climb in. Knocking the remnants of the glass from the frame, she launched herself inside headfirst.

The beam of the flashlight showed her the floor of the kitchen was three feet below her. She reached down, her legs still hanging out of the window, and her fingertips touched the damp floor beneath her. She tumbled forward with a sharp cry, landing with a thump on the hard floor, and lay there for a few seconds, feeling something furry tickling the side of her face. Joanna sprang up, shone the flashlight down, and saw the dead rat on the floor.

"Oh God! Oh God!" she panted, her chest heaving in shock and disgust, her shoulder aching from the brunt of the fall.

As she stood there, the atmosphere of the house curled around her. Every nerve ending in her body sensed the danger, the fear, and the death that seeped out of the walls. Instinct told her to get out and run.

"No, no," she muttered to herself. "Just get the letter. Nearly there now, nearly there."

Her hands shaking so hard that the beam of the flashlight wavered erratically in front of her, Joanna located the kitchen door, opened it, and found herself in an entrance hall with the stairs before her. She mounted them slowly, hearing the storm reach its zenith outside. Each stair creaked and groaned beneath her weight. At the top, Joanna paused, her sense of direction paralyzed by fear, uncertain of which way to turn.

"Think, Joanna, think . . . She said it was the room directly overlooking the cottage." Getting her bearings, she turned left, walked down the corridor, and opened the door at the end of the passage.

———

"Damn it, Simon! Can you tell me what the hell is going on?" Marcus followed him to the car, parked outside, and slumped into the passenger seat.

"We believed an . . . unsavory character named Ian Simpson had come across here after Joanna. We presumed you were him."

"For crying out loud, Simon, I know about Ian and I knew he was on her tail, that's why I flew over here too! But don't worry, Joanna's gone home, she's safe. Margaret at the hotel told me. I was just about to check out and follow her back to London when the officers picked me up."

"She didn't depart from Cork Airport. I waited for her there and she never showed up for her flight."

"Christ!" Fear was written on Marcus's face. "Do you know where she is? What if that bastard's got her— Jesus, Simon, he's an animal!"

"Don't worry, I'll track her down. Look, I'll drive you back to the hotel. I want to check Joanna's room anyway."

"I've wasted all this time locked in the bloody police station, when I could have been looking for her! Those idiots had an entire cache of credit cards with my name on them and they still wouldn't believe I was me!"

"You also had Ian Simpson's pen with his initials engraved on it by your bed."

"Jo left the pen at my apartment and all I did was pick it up! What a bloody mess."

"Apologies for the misunderstanding, Marcus. The most important thing now is to locate the real Ian Simpson, and Joanna."

Marcus shook his head in anguish as Simon parked in front of the hotel. "Christ knows where she is, but we have to find her before he does," he said as the two of them entered the hotel.

Panic crossed Margaret's face as she saw Marcus. "Is he . . . safe?"

"Perfectly." Simon nodded. "A case of mistaken identity, nothing more. Could I have the keys to Miss Haslam's room? We're concerned for her. She didn't get on the flight at Cork Airport this evening."

"Of course. I haven't touched it yet, so. It's been too busy in here." Margaret handed Simon the key.

"Thanks."

"I'll come up with you," Marcus said, as he bounded ahead of Simon up the stairs.

Simon unlocked Joanna's room and went about methodically checking the usual places, while Marcus began sweeping up objects haphazardly. Finding nothing, Marcus sat on the bed and put his head in his hands. "Come on, Jo, where are you?"

Simon's eyes caught the wastepaper basket. He emptied the contents onto the floor and fished out a tightly balled piece of paper. Flattening it out, he deciphered the text.

"She's gone to meet a woman," Simon said, "in a pink cottage opposite the house in the bay."

"Who . . . where . . . ?"

"Marcus, I'll sort this out. You stay here, keep out of trouble, and I'll see you later."

"Wait—" But before Marcus could finish, Simon was through the door and gone.

Simon drove along the causeway to the estuary as Margaret had instructed, and found Ciara Deasy's cottage, standing alone overlooking the sandbanks and the ominous black shape of the house in the bay. He jumped out of the car and walked toward the door.

33

Joanna stood in the room, as still as the walls around her. The room was bare, stripped by unknown hands of everything it had ever contained.

She shone the flashlight onto the ground, looking at the thick wooden floorboards, and walked toward the window facing Ciara's cottage. She crouched down, pulling at a floorboard with her hands. It crunched, then came free easily. Joanna gulped as she heard a sudden scratching, a patter of small paws scurrying away.

Settling herself down on the floor, her fingers numb with cold, she pulled at another rotten board, which put up little resistance as the damp air filled with dust and wood splinters. As she shone her flashlight into the gap beneath, she saw the gleam of a rusted tin. She snatched it up, her shaking fingers straining to prise open the lid.

Then she heard the footsteps outside the door. They were slow and measured, as if the owner of the feet was commanding them to move forward as quietly as they could. On instinct, Joanna dropped the tin back into its hiding place, switched off her flashlight, and froze. There was nowhere to hide, nowhere to run to. Her hands reached for a broken floorboard, her breathing coming in short, sharp gasps as she heard the door creak open.

———

Simon stepped inside the pink cottage and saw the sitting room was empty. The fire had died, leaving only a pile of glowing embers. He opened the latch door into the kitchen. There was an enamel sink with a pump above it and a pantry containing a collection of tinned vegetables, half a loaf of soda bread, some butter, and cheese.

The back door took him outside to a lavatory. Simon walked back through the sitting room and mounted the stairs. The door at the top was shut. He tapped on it gently, fearful of frightening the old lady out of her wits if she was asleep. He tapped louder, considering she might be deaf. Still there was no reply. Simon pulled up the latch and opened the door. The room was in darkness.

"Miss Deasy?" he whispered into the ether. He felt for the flashlight in his pocket and switched it on. Seeing there was a shape in the bed, Simon walked toward it, leaned over, and shone the flashlight onto the face. The mouth was open and slack, and a pair of green eyes stared unblinkingly back at him.

Simon found a light switch and turned it on, his heart heavy with dread. Checking for signs of bruising or a wound on the body, he found none, but the terror—fixed for eternity in the eyes—told Simon its own story. This was not death by natural causes, but the work of an expert.

———

Joanna heard the feet enter the room. It was pitch-black, but by the heaviness of the tread, she knew it was a man who was approaching her. A beam of light shone suddenly and brightly into her eyes. She raised the floorboard and swung at the air in front of her.

"Whoa! Lucy?"

The feet came toward her, the flashlight burning into her retinas. She swung again.

"Please! Stop! Stop! Lucy, it's me, it's Kurt. Calm down, I won't hurt you, honest."

It took a while for her brain to break through the blinding fear and recognize that, yes, this was a voice she knew. Her hands shaking violently, she dropped the floorboard, and lifted her own flashlight to shine the light on his face.

"Wh-what are you doing . . . h-here?" She was shivering, her teeth chattering from fear and cold.

"I'm sorry to have startled you, honey. I was just concerned about you, that's all. You seemed . . . a little jumpy when I saw you earlier. So I followed you down here to make sure you were okay."

"You followed me?"

"Jeez, Lu, you're soaked. You're gonna catch your death. Here." Kurt placed his flashlight on the floor, then reached into a pocket and took out a flask. "Drink some of this." He stepped forward, then seized the back of her head suddenly and forced the flask to her lips. She pursed her mouth to stop the disgusting liquid from entering, and it splashed down her shirt.

"Come on, Lu," Kurt encouraged. "It's just a little poteen. It'll warm you."

With his flashlight now on the floor, and her own lowered by her side, her eyes adjusted to the shadows and traced a path to the door. "Sorry, I'm not good with hard liquor." She forced a shaky laugh, and angled her body to where the door stood open, but he had her cornered. "What are you doing here?"

He retrieved his flashlight and his teeth looked suddenly sharp and white as the beam flashed briefly across his face. "I told you—I was real worried about you. And I could ask you the same question. Just what are you doing in an abandoned house in the middle of the night?"

"It's a long story. Why don't we head back outside and I'll explain when we get to the hotel?"

"You're searching for something you think is here, right?" Kurt shone his flashlight across the uprooted floorboards. "Buried treasure?"

"Yes, that's it, but I haven't found any yet. It could be under any of them." Joanna indicated the floorboards.

"Fine, then why don't I help you? And then we're out of here and back to the nearest fire before you catch your death."

Joanna turned exit strategies over in her mind. He was too tall, too broad, for her to physically take him on. All she had on her side was that he wouldn't see it coming. "Okay . . . I'll continue at my end, you can start over there." She nodded to the far end of the room, away from where the rusted tin lay in its hiding place close to her feet.

"Then we'll meet in the goddamned middle," he laughed.

As he bent down to pull up floorboards, she bent too and surreptitiously nudged the tin further under the still-remaining boards.

"I have zip so far. You find anything yet?" he called.

"No. Let's leave it and head back," she shouted to him, trying to make herself heard above the screaming wind. The house felt as though it was being shaken at its very foundations by the battering it was taking.

"Nah, we're here now, might as well see it through. I'm done on my side, I'll help you on yours."

"No, I'm almost done too—"

But he was already at her side, rummaging among the broken floorboards. He emerged with the tin, his eyes slanted in a knowing look.

"Well, looky here, Jo," he crowed. His large hands gripped the tin and popped open the lid with little effort. An envelope fluttered out and onto the floor.

"Wait . . . ," she said.

"I'll keep it safe for you, Jo."

"No, I . . ."

With mounting horror, she realized that he had used her real name. She watched as Kurt tucked the letter into a pocket of his waterproof, zipping it shut.

"Well, that was easier than expected." He smirked and moved toward her. She stumbled back, struggling not to trip over the holes in the floor. "Let's stop playing, Jo," he said, his voice holding no trace of its former American warmth.

In the near darkness, his features were carved in shadow, his body solid and forbidding. She found her footing, her body tense, her heart beating rapidly.

"What game is it?" She smiled at him as confidently as she could. "Here, I found something else too. Look down there." She pointed her flashlight into the space beneath the floorboards. As he turned from her to follow the beam, Joanna launched her full weight onto him, her hands shoving him forward.

With a grunt of surprise, he lost his footing and stumbled, but his fall was broken by the wall. Recovering himself, he turned back to her, and she rammed a punishing knee into his crotch.

"Aargh! You bitch!" he groaned, doubling over.

She was running toward the door, realizing she'd dropped her flashlight and was unable to see anything, when he caught her ankle and sent her down. As she hesitated to recover her bearings, a pair of arms grabbed her from behind, tightening in a viselike grip around her waist. Kicking and screaming, she was dragged along until one hard shove sent her toppling down some stairs into the darkness below.

Simon stood outside the cottage, still nauseated from what he'd discovered upstairs. The wind was wailing like a banshee in his ears, the rain driving into his face.

"Joanna, for God's sake, where are you?" he screamed into the wind.

Above its wailing came another sound. A woman was screaming in terror or agony, he couldn't decipher which. As the moon appeared from behind a fast-scudding cloud, Simon glanced at the big house out alone in the estuary, the tops of waves around it frothing and dancing with wind-whipped foam. The screaming was coming from inside the house. Seeing that the water in front of him was too deep to wade across, he raced back to his car and turned on the engine.

Joanna came to with a moan of pain, revived by the rain splattering on her face. Her brain felt wrapped in thick fog and through her blurred vision the moon above her was a shifting, snowy sky-island. She raised herself up, forcing her brain to recover her bearings. She realized she was lying outside the front door of the house. She breathed in and felt an excruciating pain in her left-hand side as she did so. A cry escaped her as she fell back on the rough gravel, another dizzy spell threatening to rob her of consciousness. Immediately, hands grabbed her under the shoulders and someone began to drag her across the gravel.

"What . . . ? Stop . . . please . . ." She fought and kicked against the ground, but she had little strength left and the iron grip was unbreakable.

"You silly little girl! Thought you were so damned clever, didn't you?!"

Ahead of her, she could see the rough steps leading down into the estuary. The water was already lapping against the top stair.

"Who are you? Let me go!"

"No can do, babe," Kurt laughed.

He dropped her on the cold, hard stone slabs by the water's edge. Turning her facedown and pinning her arms roughly behind her back, he pushed her down and angled her so her head and shoulders hung over the water. Her terrified eyes looked straight down into the angry waves just below her. The tide had risen, and the water rippled with the strong current.

"Do you know how much trouble you've caused everyone? Do you?" He yanked her head back by her hair until she felt her neck might break.

"Who are you working for?" she gasped. "What do you—"

She barely managed to snatch in a painful breath before her face was submerged in the icy-cold water. She fought to release her arms, but her lungs had nothing left. Bright lights exploded in front of her vision as she had no further energy to struggle.

Then, just as her last shred of consciousness was about to leave her, the grip on her head was removed abruptly. Joanna came up for air, gasping and spluttering as she rolled away unhindered from the water's edge. As she sucked in huge gulps of air, she saw Kurt staring up at the house behind them as if in a trance.

"Who is it?" he shouted. "Who's there?"

Joanna's brain vaguely registered a distant high-pitched sound alongside that of her own ragged breathing and the water swirling beneath her in the gale.

Kurt put his hands to his ears and began shaking his head. "Stop the noise! *Stop it!*" He keeled over to one side, screaming in agony, his hands still over his ears.

This was her chance for escape. *But the letter . . .*

Leave it, a voice told her, *leave it and run.*

Staggering upright on the wet, slippery stone, the agonizing pain in her side ripping through her, Joanna realized her only path to safety was through the water beneath her. If she could swim to the estuary wall and climb over it, she had a chance. With her lungs still screaming for oxygen, and every breath excruciating, she plunged into the icy-cold water. She went under from shock and to her relief found a solid base beneath her. The water was up to her neck, but at least she could wade across, rather than swim.

Come on, Jo, come on! You can do it, she told herself as further dizziness and nausea heralded a blackout. She turned round to check whether Kurt had noticed her leaving, and it was then she saw the figure, in the upstairs bedroom of the house, arms outstretched, as if beckoning Joanna to her. She blinked and shook her head, sure it was just another trick of her oxygen-starved brain. But the figure was still there when she opened her eyes. The figure nodded, then turned and receded from the window.

As Joanna forced her legs forward, she noticed that the storm's ferocity had suddenly died down. The water around her had calmed and in place of the howling wind, there was an eerie silence. She dragged herself through the water, heartened that the estuary wall was getting closer.

Come on, Jo, nearly there now, nearly there . . .

A sudden splash behind her alerted her to company and she forced her body to wade forward faster.

A few feet now, just a few feet . . .

"JOANNA!"

There was a familiar voice shouting her name. She stopped for an instant, listening. Then a body launched itself on top of her and she went under once more. Her lungs took in cold, salty water as she struggled for air.

I have nothing left . . .

Under the water, her body jerked and shuddered, then she struggled no more.

———

When Simon had left fifteen minutes ago, Marcus had made his way down to the bar. He'd necked a double whiskey and glanced at his mobile for the umpteenth time, willing it to ring.

He should have forced Simon to take him along. If anything happened to Jo, he'd wring Simon's neck with his own bare hands.

The barmaid glanced at him sympathetically, indicating the windows, completely obscured by pounding rain. "Your man's mad to go out on a night like this. 'Twas only a month ago that someone ended up in the estuary in a storm." She shook her head. "Fancy another?"

"Make it a double. Thanks."

"And what business has your man got with crazy Ciara?" came a voice from a table behind him.

"Excuse me?" Marcus turned to look at the old man, who was nursing his stout beneath a thick moustache.

"Saw his car going off down the causeway toward the Deasy girl's cottage—what's he want with her? She's best left alone."

"No clue, mate, we're just trying to find my girlf—" He broke off, a lump building in his throat. She was missing and here was he, sitting on his backside doing nothing . . . "Who is this Deasy woman? Where does she live?"

"About half a mile down, opposite the big house in the estuary. A pink cottage that you can't miss," said Margaret.

"Right." Marcus drained his whiskey and made for the door.

"You're not going out there, are ye?" said the old man. "'Tis dangerous down there on nights like this."

Marcus ignored him and stepped out into the howling wind. He braced himself to walk against it, the rain soaking him through after only a few steps. The whiskey and anxiety burned inside him, and he broke into a run, his heart pounding. The streetlights reflected off the puddles in the uneven road, and to his left he saw the black water of the estuary rising up, the waves breaking against the seawall.

A scream pierced the night, making him freeze. In the distance he saw a dark house standing alone in the estuary. The screaming seemed to be coming from there. As he drew closer, he stopped to catch his breath and listened. The wind had suddenly died, and there was silence. Running again, and approaching the house, he heard a loud splash and looked down into the water next to him. He could see two figures in the moonlight, and recognized Joanna's dark hair, now wet like a seal's coat. The second figure in the water was fast gaining on her.

Terror gripped his whole body. "*JOANNA!*" Marcus ran round to the spot where he could jump in closest to them and launched himself into the sea. He swam toward them, barely feeling the freezing water, and watched as the second figure grabbed Joanna from behind and pushed her under. Marcus recognized Ian immediately. "Let her go!" he screamed as he reached him.

Ian kept a firm grip on her body, which had stopped resisting. He began to laugh. "Thought I'd dealt with you in London, mate."

With a howl of anger, Marcus jumped onto him, both of them going under, a tangle of limbs as they fought. Marcus was half-blind, the salt water stinging his eyes as he tried to get a grip on Ian's jacket and get in a kick, when he saw a flash of steel and reeled back. He heard two shots echo out over the water and felt excruciating pain reverberate in his abdomen.

He tried to force his limbs to fight against it, but could no longer marshal the strength. He blinked and looked up at Ian's triumphant face as he felt himself fall back into the water like a stone.

———

Simon swung the car to a halt, and, hearing the gunshots ring out in the now-silent night, followed the sound to the water's edge. Shining his flashlight on the water, he saw two figures. Jumping in, Simon swam as fast as he could across to them.

"Don't come any nearer, Warburton. I've got a gun and I'll blast you where you stand."

"Ian, for Christ's sake! What are you doing? Who just got hurt?" Simon swept the flashlight beam around him and saw a body resting against the estuary steps, and another floating faceup in the water.

"Your friend led me straight to it, just like I knew she would."

"Where is she?"

Ian nodded to the steps. "Bloody awful swimmer," he chuckled. "But I got it. Reckon I'll have my old job back next week, don't you? This'll show them I can still cut it, won't it?"

"Course it will." Simon nodded, wading forward and seeing the gun in Ian's trembling hands aimed directly at him.

"Sorry, Warburton, can't have you stealing—"

Simon raised his fist and punched Ian on his nose, hearing a satisfying crunch and sending him backward into the water, the gun flying out of his hand. Swiftly, Simon reached for it and two further gunshots rang out in the night air. A few seconds later, Ian disappeared beneath the waves for the last time.

Simon waded over to Joanna and saw that the tide had carried her onto a set of semisubmerged steps, which were supporting her body. He carried her up to safety and checked her pulse. It was weak, but it was there.

His training automatically kicked in and he pinched her nostrils closed with his fingers as he administered several breaths mouth-to-mouth, before commencing CPR.

"Breathe, for God's sake! Breathe!" he mumbled, as he pumped his flattened palms rhythmically against her chest.

Eventually, a lungful of water spewed from Joanna's mouth. She coughed and choked, and Simon thought he had never heard such a beautiful sound.

"You're going to be fine, sweetheart," he said soothingly as she began to shiver uncontrollably.

"Thanks," she mouthed, and gave him a weak smile.

"Stay there and rest. Someone else needs help," he said as he stood up and waded back in to collect the other body.

"Marcus—Jesus Christ!" Dragging him to the steps, Simon hauled him out. Marcus's face was white in the moonlight, and a slick dark liquid was seeping out of his mouth. His pulse was weaker than Joanna's, but he was still alive. Once again Simon began resuscitation, holding out little hope. Yet Marcus finally stirred and his eyes flickered open.

"So this is what it's like to get shot," he whispered. "Joanna?"

"I'll be fine."

Simon looked up and saw Joanna had appeared beside them. She slumped down next to Marcus, the few steps she'd taken exhausting her.

"I'm running to the car to call for help. Stay with him . . . keep talking to him . . ." Simon disappeared into the darkness.

"Marcus, it's all right," she said softly.

"Tried to save you . . ." Marcus coughed and groaned as more blood trickled from his lips.

"I know. And you did. Thank you, Marcus, but try not to talk."

"So-sorry for everything. I . . . love you."

Marcus smiled up at her, before his eyes closed once more.

"And I love you too," she whispered. Then she wrapped her arms around him and sobbed into his shoulder.

CHECK

When the king is under threat of
capture on the opponent's next turn

34

North Yorkshire, April 1996

Joanna sat stiffly on the coarse moorland grass. She looked up at the Yorkshire sky and knew she had, at best, half an hour before the blue above gave way to the gray clouds coming in from the west. She moved gingerly, trying to find a more comfortable position to sit in. It was still painful to breathe or move much—the X-rays had revealed she had cracked two ribs on her left-hand side in her fall down the stairs. At least the huge purple bruises that had covered her body had faded, and the doctor had assured her that as long as she rested for a while, she would make a full recovery. Joanna felt a sick lurch in her stomach at the thought. She couldn't *ever* imagine recovering fully.

Images of the night she had so very nearly lost her life assailed her day and night—memories that had come filtering back in no particular order and that haunted her dreams. It was only in the last couple of days she'd had the mental strength to begin to contemplate what had happened and try to put the facts together.

The few hours after Simon had saved her life were still a blur. The paramedics had arrived and given her a large pain-dulling injection, which had knocked her out on the drive to the hospital. There were vague memories of X-ray machines, faces of strangers peering down at her, asking if this or that hurt, the prick of a needle as a drip was inserted into her arm. And then finally, when they had left her alone, a blissful sleep.

And then, waking up disoriented the next morning, hardly able to believe she was still alive . . . And—despite the pain she was in—feeling euphoric that she was, until Simon appeared by her bedside, looking grave. And she'd known there was worse to come . . .

"Hi, Jo, how are you?"

"I've been better," she'd quipped, studying his face for a glimmer of a smile in return.

"Yes. Look, this whole thing . . . well, it's not for now. We'll discuss it when you're stronger. I'm just so very sorry you ever got involved. And that I didn't do enough to protect you."

Joanna had seen Simon's hands clenching and unclenching. A sign of agitation she knew from years back, when he had bad news to break.

"What is it, Simon?" she asked him. "Spit it out."

Simon cleared his throat and looked away. "Jo, I need to . . . I need to tell you something difficult."

Joanna remembered wondering if *anything* could be more "difficult" at this moment. "Go on then, shoot."

"I don't know how much you remember from last night . . ."

"I don't know either. Just *say* it, Simon," she'd urged him.

"Okay, okay. Do you remember Marcus being there?"

"I . . . vaguely," Joanna had replied. And then a snapshot of him lying on the ground, blood dribbling from the corner of his mouth. "Oh God . . ." She'd looked up at Simon's expression as he shook his head and put his hand over hers.

"I'm sorry, I'm so sorry, Jo. He didn't make it."

Simon had continued to tell her of the fatal internal injuries Marcus had sustained, that he'd been pronounced dead on arrival at the hospital, but she wasn't listening.

"I love you . . . ," he'd said to her as he'd closed his eyes, perhaps for the final time. A small tear made its way from the corner of one of her eyes.

JOANNA!

"Oh my God," she'd muttered, as she realized the voice she'd heard when she'd been wading across the estuary had been Marcus's. He'd been there before Simon, she was sure of it. She hadn't seen who it was who had pulled her attacker off her just before she'd lost consciousness . . . but suddenly it became clear.

"He saved my life," she'd whispered.

"He did, yes."

Joanna had closed her eyes, thinking that perhaps, if she didn't move at all, the whole nightmare would go away. But it never would, and nor would Marcus ever be back to irritate her, excite her, and love her because he was dead, gone . . . And now she could never thank him for what he'd done.

The following morning, Joanna had been stretchered onto an RAF plane at Cork Airport and then taken to Guy's Hospital in London. During the flight, Simon had apologized for having to prep her on their cover story of what had happened in Ireland, but she'd hardly heard him.

Zoe had arrived beside her bed the following day, and put her small hand in Joanna's. Joanna had looked up and met her blue eyes, so like Marcus's, and glassy with grief.

"I can't believe he's gone," Zoe'd whispered. Then she'd reached for Joanna and the two women had held each other and wept.

"Simon said you were on holiday when it happened," Zoe had said as she composed herself.

"Yes." Simon had schooled her to say that it had been an accident—duck hunters in the estuary, but they hadn't caught the shooter. She had been knocked into the water and almost drowned in the treacherous waves, and had eventually managed to call Simon, who had organized an RAF jet to bring them back to England. Joanna could still barely fathom how anyone would believe it, but then, who would believe the *truth* anyway?

"He really loved you, Jo," Zoe had said quietly. "He could be a selfish piece of work, as you know, but I really think that he was trying to change. And you helped him do it."

Joanna had sat silently, numb from shock and grief, not wanting to add anything further to the web of lies that seemed so tightly spun and inescapable. It felt like a physical pressure on her chest and she doubted it'd ever be loosened.

Joanna had not attended Marcus's funeral, which had taken place a few days later. Simon had told her it was best she kept a low profile. She'd been released from hospital and driven up to Yorkshire to stay with her parents. Her mother had fed her endless homemade soups, helped her wash and dress, and generally enjoyed nurturing her like she was a child once more.

Zoe had called her at home to tell her the funeral had been a small affair, with just family and a few friends. He'd been buried in the family plot in Dorset, next to James, his grandfather.

Over a month had now passed since that terrible night. But the horror of it was not abating in her memory. She sighed. Maybe tomorrow some of her questions would be answered. Simon had called her to say he was coming up to stay with his parents for a few days and would pop in to see her. He'd been away on leave, apparently, which was why he hadn't been up to Yorkshire before.

Joanna gazed at the hundreds of white dots on the hillside. It was lambing season and the hillside resembled an overcrowded, woolly crèche.

"The circle of life," Joanna murmured, swallowing the lump in her throat—just now she was prone to crying over the tiniest thing. "Marcus didn't complete his because of me . . . ," she muttered, gulping back the tears. She'd been unable to even *begin* to process his death, the fact he'd made the ultimate sacrifice for *her* haunting her day and night. And just how wrong she'd been when she'd called him a coward the last time she'd seen him. It had turned out he'd been anything but . . .

"Jo! How are you?" A tanned and healthy-looking Simon walked into the farmhouse kitchen.

"Okay." She shrugged as Simon kissed her on both cheeks.

"Good. And you, Mrs. Haslam?"

"Same as always, Simon, love. Nothing much changes up here,

as you know." Laura, Joanna's mother, smiled at him, kettle in hand. "Tea? Coffee? A slice of cake?"

"Later maybe, thanks, Mrs. Haslam. How about we go out for a pub lunch, Jo?"

"I'd prefer to stay home, if you don't mind."

"Go on, love," her mother encouraged her, shooting Simon an anxious glance. "You haven't been out since you got here."

"Mum, I've been out for walks every afternoon."

"You know what I mean, Jo. Places with people, not sheep. Now go on with you and have a nice time."

"Means I can have a foaming pint of John Smith's as well. It doesn't taste the same in London," Simon said as Joanna stood up and reluctantly went to get her jacket from the boot room. "How is she?" he asked Laura, lowering his voice.

"Her body's healing, but . . . I've never known her so quiet. This whole business with that poor young man of hers has really knocked the stuffing out of her."

"I'm sure. Well, I'll do my best to cheer her up."

They drove across the moors to Haworth and opted for the Black Bull, an old haunt of theirs when they'd been teenagers.

Simon put a pint and a glass of orange juice on the table.

"Cheers, Jo," he toasted her. "It's good to see you."

"Cheers." She clinked her glass half-heartedly against his.

He put his hand over hers. "I'm so proud of you. You survived a terrible ordeal. You fought hard, and what happened to Marcus—"

"He would never have been there if it hadn't been for me, Simon. The whole night is so . . . confused in my mind, but I remember his face as he lay there. He said he loved me . . ." She fiercely brushed a tear from her eye. "I can't bear that I've caused his death."

"Jo, none of this is your fault. If it's anyone's, it's mine. I should have got to you sooner. I knew the danger you were in." Simon had been haunted, too, by the moment he'd done a U-turn at Hammersmith to help Zoe find Jamie.

"But if I'd never gone to see Ciara that night, just got on the plane, or not been so pigheaded about investigating this whole bloody mess to begin with, when you'd warned me off—a 'vigilante Sherlock Holmes' as you called me . . ."

They both managed a weak smile at the memory.

"I'm also sorry I lost it with you that day at my apartment after the story about the prince and Zoe was leaked. I should have trusted your integrity."

"Yes, you should have done," Joanna replied firmly. "Not that it matters now. It's nothing compared to Marcus being dead."

"No. Well, just try to remember, you were not the one who pulled the trigger."

"No, that was 'Kurt,' " Joanna said grimly. "Tell me, Simon, please, it's been driving me mad ever since I woke up in hospital. Who was he?"

"A colleague of mine. His name was Ian Simpson."

Joanna paused. "Oh my God. The one who turned over my apartment originally?"

"He was certainly there at the time, yes." Simon sighed. "Look, Jo, I understand how you feel; obviously you want to know and understand everything, but sometimes, as you've found out, it's better to leave it be."

"No!" Her eyes blazed. "I know he was working for your lot, trying to stop me from getting to the truth. And then, when I was almost there, he wanted me dead and he shot Marcus!"

"Jo, Ian was not working for 'our lot' at that point anymore. He'd been placed on sick leave because of his associated mental problems, exacerbated by drink. He was a dangerous loose cannon who wanted to cover himself in glory and get his job back. He was also the one who fed the news about Zoe and the prince to the *Morning Mail*. The Welbeck Street house was bugged, so Ian knew everything. He'd apparently been taking 'bungs'—as he called them—from journalists for years. We found over four hundred thousand pounds in his bank account, the most recent deposit for seventy thousand, which was placed the day after the story made the front page. Put simply, his moral compass had been blown to shreds."

"Oh, Simon!" Joanna put her hands to her burning cheeks. "I told Marcus I suspected *him*. I . . ."

"I'm so sorry." Simon took her hand as tears filled her eyes again. He could have easily wept for her too.

"Where is that bastard now?" she asked.

"He died, Jo."

The color drained from her face. "That night?"

"Yes."

"How?"

"He was shot."

"Who by?"

"Me."

"Oh God." She covered her face with her hands. "Is that what you do for a living?"

"No, but these things happen in the course of duty, just like when you work for the police. Actually, it was the first time I'd ever had to do it, but better him than you. I'll get us both another drink. G and T this time?"

Joanna shrugged and watched as Simon headed to the bar, then came back with another round. She sipped her gin and stared at him.

"I know what it was all about, Simon."

"Do you?"

"Yes. Not that it matters anymore. The letter I discovered is presumably at the bottom of the sea with Ian. And if it isn't, then it's gone to a place where I'll never be able to find it."

"I retrieved the letter, actually, for what use it was. A soggy, pulpy mess."

"Is this Simon, Jo's oldest friend, speaking, or Simon, crack secret-service agent?" Joanna eyed him.

"Both." Simon fished in his pocket and drew out a plastic envelope. "I knew you'd ask, so I brought the remains for you to see."

Joanna took the envelope and glanced inside at the pieces of disintegrated, water-marked paper it contained.

"Take a closer look," Simon urged her. "It's important you believe me."

"What's the point? It would be easy to fake." She waved the envelope at Simon. "So all the fuss, Marcus's life . . . for this?"

"I don't know what to say," he said quietly. "To be fair, it wouldn't have happened if we hadn't had a crazed renegade agent on the rampage. At least it's made those above me sit up and take notice. They forget the psychological toll a career like this can take. Agents can't simply be spat out at the other end and told their services are no longer required. I know you won't want to hear it, but when I joined the service, I looked up to Ian. He was a brilliant agent in his time—one of the best."

"I know that. Even in his crazed state, standing in a choppy sea, he managed to take perfect shots. And took Marcus's life with it," Joanna muttered. "So, will you end up like that?"

"Christ, I hope not. This whole episode has made me think very hard about my future, I can tell you."

"Good. At least that's one positive out of all of this."

"I'm just glad that you're alive at least, and that it's over. Now, let's get you something to eat, you're skin and bones."

He ordered them both a lamb hotpot. Simon devoured his while Joanna hardly touched hers.

"Not hungry?"

"No." Joanna stood up, wincing at the still-nagging pain in her ribs. "Let's get out of here. I want to know once and for all if I've got my facts right, and I'm so paranoid, I want to do it somewhere I'm positive no one is listening in. Then, maybe, I can start putting my life back on track."

They walked slowly up the hill, Joanna hanging on to Simon for support, past Haworth church and up onto the moors behind the village.

"I have to sit down," she panted, lowering herself gingerly onto the coarse grass. She lay back and tried to relax and still her breathing. "There's a lot that doesn't fit," she said after some time, "but I reckon I've got most of the gist." Joanna took a deep breath. "My little old lady with the tea chests was in the employ of the royal household. She was a lady-in-waiting called Rose Fitzgerald, who had met and fallen in love with an Irish actor called Michael O'Connell. Or as we know him now, Sir James Harrison. Their relationship was clandestine, because of her high birth. The letter she sent to me was from her to him, but if I'm right, that was the 'red herring,' because it certainly wasn't the letter you lot were after, was it?"

"No. Go on."

"What if Michael—when he visited his relatives in Ireland— heard that there was an English gentleman staying at the coastguard's house nearby and having an affair with a local girl, and had recognized him?"

"And who was the gentleman, Joanna?"

"Ciara Deasy told me. She'd seen his photograph on the front of the *Irish Times*, the day of his coronation ten years later." Joanna glanced into the distance. "It was the Duke of York. The man who would, when his brother abdicated, become the king of England."

"Yes." He nodded slowly. "Well done."

"Michael then finds out the girl is pregnant. And that is really as far as I've managed to get. Could you . . . would you fill in the details? How you knew about the letter Niamh Deasy had written, which must have spilled the beans on the duke's affair with her. And of course, her pregnancy. I can only presume Michael O'Connell knew of its existence and used it as blackmail to safeguard himself and his family until he died? It would have caused an unbelievable scandal if it had got out, especially after the duke became the king."

"Yes. The deal was, the letter was to be returned to us on Michael/ James's death. When that didn't happen, mass panic broke out."

"So, why didn't you lot look in the coastguard's house where Niamh had died? Surely it was the most obvious place?"

"Sometimes people don't see the things that are right under their noses, Jo. Everyone assumed that Michael would have kept it close, in his immediate possession." Simon regarded her with pride. "Well done! Do you want my job?"

"Not in a million years." Joanna gave Simon a weak smile. "Ciara told me the baby died. Can you imagine if it had lived? After all, it was the child of the future king of England. Half sibling to our queen!"

"Yes." Simon paused for a moment. "I can imagine."

"And poor Ciara Deasy was told she was mad. I must write to her, maybe go and see her to tell her the letter is gone, that it's all finally over."

Simon covered Joanna's hand with his own and squeezed it. "I'm afraid Ciara died that night, too, Jo. At Ian's hands."

"Oh God, no!" Joanna shook her head, wondering if she could cope with more horror. "This is all so ghastly. Something that happened over seventy years ago destroying so many people."

"I know, and I agree. But as you just said, if it had leaked out, it would have caused an enormous scandal, even seventy years on."

"Still . . ." Joanna took a deep breath, feeling her lungs laboring from all the speaking. "There are things that still don't seem right. For example, why on earth would the palace send the Duke of York over to Ireland just after Partition? I mean, the English were hated, and the son of the sovereign must have been a prime target for the IRA. Why not Switzerland? Or at least somewhere warm?"

"I can't say for sure. Possibly because it really was the last place anyone would think of looking for him. He was sick, and needed time to recover in complete peace. Whatever," Simon sighed, "it's time to close the book now."

"Something is still not right." Joanna ground a tuft of grass with her boot. "However, you'll be glad to know I'm officially giving up. I feel so . . . so bitter, and angry."

"You have a right to feel that. But it will pass—the grief, the anger . . . One day you'll wake up and it won't control you," he reassured her. "And I do have one bit of good news for you." Simon fished in his jacket pocket and handed her a letter. "Go on, open it."

She did so. The letter was from the editor of her newspaper offering her her job back on the news desk with Alec, as soon as she was fit enough to return. She looked at Simon, her mouth open in surprise. "How did you get hold of this?"

"It was passed on to me to give to you. Obviously the situation was explained to those who needed to know and has been rectified. Personally, I'm only sorry you can't go back in a blaze of glory with the scoop of the century. After all, it was you who beat us lot to the pot of gold. Right, let's go. I don't want you getting a chill." He helped her gently to standing and gave her a careful hug. "I've missed you, you know. I hated it when we weren't friends."

"So did I."

They walked back down the hill arm in arm.

"Simon, there's one last thing I wanted to ask you about that night."

"What?"

"Well, this sounds very silly, and you know I'm not a believer in any of this kind of thing, but . . . did you hear a woman's scream coming from the house?"

"I did. I thought it was you, to be honest. That's what alerted me to where you were."

"Well, it wasn't me, but I think Ian heard it too. He had my head underwater, then all of a sudden he let me go and put his hands over his ears, like he was hearing something unbearable. You . . . didn't see a woman's face at an upstairs window, did you?"

"No, Jo, I didn't." Simon grinned at her. "I reckon you were hallucinating, sweetheart."

"Maybe," Joanna acknowledged as she stepped into the car. She sighed as she saw the woman's face as clear as day in her mind's eye. "Maybe."

An hour later, Simon pulled his car away from the farmhouse, giving a last wave to Joanna and her parents. Before he headed back to his own parents' house across the lane, he had to make a telephone call.

"Sir? It's Warburton."

"How did it go?"

"She came close, but not close enough for any panic."

"Thank God. You've encouraged her to drop the whole thing, have you?"

"I didn't need to," Simon reassured him. "She's finished with it. Although she did tell me something that I think you should know. Something that William Fielding told Zoe Harrison before he died."

"What?"

"The full name of our 'lady's' emissary. I think we may have got our wires crossed there."

"Not over the phone, Warburton. Use the usual protocol and I'll see you in the office at nine tomorrow."

"Right, sir. Goodbye."

35

The day before Joanna was leaving to return to London to pick up the pieces of her life, she drove over to see Dora, her paternal grandmother, in nearby Keighley. In her mid-eighties, but with her wits as sharp as a knife, Dora lived in a comfortable apartment in a housing development for senior citizens.

As she was hugged and welcomed inside to great delight and a plate of freshly made scones, Joanna immediately felt guilty that she did not visit more regularly. Dora had always been a constant in her life, having lived only four miles down the road from her son and his family up until five years ago. Joanna had treated her cozy cottage as a second home, her granny as a second mother.

"So, young lady, tell me exactly how you landed yourself in hospital, will you?" Dora smiled as she poured tea into two fine bone-china teacups. "And I'm ever so sorry about your young man." Her warm brown eyes were full of concern. "You know your grandpa died at thirty-two in the war. Broke my heart, it did."

Joanna provided the cursory explanation she'd been drilled by Simon to give everyone who asked.

"That's what your dad told me. That you almost drowned." Dora's intelligent eyes studied Joanna. "But you can't fool me. I remember all them badges and shields you won at school for swimming, even if they don't. *Dora*, I thought to myself when I heard, *there's more to this than meets the eye*. So, love"—she took a sip of her tea and eyed her granddaughter—"who tried to drown you?"

Joanna could not help but give a weak smile—her grandmother was such a wily old bird. "It's a long, long story, Granny," she murmured as she polished off her second scone.

"I love a good story. And the longer the better," she said encouragingly. "Sadly, time is something I have in spades these days."

Joanna weighed the situation up in her mind. Then, thinking that there was no one on earth whom she trusted more, and eager to put her still-confused thoughts into words, she began to talk. Dora was the perfect listener. She rarely interrupted, stopping Joanna only if there was something her failing left ear had missed.

"So, that's it, really," Joanna concluded. "Mum and Dad know nothing, of course. I didn't want to worry them."

Dora clasped Joanna's hands in hers. "Oh, love . . ." She shook her head, a mixture of anger and sympathy in her eyes. "I'm proud of you for pulling through as well as you have. What a dreadful thing to happen. But, my, what a tale! The best I've heard for years. Takes me back to the war and Bletchley Park. I spent two years there on the Morse code machines during the war."

This was a story Joanna had heard many times before. If one was to believe Dora, her decoding skills were what had won the Second World War. "It must have been an amazing time."

"The things I could tell you that went on behind closed doors, love, but I signed the Official Secrets Act and they'll stay with me until the grave. However, it made me believe that anything is possible, that Joe Public'll never know the half of it. More tea?"

"I'll make it."

"I'll help."

The two of them wandered into the immaculate kitchen. Joanna put on the kettle as Dora rinsed the teapot under the tap.

"So, what'll you do?" Dora asked her.

"About what?"

"Your story. *You* haven't signed any Secrets Act. You could go public and make a pretty penny."

"I don't have enough proof, Granny. Besides, this is a secret that those in high places are prepared to kill people to protect, as I know to my cost. Too many people have died already."

"What do you have in the way of proof?"

"Rose's original letter to me, a photocopy of the love letter she wrote to Michael O'Connell, and a theater program from the Hackney Empire that seems to have little relevance to the story, apart from showing James Harrison using another name."

"You got them with you?"

"Yes. They're in my rucksack and they go under my pillow at night. I'm still looking behind me to see if someone's lurking in the shadows. They're no use to me anymore. Maybe you'd like them to put with the rest of your royal memorabilia?"

Dora's collection of old newspaper clippings and photos, betraying her status as an ardent monarchist, was a family joke.

"Let's have a look-see then." Dora walked back into the sitting room with the teapot, poured them each a fresh cup, and settled herself in her favorite armchair.

"I'm surprised you'd allow yourself to think that one of your precious kings might have had a fling outside the marital bed, especially one that was married to your favorite royal," Joanna commented as she dug inside her rucksack for the brown envelope.

"Men will be men," countered Dora. "Besides, up until recently, it was the done thing for kings and queens to have mistresses and lovers. It's a well-known fact there were a good few monarchs whose parentage was questionable. No birth control in those days, you know, love. I had a friend at Bletchley Park whose mother had been an undermaid at Windsor. The things she told me about that Edward VII. He had a string of mistresses, and according to her, he put at least two of them in the family way. Thanks, love." Dora reached out for the envelope and removed its contents. "Now, what have we here?"

Joanna watched as Dora studied the two letters, then opened the theater program.

"I saw Sir James a good few times in the theater. Looks different here, though, doesn't he? I thought he was a dark-haired fellow. He's blond in this picture."

"He dyed it black and added a moustache when he became James Harrison and assumed his new identity."

"What's this?" Dora was studying the photograph Joanna had found in the attic of Haycroft House.

"That's James Harrison, Noël Coward, and Gertrude Lawrence. Given their evening dress, at some kind of first-night party, I'd imagine."

Dora studied the photo intently, then glanced at the other photo of James Harrison in the theater program. "Good Lord!" She let out a sigh and shook her head in wonderment. "Oh no, it's not!"

"Not what?"

"That man standing next to Noël Coward is definitely not James Harrison. You wait here a minute and I'll prove it to you."

Dora rose and left the room. Joanna heard the sound of a drawer opening, then a scuffling, papery noise before Dora arrived back, her eyes glinting in triumph. She sat down, laid a heap of yellowing newspaper cuttings on the table, and beckoned Joanna to her. She pointed at one faded, grainy photograph and then at the others. Then she put Joanna's photograph next to them.

"See? It's one and the same person. No doubt about it at all. A case of mistaken identity there, love."

"But . . ." Joanna felt breathless and slightly sick as her brain tried to make sense of what she saw. She pointed to the face in the program, the face of the young Michael O'Connell. "Surely that can't be him too?"

Dora took her glasses off her nose and looked at Joanna intently. "I doubt that the then-second in line to the throne would be performing in a play at the Hackney Empire, don't you?"

"You're saying the man standing next to Noël Coward is the Duke of York?"

"Compare that photo of him with these: on his wedding day, in his navy officer's uniform, on his coronation . . ." Dora stabbed her finger at the face. "I'm telling you, it's him."

"But the photograph of Michael O'Connell in the theater program . . . I mean, they look like one and the same person."

"Seems like we're seeing double, dear, doesn't it? Oh, and I brought you something else to look at too." Dora pulled out another cutting. "I thought it sounded odd when you mentioned the 'visitor' arriving in Ireland in early January 1926. See, this shows the duke and duchess on a visit to York Minster in January 1926. My parents went to wave in the crowd. So it's very doubtful the duke could have been in southern Ireland around the same time, it was a long way to travel in those days. And besides, the duchess was six months along with her first pregnancy. Far as I know, the pair of them didn't leave England's shores until their tour of Australia the following year."

Joanna's hands went to her head as her brain struggled to compute it all. "So, I . . . then it couldn't have been the Duke of York in Ireland after all?"

"You know," Dora said slowly, "in those days, a lot of famous people used doubles. Monty was known for it, and Hitler, of course. That's why they couldn't get him. They'd never know whether they'd killed the right man."

"You're saying that Michael O'Connell might have been used as a double for the Duke of York? But why?"

"Search me. The duke's health was never good, mind. He was sick as a young boy. And he always had that dreadful stutter. He suffered from bouts of bronchitis all his life."

"Surely someone would have noticed? All the photographs in the newspapers . . ."

"The quality was not like it is these days, dear. No newfangled lenses pointing up your nose, and no television. You'd see the royals from a distance, if you were lucky, or hear them on the radio. I'd reckon if there was some reason they wanted a stand-in—say, if the duke was sick and they didn't want the country to know—they'd have got away with it easily."

"Okay, okay." Joanna tried to take in this new information. "So, if that was the case, and Michael O'Connell was used as a double for the Duke of York, why all this fuss?"

"Don't ask me, dear. You're the investigative journalist."

"Christ!" Joanna shook her head in frustration. "I thought I'd made sense of it all, and if what you've pointed out is right, then I'm back to square one. Why all the deaths? And what on earth was in that letter they were so desperate to get their hands on?" She stared into space, her heart beating hard against her chest. "If . . . *if* you're right, Simon has sold me completely down the river."

"Maybe he thought it was better than having you drown in it," Dora said sagely. "Simon's a straight Yorkshireman and you're like a sister to him. Whatever he's done, he's done to protect you."

"You're wrong. Simon may care for me, but I've learned where his true allegiance lies in the past few weeks. Oh Christ, Granny. I'm so confused. I thought it was all over, that maybe I could forget about it and get on with my life."

"Well, you can, of course, love. All we've done is spot a similarity between one young man and t'other . . ."

"Similarity? In those photos anyone would be pushed to tell the difference! It's too much of a coincidence. I'm going to have to go back to London and rethink everything. Can I borrow these cuttings?"

"With pleasure, as long as you return them."

"Thank you." Joanna scooped the cuttings up and folded them into her rucksack.

"Let me know how it goes, love. My instincts tell me you're on the right track now."

"God help me, so do mine." She kissed Dora warmly. "This may sound rather overdramatic, but please don't say a *word* to anyone about what we've discussed today, Granny. People involved in this have a horrid habit of getting hurt."

"I won't, even though half the old biddies living around me are too senile to remember what day it is, let alone a story like this." Dora chuckled.

"I'll see myself out."

"Yes. You take care, Joanna. And whatever you say, if you trust anyone, trust Simon."

Joanna called goodbye from the hall, opened the front door, and headed for the car. As she drove away, she mused that Dora may have unwittingly led her to the truth of the matter, but that her final words of advice about Simon were fatally flawed.

36

When Simon arrived back at the office, he noticed a faint smell of expensive perfume that hung around Ian's old desk, while his overflowing ashtrays and half-drunk coffee mugs had been replaced by an orchid in a pot. A Chanel handbag was slung by its elegant chain on the back of the chair.

"Who's the new boy?" Simon asked Richard, the office's systems manager and resident gossip.

"Monica Burrows." Richard raised an eyebrow. "She's on secondment from the CIA."

"I see." Simon sat down at his own desk and switched on his computer to check his emails. He'd been out of the office for most of the past month. He glanced at Ian's desk and a gamut of mixed emotions assailed him. A gut-wrenching guilt that it was *he* who had ended Ian's life . . .

There were no words he could ever write that could put his feelings onto a page, nothing he could say to explain. He was his own judge and jury—never outwardly tried for his crime, but neither pardoned nor condemned and in a moral limbo for the rest of his life. And doubting more and more that this was the career for him.

Simon checked himself. It wasn't Monica's fault she'd been given the desk of a man who no longer existed . . .

"Human life is like a bucket of water. Take out a cupful of it and the bucket fills over," someone had once said to him.

Pulling himself out of his reverie, he checked the time and realized he had only fifteen minutes before reporting for his meeting.

"Hi," said an unfamiliar voice from behind him.

Simon turned round to see a tall brunette in a well-cut jacket and skirt. The woman was immaculate—blow-dried from head to toe. She held out her hand. "Monica Burrows, good to meet you."

"Simon Warburton." Simon shook her hand, noticing her smile was warm, but the perfectly made-up green eyes were cold.

"Seems we're desk neighbors," Monica purred as she sat down and crossed her long, slim legs. "Maybe you'll help show me the ropes."

"Sure, but I'm afraid I'm on my way out." Simon stood up, nodded at her, then headed for the door.

"See you around," he heard her say as he pushed it open.

Life goes on . . . , he thought as he emerged from the elevator on the top floor and walked along the thickly carpeted corridor. "Even when it doesn't," he muttered as he went to make himself known to the faithful receptionist who sat in state alone on the top floor.

The strong morning sunlight was pouring in through the high windows. As he entered the room, Simon thought how frail the man looked, the bright light accentuating the deeply engraved lines on his face.

"Good morning, sir," he said as he walked toward the desk.

"Sit down, Warburton. Before we go any further, did you turn up anything on that private detective agency that James Harrison had engaged?"

"The chap I interviewed from the agency told me that James Harrison had asked him to investigate what had happened to Niamh Deasy all those years ago in Ireland."

"Guilt in the last stages of his life," sighed the old man. "I presume they came up with nothing?"

"No more than that she and the child died at the birth, sir."

"Well, at least I can take comfort that the British security service managed to cover their tracks sufficiently on *that* one. And the Marcus Harrison situation has been smoothed over, I take it?"

"Yes, it's been reported as a shooting accident, and I doubt anyone will dig deeper. His funeral was last month."

"Good. Now, this name that Miss Haslam gave you is interesting, very interesting indeed. I'd always wondered who it was our 'lady' trusted enough to deliver the damned letters. Of course, I should have thought of her long ago. She was certainly a close friend of our 'lady,' though if memory serves me, she'd left to marry by the time all this happened. I've got some men on it, but the chances are, she's probably dead anyway."

"Probably, sir, but at this point any avenue is worth a shot."

"We've looked through every damned piece of paper in that attic. Any other hiding place that's struck you, Warburton?"

"I'm afraid not, although I'm seriously beginning to wonder whether he destroyed the letter, that maybe it just doesn't exist anymore. It's obvious to me that the Harrison family know nothing of Sir James's past."

"Look how close the Haslam girl came to discovering the truth. We were only lucky that Harrison's Irish affair provided the perfect smokescreen." The old man sighed again. "He would have kept the damned thing and I cannot rest until that letter is found and destroyed. Mark my words, if we don't get hold of it, then someone else will."

"Yes, sir."

"As there seem to be few other options, I'm putting you back on duty with Zoe Harrison. The palace is dithering as to how to play the situation. HRH is still resisting all attempts to bring him to his senses. They're having to go along with him for the present and hope the relationship peters out."

Simon studied his hands, his heart sinking. "Yes, sir."

"He is also insisting that Miss Harrison and he begin to be seen out officially in public together. The palace has agreed to her attending a film premiere with him in a couple of weeks' time. He's also eager to move her, but they are resisting. She's been away on a short holiday with her son for the past week, but she's been told to expect you at Welbeck Street on Monday morning."

"Yes, sir. One last thing: Monica Burrows from the CIA—Jenkins told me she'll be working alongside us. I presume she knows nothing?"

"Absolutely not. Personally, I disapprove of all this getting into bed with other intelligence agencies, sharing methods and pooling ideas. Jenkins will put her on light surveillance work, spending time with members of the department, shadowing them, that sort of thing. Thank you, Warburton. We'll speak at the usual time tomorrow."

Simon left the office thinking how weary the old man seemed. But then he'd carried the secret alone for many, many years. And the burden of that was enough to sap the strength of the strongest constitution.

It was certainly sapping *his*.

———

"Joanna!" A pair of thick, hairy arms went around her shoulders and clasped her in a bear hug.

"Hi, Alec." She was taken aback by his display of affection.

He dropped his arms and stood back to look at her. "How are you, love?"

"I'm fine."

"You look terrible, girl. Skin and bone. Sure you're okay?"

"Yes. Honestly, Alec, I just want to get on with some work, try to forget all about the past few weeks."

"Right, well, I'll see you for a sandwich in the local at one o'clock. There's a few things I should fill you in on. Some . . . changes that have occurred since you went away. Go on, get off with you to your old desk and catch up with your emails." He winked at her and returned to his computer.

Joanna wandered across the office, breathing in its fuggy smell.

No matter how many No Smoking notices the management posted, a cloud of cigarette smoke still hung permanently above the desks in the newsroom. Glad Alice's chair next door to her was empty—she wanted some time to settle in without a barrage of questions—Joanna sat down and turned on her computer.

She stared sightlessly at the screen, as her mind continued to run over the new facts. Since she'd seen Dora, she'd compared further photos of the young duke with that of the young Michael O'Connell in the program. Any differences between the two men were virtually indistinguishable.

Taking Dora's idea of a "double," Joanna had come up with a vague outline of what might have happened: a young actor, very similar in looks and age to the Duke of York, plucked to play the part of his life. The duke could not have been in Ireland at the time in question due to official engagements and the fact that his wife was pregnant, so it *had* to have been Michael O'Connell who had stayed in the coastguard's house. And therefore it was Michael O'Connell who had the affair with Niamh Deasy. Poor Ciara had seen the picture of the Duke of York's coronation on the front of the *Irish Times* ten years later and understandably thought it was *he* who had been staying at the house across the estuary, *he* who'd had an affair with her dead sister. And, Joanna thought sadly, the letter, hidden for so many years under the floorboards of the house, had probably been no more than the last few sad words of a dying woman to Michael, the man she loved.

If this was the case, why had Michael O'Connell changed his identity? What had he known that had provided him with a house the size of Welbeck Street, money, an aristocratic wife, and huge success as an actor? And what about the love letter to "Siam" from the mysterious lady—the letter that had begun her quest in the first place? Had Rose written it, as she'd previously thought, or someone else . . . ?

Joanna sighed in frustration. The bottom line was that, even though the similarity between the two men was incredible, there was absolutely no proof of anything.

Joanna glanced around trying to bring herself back to reality. The chances were that if she gave anyone so much as a sniff of the fact she was still "interested," they'd be onto her immediately. They'd only given her back her life because they thought what she knew was safe. The big question was, did she have the strength and courage to continue to pursue the truth? Even if she had no firm answers, Joanna's instincts told her she was dangerously close to finding out what it was.

Despite her protestations, Alec pushed her into the nearby pub at one o'clock on the dot, eager to hear the whole story.

"So, tell all." Alec eyed her over his pint.

"Nothing to tell," Joanna said. "There were some duck hunters out, and Marcus and I got caught in the midst of it. He was shot. I ran away from the gunfire and fell into the estuary, then got carried away by the current and nearly drowned," she repeated like a mantra.

"Duck hunters!" Alec snorted. "For God's sake, Jo! It's *me* you're talking to here. What was it you found out that had you fighting for your life? And Marcus losing his?"

"Nothing, Alec, really," she said wearily. "All my leads led to nothing. As far as I'm concerned, the chapter's closed. I've got the job I love back and I intend to concentrate on digging the dirt on supermodels and soap stars, rather than getting carried away imagining fantastical plots fertilized by little old ladies."

"Haslam, you are a bloody shit liar, but I accept that them upstairs have done a good job and you've been well and truly scared off. Which is a shame, because I've done a little further digging myself."

"I wouldn't bother if I were you, Alec. The road leads to nowhere."

"I don't like to pull rank on you, sweetheart, but I've been in this business longer than you've been on the planet and I can smell a scandal from a mile off. Do you want to hear or not?"

Joanna shrugged casually. "Not really, no."

"Ah, go on, I'll tell you anyway. I was reading through one of those autobiographies of our Sir James and something struck me as odd."

Joanna focused on looking disinterested as Alec went on. "It recalls how close Sir James was to his wife, Grace. How strong their marriage was and how devastated he was when she died."

"Yes. So?"

"Grace died in France apparently. I mean, if your beloved died abroad, surely you'd want to collect the body and have it buried on home soil? So that one day you could lie together for eternity? And we know Sir Jim is buried in Dorset. Alone," he added.

"Maybe. Marcus certainly came home from Ireland." Joanna swallowed hard. "Though I was too ill to go to the funeral."

"So sorry about that, love. But there you go. So why didn't Sir James do the same with his beloved? Could it be that she didn't die after all?"

"I don't know. Can I have my sandwich? I'm starving."

"Sure. Cheese do?"

"Fine."

Alec shouted over the noisy hubbub to order the sandwich and a couple more drinks. "Anyway, she'd be over ninety by now, so the chances of her being either alive or compos mentis are slim."

"You really think she could still be alive? That she was involved in all this too?"

"Could be, Jo, could be." Alec slurped his pint.

"Alec, this is all very interesting, but as I said, I've come to the end of the line."

"Well, your call, darling."

"Besides, how would you go about trying to locate someone who's supposedly been dead for nearly sixty years?"

"Ah now, Jo, them's the tricks of the trade. There's always a way to reel 'em in, if you word it right."

"Word what right?"

"An advertisement placed on the obituaries page. Every old crone reads those to see if anyone they know has copped the Big D. Come on, Jo, eat your sandwich. Looks like you could do with putting on a few pounds."

———

Joanna let herself into her apartment that night, feeling utterly exhausted, and went to run a bath. Coming back from the clean Yorkshire air made London—and her—feel grimy. Once she had bathed and donned her bathrobe and furry slippers, she sat on the sofa in the sitting room. She wondered now if she had returned too quickly—at least in Yorkshire she had felt safe and secure, and never as alone as she felt right now.

Reaching for the pile of post that had gathered while she was away, she began to open it. There was a sweet letter from Zoe Harrison, welcoming her back to London and asking Joanna to ring her so they could get together for lunch. There were also a frightful number of unpaid bills, and Joanna was grateful to have her job back. As she sorted the pile into "important" and "wastepaper" piles, a slim white envelope slipped onto the floor. She picked it up, and seeing it was a handwritten note with just her name on it, she opened it.

Dear Jo,

Please don't tear up this letter yet. I've been an utter shit, I know. I saw how hurt and angry you were; I've honestly never hated myself more than I do now.

    I've spent my whole life blaming other people for my problems, and I realize now that I'm a coward. I'm such a coward for not telling you the truth about the money. I never deserved you.

    From the moment that I saw you in that restaurant, I knew I wanted you. That you were special and different. You're an incredible woman, and with your strength and bravery, you make me feel like the pathetic creature I am.

    I know you're probably shaking your head as you read this—

if you haven't already thrown it in the bin. I'm not the most articulate or romantic person, but I'm laying my heart bare here. It's true. Joanna Haslam, I love you. There's nothing I can do to change the past. But I hope I can change the future.

If you can find it in your heart to forgive me, I want to be a better man for you. And to show you who I can be.

Again, I love you.

Marcus

P.S. I didn't tell the papers about Zoe, by the way. She's my sister. I'd never do that to her.

"Oh God, oh God, Marcus . . ." Tears spilled out of Joanna's eyes. "But you did show me, darling, *you did*!"

She cried some more, the awful finality of death—the fact she could never thank him for what he had done for her—hitting her acutely as she reread his last words to her. She realized that, despite his flaws, never in her life had she been loved as much as she had been by Marcus. And now he was gone.

"I'm not strong, or brave," she muttered, as she wandered into the bedroom and looked in her rucksack for the sleeping pills the doctor had given her when she'd left the hospital. She would definitely need them tonight.

Pulling out the old newspaper cuttings and the envelope containing all her "evidence," Joanna climbed into bed and looked at the pile. Yet again she was compelled to compare the photographs, and yet again her mind reached for answers.

"This was *your* grandfather, Marcus," she whispered into the silent room as she swallowed a pill and tried to get comfortable on the new mattress.

"Who *was* he?" she asked the ether.

An hour later, still unable to sleep despite the pill, Joanna sat up.

Surely . . . *surely* she owed it to Marcus, who had lost his life on the search, to find out?

Following Alec's advice about posting an advert in the small ads, Joanna set to work on her computer. Over a dozen national French newspapers were listed, plus numerous local papers. She decided she'd start with *Le Monde* and the *Times*, which, being of English origin, Grace might buy to keep in touch. If she received no joy from adverts in those, she'd move on to the next two, and so on. After all, there was no guarantee that Grace was still living in France. She might well have left soon after her faked "death" all those years ago.

But how to word the advert so that Grace would know it was safe to reveal herself? And, by the same token, not alert anyone who might be watching and waiting? Joanna sat cross-legged on her bed far into the night, the pile of discarded scraps of paper—each one of which she knew she must burn to a cinder before morning came—growing as she racked her brains to find the right words to use.

As the sun rose, Joanna typed up the advert, then deleted it immediately after it had printed. When she arrived at work, she used the office fax machine to send it through, with a note to both newspapers to place the ad as soon as possible. The ads would appear in two days' time. It was a long shot, she knew, and all she could do now was to wait.

———

Lunchtime found her in the local library in Hornton Street to work, the table full of books on the history of the royal family. She studied yet another photograph of the young Duke of York and his bride. Then, casting her eyes down, she noticed a ring on a finger of his left hand. Even though it was partly in shadow, the shape and the insignia looked familiar.

Joanna closed her eyes and scoured her brain. Where had she seen that ring before? Cursing out loud because the answer would not come to her, Joanna looked at the clock and realized her lunch break was over.

At four o'clock, as she drank a cup of tea, she thumped her desk in exhilaration.

"Of course!"

She picked up the receiver and dialed Zoe's number.

———

"How are you?" Zoe opened the door to the Welbeck Street house that evening, made a fast check of the street, then ushered Joanna inside and embraced her warmly.

"I'm . . . okay."

"Sure? You look very thin, Jo."

"I guess. How are you?"

"Yes, well . . . you know, the same. Tea? Coffee? Wine? I'm opting for the latter, as the sun has long passed the yardarm."

"I'll join you," Joanna said as she followed Zoe into the kitchen. She grabbed a half-drunk bottle and sloshed the wine into two glasses.

"You don't look that great either," Joanna said.

"To be honest, I feel like crap."

"Me too."

"Cheers." They clinked glasses in mock celebration and sat down at the kitchen table.

"How's it been, coming back to London?" Zoe asked her.

"Difficult," Joanna admitted. "And I found this last night in my post," she said quietly, handing Zoe the letter. "It's from Marcus. He must have written it to me after our fight . . . I thought you'd . . . well, I thought you might want to read it."

"Thanks." Zoe opened the envelope. Joanna watched her read it and could see the tears sparkling in her blue eyes. "Thank you for showing me this." She took Joanna's hand. "It means a lot to me that Marcus loved you so deeply. I didn't think he would ever experience it, and I'm so happy he did, even if it was only for a short time."

"I just wish I'd believed he loved me, but it was very difficult, given his behavior and past reputation. We also had an argument. I feel so dreadful. I accused him of shopping you and Art to the papers." At least it was a half-truth.

"I see. I thought it might have been you, but Simon swore it wouldn't be."

"That's nice of him. Anyway, as it happens, it wasn't either of us."

"Then who was it?"

"Who knows? A neighbor maybe, who saw Art coming in and out of your house? God, Zoe, I'm so ashamed I accused Marcus."

"Well, at least you two made up in Ireland."

"Yes, we did," Joanna lied, hating the fact she could never tell his sister that Marcus had saved her life. "And I miss him terribly."

"So do I. Even though he was irritating, self-indulgent, and useless with money, he was so *passionate*. And alive. Now, let's change the subject before we both end up having another sob-fest. You said you wanted to see William Fielding's ring?"

"Yes."

Zoe reached into her handbag, pulled out a small leather box, and passed it to Joanna, who opened the box and studied the ring inside it.

"Well? Is it the one you saw in the catalog you mentioned on the phone earlier? A lost heirloom from tsarist Russia? A priceless ring stolen directly from the finger of some murdered archbishop during the Reformation?"

"I'm not absolutely sure, but it certainly might be valuable . . . Would you let me borrow it for a few days so I can check if it is the same one? I promise not to let it out of my sight."

"Of course you can. It's not even mine to keep anyway. Poor old William had no living relatives. I did ask at the funeral, but all the people there were either old actor friends or others who knew him from the business. Maybe, if the ring is worth something, he'd like the money to go to the Actors' Benevolent Fund."

"That's a nice idea." Joanna closed the box and stowed it away in her rucksack. "I'll let you know as soon as I find out for sure. Now, tell me all about your prince."

"He's fine." Zoe took a large slug of wine.

"Only 'fine'? Not an apt word for the love of your life, the fairy-tale relationship of the decade, the—"

"I've not seen him in a while. I've been spending some time with Jamie over the Easter holidays. He's still shaken after what happened and he's nervous about going back to school and being ribbed about his mum."

"Poor Jamie. Sorry, Zoe. I've been away for weeks, so I've rather lost touch."

"Well, he got teased at school about my relationship with Art. I hadn't told him about it and while Art and I were away in Spain to-gether, he ran away from school. It was Simon who found him, actu-ally, lying asleep on his great-grandfather's grave." Zoe's face softened. "I'm still amazed Simon knew Jamie well enough to know where to look. He's such a kind man, Joanna. Jamie adores him."

"But you and Art, you're still okay, aren't you?"

"If I'm truthful, I was very angry with him when I left Spain. He just didn't seem to understand how frightened I was, or, to be honest, care that Jamie was missing. Although when he flew back to London, he did the bouquet thing, apologized profusely for his insensitivity, and promised to make sure Jamie was better protected in the future."

"So, everything's fine again now?"

"Supposedly, yes. Art's moving heaven and earth to have his parents and the rest of the family accept me. But"—Zoe twirled a finger around the base of her wineglass—"between you and me, I'm seriously beginning to question my own feelings for him. I'm des-perate to believe that what I've felt for so long is real. Art is all I've wanted for years, and now that I've got him . . . well"—Zoe shook her head—"I'm beginning to find fault with him."

"Personally, I think that's understandable, Zoe. No one could live up to the imaginary prince of your dreams."

"I keep telling myself that, but the truth is, Jo, I don't know how much we have in common. He never finds things that I find funny even vaguely amusing. In fact, to be honest, he rarely laughs. And he's so"—Zoe searched for the word—"rigid. There's no spontaneity at all."

"Surely that's more to do with his position rather than his personality?"

"Perhaps. But you know how with some men you don't feel you're your true self? How you feel you're always acting? That you can never really relax?"

"Totally. I had one like that for five years, although I didn't realize it until he dumped me. Matthew—my ex—just didn't bring out the best in me. We rarely had fun."

"That's just it, Jo. Art and I spend our lives having intense conversations about the future and we never just enjoy the moment. And I still haven't got up the courage to introduce him to Jamie. I just have this awful feeling that my son won't like him much. He's so . . . stiff. Besides all that"—Zoe sighed—"it's the thought of the scrutiny I'll be placed under for the rest of my life. Having the media analyzing my every move, having a camera lens pointed up my nostrils everywhere I turn."

"I'm sure if you love Art enough, he can help you through all that. It's your *feelings* for him that you must get straight in your mind."

"Love conquers all, you mean?"

"Exactly."

"Well, that's the bottom line, I suppose. I feel a bit like Pooh Bear stuck in Rabbit's hole; I'm so far in that I'm wondering how on earth I can get out. God, it's times like this when I really wish my grandfather was still alive. He'd be bound to have some sane, wise words to throw on the subject."

"You really were close, weren't you?"

"Absolutely. I wish you could have met him, Jo. You'd have loved him and he'd have loved you. He adored feisty women."

"Was your grandmother feisty?" Joanna probed.

"I'm not really sure. I do know she came from a wealthy English background. The White family were awfully grand—she was a 'lady.'

Of course she lost her title when she married my grandfather. Quite a catch for an actor, especially one with supposed Irish origins."

Joanna's heart skipped a beat.

Talk to the White Knight's Lady . . .

"Grace's maiden name was White?"

"Yes. She was really pretty . . . petite and dainty."

"Like you."

"Maybe. Perhaps that's why James was so fond of me. Speaking of dead wives, there's something else I wanted to tell you. I've been asked to play one."

"Sorry?" Joanna forced herself to concentrate on what Zoe was saying.

"Paramount is doing a major, multimillion-pound remake of *Blithe Spirit*. They want me for Elvira."

"Blimey, Zoe, are we talking Hollywood here?"

"We sure are, and the part's mine if I want it. They saw a rough cut of *Tess*, called me in for a quick read-through, then came through to my agent yesterday with an offer that borders on the obscene."

"Zoe, that's fantastic! Well done, you! You totally deserve it."

"Come on, Jo." Zoe rolled her eyes. "They probably think their American audiences will flock to see it, with my being the girlfriend of an English prince. I don't wish to be cynical, but I hardly believe the offer would have come through if my face hadn't been plastered all over the US papers with Art next to me."

"Zoe, don't belittle yourself," Joanna urged her. "You're an extremely talented actress. Hollywood would have come calling eventually, with or without Arthur."

"Yes. But I can't do it, can I?"

"Why not?"

"Jo, get real. If I marry Art, the most I'm going to be doing is chomping my way through canapés and shaking endless hands at charity functions, *if* they can't get one of my higher-profile prospective in-laws to do it."

"Times are changing, Zoe, and you could be just what the royal family needs to bring them kicking and screaming into the new millennium. Women have careers these days. End of story."

"Perhaps, but not careers where they may have to take their clothes off, or kiss their leading man."

"I don't recall any nudity in *Blithe Spirit*," Joanna chuckled.

"There isn't, but you get my drift. No," sighed Zoe. "If I go ahead and marry him, I'd have to kiss my career goodbye. I mean, look at Grace Kelly."

"That was in the 1950s, Zoe! Have you discussed it with Art?"

"Er, no, not yet."

"Then I suggest you do. Fast, or someone'll leak it to the press."

"That's exactly my point!" Zoe's blue eyes flashed. "My life's not my own anymore. I get papped walking down the street to buy a pint of milk. Anyway, I have two weeks to decide if I want the part. I'm taking Jamie back to school this Sunday, and then I'm going to go down to Dorset for a couple of days to try to get my head straight."

"Alone?"

"Of course not." Zoe raised an eyebrow. "Those days are long gone. Simon is joining me, not that I mind him being around. He's a great cook actually. And a great listener."

Joanna looked at Zoe's eyes and how the expression in them had suddenly softened.

"You know, I think this comes down to whether you love Art enough to give up everything for him. Whether your life would be meaningless if he wasn't by your side."

"I know. And that's the decision I've got to make. Jo, did you love Marcus?"

"I think I was definitely falling in love with him, yes. The problem was that by the time I managed to trust him, ignore his reputation, and believe he really *did* have feelings for me, it was too late. I just wish we'd had longer together . . . he was a very special man."

"Oh, Jo." Zoe reached a hand across the table. "It's so, so sad. You brought out the best in him."

"He made me laugh, never took things too seriously, except his precious films, of course. I was completely myself with him and I miss him dreadfully," Joanna admitted. "Anyway, I'd better be off. I have some . . . work to do back at the office."

"Okay. And I'm sorry I even thought for one minute it was you that gave me and Art away to your paper."

"Don't worry about it. To be honest, *I* thought about doing it for at *least* one minute!" She smiled as she stood up and kissed Zoe. "You know where I am if you need to talk."

"I do. And you. Can you come to the launch of the memorial fund at the end of the week? I'm speaking in Marcus's place." Zoe handed her an invitation from a pile on the worktop.

"Of course."

"And also, would you come to dinner here next weekend when I'm back from Dorset? I think it's about time Art met some of my friends. Then you can judge for yourself. I could do with a second opinion."

"Okay. Give me a buzz during the week. You take care."

Joanna left the house, and seeing a bus pulling into the stop opposite, she dodged through the traffic and jumped aboard. Finding a seat at the back of the top deck, she sat down and opened her rucksack. Pulling out the photograph she had been studying so hard last night, her fingers shook as she opened the box containing the ring.

There was absolutely no doubt. The ring she held in her palm matched the one that the Duke of York once wore on his little finger.

Joanna stared out of the window as the bus wended its way along Oxford Street. Was this the proof she needed? Was this ring enough to guarantee that what her dear old granny had so innocently pointed out was the truth? That Michael O'Connell had been used as a double for the ailing Duke of York?

And there was something else too . . .

Tucking the ring safely back into its box and into her rucksack, Joanna removed Rose's letter and read it again.

If I am gone, talk to the White Knight's Lady . . .

James had been knighted. Grace, his wife, was not only a "lady" but a "White."

Joanna felt her stomach flip. It seemed Alec had been spot-on.

37

The front doorbell rang and Zoe went to answer it. She smiled as she saw who it was.

"Hello, Simon." Zoe reached up on tiptoe as he came inside and planted a kiss on his cheek. "It's lovely to see you. How have you been?"

"Well. You?"

"Coping, just," she sighed as Simon headed for the stairs with his holdall. "Jamie was sorry to have missed you," she added, following in his wake up the stairs. "I took him back to school yesterday. He was so nervous, poor thing, but I had a good chat with the headmaster and he promised to keep an eye on him." Zoe watched as Simon placed his holdall down on his bed and she picked up a card with a felt-tip picture of two people playing on a computer to hand it to Simon. "It's from Jamie, to welcome you back. He wasn't so keen on the man who replaced you while you were gone—not as fun as you, he said."

Simon smiled as he read the words inside. "That's sweet of him."

"Now, you get settled, then come downstairs and have a drink. I've cooked us supper, seeing as I owe you one."

"Zoe, sorry to be a party pooper, but I've already eaten and I have a heap of work to do tonight. It's very kind of you, but maybe some other time, okay?"

Her face fell. "I've spent all afternoon cooking. I . . ." She fell silent as she saw his closed face. "Oh well. Never mind."

Simon did not reply, but instead busied himself with unpacking his few possessions from his holdall.

"Is it okay if we go down to the house in Dorset tomorrow?" she continued into the silence. "I need a bit of time to think some stuff over. I have to come back to London for the launch of the memorial fund on Thursday, but we could do a day trip, couldn't we?"

"Of course. Whatever you'd prefer."

Zoe got the strongest feeling that her presence was not required. "Well, I'll leave you to it then. Come down for a cup of coffee when you've finished your work."

"Thanks."

Zoe shut Simon's door behind her, feeling deflated. She wandered down the stairs toward the yummy aroma wafting from the kitchen. She poured herself a glass of wine out of the bottle she'd chosen earlier from the vintage collection in the cellar and sat down at the table.

She'd been filled with such manic energy all day, running around the house tidying up, shopping at Berwick Street market to get fresh ingredients for supper, and coming home with armfuls of flowers to let spring inside.

She groaned, as realization hit her properly for the first time. Her actions today had been those of a woman excited by the thought of seeing a man she really liked tonight . . .

Simon did not appear downstairs for a cup of coffee later that night. Zoe left most of the moussaka and Greek salad on the plate in front of her, preferring to drown her sorrows with the excellent bottle of wine.

Art called her at ten, telling her he loved her and missed her, reminding her that she was to face her first public outing with him in a week's time and should do something about a dress—which shouldn't be all that "revealing," as he put it—which only aggravated her tension further. She tersely wished him good night and took herself off to bed.

Lying sleepless, she berated herself for allowing her imagination to run riot about Simon, just as she had done with Art for all those years. She'd thought Simon cared for her, thought she'd felt his warmth during all the time they'd spent together. But tonight he'd been cold, distant . . . made it obvious he was here to do his job and nothing more. Tears of frustration fell down her cheeks as she realized for certain that it was not the love of her life she longed for beside her, but the man sleeping only a few feet from her in his upstairs bedroom.

The journey down to Dorset the following day was conducted in virtual silence. Zoe, hungover and tense, sat in the backseat trying to both concentrate on the film script of *Blithe Spirit* and make a decision.

Having stopped off for supplies at the supermarket in Blandford Forum, they drove to Haycroft House. After Simon had carried in her holdall and the shopping, he asked her curtly if there was anything else she required, then disappeared upstairs to his bedroom.

At seven that evening, as she sat toying with an uninspired pork chop covered in lumpy gravy, Simon wandered into the kitchen.

"Mind if I make myself a coffee?"

"Of course not," she replied. "There's a pork chop and potatoes keeping warm in the Aga if you want them."

"Thanks, Zoe, but there's no reason for you to cook for me. It's not your responsibility, so really don't bother in future."

"Come on, Simon, you've cooked for me. And I was cooking for myself anyway."

"Well . . . thanks. I'll take it upstairs, if that's okay."

Zoe watched him reach inside the range and retrieve the plate. "Have I done something wrong?" she asked him plaintively.

"No."

"Are you sure? Because it feels like you're trying to avoid me."

He didn't meet her eyes. "Not at all. I realize that it's difficult enough having a stranger staying in your house and invading your privacy, without him foisting himself on you when you want some time alone."

"You're hardly a stranger, Simon. I regard you as a friend as much as anything. After what you did for Jamie, well . . . how could I not?"

"All in the line of duty, Zoe." Simon put his coffee and his plate on a tray and headed toward the door. "You know where I am if you need me. Good night." The kitchen door closed behind him.

Zoe moved her untouched meal to one side and laid her head on her arms. "All in the line of duty," she muttered sadly.

———

"Good news. Our 'messenger' is still alive."

"Have you found her?" Simon asked into his mobile, pacing across his bedroom floor.

"No, but we have located where she used to live. She moved several years ago when her husband died. There have been three owners since and the present ones don't have a forwarding address. However, I reckon we'll have tracked her down by tomorrow. Then we might be getting somewhere. I'll want you to fly across to France, Warburton. I'll be in touch as soon as we've pinpointed her whereabouts."

"Right, sir."

"I'll call you in the morning. Good night."

———

"Get your backside over to the South Bank. It's the launch of the James Harrison memorial fund in the foyer of the National."

"I know, Alec. I was going anyway, to support Zoe," Joanna replied tensely.

"We're running the interview you did with Marcus Harrison tomorrow, as a follow-up to his obituary. As you wrote the piece, you can cover the launch while you're there."

"Alec, please . . . I'd really prefer just to go as a friend. Of . . . both of them."

"Come on, Jo."

"Anyway, I thought my interview with Marcus had been canned. Why put it in now?"

"Because, sweetheart, the Harrison family has suddenly become newsworthy again. A shot of Zoe speaking in her dead brother's place at the launch'll look good on the front pages."

"Jesus, Alec! Have you no heart?" Joanna shook her head in despair.

"Sorry, Jo, I know you're grieving." Alec softened his tone. "Surely you wouldn't want anyone who didn't know him to write this up, would you? Steve'll come with you for the piccies. See you later."

———

The foyer of the National Theatre was jam-packed with journalists and photographers, plus the odd television camera. It was a huge turnout for an event that would normally have warranted a handful of barely interested cub reporters.

Joanna grabbed a glass of Buck's Fizz from a passing waiter and took a gulp. After her month in Yorkshire, she was unused to this mass of loud, effusive people. She saw Simon across the foyer. He gave her a small nod of acknowledgment.

"Thank God you're here," a voice breathed in her ear.

She turned, startled. It was Zoe, looking elegant in a turquoise dress.

"I didn't realize this was going to be such a big thing," Joanna said, after giving Zoe a hug.

"Me neither, and I don't think any of them are here in Marcus's or James's memory—but rather hoping that you-know-who will show up." Zoe wrinkled her nose in disgust. "Anyway, *I'm* doing it for my brother and grandfather."

"Course you are, and at least I can write a lovely piece on Marcus and his passion for the memorial fund."

"Thanks, Jo. That would be great. Wait for me and we can grab a drink afterward."

As Zoe spoke to other members of the press, Joanna studied the photographs of Sir James Harrison that had been blown up and placed on boards around the foyer. There he was as Lear, in dramatic pose, hands reaching to the heavens, a heavy gold crown placed on his head.

Art imitating life, or life imitating art? she mused.

Amid the photographs hung a print of Marcus, Sir James, and Zoe standing together, at what must have been a movie premiere. Joanna fought the urge to trace her fingers over Marcus's carefree expression, his gaze aimed confidently at the camera. She turned and saw an attractive woman of similar age to her standing no more than a few feet away from her. As their eyes met, the woman smiled at her, then moved away.

It was two o'clock before the last journalist left Zoe alone. Joanna was sitting quietly in a corner of the empty foyer scribbling notes on the launch taken from Zoe's short and emotional speech, and the press statement she'd been issued with.

"Was I okay? I was holding back the tears all the way through that speech." Zoe sank down beside her on one of the purple seats.

"You were perfect. I reckon you and the memorial fund will get blanket coverage tomorrow."

Zoe rolled her eyes. "All for a good cause at least."

As they left the theater, Joanna noticed the woman she had seen earlier reading a pamphlet on forthcoming productions.

"Who is she?" Joanna asked as they strolled into the warm sunlight of a spring afternoon on the South Bank, the Thames sparkling beneath them.

Zoe turned to look. "No idea. A journalist probably."

"I don't recognize her. And few newspaper journalists I know wear expensive designer suits."

"Just because you live in jeans and sweaters doesn't mean others don't make fashion a priority," Zoe teased her. "Come on, let's go and have a drink."

Linking arms, they walked along the river and stopped at a wine bar. Zoe turned back to Simon, hovering a few yards behind them. "Girl talk, I'm afraid. We won't be long."

"I'll be over there." He pointed at a table as they entered.

"Wow," Joanna murmured as they sat down at a table and ordered two glasses of wine. "Even though it's Simon, being tailed all the time would drive me nuts."

"See what I mean?" Zoe picked up a menu and hid behind it.

Joanna saw that every eye in the café had turned to stare at Zoe. She watched Simon walk to the back of the café and then disappear into the kitchen. "Where's he going?"

"Oh, to check out an escape route just in case. He has a thing for back entrances. I mean . . ."

Both women giggled as two glasses of wine arrived with the attentive waiter.

"Seriously, Jo"—Zoe leaned forward—"I just don't know whether I can do this. Anyway, cheers."

"Cheers," Joanna repeated.

It was past four o'clock by the time Joanna said goodbye to Zoe and took a bus back to the office.

"And what time do you call this?" Alec growled at her as she stepped out of the elevator.

"I got an exclusive with Zoe Harrison, Alec, okay?"

"Attagirl."

As she sat down and turned on her screen, Alec handed her a small package.

"This arrived at reception for you today."

"Oh. Thanks." She took it from him and placed it by her keyboard.

"You going to open it then?" he asked.

"Yes, in a second. I want to get this piece typed up." Joanna turned her attention to the screen.

"Looks like a small incendiary device to me."

"What?!" She saw he was smiling, then gave a resigned sigh and handed it to him. "You open it then."

"Sure?"

"Yes."

Alec tore the flap of the parcel open, and pulled out a small box and a letter.

"Who's it from?" Joanna continued typing. "Does it tick?"

"Not so far. The letter says, '*Dear Joanna, I have been trying to contact you, but I didn't have an address or telephone number. Then yesterday I saw your name under a story in my daily paper. Inside is the locket that your aunt Rose gave me last Christmas. I was having a bit of a spring clean and found it in a drawer. And I was thinking that this belongs to you rather than me, given as you got nothing from her. Could you let me know you received it safely? Pop round for a cuppa sometime. It would be nice to see you. Hope you found your aunt, God rest her soul. Best, Muriel Bateman.*'"

Alec handed Joanna the box. "There you go. Want me to open it?"

"No, I can do it, thanks."

Joanna took the lid off and removed the layer of protective cotton wool, revealing the gold locket with its delicate filigree pattern and thick, heavy rose-gold chain. Joanna took it carefully out of its box and laid the locket on her palm. "It's beautiful."

"Victorian, I'd guess." Alec studied it. "Worth a bomb, especially that chain. So, this belonged to the mysterious Rose."

"Apparently, yes." Joanna fiddled with the clasp that would open the locket.

"If it's anyone, my guess would be that there's a picture of Sir James in there," remarked Alec as Joanna's fingertips finally managed to win the war of attrition.

Alec watched as she stared at whatever was inside. Her eyebrows puckered as her cheeks drained of color.

"Jo, you okay? What is it?"

When she finally raised her head to look at him, her hazel eyes shone in her pale face.

"I . . ." There was a catch in her throat as she tried to steady her voice. "I know, Alec. God help me, I know."

38

"I've lost her, I'm afraid."

Monica Burrows sat clicking her pen as if she had a nervous tic across the desk from Jenkins.

"Where? At what time?"

"I followed her home last night after work and in Kensington yesterday morning. She went inside her office building and, hey, just hasn't reappeared."

"She might have spent the night working on a story."

"Sure, that's what I thought, too, but this morning I went to reception and asked to see her. I was told she wasn't in the building, but off sick."

"Have you tried her apartment?"

"Of course, but it's deserted. I don't know how she got out, Mr. Jenkins, but she sure slipped the net somehow."

"I don't need to tell you that's not good enough, Burrows. Write your report and I'll be down as soon as I've spoken to my colleague."

"Yes, sir. Sorry, Mr. Jenkins."

Monica left the office and Lawrence Jenkins dialed for the top floor. "It's Jenkins. The Haslam girl's gone AWOL again. I put Burrows on her, seeing as you said it was a light surveillance job, and she lost her last night. Yes, sir, I'll be up right away."

Simon walked to the window of his bedroom under the eaves at Haycroft House and stared out at the garden below. Zoe was sitting in the rose arbor, a straw hat on her head, her lovely face tipped up to catch the sun. They'd arrived back from London late last night and Simon had gone straight up to his bedroom. He sighed heavily. The past few days had been bloody awful. Trapped with her twenty-four hours a day, the very nature of his job precluding any kind of escape or respite from the nearness of the woman he now knew he loved; yet she was untouchable. So, he'd done what he thought best to preserve his sanity and cut himself off, refusing all her kindnesses, loathing himself for the confusion and hurt he saw in her eyes.

His mobile vibrated in his pocket and he pulled it out. "Sir?"

"You heard from Haslam?"

"No. Why?"

"She's on the missing list again. I thought you said she was off the scent."

"She was, sir, really. Are you sure she's missing on purpose? Her absence could be perfectly innocent."

"Nothing about this situation is innocent, Warburton. When are you returning to London?"

"I'm driving Miss Harrison back from Dorset this afternoon."

"Contact me as soon as you arrive."

"Yes, sir. Any news on the 'messenger'?"

"The house we'd tracked her down to was deserted. Gone away on a long holiday, the neighbors said. Either it's a coincidence, or she's on the move. We're doing our best to locate her, but even these days, the world is a big place."

"I see," Simon answered, unable to keep the disappointment out of his voice.

"Haslam's onto something, I know she is, Warburton. We'd better bloody well find out what it is."

"Yes, sir."

The phone went dead.

———

Joanna put the menu down and glanced at her watch. The string quartet in the Palm Court tea room began to play the first dance. From the tables around her, elderly ladies and gentlemen, dressed in finery reminiscent of a more graceful age, stood up and took to the floor.

"Would madam like to order?"

"Yes. Afternoon tea for two, please."

"Very good, madam."

Joanna fiddled nervously with the locket round her neck, feeling uncomfortable in the summer dress she had bought with cash that morning in order to be allowed into the Waldorf's famous tea room. She had positioned herself so she had a perfect uninterrupted view of the entrance. It was twenty past three. With every minute that ticked by, her confidence was waning, her heartbeat growing ever faster.

Half an hour later, the Earl Grey tea had grown cool in the shiny silver teapot. The edges of the cucumber-and-cream-cheese sandwiches, untouched on the fine bone-china plate, began to curl. At half past four, nerves and the fact that she'd drunk numerous cups of tea were making a trip to the lavatory an urgent necessity. The tea dance finished in half an hour. She had to hold out until then, just in case.

At five o'clock, after rousing applause for the musicians, the guests began to disperse. Joanna paid the bill, picked up her handbag, and headed for the ladies'. She straightened her hair, which she had rather inexpertly piled on top of her head with combs, and reapplied some lipstick.

Of course, she admitted to herself, it had been a ridiculous long shot. Grace Harrison was probably long dead and buried. And even if she wasn't, the chances of her seeing the advertisement, *or* responding to it, were minuscule.

She was suddenly aware of a face behind her staring into the mirror. A face that, despite its age, still showed traces of a noble lineage. Gray hair immaculately coifed, makeup carefully applied.

"I hear tell the Knight once stayed at the Waldorf?" the woman said.

Joanna turned round slowly, gazed into the faded but intelligent green eyes, and nodded.

"And his Lady in White came with him."

The woman led her up several staircases and down a thickly carpeted corridor, until they reached the door to her suite. Joanna unlocked the door with the key the woman offered her, then ushered her through the door, and closed and locked it behind them. She immediately went to the window, with its view of the busy London street below, full of theatergoers and tourists, and shut the curtains.

"Please, do sit down," the woman said.

"Thank you . . . Er, may I call you Grace?"

"You may, my dear, of course, if it pleases you to do so." The woman gave a short chuckle, then eased herself into one of the comfortable armchairs in the ornate sitting room.

Joanna sat down opposite her. "You *are* Grace Harrison, née White? Wife of Sir James Harrison, who died in France over sixty years ago?"

"No."

"Then who are you?"

The old lady smiled at her. "I think, if we are to be friends, which I'm sure we are, you should just call me Rose."

As soon as Simon arrived with Zoe in London, he ran upstairs to his bedroom, shut the door, and checked his mobile. Seeing he had four missed calls, he dialed the number back.

"I've just spoken to the editor of Haslam's paper," Jenkins snapped. "It seems it's not only her that's missing. It's the news-desk editor as well—one Alec O'Farrell. He told his boss he had something big and needed a couple of days to follow it up. They're onto us, Warburton."

Simon could hear the barely disguised panic in his boss's voice.

"I'm putting every available man on this as of now," Jenkins continued. "If we can find O'Farrell, we'll make sure he tells us where Haslam has gone."

"Surely they won't be able to break the story, sir? You can control that?"

"Warburton, there are two or three subversive editors who would clap their hands in joy to get hold of a story like this, not to mention the foreign papers. For God's sake, it's the story of the bloody century!"

"What would you like me to do, sir?"

"Ask Miss Harrison if she's heard from Haslam. They met at the memorial fund launch and went for a drink together afterward. Haslam returned to her office, before Burrows lost her. Hold fast where you are. I'll be in touch later."

———

Joanna stared at the woman.

"But you can't be Rose. I met Rose at a memorial service for James Harrison. And she wasn't you. Besides, she's dead."

"Rose is a common enough name, especially for the era in which I was born. You are quite correct, my dear. You did meet a Rose. Except the one you met was Grace Rose Harrison, the long-departed wife of Sir James Harrison."

"That little old lady was Grace Harrison? James Harrison's dead wife?" Joanna confirmed in amazement.

"Yes."

"Why did she use her middle instead of her first name?"

"A flimsy attempt at protection. She would insist on going to England after James died. And then, a few weeks later, she wrote to me from London to say she was attending his memorial service. She was terribly sick, you see, had very little time left. She thought it the perfect opportunity to see her son, Charles, for the last time, and view her grandchildren—Marcus and Zoe—for the first. I knew it would stir up trouble, that it was dangerous, but she was determined. She didn't think anyone would be there to recognize her, that they'd all be dead and buried by now. Of course, she was wrong."

"I was sitting next to her in the pew when she saw the man in the wheelchair. Rose . . . I mean, Grace had some form of seizure. She couldn't breathe and I had to help her out of the church."

"I know. She told me all about you in the last letter she wrote to me, and about the clues she had given you. I was expecting to hear from you sooner, although I knew it might take you time to work it all out. Grace couldn't give you too much, you see, put you or me in danger."

"How did you know I was looking for you? I'd written my advertisement especially for Grace."

"Because I knew everything, my dear. Right from the beginning. When I saw your advertisement in the paper, asking for the 'Lady in White' to join her 'Knight' at the Waldorf for tea, I knew it was meant for me."

"But the clue in Grace's letter—'Talk to the White Knight's Lady'—how did that refer to you?"

"Because, my dear, I married a French count. His name was Le Blanc and—"

"'*Blanc*' is French for 'white.' Oh my God! I got it completely wrong."

"No, you didn't. I'm here and all is well," Rose said with a smile.

"Why did Grace choose me to tell?"

"She said you were a clever and kind girl, and that she didn't have much time. She knew it was over, you see, the minute he saw her. That he'd find her and kill her." Rose sighed. "Why she had to stir this up again, I really don't know. She was so terribly bitter . . . I suppose it was an act of revenge."

"I think I know why she was bitter," Joanna said quietly.

Rose regarded her quizzically. "Do you? You must have been doing some very careful investigation since poor Grace died."

"Yes. You could say it's rather taken over my life."

Rose laid her small hands neatly in her lap. "May I ask you exactly what you're going to do with the information you've gathered?"

This was no time for lies. "I'm going to publish it."

"I see." Rose was silent as she digested this. "Of course, it was the reason Grace wrote to you in the first place. It was what she wanted. Retribution, against those who destroyed her life, to blow the establishment sky-high. Myself, well, let us say I still have some loyalty, though goodness knows why."

"Are you saying you won't help me fit the pieces together? I think we're going to be offered an awful lot of money for this story. It would make you rich."

"And what would an old woman like me do with money? Buy a sports car?" Rose chuckled and shook her head. "Besides, I'm rich enough already. My late husband left me excellently provided for. My dear, have you not wondered why so many around me have died? And yet here I am, still alive to tell the tale." She leaned forward. "The thing that has kept me alive is discretion. I've always been able to keep a secret. Of course, I didn't expect to be harboring the best-kept secret of the century, but such is life. What I'm saying is that, for Grace's sake, I can lead you there, but for mine, I can't tell you outright."

"I see."

"However, Grace trusted you, and therefore, so must I, but I absolutely insist on anonymity. If my name, or my visit here, is ever mentioned, then my subsequent death will be on your conscience. Every second I'm here in England with you, we are both in great danger."

"Then why did you come?"

Rose sighed. "Partly because of James, but mostly because of Grace. I may have been part of the establishment by accident of birth, but that does not mean to say I approve of the things they have done, the way other people's lives have been destroyed to keep the silence. I know I must meet my maker in the next few years. I'd like Him to know I did the best I could for those I cared for on earth."

"I understand."

"Why don't you order us both a drink? I would like a nice cup of tea. Then you'd better tell me what you know and we'll take it from there."

Once room service had arrived and been dispatched, it took Joanna almost an hour to tell Rose everything—partly due to discovering her companion was a little deaf, as well as Rose's wanting to clarify every fact Joanna had discovered twice.

"And when the locket arrived at the office and I saw the photograph of the duchess inside, everything fell into place." Joanna sighed, and took a gulp of her white wine, feeling breathless with tension.

Rose nodded sagely. "Of course, it was the locket at your neck that convinced me that you were the young lady who had placed the advertisement. You could only have obtained it from Grace herself."

"As a matter of fact, she gave it to her next-door neighbor, Muriel, as a gift for being so kind."

"Then she must have known they were on their way for her. The locket was mine, you see, a gift from her. Grace always loved it. I gave it to her when she left for London, as a talisman. For some reason, I'd always felt it had protected me. Unfortunately, as we know, it did not work the same magic for her . . ."

———

Later that evening, Simon wandered down to the kitchen. Zoe was at the table, writing a list and drinking a glass of wine.

"Hello," he said.

"Hi." She didn't look up.

"Okay to make myself a coffee?"

"Of course it is, Simon. You know you don't have to ask," she replied irritably.

"Sorry." Simon went to the kettle.

Zoe put her pen down and stared at Simon's back. "I'm sorry too. I'm tense, that's all."

"You have a lot on your plate." He spooned some coffee powder and sugar into a mug. "Heard from Joanna recently?"

"No, not since the memorial fund. Should I have done?"

He shrugged. "No."

"Are you sure you're okay, Simon? I mean, I've not done anything to upset you, have I?"

"No, not at all. I've just been . . . dealing with some problems, that's all."

"Women problems?" She tried to keep her voice light.

"I suppose you could say that, yes."

"Oh." Zoe disconsolately refilled her wineglass. "Love. It makes life so bloody difficult, doesn't it?"

"Yes."

"I mean . . ." She looked straight at him. "What would you do if you were meant to be in love with one person, then found you were actually in love with someone else?"

"May I ask who?" The way she was gazing at him made Simon's heart begin to thump.

"Yes." She blushed and lowered her eyes. "It's—"

Simon's mobile rang in his pocket. "Sorry, Zoe, I'll have to take this upstairs." He raced from the room and shut the door behind him.

Zoe could have wept.

He was back down ten minutes later, his jacket on. "I have to go, I'm afraid. My temporary replacement will be here any second. Monica's a nice girl, American. I'm sure you'll get on."

"Okay." Zoe shrugged. "Bye then."

"Bye." Simon could barely bring himself to look her in the eyes as he left the kitchen.

39

At Rose's request, Joanna had taken a couple of small bottles of whiskey from the mini-fridge, poured them into two glasses, and added ice.

"Thank you, my dear." Rose took a sip. "Far too much excitement for an old lady like me." She settled back more comfortably in her chair, cradling her whiskey glass in her hands. "As you already know, I was working for a time as a lady-in-waiting for the Duchess of York. Our families had known each other for years and so it was natural that I traveled down from Scotland with her when she married the duke. They were very happy, living between their houses in Sandringham and London. Then the duke's health began to deteriorate. He had a bronchial condition, which, given the health problems he'd had as a child, was cause for some concern. The doctors advised complete rest and fresh air for a number of months to help him recover. But there was the problem of what to tell the country. In those days, the royal family were in some ways regarded as immortal, you see."

"So the idea of a double to stand in for him during his absence was put forward?" Joanna confirmed.

"Yes. It used to be quite common among public figures, as I'm sure you know. Coincidentally, a senior adviser at the palace happened to visit the theater one night. And there he saw a young actor who he thought could pass perfectly adequately for the Duke of York at state functions, factory openings, and the like. The young man, one Michael O'Connell, was brought in and given 'duke lessons' for a few weeks, as the duchess and I used to giggle. Once he'd passed the 'test,' the real duke was shipped off to Switzerland to recover forthwith."

"He was the image of him," said Joanna. "I was completely convinced they were one and the same person."

"Yes. Michael O'Connell was already an extremely talented actor. He had always been good at impersonations—it was his 'act' back then. He lost his Irish brogue completely, even perfected the slight stutter." Rose smiled. "And literally, my dear, he *became* the duke. He was duly installed in the royal household and it all worked like a charm."

"How many people knew about this?"

"Only those that absolutely had to. I'm sure some of the servants thought it odd when they heard the 'duke' singing Irish ballads while shaving in the morning, but they were paid to be discreet."

"Was that when you and Michael became friends?"

"Yes. He was such a nice man, so eager to please, and took the whole situation in his stride. Yet I always felt rather sorry for him. I knew he was being used, and once he was no longer needed, he'd be paid off and waved away without so much as a backward glance."

"But it didn't quite happen like that, did it?"

"No," Rose sighed. "The thing was, he had such charisma. He was the duke, with an added dimension. He had a great sense of humor, used to send the duchess into fits just before they were about to attend a function. I was always convinced that he laughed her into bed, if you'll excuse the tasteless expression."

"When did you realize they were lovers?"

"Not for a long time afterward. I thought, just like everyone else who knew her, that the duchess was playing her part like the trouper she was. Then the duke came home a few months later, fit and well, and Michael O'Connell was packed off back to his life. And that would have been the end of it if it hadn't been for the fact that . . ." Rose caught her breath.

"What?"

"The duchess believed that she had fallen head over heels in love with Michael. At the time, I'd left the palace in order to prepare for my wedding to François. I went back to visit her one day and she asked whether I'd be prepared to help her, if I would be a 'messenger' for her so she and Michael could keep in contact. She was quite desperate. What else could I do but agree?"

"So you began to meet with William Fielding outside Swan and Edgar?"

"Was that his name? The young boy from the theater, anyway," Rose clarified.

"He became quite a well-known actor too."

"Not in France," Rose said with a sniff of hauteur. "Of course, at the time I was madly in love with François, so the fact that the duchess was so in love too rather gave us a bond. We were both so young." Rose sighed. "We believed in romance. And because Michael and the duchess had been put together, then torn apart, with no possibility of a future, it made the situation all the more poignant."

"Did they see each other after he left the employ of the royal household?"

"Only once. The duchess was terribly concerned for him, for his safety, especially when her secret, one might say, exploded into public view."

"Someone found out about the affair?"

Rose's eyes twinkled. "Oh yes, my dear. More than one."

"Was that when they sent Michael O'Connell off to Ireland to stay at the coastguard's house?"

"Yes. You see?" Rose gave her an approving smile. "You know most of the story already. The duchess came crying to me one day, saying that he'd written to say he was being sent away back to Ireland. He didn't want to compromise her sensitive position, so he thought it best if he agreed and left the country as they wished him to do. Of course"—she raised her eyebrows—"he was never meant to return."

"What do you mean?"

"Don't you see that it was perfect for them? Michael returning to Ireland, bearing an extraordinary resemblance to the Duke of York. Remember, Partition had just taken place. The Irish loathed the English. All they had to do was put it about locally that there was a member of the British royal family staying in the area and the rest would happen naturally. It was the perfect 'scalp' for the Irish Republican movement at the time."

"You mean the establishment wanted him dead?"

"Of course. Under the circumstances, it was imperative they put him out of the way permanently. But it needed to be done discreetly, presented to the duchess in a way she couldn't question. No one quite knew how she'd react, you see, given her"—Rose checked herself—"state of mind at the time."

"So what happened then?"

"The one who saved Michael from certain death was his Irish lady love—Niamh, I think her name was—whom he'd met when she came to keep house for him there. Apparently, one night, she heard her own—and I might add highly Republican—father plotting and planning to kill Michael. So, between the two of them, Niamh and Michael organized his escape on a cotton boat back to England."

"I know who she was. I met her sister Ciara in Rosscarbery. Niamh Deasy died. In childbirth, along with her baby," Joanna added.

"Oh my." A tear came to Rose's eye. She reached into her sleeve for a hanky and dabbed her eyes. "Another tragic casualty in this twisted web of deceit. Michael always wondered what had happened to her after he left Ireland. He was expecting her to follow him to England, but of course, he couldn't write to her to find out when. Or put in writing where he was. But she never came. Now I know why. He was very fond of her, although I doubt it was love. I never heard him mention a child, mind you."

"Perhaps he didn't know," mused Joanna. "Maybe Niamh never told him."

"And maybe she didn't realize herself until a bump appeared in her stomach." Rose sighed. "It was a much more innocent time back then. None of us girls were really taught in any detail about the facts of life. Especially not Catholic girls."

"Poor Niamh, and her baby. She was so innocent . . . she had no idea of the complex man she had fallen in love with. Please go on," Joanna urged.

"Well, Michael came back to London and managed to contact the duchess. They met at my London house. He told her how the establishment had tried to engineer his death. The duchess was understandably hysterical with anger. Having spent a sleepless night trying to think how she could protect him, she returned to see me. When she told me what she was going to do, I told her that it would put both herself and her family in the most compromising position if it was ever discovered. But she'd have none of it. Michael O'Connell had to be kept from harm, and that was an end to it. After all, no one else was there to protect him. He'd been used and discarded. And the duchess was—out of love, or scruples—wishing to do the right thing."

"What was it the duchess did?"

"She wrote him another letter, which I delivered personally to his lodgings, concealed in the usual way."

"I see." Joanna was doing her best to compute the facts as they were spoken. "And Michael O'Connell used whatever was in this letter to buy himself his safety. A new identity, a substantial house, and a brilliant future?"

"Spot-on, young lady. I doubt if he'd have asked for anything, had they not tried so obviously to get rid of him. He was never a greedy man. But"—Rose sighed—"he thought he'd be safer, the more noticeable he was. Besides, he deserved the success he achieved. He'd pulled off one of the greatest acting roles of the twentieth century."

"Yes, he had. And I suppose that it's much easier to murder a nobody than it is a rich and successful actor. You obviously knew him well, Rose."

"I did, and I feel I did my best for him, he was a good man. Anyway, after that, everything seemed to settle down. The duchess accepted he was gone, that she had done her best to protect him, and she and the real duke resumed their relationship."

"May I say, Rose, that this is what has puzzled me in the past few days?" queried Joanna. "The duke and duchess's marriage was always regarded as one of the biggest success stories of the monarchy."

"And I truly believe it was. There are different types of love, Miss Haslam," said Rose. "Michael and the duchess's relationship was what one might call a brief but passionate affair. Whether it would have endured beyond those few months, we will never know. Certainly, once the duchess knew he was safe, she stood by the duke during all the trials and tribulations that followed. She never mentioned Michael's name again."

"When he later became famous as James Harrison, surely their paths must have crossed?"

"Yes, but thankfully, by then he'd met Grace. By complete coincidence, I'd known her for years. We were presented at court together. She always *was* as mad as a hatter, but James fell for her hook, line, and sinker."

"It was a real love match then?"

"Absolutely. They worshipped each other. Grace needed James to protect her against a world she'd never been very comfortable being a part of."

"What do you mean?"

"As I said, Grace White was emotionally unstable. Always had been. If she hadn't been part of the aristocracy, she'd have been tucked away in a funny farm years before. Her parents were just thankful to get her off their hands. However, with James she seemed to blossom. His love steadied her . . . somewhat erratic personality traits. They had their son, Charles, and all was going well for both of them . . . until the king's abdication."

"Of course. The duke became the king, the duchess the queen. I suppose then that it was even more vital that the secret affair never came out?"

"Oh yes, my dear, it certainly was. Confidence in the royal family was at an all-time low. The old king had done the unthinkable and given up the throne of England to marry an American."

"Which meant his brother—the Duke of York—was left to take over," mused Joanna.

"Quite. Even though I was in France at the time, having married François, I felt the shock waves over there. Neither the duke nor the duchess had ever even considered that one day they would be crowned king and queen of England. Nor, and perhaps more importantly, had those who worked behind the scenes, those who knew exactly what had happened ten years earlier."

"So what did they do?"

"You remember the gentleman in the wheelchair who so frightened Grace at the memorial service?"

"How could I forget?" Joanna remembered the cold eyes that had swept over Grace as they had left the church.

"He was a very senior member of the British Secret Intelligence Service. His remit at the time was the safeguarding of the royal family. He went to the Harrison homestead and demanded James give up the letter the duchess had written to him, for the sake of the future of the monarchy. James, understandably, refused. He knew that without the letter he was unprotected. Unfortunately, Grace was listening behind closed doors and heard the gist of the conversation."

"Oh dear."

"Perhaps it wouldn't have been so bad if she wasn't as neurotic and needy a character, but she felt betrayed by the one human being she had placed all her trust in. Here was absolute evidence of her husband's previous—and obviously powerful—liaison with another woman. A woman whom Grace could never hope to compete with. She accused him of keeping secrets, of still being in love with the duchess. You have to understand, Joanna, we are not talking about a rational woman here. This discovery sent her completely off the rails. She'd always liked a drink and she started making drunken references in public to a secret that *had* to be kept at any cost. In short, she became a liability."

"Oh God. How awful. What did James do?"

"He told me later that Grace went absolutely mad after the meeting had ended. She confronted him and demanded to see the letter. When he refused, she began to tear the house apart in an attempt to find where he had hidden it. So James did the only thing he could, and tore one of the letters the duchess had sent him from its hiding place. Of course, it was not the letter they wanted back, but a decoy."

"But Grace believed it was the letter they wanted?"

"Yes."

"Was it the letter she sent to me?"

"Yes." Rose sighed. "Of course, it said nothing of real importance, but she was not to know that. She refused to give it back to James, telling him she would hold it with her forever as proof of his unfaithfulness. That letter stayed with her for the rest of her life. Where she hid it when she was in the sanatorium remains a mystery, but she certainly showed it to me just before she left for England last November."

"But this affair was years before James had even met Grace!"

"I know, my dear, but as I said, she had gone quite mad. He wrote to me in France, confiding his fears, knowing I was a friend of Grace's and one of the only people who also knew the truth. He knew it wouldn't be long before our friend in the wheelchair and his cronies got wind of the fact Grace knew, of her indiscreet behavior. She had also tried to take her own life by then, blaming the attempted suicide on James for his affair with the duchess. He was desperately aware of what lengths they would go to, that even the letter in his possession could not save a woman who might give the game away. So he decided to act before they did."

"How did he get her out of danger?"

"He brought Grace to France. They stayed with me for a while, then James made arrangements to install her in a comfortable institution near Berne in Switzerland. I'm sure that these days the poor lamb would have been diagnosed with manic depression or some such, but I assure you, at the time, it was the kindest thing to do. She was known there as 'Rose White'—James using her middle name. A few months later, he then made it known to those in England that Grace had taken her own life while on holiday with me, her oldest friend. At the time, most of London was aware of her instability. It made a believable story. We held a funeral in Paris with an empty coffin." Rose gazed into the distance. "Let me tell you, my dear, she might as well have been in there for the difference it made to James. I've never seen a man so distraught. For her own safety, he could never see her again, he knew that."

"Good God." Joanna shook her head sadly. "No wonder he never remarried afterward. His wife was still living."

"Exactly, but no one else knew that. Then, of course, the war came. The Germans invaded France and my husband and I left for our house in Switzerland. We were close by and I'd see Grace at the sanatorium as often as I could. She ranted and raved, asking where James was, begging me constantly to take her home. My husband and I rather hoped that, for her sake, her health would fail, for it was no life, but she always was a tough old boot, physically anyway."

"Did she stay in the Swiss institution for all those years?"

"Yes. And I admit I stopped going to see her as often as I had before, because it all seemed rather pointless. And dreadfully upsetting. Then, one morning, seven years ago, I received a letter. It was from one of the doctors at the institution, asking me to go and see him. When I arrived, the doctor told me that Grace had improved. My guess would be that with all the advances in medical science, they had found a drug to stabilize her condition. She was better to the point where he suggested she was well enough to take a step into the outside world. I admit to being dubious, but I went to see her and talked to her, and there was absolutely no doubt that she was. She was able to talk rationally about the past and what had happened. And she begged me to help her at least enjoy the final years of her life in some semblance of normality." Rose raised her arms in an elegant shrug. "What could I do? My beloved husband had died a few months before. I was rattling around in a huge château all by myself. So I decided I'd buy a smaller house and have Grace come and live with me. We agreed with the doctor that if there was any deterioration, Grace would go straight back to the institution."

"How on earth did she cope with the outside world after all those years of being locked away?" Joanna muttered, more to herself than Rose.

"She was absolutely delighted with everything. Simply the treat of making her own decisions about what she should eat for breakfast, and when, thrilled her. She had her freedom, after all those long years, bless her."

Joanna smiled. "Yes."

"So, we settled down to a life together; two old ladies grateful for each other's company, sharing a past that bound us tightly. And then, a year ago or so, Grace began to develop a cough that wouldn't go away. It took me months to convince her to go to the doctor—you can imagine how frightened she was of going anywhere near them. When she finally did, tests revealed she had cancer of the lung. The doctor wanted to hospitalize her, of course, and operate, but you can imagine Grace's reaction to that idea. She refused point-blank. I think that was the most tragic part of the whole tale. After all those years of incarceration, to finally find some peace, a little happiness, and then be given a year to live." Rose fumbled for her hanky and wiped her eyes. "Sorry, my dear. It's all still very fresh in my mind. I miss her dreadfully."

"Of course you must." Joanna watched Rose compose herself before she continued.

"It was a few months later when Grace saw the article about James dying in the English *Times*. And took it into her head that she wanted to go back to England. I knew it would kill her if she did. She was seriously ill by then."

"Yes, and you should have seen the squalor she was living in. What on earth was in those tea chests?"

The comment brought a smile to Rose's face. "Her life, my dear. She was the most dreadful magpie; she'd steal spoons from restaurants, toilet rolls and soap from powder rooms, and even hide food from our kitchen under the bed in her room. Perhaps it was due to material deprivation in the institution, but she hoarded everything. When she left France, she insisted on having the tea chests shipped over with her. When I kissed her goodbye, I . . . knew I would never see her again. But I understood she felt she had nothing to lose."

Joanna watched Rose sink lower into the chair, as grief overwhelmed her. From the way her energy was visibly ebbing, Joanna knew it was now or never. "Rose, do you know where this letter is?"

"I really can't talk anymore until I have a good meal inside me. We shall send for room service," Rose decreed. "Be a dear and pass the menu, would you?"

Joanna did so, knowing there were so many more questions she wanted to ask. She willed herself to garner patience as Rose searched in her handbag for her glasses, and studied the menu intently. Then she stood up wearily and crossed to the telephone by the bed. "Hello there, could you send up two rare sirloin steaks with béarnaise sauce, and a bottle of Côte-Rôtie. Thank you." She put the receiver down and smiled at Joanna, then clasped her hands together like an excited child. "Oh, I do so love hotel-room food, don't you?"

If it was possible to mentally pace while sedentary in a wheelchair, then the old man was doing just that. He was not behind his desk; in fact, he wheeled himself toward Simon as he opened the door, comforted by the sight of the only other human being who could share his anxiety.

"Any news?"

"No, sir. We'll try again tomorrow."

"Tomorrow may be too late, damn it!" he snapped.

"No sign of Haslam or Alec O'Farrell your end?" Simon asked.

"There's been a lead on O'Farrell's whereabouts, which is being followed up as we speak. My bet is that they're holed up in a hotel somewhere, probably planning the sale of the century for their sordid little story. They're certainly still in the country at least. I've had all my people scouring passenger lists at airports and ferry terminals. Unless of course they've left under forged passports." He sighed.

"What about our 'messenger'? Rose Le Blanc, née Fitzgerald?"

"No flights into England have confirmed a passenger by that name, but of course that means nothing. She could have easily traveled in by car or train. We will find her if she's here, but—Christ!—if Haslam gets to her first . . . I'm positive Madame Le Blanc knows where that damned letter is."

"Sir, until they've actually got it in their hands, they don't have proof."

He did not seem to be listening. "I always knew we were headed for disaster, that the fool would never give it up. The devil even got a knighthood on the strength of his promise!"

"Sir, I think you're going to have to widen the net, let others know what it is they're looking for."

"No! They have to work blind. We just cannot risk further leaks. I'm depending on you, Warburton. I want you to stay exactly where you are. My gut has always told me, if that letter is anywhere, it's in one of Harrison's houses. If Haslam finds out where it is, she'll come to get it. Both houses are under heavy surveillance. If she does, she must be dealt with. Do not under any circumstances let emotion cloud your judgment. Tell me now if you feel you are unable to finish the job."

There was a pause before Simon said, "No, sir, I can handle it."

"If you don't, then someone else will. I hope you realize that."

"Yes, sir."

"Make sure you carry on as normal. I don't want either Haslam or O'Farrell getting wind of the fact we're onto them. Let them lead us to it, understand?"

"I do, sir."

He angled his wheelchair to face the river. After a long silence, he sighed heavily. "You do realize that if this gets out, it will be the end of the British monarchy. Good night, Warburton."

Joanna watched in an agony of suspense as Rose chewed her way through everything on her plate so slowly it was painful. She'd wolfed her own food down, not even registering the taste, but knowing she needed to eat.

Eventually, Rose patted her lips with her napkin. "Now I feel more like it. A cup of coffee while we chat, I think, my dear."

Trying to control her frustration, Joanna rang down for room service once more.

Finally, once the coffee had arrived, Rose began to talk again. "Now, it's well-known that royals have had mistresses and lovers since the monarchy came into being. The fact the Duchess of York fell in love with her husband's double was not what the palace would have cared for, of course, but it could be dealt with. Even the fact that she insisted on writing him dangerous love letters, one of which you yourself saw, could be contained. At the time, it was unlikely she would ever be queen, or her husband king." Rose paused and gave a small smile. "Ironically, history was changed overnight by the most simple, yet potent force in the world."

"Love."

"Yes, my dear. Love."

"And she *did* become queen."

Rose nodded and took a sip of coffee. "So ask yourself, Joanna, what could it be, what could have happened between Michael O'Connell and the Duchess of York that could in turn become the most closely guarded secret of the twentieth century? And what would happen if proof of this secret was in a simple letter? Written by design, by a woman who, in the midst of an infatuation, wished to save him. Then hidden somewhere and used as his only method of protection against the vast armory of those who wanted and needed him dead?"

Joanna searched the air, then looked around the room for an answer. Then, the sound of the traffic on the street outside disappeared as realization hit her.

"Oh my God! Surely not?"

"Yes." It was Rose's turn to pour whiskey for a shocked and shaking Joanna.

"Never let it be said I told you. You guessed." Rose shook her head. "I've only seen that kind of shock on one other face, and that was when I confirmed to Grace what she had heard through the study door at Welbeck Street."

"Surely it would've been best to lie to Grace? To make her believe she'd misheard? My God." Joanna swallowed the whiskey. "I class myself as perfectly sane, but having finally discovered the truth . . . I'm a gibbering wreck."

"I'm sure. And yes, I did consider trying to convince Grace she'd misheard, but of course I knew she wouldn't leave it there. There was a chance she'd go to the horse's mouth, to the man whom she'd heard James talking to that day in the study. A man who later became Sir Henry Scott-Thomas, head of MI5. A man capable of destroying both her and James if he found out she knew. A man who was later paralyzed from the waist down in a riding accident."

"The man in the wheelchair . . ." Joanna felt as though her brain was frozen. She searched through the gray mists, knowing there were further questions she must ask.

"The letter . . . does it confirm what . . . we've just talked about?" Joanna could not bring herself to voice the words.

"I may have delivered it, but it was already well hidden inside the package when I did. However, if it kept James alive all those years, allowed him to amass fame and fortune right beneath the noses of those who wanted him dead, then yes, I rather believe it does."

"And why did they never get to you? After all, you delivered the letters."

"By then, I was engaged to my beloved François and had left the palace. I married and left for the Loire only after the package had been delivered. No one knew I was ever involved." Rose chuckled softly. "The duchess was awfully clever, until she couldn't hide her secret any longer."

Joanna realized with a jolt that she herself had told Simon the name of the "messenger" in Yorkshire only two weeks ago.

"Rose, you really are in terrible danger! I told someone your name recently. Oh God, I'm so very sorry." Joanna stood up. "So many people have died already. They'll stop at nothing . . . you have to leave immediately!"

"I'm safe, at least for now, my dear. After all, I am the only person who knows where that letter is. And besides, my old World War Two forged identity papers proved a godsend after all these years. François paid an expert a lot of money to ensure we were known as Madame et Monsieur Levoy—Swiss citizens. He had some Jewish blood on his maternal side, you see. I've always kept a passport in that name, just in case. François insisted." Rose gave a small smile. "And that is how I came into the country and how I am known here at this hotel."

Joanna looked with admiration at this extraordinary woman, who had kept the secret for so long, and was putting her life at risk out of love for her old friend. "You mentioned earlier you delivered a package, rather than a letter?"

"Correct."

"What was in that package?"

"Dearie me." Rose yawned. "I'm getting terribly sleepy. Well now, the thing was that obviously the letters were highly sensitive, and that one in particular. If they had fallen into the wrong hands, it could have been disastrous. So the duchess thought up a very clever way to disguise them."

"How?"

"You saw the letter that Grace sent you. Even though it was old, there must have been something odd that you noticed about it?"

Joanna racked her brains. "I . . . yes, if I remember, there were tiny holes around the edges."

Rose gave a slight nod of approval. "Now, as we are running out of time, perhaps I must help you with the final piece of the jigsaw. Remember, I am only doing it for poor Grace's sake."

"Of course." Joanna nodded her head wearily.

"The duchess had two passions in life. One of them was the cultivation of the most marvelous roses in her gardens; the other, exquisite embroidery." She eyed Joanna, who looked back at her blankly. "Now, I think it's high time I was in bed. I intend to leave England shortly to stay with some friends in America until all this blows over. I thought it best if I made myself scarce for the next few months, until the dust settles."

"Rose, please! Don't do this to me! Tell me where the letter is!" Joanna entreated her.

"My dear, I *have* just told you. All you must do now is use that quick brain and those pretty eyes of yours."

Joanna knew there was no point in begging further. "Will I see you again?"

"I doubt it, don't you?" Rose's eyes twinkled. "I have every confidence you will find it."

"I don't! Roses, embroidery . . ."

"Yes, my dear. Now, the minute you have it, I should leave England tout de suite. Are you really going to publish and be damned, as they say?"

"That's my intention, yes. So many people have died because of it. And I . . . owe it to someone." Joanna's eyes filled with spontaneous tears.

"Someone you loved?"

"I . . . yes," she sighed, "but he died trying to save my life. And it was all because of the letter."

"Well then, there we go. Love has us make the most reckless—and often misguided—decisions, as you have already seen."

"Yes."

Rose stood up and laid a gentle hand on Joanna's shoulder. "I leave it to your conscience. And to fate. Goodbye, my dear. If you survive to tell the tale, you'll leave your mark on the world one way or another, of that there's no doubt. See yourself out, will you?" Rose walked toward the bedroom and closed the door behind her.

ENDGAME

The stage of the game when few
pieces remain on the board

40

"Hi, Simon," Zoe said as he appeared the following lunchtime in the Welbeck Street kitchen.

"Hi. Everything okay?"

"Yes." Zoe thought Simon looked tense and strained. "Has Miss Burrows gone now that you're back?"

"Yes, she left as I arrived. I somehow didn't fancy sharing quarters with her."

"Right." Zoe dipped her finger into the sauce she was stirring on the hob. "She's an attractive girl."

"Not my type, I'm afraid," Simon answered shortly, as he filled a cup with instant coffee granules and hot water. "What are you cooking?"

"What do you cook for a prince?" she sighed. "I'm going for my dinner party staple of Stroganoff. Not exactly lobster thermidor, but it'll have to do."

"Oh God, of course! Your supper's tonight! I'd forgotten all about it."

"Art called me last night. He said he was expecting you down at Sandringham late afternoon to bring him here. I left a message asking Joanna to arrive at eight, so that should time nicely. Sadly, two of my friends have cried off, so it will just be the three of us."

Simon's heart missed a beat. "Joanna's coming?"

"Yes, but even she hasn't replied to my message. We've become really close and I'd love to know what she thinks of Art."

"Do you think you should call her again to find out?"

"Yes, I suppose I should." She wiped her hands on her apron. "Keep stirring, will you?"

Zoe was back a few minutes later. "Straight to the answering machine," she said as she watched Simon search her cupboards. He turned around with a bottle in his hand. "Add some Tabasco, it gives the sauce that extra zing."

Later that day, Simon's mobile rang. "We've located O'Farrell. Knew he couldn't stay without whiskey too long. He signed a credit-card slip to buy supplies at a liquor store in the Docklands."

"Right."

"We ran a check on his acquaintances and it seems he has a journalist pal in the States who owns an apartment near the liquor store. My men have checked, and there are signs of life in the apartment. They have it under heavy surveillance at the moment. We've got hold of the telephone number of the place. If he's going online to send the story, we can stop it instantly."

"And Haslam?"

"Not a sniff."

"Haslam's been invited here to supper tonight, although I doubt she'll turn up. It would be rather like walking into the lion's den. Do I continue as usual for the present?"

"Yes. If nothing comes to light, collect HRH from Norfolk as planned. Burrows will be in situ while you do so. Just make sure you're both armed, Warburton. I'll be in touch."

Just before five o'clock that afternoon, Simon arrived outside the beautiful secluded house on the Sandringham estate and pulled the car to a halt. He opened the door, got out, and saw the butler was already opening the front door.

"His Royal Highness will be slightly delayed, I'm afraid. As he might be some time, he suggested you might wish to wait inside and take some tea."

"Thank you." Simon followed the butler into the house, along the hall, and into a small but richly furnished sitting room.

"Earl Grey or Darjeeling?"

"I really don't mind."

"Very good, sir."

The butler left the room and Simon paced around it, wondering why on earth, on today of all days, the duke had to be delayed. Every second he was away from Welbeck Street was making him more and more edgy.

The butler brought his tea and left again. Simon drank it, still pacing distractedly up and down the room. Then something on the wall, sitting innocently amid the myriad of other, probably priceless, paintings, caught his eye. It looked similar to something he'd seen recently. He moved closer to study it, and the hand holding his teacup began to shake.

He was pretty sure it was identical, down to the last detail.

Simon pulled out his mobile phone to make a call, but at that moment, the butler arrived.

"His Royal Highness is ready to leave now."

The teacup was firmly removed from his hand and he was ushered out of the room.

———

From her vantage point inside the telephone box on the opposite side of Welbeck Street, Joanna dialed a mobile number. "Steve? It's Jo. Don't ask where I am, but if you want a pretty piccie, get your backside to Zoe Harrison's house. The duke is about to arrive. Yes, really! Oh, and there's a back entrance if you want an interior shot, though you'll have to scale a few walls to get to it. Then wait outside the house until you hear from me. Bye."

She dialed another number, and another, until she had informed every picture desk of every daily London newspaper of the whereabouts of Prince Arthur, the Duke of York's supper engagement that evening. Now all she had to do was wait for them to arrive.

One of the photographers spotted the car as soon as Simon turned into Welbeck Street just before eight o'clock.

"Oh Christ!" the duke swore as he saw the barrage of cameras positioned outside Zoe's house.

"Would you like to move on, Your Royal Highness?"

"Bit late for that now, isn't it? Come on, let's get on with it."

Joanna watched as the door to the Jaguar opened and the photographers clustered round the car. She made a run for it across the road and into the scrum, emerging just in front of the duke and Simon. As she knew it would, the door opened like magic and she stumbled inside.

"Jo! You did manage to make it after all!" Zoe greeted her distractedly, looking anxiously at Art as Simon slammed the door and locked it behind him.

"Yes," she panted, removing her trilby hat and shaking her hair out. "It's a scrum out there."

"What a pretty dress. I've only ever seen you in jeans before."

"That's 'cause it's all I ever wear. Thought I'd make an effort for tonight."

"And those glasses really suit you. You look different."

"Good," said Joanna, and she meant it.

Zoe kissed her on the cheek, then turned her attention to Art, who was standing behind her. "Hello, darling. How are you?" she began, then they all jumped as the letter box was prized open and the end of a telephoto lens appeared through it. Simon immediately snapped it shut and there was a satisfying crack of plastic as the camera withdrew.

"I suggest you all move into the drawing room. Give me a few seconds to draw the curtains," said Simon to the disgruntled prince.

"Thank you, Warburton." Art followed Simon along the hall, as Zoe put a hand on Joanna's arm.

"I'll formally introduce you to Art in a second," Zoe whispered.

"Do I curtsey? What do I call him?" Joanna asked.

Zoe suppressed a laugh. "Just be yourself. And he'll let you know what to call him. Although it might be best if you don't mention you're a journalist," she said with a hint of irony.

"Understood. I'll be a dog handler for the night instead." Joanna nodded as they walked together toward the drawing room. She turned to Zoe at the door. "Excuse me, I must just go to the loo." And dashed up the stairs before Zoe could reply.

"Simon, would you mind bringing the champagne through?" Zoe asked him as he emerged from the drawing room. "It's on ice in the kitchen."

"Of course."

Simon zoomed into the kitchen and collected the champagne, depositing it on the drawing-room table. "I'll leave you to it now." Then he left and mounted the stairs two at a time.

Monica Burrows was waiting on the second floor of the house. "She's here. I've just seen her, in the boy's bedroom. She went into the next-door bathroom when she saw me," she whispered.

"Okay. Leave this to me. Go downstairs and station yourself by the front door."

"Sure. Shout if you need me."

Simon watched Monica run down the stairs. Then he settled himself outside the bathroom door to wait for Joanna.

A scream from Zoe echoed up from the kitchen. "Simon!" she yelled. "In the kitchen!"

"Warburton!" The duke's voice joined hers.

Simon careered down the two flights of stairs, along the hall, and into the kitchen.

"Get him out of here!" Zoe shouted, aghast at the man standing in the back doorway of the kitchen, stoically taking photos even as Simon manhandled him to the ground and removed the camera from his grasp.

"Only doing my job, guv." He grimaced as Simon shoved the camera back into his grasp, minus the film roll, and marched him through the house to the front door. He pulled the man's wallet from his jeans pocket and took a note of the name on his driver's license.

"You'll be charged with breaking and entering. Now get the hell out." Simon opened the front door, threw the photographer out, and slammed the door behind him. A shaken Zoe was being comforted by the duke in the kitchen.

"You okay?" he asked her.

"Yes. It's my own fault. I hadn't locked the back door."

"Hardly. It's Warburton's job to attend to security matters. Bloody shoddy of you."

"My apologies, sir."

"Don't blame Simon, Art. He's always reminding me to lock everything. He's been absolutely wonderful, and I don't know what I'd do without him," Zoe said defensively.

"Hear! Hear! He's a great guy, aren't you, Simon?" Joanna entered the kitchen behind him.

Simon turned and knew then, in that instant, that she'd found it.

"Well, I'd rather like to settle down and get on with the evening," the duke remarked irritably. "We'll call you if we need you, Warburton, okay?"

"Yes, sir." Simon left the kitchen and made his way upstairs to Jamie's bedroom. It was as he'd expected. It had vanished. Walking into the bathroom, he saw the empty frame in the wastepaper basket. The exquisitely embroidered nursery rhyme, which had lain inside the glass for all these years, innocently holding its secret, was gone.

"We all fall down," muttered Simon under his breath as he left the bathroom and went up the stairs to his bedroom. Hastily digging in his pocket for his mobile, he dialed a number.

"She's here, sir, and she has it."

"Where is she?"

"Downstairs, enjoying a pleasant dinner party with the third in line to the throne. We can't touch her and she knows it."

"We've made sure O'Farrell won't help her. We found the story on his computer. All he was waiting for was the letter. And we have Welbeck Street surrounded. She can't escape this time."

"No, but at present, with HRH in the house, there's very little we can do."

"Then we must remove him immediately."

"Yes, sir. And, if you'll excuse me, I have an idea."

"Fire away."

Simon told him.

———

"Tonight has only proved to me what I already know. Zoe, you can't continue to stay here. I'm moving you into the palace immediately, where at least you'll be safe." Art put together his knife and fork. "That was delicious, by the way. Now, do excuse me, ladies. I must use the facilities."

Joanna and Zoe watched him leave the dining room.

"So, what do you think?" Zoe asked.

"Of what?"

"Art, of course! You're awfully jumpy tonight, Jo. You hardly said a word over dinner. Are you okay?"

"Yes, sorry, just tired, that's all. I think your prince is . . . very nice."

"Really? You don't sound convinced," Zoe said with a frown.

"Well, he's a bit . . . royal and everything, but that's not his fault," Joanna said distractedly.

"He is, isn't he?" She laughed uncertainly. "I . . . I'm really just not sure anymore," she whispered.

"Why?"

"Oh, I don't know."

"Is there someone else?" Joanna decided to give her hunch a whirl. She had already seen the way Zoe had looked at Simon tonight.

"Yes . . . there might be, but I'm not sure he's very keen on me."

"Well, I don't know who'll be more disappointed if you end it: Art or your gallant protector," Joanna said lightly.

"What do you mean?"

Joanna glanced at her watch nervously. "I . . . er, nothing. Simon is very fond of you."

"Really?" There was a light in Zoe's eyes.

"Yes, and I think you should follow your heart. I only wish now I'd had more time with Marcus. Don't waste any of yours," Joanna whispered in her ear as Art reappeared. "Right, my turn to pop to the bathroom. I'll be back in a second."

Joanna's eyes filled with unprompted tears as she stood up, gave Zoe a last glance, then disappeared from the room.

Monica signaled to Simon, who was stationed behind the dining room door, as Joanna passed her in the hall and went up the stairs. He nodded and picked up his mobile.

"Now, sir."

Locked in the bathroom, Joanna feverishly dialed Steve's number.

"It's me. I'll be out in two minutes. Get the bike ready, okay? And just don't hang around to ask questions."

She'd just unlocked the bathroom door when she heard the sirens wailing and a voice booming out of a megaphone.

"This is the police. We have a bomb alert in Welbeck Street. Would all residents leave their homes immediately. I repeat, would all resi—"

Joanna banged her knuckles against the wall in despair. "Shit! Shit! Shit!"

———

Simon appeared in the dining room. "We need to leave now, Your Royal Highness, Miss Harrison, please."

"What is it? What's happened?" Zoe asked as she stood up.

"What's going on out there?" asked the duke irritably.

"Bomb alert, sir. I'm afraid we have to evacuate the building. If you'd like to follow me, there's a car already waiting outside."

"Where's Joanna?" asked Zoe, as she walked with Art behind Simon.

"She's up here, in the bathroom. I'll see her out," called Monica Burrows from the top of the stairs.

"We should wait for her," said Zoe.

Upstairs, Joanna felt cool hard steel press into her back.

"Tell them to leave," the woman whispered.

"I'll see you outside, Zoe, okay?" Joanna called out shakily.

"Okay!" she heard Zoe shout, then the front door slammed and the house fell silent.

"Don't move. I'm under orders to shoot to kill." Monica steered her into Jamie's bedroom, holding the gun to her lower spine. Simon joined them a few minutes later.

"Let her go, Monica, I've got her covered." Simon raised his arm and Joanna saw his gun. The muzzle poking into her back was removed and Joanna sank down onto the bed. She looked at the woman and recognized her from the launch of the memorial fund.

"Joanna."

She stared at him. "What?"

"Why couldn't you leave it alone when you had the chance?"

"Why did you lie to me?! All that bullshit up in Yorkshire! I . . . you let me believe I was right."

"Because I was trying to save your life."

"You're too late, anyway," Joanna said, with a bravado she didn't feel. "Alec knows it all. By now, he's probably sent the story down the line. And if anything happens to me, he'll know why."

"Alec's dead, Joanna. They found him at his mate's apartment in the Docklands and stopped him in time. The game's up, I'm afraid."

A horrified gasp escaped her. "You bastard! But . . . I have the letter and you don't," she added defiantly.

"Search her, Burrows."

"Get off me!" As Joanna tried to struggle free from the woman's grasp, the sound of a bullet rang out from Simon's gun. Joanna and Burrows turned and saw the bullet had shot into the wall and embedded itself in the plaster. Raw fear appeared on Joanna's face as she saw Simon's cold, hard eyes. And the gun in his hand pointed straight at her.

"Rather than putting you through the indignity of a body search, Jo, why don't you just give us what we want? Then no one will get hurt."

Joanna nodded brokenly, not trusting herself to speak. She delved into the pocket of her dress, withdrawing a small square of material. She offered it to Simon. "There. You've finally got what you wanted. How many have you had to kill to retrieve it, Simon?"

Simon ignored her, indicating to Burrows that she should take over covering Joanna with her weapon, and concentrated instead on the square of material in his hand.

Ring a Ring o' Roses . . .

The words—and their subject matter—were exquisitely embroidered onto the material. Simon turned it over, and despite her gnawing fear, Joanna was mesmerized by the fact that, after all these years, the truth would finally be revealed. She watched as Simon carefully removed the backing, and there, tacked onto the back of the embroidery itself, was a piece of thick cream vellum paper, identical to that of the other letter Grace had sent her.

Simon took out a penknife and cut the neat tacking stitches. The paper finally came loose. He read it and nodded to Monica. "It's the one."

Carefully folding the letter into his inner jacket pocket, he aimed his gun at her once more. "So, what are we to do with you? Strikes me you know a bit too much."

She couldn't look up any longer into the eyes that had become cold and flinty. "Surely you can't kill me in cold blood, Simon? Jesus, we've known each other for years, been best friends for most of our lives. I . . . Give me a chance to run away. I'll . . . I'll disappear. You'll never see me again."

Monica Burrows watched Simon waver. "I'll do it," she said.

"No! This is my job." Simon took a step forward as Joanna backed away, her heart racing, her head spinning.

"Simon, for God's sake!" she screamed as she cowered in the corner of the room. He leaned over her until his face was close to hers, the gun pointed at her chest.

"Simon, please!" she cried.

He shook his head. "Remember, Joanna. This is *my* game. We play by *my* rules."

She stared at him, her voice husky with dread. "I surrender."

"Bang, bang! You're dead!"

She barely had time to scream as he fired two shots at point-blank range, before she slumped to the floor.

Simon knelt down and took her pulse, then listened for a heartbeat. "She's dead. Call in, tell them mission accomplished in all respects. I'll clean up and then get her out to the car."

Burrows studied Joanna's prone body from where she stood. "You knew her from way back?"

"Yes."

"Jeez," she breathed, "that sure took some guts." She moved nearer to the body and bent down, about to check Joanna's pulse.

He turned to look at her. "You know the rules of service, Burrows. No room for sentiment. I'll make double sure." Then he fired again.

Fifteen minutes later, Welbeck Street was deserted as the front door opened. The surveillance team across the road monitored Warburton and Burrows as they supported the figure between them, heading to a car that was parked a few feet along the road.

"They're en route now," one of them said into his walkie-talkie.

Ten minutes later, with a backup car tailing them some distance behind, they parked in a street on the edge of a gated industrial estate. Transferring the body from their car to one parked a few feet away, they climbed back into another and drove off at top speed. Twenty minutes later, the sound of a huge explosion shattered the peace of the surrounding streets.

41

Simon reached into his pocket and pulled out the letter. He handed it across the desk.

"There you are, sir. Safe and sound at last."

Sir Henry Scott-Thomas read it through without a hint of emotion. "Thank you, Warburton. And her body was placed successfully?"

"Yes."

Sir Henry studied Warburton. "You look exhausted, man."

"I admit it was an extremely unpleasant thing I had to do, sir. She was my childhood friend."

"And I assure you that it won't be forgotten. That kind of loyalty is rare, let me tell you. I'll be recommending you for immediate promotion. There'll also be an excellent bonus in your bank account at the end of the month for all your hard work."

"I think I need to go home and get some sleep." Simon's stomach was churning. "Tomorrow will be another difficult day when they discover exactly who was killed in the bomb blast."

Sir Henry nodded. "After the funeral, I suggest you take a short sabbatical; fly away somewhere hot and sunny."

"I was thinking of doing just that, sir."

"Just two other questions before you go: how did Burrows cope?"

"She was pretty shaken up afterward. I got the feeling she'd never seen anyone killed at close range before."

"This kind of thing does tend to sort out the men from the boys, so to speak. Did she see the contents of the letter?"

"No, sir, she didn't. I can assure you she had no idea what the hell was going on," Simon replied.

"Good chap. You've done a fine job, Warburton, a fine job. Now, good night."

"Good night, sir." Simon stood up and walked toward the door. Then he paused and turned back.

"Just one more thing, sir."

"Yes?"

"Perhaps I'm being sentimental, but do you by any chance happen to know where Grace's remains are? I rather thought that after all this, it might be the right thing to do to reunite her with the husband she loved."

There was a pause before the old man answered. "Quite. I will see to it. Good night, Warburton."

Simon just managed to hold it together until he reached the men's toilets further along the corridor. There, he vomited copiously, then sank to the floor, wiping his mouth on his sleeve, empathizing completely with what had driven Ian Simpson over the edge.

He'd never forget the fear in her eyes, the look of betrayal as he'd pulled the trigger. Simon put his head in his hands and sobbed.

On the drive down to Dorset at dawn the following morning, Sir Henry Scott-Thomas studied the short article on the third page of the *Times* newspaper.

JOURNALISTS KILLED IN BOMB BLAST

A car bomb exploded near an industrial estate in Bermondsey last night, killing both the driver, a twenty-seven-year-old journalist, and her editor. The explosion came after an evening of hoax calls, which resulted in part of the West End being closed to traffic for two hours due to bomb alerts. The victims are believed to have been Joanna Haslam, who worked for the *Morning Mail*, and Alec O'Farrell, the editor of the news desk at the same publication. Police suspect they may have been close to uncovering an IRA plot. After the bomb attack at Canary Wharf in February, police have been on high alert . . .

He sifted through the other articles in the newspaper, until his eyes fell on a short piece at the bottom of page fourteen.

RAVENS RETURN TO TOWER

It was announced this morning by the beefeaters at the Tower of London that the world-famous ravens have returned home. The ravens, who have by tradition guarded the Tower for nine hundred years, mysteriously vanished six months ago. A nationwide hunt ensued, but to no avail. Although during the Second World War the disturbances caused by the Luftwaffe bombing raids reduced their number to one bird only, at no time has the Tower been without a raven to guard it. Protected by the royal decree of King Charles II, legend has it that should these birds ever leave the Tower for good, the monarchy will fall.

It was with considerable relief that the raven keeper found Cedric, Gwylum, Hardey, and the rest of the ravens back at their lodgings near Tower Green late last night. After they'd had a good meal, the keeper pronounced them in excellent physical condition, but was at a loss to explain their temporary disappearance.

———

"We are here, sir."

"Thank you."

The driver made the necessary maneuvers to remove Sir Henry and his wheelchair from the car.

"Where to, sir?"

Sir Henry pointed in the direction of the spot.

"You can leave me here and collect me in ten minutes."

"Very good, sir."

Once the driver had gone, Sir Henry studied the grave in front of him.

"So, Michael, we meet once again."

It took all of his energy to twist the top off the canister he clutched in his hand.

"Rest in peace," he muttered, as he threw the contents of the canister onto the grave. The particles seemed to dance in the glow of the early morning sun, many of them settling on the rosebush that grew atop the grave.

Sir Henry saw his gnarled hands were shaking and he was aware of a steady and increasing pain across his chest.

No matter. At long last, it was over.

42

Zoe watched the coffin as it made its way into the ground, trying to suppress her sobs. She looked at the drawn, pale faces of Joanna's parents, standing opposite her by the head of the grave, and at Simon, whose face was a mask of misery.

When it was over, the crowd began to disperse, some heading for the tea provided at the Haslams' farmhouse, others straight back to London and their newspapers. Zoe walked back slowly toward the church gate, thinking what a peaceful, beautiful spot this was, tucked away on the edge of the small moorland village.

"Hello, Zoe. How are you?" Simon caught up with her.

"Middling to absolutely ghastly," she sighed. "I just can't accept it. I remember her hugging me in the kitchen, and now . . . oh God, she's not here anymore. And James isn't, and Marcus . . . I'm starting to wonder if our family is cursed."

"You can berate yourself forever and a day, but nothing's going to bring Joanna back, or your grandfather or Marcus."

"I know the papers said she was onto a terrorist plot with her editor. She never mentioned a word to me."

"Well, you can't be surprised by that."

"No. So." Zoe swallowed, conflicting emotions rendering her mouth dry. "How are you?"

"Pretty low too, to be honest. I keep going over and over that night in my mind, wishing I'd waited for her to come with us, as you suggested." Simon stopped by the gate and looked back at the grave, the bright Yorkshire sun shining on the fresh earth that covered it. "I've asked for a sabbatical, I want to take some time to think things through."

"Where will you go?"

"I don't know. Maybe do a bit of traveling." He smiled at her wanly. "I don't feel there's anything to keep me here in England."

"When are you going?"

"In the next couple of days."

"I'll miss you." The words were out of her mouth before she could stop them.

"I'll miss you too." He cleared his throat. "How's the prince and living at the palace?"

"Okay," she said. "I suppose it was sensible to move me in there after what happened. To be honest, I haven't really settled, but it's early days yet. I have my first official public engagement with him tomorrow. A film premiere, of all things." She smiled.

"Ain't life ironic." Simon shrugged.

"It sure is."

"Are you coming back to Joanna's parents' place for some tea?" he asked her. "I can introduce you to my mum and dad. They're very impressed that I know you."

"I'm afraid I can't. I promised Art I'd get straight back. My new driver awaits." She indicated the Jaguar in the small car park. "Well then. I suppose this is goodbye. Thank you so much for everything." She reached up and kissed him on the cheek.

He squeezed her hand tightly. "Thanks. Goodbye, Zoe. It's been an absolute pleasure looking after you."

She walked swiftly away from him, not wanting him to see her tears. She heard him mumble something under his breath, so she stopped and turned back, her expression hopeful. "Did you say something, Simon?"

"No. Just . . . good luck."

"Okay. Thanks." Zoe smiled up at him sadly. "Bye."

He watched as she got into the Jaguar. "My darling," he added as the car drove away and out of sight.

———

The following afternoon, Simon walked along the heavily carpeted top corridor of Thames House toward the elderly receptionist.

"Hello, I have an appointment with Sir Henry at three," he said, but she did not respond. Instead her eyes filled with tears.

"Oh, Mr. Warburton!"

"What?"

"It's Sir Henry. He died last night at home. A fatal heart attack, apparently. Nothing anybody could do." The woman's face disappeared into her sodden lace handkerchief.

"I see. How . . . tragic." Simon only just managed to stop the word "ironic" from falling from his lips. "It's unfortunate I wasn't told."

"No one has been. They're announcing it on the six o'clock news tonight. But," she sniffed, "we've all been told to continue as normal. Mr. Jenkins is waiting for you in Sir Henry's office. Do go through."

"Thank you." He walked to the heavy oak-paneled door and knocked.

"Warburton! Do come in, old chap."

"Hello, sir." Simon wasn't surprised to see Jenkins grinning at him like a schoolboy from behind the huge desk. "Fancy meeting you here."

"Want a drink? Been a bit of a roller-coaster day, as you can imagine. Sorry to see the old boy gone, but I have to admit we're all a little relieved downstairs. Sir Henry would hang in here. We all indulged him, of course, but I've been effectively doing his job for years. Not that I'd want that to go out of this office, of course. There we go." Jenkins handed him a tumbler of brandy. "Your health."

"To your new position?" Simon raised an eyebrow questioningly as they clinked glasses.

Jenkins tapped his nose. "You'll have to wait for the official announcement."

"Congratulations." Simon looked at his watch. "Sorry to hurry you, sir, but I'm leaving tonight for my sabbatical and I still haven't been home to pack yet. Why did you want to see me?"

"Let's sit down." Jenkins indicated the leather chairs in a corner of the room. "The thing is, there's no doubt you fully deserve your holiday, after that, er, little upset. But it just so happens we might have a job for you while you're abroad. And I don't wish to alert anyone else to the situation, given its delicacy."

"Sir, I—"

"Monica Burrows has gone AWOL. We know she flew back to the States the day after the Welbeck Street affair, because passport control in Washington have a record of her entry. But so far, she has not turned up at her office."

"Surely, sir, if she's returned to the States, then she's no longer our responsibility? We can't be accountable for the fact she's decided to go home."

"True, but are you absolutely sure she had no idea what it was all about?"

"I'm certain," Simon said firmly.

"Even so, under the circumstances, I'm uncomfortable about information of such a sensitive nature escaping across the Atlantic. The last thing we need after all this is loose ends."

"I can understand that, but rest assured there are none."

"Besides that, the CIA want to know what happened to Monica. As a gesture of détente, I promised to send you over to see them. And given you're heading stateside anyway, I can't see it's an issue."

"How did you know? I only booked the flight to New York this morning!"

"I won't even grace that statement with a response." Jenkins raised an eyebrow. "Now, given the flight to Washington is a short hop from NYC, for the sake of both the CIA—with whom I hope to maintain a much closer relationship than my predecessor—and for the unfortunate situation that you so expertly handled for us this end, I have to send someone. On all levels, it's best if it's you. They'll want a full debrief of what happened that night, Burrows's state of mind, et cetera. The good news is, it would mean your entire sabbatical would be all expenses paid—first class all the way. We've already upgraded your current ticket and it's two or three days at most, placating them."

"Right." Simon swallowed hard. "To be honest, sir, I just wanted some time out. Off duty," he added firmly.

"And you will have it. However, once an agent, always an agent. You know the rules of the game, Warburton."

"Yes, sir."

"Good. Sign for a company credit card on your way out. Don't go too mad."

"I'll do my best not to, sir." Simon put his glass on the table and stood up.

"And when you return, there'll be a nice promotion waiting for you." Jenkins stood, too, and shook his hand. "Goodbye, Warburton. Keep in touch."

Jenkins watched Warburton leave the room. He was a talented agent, and both Sir Henry and he had him earmarked for great things. Given the Haslam saga, the chap had certainly shown his mettle. Perhaps a luxury sabbatical would ease the pain. He treated himself to a top-up from Sir Henry's decanter and surveyed his new domain with pleasure.

———

Zoe looked at her reflection in the mirror. She tugged at her hair, piled tightly into a French plait by the hairdresser who had come to her rooms at the palace. "*Too* tight," she muttered irritably as she attempted to loosen and soften the style. Her makeup was too heavy as well, so she scrubbed it all off and started again. At least her dress—a sea of Givenchy midnight-blue chiffon—was stunning, even if it was not what she would have chosen herself.

"I feel like a doll, being all dressed up," she whispered miserably to her reflection.

And to cap it all, Art had called her an hour ago to say he was running late at another function. This meant they'd have to rendezvous inside the cinema. Which in turn meant that when she stepped out of the car, she'd have to face the press all alone. And even worse, Jamie had called her, sounding downright miserable. He just wasn't settling back down at school, finding the jibes of the boys too hard to take.

And besides all that, she had twenty-four hours before she had to say no to Hollywood, and she still hadn't told Art . . .

"James, Joanna, and Marcus are dead and Simon's gone!" she shouted, then sank to the floor in despair, thinking back to yesterday and seeing Simon . . .

I'll miss you too, he'd said.

"Oh God! I bloody love him!" she moaned, knowing she was wallowing in self-pity, when no one in the world would feel anything but envy for her. Yet she currently felt like the loneliest person on Earth . . .

Her mobile rang. Standing up, she saw it was Jamie and grabbed it.

"Hi, darling," she said as brightly as she could. "How are you?"

"Oh, okay. Just wondered what we were doing for half-term next week?"

"I . . . well, what would you like to do?"

"Dunno. Just get away from school. And England."

"Okay, darling. Then yes, let's book something."

"Can you do that? Now that you're living at the palace?"

"I . . ." It was a good point. "I'll find out."

"Okay. At least Simon can come and collect us, can't he?"

"Jamie, Simon's not here anymore."

"Oh." Zoe heard the catch in her son's voice. "I'll miss him."

"Yes. So will I. Listen, I'll talk to Art and see what we can do."

"Okay," Jamie repeated, sounding as miserable as she felt. "Love you, Mumma."

"I love you too. See you next Friday."

"Yeah. Bye."

Zoe ended the call and walked to the windows, which overlooked the glorious palace gardens. And longed to open the door, run down God-knew-how-many flights of stairs and along countless corridors covered in priceless rugs, and escape into them. In the past ten days, she'd nearly gone mad with claustrophobia—which sounded ridiculous as the palace was enormous. It had felt like the day when she had been trapped at the Welbeck Street house. Except then, she'd been with Simon, who had made it okay.

How she longed to be beyond those high walls, to be allowed to walk out of her front door and along the road to the shop, alone, to buy a pint of milk. In here, her every wish was the staff's command—anything she wanted was hers. Except for the freedom to come and go as she chose.

"I can't do this," she whispered to herself, and then felt shocked by voicing her feelings for the first time. "I'll go mad. Oh God, I'll go mad . . ."

Zoe left the window, then paced up and down the enormous bedroom, trying to think what to do.

Did she love Art enough to sacrifice everything else that she was? Let alone the happiness of her child? What life would it be for him? She was aware after ten days at the palace that the "family" view was that he should be kept well in the background. She'd tried to ask Art what that meant in reality.

"He's got another eight years at boarding school anyway, darling. And we can sort out the holidays as we go."

"This is your son," Zoe had hissed.

There was a knock at her door.

"Coming," she shouted through it. Stuffing her mobile into the tiny bag that the stylist had chosen to match her dress, Zoe took a deep breath and walked to the door.

———

Simon barely made it to the gate on time.

"Can you board now, Mr. Warburton? Your flight is already closing."

"Of course." Simon was handing over his boarding pass and passport when he heard his mobile ring.

He looked at the number and saw it was Zoe. He answered immediately. He couldn't help it.

"Zoe, how are you?"

"Rubbish," he heard her sob. "I've run away."

"Run away from where?"

"The palace."

"Why? How . . . ? Where are you?"

"Hiding in a toilet in a café in Soho."

"You're doing what?!" Simon could hardly hear her.

"I was on my way to a premiere and told the driver I needed the toilet urgently before I arrived. I can't do this. I just . . . *can't*. Simon, what do I do?"

He ignored the anxious signals of the staff at the boarding gate as he heard her sobs down the line.

"I really don't know, Zoe. What do you want to do?"

"I want to . . ."

There was a pause on the line, and the woman on the gate mimed slitting her throat as she indicated the door that led to the plane.

"Yes?" he said.

"Oh, Simon, I want to be with you!"

"I . . ." He gulped. "Are you sure?"

"Yes! Why else would I be standing here in a smelly toilet in a dress worth thousands? I . . . love you!"

The woman on the gate shook her head, shrugged, and closed the door. Simon smiled at her.

"So," he continued, "where do you need rescuing from this time?"

She told him.

"Okay," he said, as he retraced his footsteps through the corridors that led to landside. "Try to find a back entrance—it's normally through the kitchens—and let me know."

"I know, and I will. Thank you, Simon." Zoe grinned into the receiver.

"I should be with you in under an hour. Oh, and by the way . . ."

"Yes?"

"I love you too."

PAWN TO QUEEN

Promotion of a pawn that reaches
its eighth rank to become the most
powerful piece on the board: the queen

43

La Paz, Mexico, June 1996

Simon walked into the Cabana Café, its exotic name belying its scruffiness. The streets he had driven through in the taxi had bypassed the scenic boardwalk and the tourist areas and had stopped in a seedier part of the otherwise beautiful town, graffiti sprayed on the wall opposite, a group of young men lolling against it looking for action. But the beach in front of him was stunning, the ocean an aquamarine glimmer behind a stretch of white sand, dotted with a few tourists tanning in the bright sunshine.

He ordered a double espresso from the Mexican sweating behind the bar, then took himself off to a table by the open window.

He glanced around but the only female in the place was a tall blonde with the lithe-limbed, golden-brown body of a Californian. He watched as she slipped off her stool at the bar.

"Anyone sitting with you?" she asked in an American accent as she strolled across to him.

"No, but I'm waiting for someone."

She sat down, and in a broad Yorkshire accent said, "Yes, Simon, you dozy git. You're waiting for me!"

Simon was stunned by her transformation. He, who had known her since she was a toddler, would not have recognized her in a million years. The only things left of her past self were her hazel eyes.

They left the café soon after, then walked down to the beach and sat on the sand. She wanted to know everything—as she always had done—in minute detail.

"Was my funeral good?"

"Extremely moving, yes. Everyone was in floods of tears. Including me."

"I'm glad to know they cared," she joked. "To be honest, I have to laugh, or else I'd cry."

"They did care, promise."

"How were my mum and dad?"

"Honestly?"

"Of course."

"Distraught."

"Oh God, Simon, I . . ." Her voice cracked and she kicked off her sandals and ground her toes into the sand. "I wish . . ." She shook her head. "I wish I could tell them."

"Joanna, it was the only way."

"I know."

The two of them sat in silence and stared out at the sea.

"How are you . . . surviving?" he asked.

"Oh, I'm managing, just, though it's pretty hard being a nameless person. I did as you asked and ditched Monica Burrows's passport and credit cards the minute I arrived in Washington, then made my way down to California and paid that contact you gave me a shedload of money to drive me across the border. I've been working in a bar near here for the last couple of weeks, but I'm fast running out of money."

"Well, at least it got you out of the UK alive."

"Yes, though part of me has begun to wonder if I'd be better off dead. Christ, this is hard, Simon. I'm trying not to give up, but . . ."

"Come here." Simon pulled her into his arms and she sobbed out all the anguish she felt. He stroked her hair gently, knowing he'd give anything for it not to have turned out the way it had.

"Sorry, I . . ." Joanna sat up and wiped her eyes roughly with her knuckles. "It's seeing you that's done it. I'll be okay now, promise."

"God, don't apologize, Jo. You've been incredible, really. I have something for you." Simon dug in his pocket and produced an envelope. "As promised."

"Thanks." Joanna took it and pulled out an American birth certificate, a United States passport, and a card with a number on it. "Margaret Jane Cunningham," Joanna read. "Born, Michigan 1967 . . . Hey, Simon! You've made me a year older! Charmed, I'm sure."

"Sorry. It was the closest I could come on an 'off the shelf' identity-kit basis. You have a social security number there, so that should sort out your work problems."

"Are you positive it's all kosher?"

"Joanna, trust me, it's kosher, but you'll have to add a photo. I left the plastic open so you could. I'm glad I did, as you now resemble something out of *Baywatch*. I rather fancy you like that."

"Well, it remains to be seen if blondes have more fun," Joanna snorted. "Speaking of blondes, how's Zoe?"

"Happily ensconced with Jamie in a very comfortable villa in Bel Air. Courtesy of Paramount."

"What?! She left Art?"

"Yes. Didn't you read about it?"

"God, no, I've been too terrified to even pick up a newspaper in the past few weeks. I kept thinking I'd see my picture on the front and a headline above it saying 'Wanted!'" Joanna gave a short laugh. "I knew Zoe was wavering about Art, though. Was it the offer of the film that finally made her decide?"

"That and, well, something else actually."

Joanna watched as the familiar hectic blush rose up Simon's neck. "You mean . . . ?"

He smiled. "Yes. And we're outrageously happy together."

"I'm absolutely thrilled for you both. Can your old pal Margaret Cunningham come to the wedding?" Joanna asked him. "Please? No one would recognize me—even *you* didn't—"

"Jo, you know the answer to that. Besides, it wouldn't be fair on

Zoe or Jamie. We've both learned what a burden keeping a secret can be. Forgive me if I sound harsh, but there it is."

"I know. I just . . . miss her. And everyone I loved." Joanna lay back and looked at the blue sky. "Well, thank God this whole dreadful saga has had one happy ending. So many people dead and gone because of it. Poor Alec too."

"You know what? In a strange sort of way, I think he'd have seen it as a fitting ending to his life. After all, he went to his grave having just uncovered the biggest scandal of the twentieth century. He was a great newshound right to the end."

"Sorry, Simon, I'm afraid I can't justify anyone dying because of it."

"No, of course you can't."

"I'm still having nightmares about the evening *I* 'died.'" Joanna shuddered. "I was absolutely convinced, right up until the very last moment, that you were going to kill me."

"I absolutely had to make it look real, Jo, to convince Monica Burrows. I needed a witness to call in and say I'd done the dirty deed."

"All those silly cowboy and Indian games we used to play on the moors when we were kids," she mused. "'This is *my* game, we play by my rules,' and then I had to say, 'I *surrender*,' and you'd say . . .'"

"'Bang, *bang*, you're dead,'" Simon finished for her. "Anyway, thank God for those games. It provided me with the perfect way of warning you to 'die.'"

"When you fired that bullet into Jamie's bedroom wall, it was real, wasn't it?"

"Absolutely." Simon nodded. "I can tell you, even though the next two were blanks, the sweat was pouring off me as I hadn't had time to go through the usual rigorous procedures. I had to load the gun on the way up the stairs to Jamie's bedroom. If I hadn't moved quickly, Monica would have killed you and I couldn't risk that."

"So how did you kill her?"

"I'm afraid Monica wasn't concentrating on her gun when she

came over to check your pulse. I whipped it out of her hand and shot her with it before she knew what was happening."

"God, Simon, she was younger than me . . ."

"The fact she was so inexperienced saved your life, Jo."

Joanna sat up on her elbows and studied Simon. "And to think I ever doubted you. What you did for me that night . . . I can never repay you."

"Well, I just hope that, when my day of judgment comes, He'll forgive me. The bottom line was, it was her or you."

"Was your boss grateful to get hold of his pot of gold after all this time?" Joanna asked.

"Extremely. It may sound stupid, but I actually felt sympathy for him toward the end. He was only doing his job. Trying to protect what he believed in."

"No, Simon, never, ever could I shed one tear. Think of those who've died—Grace, William, Ciara, Ian Simpson, Alec, poor Marcus . . ."

"But it wasn't him that caused all this in the first place, was it?"

"No, I suppose not."

"Well, the old boy died of a massive heart attack the day after I handed him back the letter."

"Don't expect me to mourn."

"I won't. But the odd thing was, only a couple of hours before you turned up at Welbeck Street, I'd suddenly realized where the letter had been hidden."

"How come?"

"I was waiting for the duke at York Cottage, to bring him back to London, and I saw a framed sampler on the wall. It was almost identical to the one I'd seen hanging above Jamie's bed a few weeks earlier. If I'd have got there sooner, then all this could have been avoided." He leaned back on the sand. "I know how you found out where it was."

"Do you?"

"Yes. A wily old bird, by all accounts." Simon's eyes twinkled.

"Is she okay?"

"I believe so. Safely in America, I hear tell."

"I'm glad. She's one hell of a lady," Joanna said quietly. "I suppose you've already thought about the irony of all this? I mean, Zoe's ex-boyfriend being his namesake?"

"Yes. Weird, isn't it? The current duke was apparently devastated when Zoe left him . . . history repeating itself, one could say."

"One absolutely could," agreed Joanna. "And besides, you must have already worked out why the palace was so dead set against Zoe and the duke's relationship? I mean, they were actually related through James. They were cousins, which means that Jamie is—"

"Just don't go there, Jo." Simon shuddered. "All I can say is that it's not unusual among the aristocracy to marry blood relatives. Most members of European royalty are related to one another."

"What a mess," sighed Joanna.

"Yes. Anyway, changing the subject, have you decided yet where you go from here?"

"No, apart from the fact that I'm certainly going to go by the name of 'Maggie'—I've always hated 'Margaret.'" Joanna gave him a wan smile. "At least now that I'm a bona fide American citizen, I can start thinking about it. You'll laugh, I'm sure, but I've always had a fancy to write a spy novel."

"Jo . . ."

"Simon, I'm serious. I mean, let's face it, no one would believe the story anyway, so why not? I'd change the names, of course."

"I'm warning you, don't."

"We'll see. Anyway, how about you?" she asked him.

"Zoe and I have decided to stay in LA for the foreseeable future. We thought it was wise to make a fresh start, and it looks like Zoe will be inundated with work offers when *Blithe Spirit* is released. We went to see a school for Jamie a couple of days ago. He was so unhappy at his last place, but there, everybody's mums and dads are celebrities and he's just normal."

"What about your job?"

Simon shrugged. "I haven't decided yet. The service has offered me a transfer over here, but Zoe has this mad idea of me opening a restaurant. She wants to back me."

Joanna giggled. "Well, we always did talk about it. But could you leave your old way of life behind, do you think?"

"The truth is, I'm not a killer. The fact that I took lives during all this will haunt me forever." Simon shook his head. "God help me if Zoe ever found out what I've done, or Jamie."

Joanna laid her hand on his. "You saved my life, Simon, that's what you did."

"Yes." He took her hand and squeezed it. "Joanna, you know that for your own sake, I can't see you again."

"I know," she said with a sad shrug.

"By the way, I have something else for you." From his shorts pocket, he drew out an envelope and handed it to her.

"What's in it?"

"Twenty thousand pounds in dollars—the bonus I was paid for finding the letter. It's yours by rights and it might help get you started."

Tears filled Joanna's eyes. "Simon, I can't take this."

"Of course you can. Zoe's earning a fortune and my boss insisted on paying for all my expenses while I was in the States investigating Monica's disappearance."

"Thank you, Simon. I promise I'll make good use of it."

"I'm sure you will." He watched Joanna fold the envelope up and put it in her rucksack.

"There's something else in there too, something I thought you should at least have the satisfaction of reading," he added. "So . . ." He pulled her to standing. "I'm afraid this is goodbye." He hugged her tightly to him.

"Oh God." She wept on his shoulder. "I can't bear the thought of never seeing you again."

"I know." He wiped her tears gently away with his finger. "So long, Butch."

"Take it easy, Sundance," she whispered.

With a small wave, he turned away from her. Only when he'd left the beach did she pick up her rucksack and walk down to the water's edge.

Kneeling on the sand, she found a tissue to blow her streaming nose. Then she reached inside the envelope he'd given her, took out the sheet of paper, and unfolded it.

York Cottage
Sandringham
10th May 1926

My darling Siam,

Understand that it is only my love for you that compels me to write this, the fear that others might wish to hurt you overriding care for myself or common sense. With God's grace, let it be delivered to you without incident in the secure hands that bear it.

I must tell you the joyful news of the arrival of our baby girl. She has your eyes already, and perhaps your nose. Even if the blood that runs through her veins is not royal, your child is a true princess. How I wish her real father could see her, hold his child in his arms, but of course that is an impossibility, a dreadful sadness I must live with for the rest of my days.

My darling, I implore you to keep this letter safe. The threat of its existence to the few who know the truth should be enough to see you safely through life. I trust you will dispose of it when the time comes for you to leave this earth, for the sake of our daughter, and so that history may never record it.

I cannot write again, my love.

I am yours forever,

The letter was signed with the famous flourish, the photocopy not diminishing the magnitude of what Joanna had just read.

A baby princess, born into royalty, sired in the most extraordinary circumstances by a commoner. A baby that at the time was third in line to the throne, the chances of her succession small. But then, through a twist of fate, which saw others putting love before duty, too, the baby princess had become a queen.

Joanna stood up with the letter in her hand, the temptation to exact revenge for her own and other lives destroyed holding her tightly in its grasp. The anger left her, as quickly as it had come.

"It's finally over," she whispered to the ghosts who might have been listening.

Joanna went to the water's edge, tore the paper up, and watched the pieces as they fluttered in the wind. Then she turned round and walked back to the Cabana Café to drown her sorrows in tequila.

Nursing her drink at the bar, Joanna knew that her new life began today. Somehow, she had to find the strength to embrace it—move on and put the past behind her.

Normally one would do that with the support of friends and family. She was totally alone.

"How can I do this?" she muttered as she ordered a second cocktail and realized that she'd been using Simon's imminent visit as a lifeline. Now that he was gone, the thread to all she had ever known was broken forever.

"Oh my God," she whispered, as the full enormity of the situation hit her.

"Hi there, got a light?"

"I don't smoke, sorry." Joanna ignored the male voice, with its strong American accent. Here in Mexico, men hovered around her like bees drawn to honey.

"Okay, I'll take a light and an orange juice, please," she heard the voice say to the bartender as, out of the corner of her eye, she saw a man climb onto the bar stool next to hers.

"Want a top-up?"

"I . . ."

The quintessentially English phrase made her turn to her neighbor. He was tanned to a deep nut-brown, wearing a pair of brightly colored shorts, a T-shirt, and a straw hat pulled down over his long dark hair. It was only when she saw his eyes—the deep tan highlighting their blueness—that she recognized him.

"Don't I know you?" He grinned at her. "Aren't you Maggie Cunningham? Think we spent a year at NYU together way back when."

"I . . ." Joanna stuttered, her heart banging against her chest. Was this some kind of weird hallucination brought on by the tequila? Or a test from Simon to see if she'd blow it? Yet, he had called her "Maggie" . . .

Joanna knew she was staring at him openmouthed, wanting to drink in everything her eyes were telling her she saw, but . . .

"I'll get you one anyway." He signaled to the bartender to fill her glass up. "Then how about we go and catch up on old times?"

As she followed him out of the café, she decided it was best to keep her mouth shut, because this just could not . . . it *could not* be real.

As he led her to a quiet table on the rickety wooden terrace, she noticed he walked with a pronounced limp. She sat down abruptly.

"Who are you?" she muttered darkly.

"You know who I am, Maggie," he said, in his familiar clipped English. "Cheers." He lifted his glass to hers.

"I . . . How did you get here?"

"Same way you did, I reckon. My name's Casper by the way—your very own friendly ghost." He looked at her and grinned. "And I'm not kidding."

"Oh my God," she breathed, as one of her hands unconsciously reached out to touch him, needing to confirm he was real.

"And my surname's 'James.' Thought it was fitting. I'm lucky—I got to choose my name myself, unlike you."

"How? Where? Why . . . ? Marcus, I thought you were—"

"Dead, yes. And please, call me Casper," he muttered. "As you know, walls tend to have ears. To be fair, they thought I *was* going to cop it—I had multiple organ failure and I was in a coma for a time after the surgery. And then, when I actually regained consciousness, they'd already announced my death to the family and the media."

"Why did they do that?"

"I've worked out since, it was probably because they didn't know how much I knew, so they carted me off to some private hospital and put me under twenty-four-hour surveillance. They couldn't take the risk of me waking up and spilling the beans to a doctor or nurse who happened to be lurking nearby at the time. Given they obviously wanted it to look like a straightforward shooting accident—no questions asked—and that they were convinced I was going to die anyway, they preempted my demise. So when I actually woke up and my body began functioning again, they had a bit of a problem."

"I'm amazed they didn't kill you off once and for all," Joanna murmured. "That's what they usually do."

"I think your mate Simon—or should I say, my long-lost distant cousin"—Marcus raised an eyebrow—"had quite a bit to do with it. He told me later that he'd mentioned to his superiors that I'd grabbed the letter from Ian Simpson and hidden it somewhere before we fell into the water. Which was why the bastard shot me. So they had to keep me alive for a bit when I did wake up to find out if I had. See?"

"Simon covered for you . . ."

"He did. And then he gave me the letter—or what was left of it—to return to them. And told me to say that I knew nothing—that Ian Simpson had simply given me some money to find it. Next thing I know, Simon's telling me I'm officially dead and asking me what I'd like to be called in my new life."

"Did you refuse?"

"Maggie," Marcus sighed, "you'll probably call me a coward again, but those people . . . wow, they'll stop at nothing. I'd just come back from the dead and I wasn't particularly keen on returning any time soon."

"You're not a coward, Marcus . . . I mean, Casper." She reached out a tentative hand and put it on his. "You saved my life that night."

"And I'm sure Simon saved mine. He's a seriously good guy, though I've still no idea what the hell was going on. Maybe one day you'll enlighten me." Marcus lit up a cigarette and Joanna saw that his left hand shook continuously.

"Maybe I will."

"So," he said, smiling, "here I am."

"Where have you been living?"

"In a rehabilitation center in Miami. Apparently the bullets I took in the abdomen grazed my spine, and I woke up with my lower body paralyzed. I'm better now, although it took a long time to learn how to walk again. And no more whiskies for me anymore, unfortunately." He gestured to the juice in front of him. "Bloody nice place Simon set me up in, though, all expenses paid . . ." He grinned.

"Good."

They sat in silence for a while, simply staring at each other.

"This is surreal," Marcus said eventually.

"You're telling me," Joanna replied.

"I thought Simon was having me on when he called to say he was bringing me down to Mexico to meet someone I knew. I just . . . I just can't believe you're here." Marcus shook his head in wonder.

"No . . . especially as we're both 'dead.'"

"Maybe this is the afterlife . . . If it is"—he swept his hand toward the beach—"I quite like it. And you know I've always had a thing for blondes . . ."

"Mar—Casper, behave, please!"

"Well, some things never change." He smiled at her, taking her hand and squeezing it. "I've missed you, Jo," he whispered. "Terribly."

"I've missed you too."

"So, where do we go from here?" he asked her.

"Anywhere we want, I suppose. The world—apart from England, of course—is our oyster."

"How about Brazil?" he suggested. "I know of a great film project."

Joanna chuckled. "Well, even MI5 might struggle to find us in the Amazon. I'm up for it."

"Good, come on," he said as he stood up. "Before we plan out the rest of our future together, why don't you help what's left of me down to the beach? I have a violent urge to lie on the sand and kiss every part of you. Even without the chocolate sauce."

"Okay." Joanna smiled and stood up too.

———

From his vantage point above the beach, Simon watched the young couple, their arms wound tightly around each other, walk slowly across the sand and into their new life.

EPILOGUE

Los Angeles, September 2017

Simon found Zoe out on a sun lounger by the pool. He looked at her still-taut body and lightly tanned skin, which didn't seem to have aged at all in twenty years and with two pregnancies since they'd met.

He kissed her on the top of her head. "Where are the kids?"

"Joanna has gone off to a friend's eighteenth party—in the shortest miniskirt I've ever seen, I might add—and Tom is at a baseball game. You're home early. Was the restaurant quieter today?"

"No, it was packed, but I came back to do some paperwork. I can't concentrate there, even in my office—everyone keeps interrupting me. What's that you're reading?" he asked as he peered over her shoulder.

"Oh, it's a new thriller that came out last week and everyone here is talking about it. It involves hidden secrets about the British royal family, so I thought I'd give it a go," she said with a smile.

His heart pounding in the way it hadn't since he'd left his old job, Simon glanced down at the cover.

The Royal Secret
BY
M. Cunningham

Joanna, no!

"Right," Simon said.

"It's gripping, actually, though utterly unbelievable, of course. I mean, this stuff just doesn't happen, does it? Does it, Simon?" she prompted him.

"No, of course it doesn't. Right, I'm going inside to get a cool drink. Want anything?"

"Some iced tea would be great."

Simon walked up to the house, sweating profusely. He went into his office and dumped the files containing the restaurant accounts on his desk, then checked his emails on his iPhone.

l.jenkins@thameshouse.gov.uk

Subject: Urgent

Call me. Something's come up.

1

I will always remember exactly where I was and what I was doing when I heard that my father had died.

I was sitting in the pretty garden of my old school friend's townhouse in London, a copy of *The Penelopiad* open but unread in my lap, enjoying the June sun while Jenny collected her little boy from kindergarten.

I felt calm and I appreciated what a good idea it had been to get away. When my cell phone rang and I glanced at the screen and saw it was Marina, I was studying the burgeoning clematis unfolding its fragile pink buds, giving birth to a riot of color, encouraged by its sunny midwife.

"Hello, Ma, how are you?" I said, hoping she could hear the sun's warmth in my voice.

"Maia, I . . ."

Marina paused, and in that instant I knew something was dreadfully wrong. "What is it?"

"Maia, there's no other way to tell you this, but your father had a heart attack here at home yesterday afternoon, and in the early hours of this morning, he . . . passed away."

I remained silent as a million different and ridiculous thoughts passed through my mind. The first one being that Marina, for some unknown reason, had decided to play some form of a tasteless joke on me.

"You're the first of the sisters I've told, Maia, as you're the eldest.

And I wanted to ask you whether you would prefer to tell the rest of your sisters yourself, or leave it to me."

"I . . ."

Still no words would form coherently on my lips, as I began to realize that Marina, dear, beloved Marina, the woman who had been the closest thing to a mother I'd ever known, would never tell me this if it weren't true. So it had to be. And at that moment, my entire world shifted on its axis.

"Maia, please, tell me you're all right. This really is the most dreadful phone call I've ever had to make, but what else could I do? God only knows how the other girls are going to take it."

It was then that I heard the suffering in *her* voice and understood she'd needed to tell me as much for her own sake as mine. So I switched into my normal comfort zone, which was to comfort others.

"Of course I'll tell my sisters if you'd prefer, Ma, although I'm not positive where they all are. Isn't Ally away training for a regatta?"

And, as we continued to discuss where each of my younger sisters was, as though we needed to get them together for a birthday party rather than to mourn the death of our father, the entire conversation took on a sense of the surreal.

"When should we plan on having the funeral, do you think? What with Electra being in Los Angeles and Ally somewhere on the high seas, surely we can't think about it until next week at the earliest," I said.

"Well"—I heard the hesitation in Marina's voice—"perhaps the best thing is for you and I to discuss it when you arrive back home. There really is no rush now, Maia, so if you'd prefer to continue the last couple of days of your holiday in London, that would be fine. There's nothing more to be done for him here . . ." Her voice trailed off miserably.

"Ma, of *course* I'll be on the next flight that I can get to Geneva! I'll call the airline immediately and let you know what time the flight is. And in the meantime, I'll do my best to get in touch with everyone."

"I'm so terribly sorry, *chérie*," Marina sighed. "I know how you adored him."

"Yes," I said, the strange calm that I had felt while we discussed arrangements suddenly deserting me like the stillness before a violent thunderstorm. "I'll call you later, when I know what time I'll be arriving."

"In the meantime, please take care of yourself, Maia. You've had a terrible shock."

I pressed the button to end the call and before the storm clouds in my heart opened up and drowned me, I went upstairs to my bedroom to retrieve my flight documents and contact the airline. As I waited in the calling queue, I glanced at the bed where I'd woken up that morning to simply another day. And I thanked God that human beings don't have the power to see into the future.

The officious woman who eventually answered wasn't helpful and I knew, as she spoke of full flights, financial penalties, and credit-card details, that my emotional dam was ready to burst. Finally, once I'd been grudgingly granted a seat on the four o'clock flight to Geneva, which would mean throwing everything into my luggage immediately and taking a taxi to Heathrow, I sat down on the bed and stared for so long at the sprigged wallpaper that the pattern began to dance in front of my eyes.

"He's gone," I whispered, "gone forever. I'll never see him again."

Expecting the spoken words to provoke a raging torrent of tears, I was surprised that nothing actually happened. Instead, I sat there numbly, my head still full of practicalities. The thought of telling my sisters—all five of them—was horrendous and I searched through my emotional filing system for the one I would call first. Inevitably, it was Tiggy, the second youngest of the six of us girls and the sibling to whom I'd always felt closest.

With trembling fingers, I scrolled down to find her number and dialed it. When her voice mail answered, I didn't know what to say, other than a few garbled words asking her to call me back urgently.

She was currently somewhere in the Scottish Highlands working at a center for orphaned and sick wild deer.

As for the other sisters . . . I knew their reactions would vary, outwardly at least, from indifference to a dramatic outpouring of emotion.

Given that I wasn't currently sure quite which way I would go on the scale of grief when I did speak to any of them, I decided to take the coward's way out and texted them all, asking them to call me as soon as they could. Then I hurriedly packed my luggage and walked down the narrow stairs to the kitchen to write a note for Jenny explaining why I'd had to leave in such a hurry.

Deciding to take my chances hailing a black cab on the London streets, I left the house, walking briskly around the leafy Chelsea crescent just as any normal person would do on any normal day. I believe I actually said hello to someone walking a dog when I passed him in the street and managed a smile.

No one would know what had just happened to me, I thought as I managed to find a taxi on the busy King's Road and climbed inside it, directing the driver to Heathrow.

Nobody would know.

———

Five hours later, just as the sun was making its leisurely descent over Lake Geneva, I arrived at our private pontoon on the shore, from where I would make the last leg of my journey home.

Christian was already waiting for me in our sleek Riva motor launch. And from the look on his face, I could see he'd heard the news.

"How are you, Mademoiselle Maia?" he asked, sympathy in his blue eyes as he helped me aboard.

"I'm . . . glad I'm here," I answered neutrally as I walked to the back of the boat and sat down on the cushioned cream leather seat that curved around the stern. Usually, I would sit with Christian in the passenger seat at the front as we sped across the calm waters on the twenty-minute journey home. But today, I felt a need for privacy. As Christian started the powerful engine, the sun glinted off the windows of the fabulous houses that lined Lake Geneva's shores. I'd often felt when I made this journey that it was the entrance to an ethereal world disconnected from reality.

The world of Pa Salt.

I noticed the first vague evidence of tears pricking at my eyes as I thought of my father's pet name, which I'd coined when I was young. He'd always loved sailing and often when he returned to me at our lakeside home, he had smelled of fresh air and the sea. Somehow, the name had stuck, and as my younger siblings had joined me, they'd called him that too.

As the launch picked up speed, the warm wind streaming through my hair, I thought of the hundreds of previous journeys I'd made to Atlantis, Pa Salt's fairy-tale castle. Inaccessible by land, due to its position on a private promontory with a crescent of mountainous terrain rising up steeply behind it, the only method of reaching it was by boat. The nearest neighbors were miles away along the lake, so Atlantis was our own private kingdom, set apart from the rest of the world. Everything it contained within it was magical . . . as if Pa Salt and we, his daughters, had lived there under an enchantment.

Each one of us had been chosen by Pa Salt as a baby, adopted from one of the four corners of the globe, and brought home to live under his protection. And each one of us, as Pa always liked to say, was special, different . . . we were *his* girls. He'd named us all after the Seven Sisters, his favorite star cluster. I was Maia, being the first and eldest.

When I was young, he'd take me up to his glass-domed observatory perched on top of the house; lift me up with his big, strong hands; and have me look through his telescope at the night sky.

"There they are," he'd say as he aligned the lens, "look, Maia, and see the beautiful shining star you're named after."

And I *would* see. As he explained the legends that were the source of my own and my sisters' names, I'd hardly listen but simply enjoy his arms tight around me, fully aware of this rare, special moment when I had him all to myself.

Marina, whom I'd presumed as I grew up was my mother—I'd even shortened her name to "Ma"—I'd realized eventually was a glorified nursemaid, employed by Pa to take care of me, because he was away so much. But of course, Marina was so much more than that to all of us girls. She was the one who had wiped our tears, berated us for sloppy table manners, and steered us calmly through the difficult transition from childhood to womanhood.

She had always been there, and I could not have loved Ma any more if she had given birth to me.

During the first three years of my childhood, Marina and I had lived alone together in our magical castle on the shores of Lake Geneva as Pa Salt traveled the seven seas to conduct his business. And then, one by one, my sisters began to arrive.

Usually, Pa would bring me a present when he returned home. I'd hear the motor launch arriving, run across the sweeping lawns and through the trees to the jetty to greet him. Like any child, I'd want to see what he had hidden inside his magical pockets to delight me. On one particular occasion, however, after he'd presented me with an exquisitely carved wooden reindeer, which he assured me came from Saint Nicholas's workshop at the North Pole itself, a uniformed woman had stepped out from behind him, and in her arms was a bundle wrapped in a shawl. And the bundle was moving.

"This time, Maia, I've brought you back the most special gift. You have a new sister." He'd smiled at me as he lifted me into his arms. "Now you'll no longer be lonely when I have to go away."

After that, life had changed. The maternity nurse who Pa had brought with him disappeared after a few weeks and Marina took over the care of my baby sister. I couldn't understand how the red, squalling thing which often smelled and diverted attention from me could possibly be a gift. Until one morning, when Alcyone—named after the second star of the Seven Sisters—smiled at me from her high chair over breakfast.

"She knows who I am," I said in wonder to Marina, who was feeding her.

"Of course she does, Maia dear. You're her big sister, the one she'll look up to. It'll be up to you to teach her lots of things that you know and she doesn't."

And as she grew, she became my shadow, following me everywhere, which pleased and irritated me in equal measure.

"Maia, wait me!" she'd demand loudly as she tottered along behind me.

Even though Ally—as I'd nicknamed her—had originally been an unwanted addition to my dreamlike existence at Atlantis, I could not have asked for a sweeter, more loveable companion. She rarely, if ever, cried and when she was a toddler there were none of the temper tantrums associated with children of her age. With her tumbling red-gold curls and her big blue eyes, Ally had a natural charm that drew people to her, including our father. On the occasions Pa Salt was home from one of his long trips abroad, I'd watch how his eyes lit up when he saw her, in a way I was sure they didn't for me. And whereas I was shy and reticent with strangers, Ally had an openness and trust that endeared her to everyone.

She was also one of those children who seemed to excel at everything—particularly music, and any sport to do with water. I remember Pa teaching her to swim in our vast pool, and whereas I had struggled to master the technique to stay afloat and hated being underwater, my little sister took to it like a mermaid. And while I struggled to find my sea legs even on the *Titan*, Pa's huge and beautiful oceangoing yacht, when we were at home, Ally would beg him to take her out in the small Laser dinghy he kept moored on our private lakeside jetty. I'd crouch in the cramped stern of the boat while Pa and Ally took control as we sped across the glassy waters. Their joint passion for sailing bonded them in a way I felt I could never replicate.

Although Ally had studied music at the Conservatoire de Musique de Genève and was a highly talented flautist who could have pursued a career with a professional orchestra, since leaving music school she had chosen the life of a full-time sailor. She now competed regularly in regattas and had represented Switzerland on a number of occasions.

When Ally was almost three, Pa arrived home with our next sibling, whom he named Asterope, after the third of the Seven Sisters.

"But we will call her Star," Pa had said, smiling at Marina, Ally, and me as we studied the newest addition to the family lying in the bassinet.

By now I was attending lessons every morning with a private tutor, so my newest sister's arrival affected me less than Ally's had. Then, only six months later, another baby girl joined us, a twelve-week-old named Celaeno, whose name Ally immediately shortened to CeCe.

There was only three months' age difference between Star and CeCe, and from as far back as I can remember, the two of them forged a close bond. They were like twins, talking in their own private baby language, some of which the two of them still used to communicate. They inhabited their own private world, to the exclusion of us others, and even now, in their twenties, nothing had changed. CeCe, the younger of the two, was always the boss, her stocky body and nut-brown skin in direct contrast to the pale, whippet-thin Star.

The following year, another baby arrived, Taygete—whom I nicknamed "Tiggy" because her short, dark hair had sprouted out at strange angles on her tiny head and reminded me of the hedgehog in Beatrix Potter's famous story.

I was by now seven years old, and I'd bonded with Tiggy from the first moment I set eyes on her. She was the most delicate of us all, suffering one childhood illness after another, but even as an infant, she was stoic and undemanding. When yet another baby girl, named Electra, was brought home by Pa a few months later, an exhausted

Marina would often ask me if I would mind sitting with Tiggy, who was continually suffering with a fever or croup. Eventually diagnosed as asthmatic, she rarely left the nursery to be wheeled outside in the pram, in case the cold air and heavy fog of a Geneva winter affected her chest.

Electra was the youngest of my siblings and her name suited her perfectly. By now, I was used to little babies and their demands, but my youngest sister was without doubt the most challenging of them all. Everything about her was electric; her innate ability to switch in an instant from dark to light and vice versa meant that our previously calm home rang daily with high-pitched screams. Her temper tantrums resonated through my childhood consciousness and as she grew older, her fiery personality did not mellow.

Privately, Ally, Tiggy, and I had our own nickname for her and she was known between the three of us as "Tricky." We all walked on eggshells around her, wishing to do nothing to set off a lightning change of mood. I can honestly say there were moments when I loathed her for the disruption she brought to Atlantis.

And yet, when Electra knew one of us was in trouble, she was the first to offer help and support. Just as she was capable of huge selfishness, her generosity on other occasions was equally pronounced.

After Electra, the entire household was expecting the arrival of the seventh sister. After all, we'd been named after Pa Salt's favorite star cluster and we wouldn't be complete without her. We even knew her name—Merope—and wondered who she would be. But a year went past, and then another, and another, and no more babies arrived home with Pa.

I remember vividly standing with my father once in his observatory. I was fourteen years old and just on the brink of womanhood. We were waiting for an eclipse, which he'd told me was a seminal moment for humankind and always brought change with it.

"Pa," I said, "will you ever bring home our seventh sister?"

At this, his strong, protective bulk had seemed to freeze for a few seconds. He'd looked suddenly as though he carried the weight of the world on his shoulders. Although he didn't turn around, for he was still concentrating on training the telescope on the coming eclipse, I knew instinctively that what I'd said had distressed him.

"No, Maia, I won't. Because I have never found her."

———

As the familiar thick hedge of spruce trees, which shielded our waterside home from prying eyes, came into view, I saw Marina standing on the jetty and the dreadful truth of losing Pa finally began to sink in.

And I realized that the man who had created the kingdom in which we had all been his princesses was no longer present to hold the enchantment in place.

2

Marina put her comforting arms gently around my shoulders as I stepped up onto the jetty from the launch. Wordlessly, we turned to walk together through the trees and across the wide, sloping lawns that led up to the house. In June, our home was at the height of its beauty. The ornate gardens were bursting into bloom, enticing its occupants to explore their hidden pathways and secret grottos.

The house itself, built in the late eighteenth century in the Louis XV style, was a vision of elegant grandeur. Four stories high, its sturdy pale pink walls were punctuated by tall multipaned windows and topped by a steeply sloping red roof with a turret at each corner. It was exquisitely furnished inside with every modern luxury, and its thick carpets and plump sofas cocooned and comforted all who lived there. We girls had slept up on the top floor, which had superb, uninterrupted views of the lake over the treetops. Marina also occupied a suite of rooms upstairs with us.

I glanced at her now and thought how exhausted she looked. Her kind brown eyes were smudged with shadows of fatigue, and her normally smiling mouth looked pinched and tense. I supposed she must be in her midsixties, but she didn't seem it. Tall, with strong aquiline features, she was an elegant, handsome woman, always immaculately attired, her effortless chic reflecting her French ancestry. When I was young, she used to wear her silky dark hair loose, but now she coiled it into a chignon at the nape of her neck.

A thousand questions were pushing for precedence in my mind, but only one demanded to be asked immediately.

"Why didn't you let me know when Pa fell sick?" I asked as we entered the house and walked into the high-ceilinged drawing room that overlooked a sweeping stone terrace, lined with urns full of vivid red and gold nasturtiums.

"Maia, believe me, I begged him to let me tell you, to tell all you girls, but he became so distressed when I mentioned it that I had to do as he wished."

And I understood that if Pa had told her not to contact us, she could have done little else. He was the king and Marina was at best his most trusted courtier, at worst his servant who must do exactly as he bade her.

"Where is he now?" I asked her. "Still upstairs in his bedroom? Should I go and see him?"

"No, *chérie*, he isn't upstairs. Would you like some tea before I tell you more?" she asked.

"To be quite honest, I think I could do with a strong gin and tonic," I admitted as I sat down heavily on one of the huge sofas.

"I'll ask Claudia to make it. And I think that, on this occasion, I may join you myself."

I watched as Marina left the room to find Claudia, our housekeeper, who had been at Atlantis as long as Marina. She was German, her outward dourness hiding a heart of gold. Like all of us, she'd adored her master. I wondered suddenly what would become of her and Marina. And in fact, what would happen to Atlantis itself now that Pa had gone.

The words still seemed incongruous in this context. Pa was always "gone": off somewhere, doing something, although none of his staff or family had any specific idea of what he actually did to make his living. I'd asked him once, when my friend Jenny had come to stay with us during the school holidays and been noticeably awed by the opulence of the way we lived.

"Your father must be fabulously wealthy," she'd whispered as we stepped off Pa's private jet, which had just landed at La Môle airport near Saint-Tropez. The chauffeur was waiting on the tarmac to take us down to the harbor, where we'd board our magnificent ten-berth yacht, the *Titan*, and sail off for our annual Mediterranean cruise to whatever destination Pa Salt fancied taking us to.

Like any child, rich or poor, given that I had grown up knowing no different, the way we lived had never really struck me as unusual. All of us girls had taken lessons with tutors at home when we were younger, and it was only when I went to boarding school at the age of thirteen that I began to realize how removed our life was from most people's.

I'd asked Pa once what exactly it was he did to provide our family with every luxury imaginable.

He'd looked at me in that secretive way he had and smiled. "I am a magician of sorts."

Which, as he'd intended, told me nothing. As I grew older, I began to realize that Pa Salt was indeed the master illusionist and nothing was as it first seemed.

When Marina came back into the drawing room carrying two gin and tonics on a tray, it occurred to me that, after thirty-three years, I had no real idea who my father had been in the world outside Atlantis. I wondered whether I would finally begin to find out now.

"There we go," Marina said, setting the glass in front of me. "Here's to your father," she said as she raised hers. "May God rest his soul."

"Yes, here's to Pa Salt. May he rest in peace."

Marina took a hefty gulp before placing the glass on the table and taking my hands in hers. "Maia, before we discuss anything else, I feel I must tell you one thing."

"What?" I asked, looking at her weary brow, furrowed with anxiety.

"You asked me earlier if your father was still here in the house. The answer is that he has already been laid to rest. It was his wish that the burial happen immediately and that none of you girls were to be present."

I stared at her as if she'd taken leave of her senses. "But, Ma, you told me only a few hours ago that he died in the early hours of this morning! How is it possible that a burial could have been arranged so soon? And *why*?"

"Maia, your father was adamant that as soon as he passed away, his body was to be flown on his jet to his yacht. Once on board, he was to be placed in a lead coffin, which had apparently sat in the hold of the *Titan* for many years in preparation for such an event. From there he was to be sailed out to sea. Naturally, given his love for the water, he wanted to be laid to rest in the ocean. And he did not wish to cause his daughters the distress of . . . watching the event."

"Oh God," I said, Marina's words sending shudders of horror through me. "But surely he knew that we'd all want to say goodbye properly? How could he do this? What will I tell the others? I—"

"*Chérie*, you and I have lived in this house the longest and we both know that where your father was concerned, ours was never to question why. I can only believe," she sighed, "that he wished to be laid to rest as he'd lived: privately."

"And in control," I added, anger flaring suddenly inside me. "It's almost as though he couldn't even trust the people who loved him to do the right thing for him."

"Whatever his reasoning," said Marina, "I only hope that in time you can all remember him as the loving father he was. The one thing I do know is that you girls were his world."

"But which of us knew him?" I asked, frustration bringing tears to my eyes. "Did a doctor come to confirm his death? You must have a death certificate. Can I see it?"

"The doctor asked me for his personal details, such as his place and year of birth. I said I was only an employee and I wasn't sure of those kinds of things. I put him in touch with Georg Hoffman, the lawyer who handles all your father's affairs."

"But *why* was he so private, Ma? I was thinking today on the plane that I don't ever remember him bringing friends here to Atlantis. Occasionally, when we were on the yacht, a business associate would come aboard for a meeting and they'd disappear downstairs into his study, but he never actually socialized."

"He wanted to keep his family life separate from business, so that when he was home, his full attention could be focused on his daughters."

"The daughters he adopted and brought here from all over the world. Why, Ma, why?"

Marina looked back at me silently, her wise, calm eyes giving me no clues as to whether or not she knew the answer.

"I mean, when you're a child," I continued, "you grow up accepting your life. But we both know it's terribly unusual, if not downright strange, for a single, middle-aged man to adopt six baby girls and bring them here to Switzerland to grow up under the same roof."

"Your father *was* an unusual man," Marina agreed. "But surely, giving needy orphans the chance of a better life under his protection couldn't be seen as a bad thing?" she equivocated. "Many wealthy people adopt children if they have none of their own."

"But usually, they're married," I said bluntly. "Ma, do you know if Pa ever had a girlfriend? Someone he loved? I knew him for thirty-three years and never once did I see him with a woman."

"*Chérie*, I understand that your father has gone, and suddenly you realize that many questions you've wanted to ask him can now never be answered, but I really can't help you. And besides, this isn't the moment," Marina added gently. "For now, we must celebrate what he was to each and every one of us and remember him as the loving and kind human being we all knew within the walls of Atlantis. Try to remember that your father was well over eighty. He'd lived a long and fulfilling life."

"But he was out sailing the Laser on the lake only three weeks ago, scrambling around the boat like a man half his age," I sighed. "It's hard to reconcile that image with someone who was dying."

"Yes, and thank God he didn't follow many others of his age and suffer a slow and lingering death. It's wonderful that you and the other girls will remember him as fit, happy, and healthy," Marina said encouragingly. "It was certainly what he would have wanted."

"He didn't suffer at the end, did he?" I asked her tentatively, knowing in my heart that even if he had, Marina would never tell me.

"No. He knew what was coming, Maia, and I believe that he'd made his peace with God. Really, I think he was happy to pass on."

"How on earth do we tell the others that their father has gone?" I entreated her. "And that they don't even have a body to bury? They'll feel like I do, that he's simply disappeared into thin air."

"Your father thought of that before he died, and Georg Hoffman, his lawyer, contacted me earlier today. I promise you that each and every one of you will get a chance to say goodbye to him."

"Even in death, Pa has everything under control," I said with a despairing sigh. "I've left messages for all the sisters, by the way, but as yet, no one has called me back."

"Well, Georg Hoffman is on standby to come here as soon as you've all arrived. And please, Maia, don't ask me what he'll have to say, for I haven't a clue. Now, I had Claudia prepare some soup for you. I doubt you've eaten anything since this morning. Would you prefer to take it to the Pavilion, or do you want to stay here in the house tonight?"

"I'll have some soup here, and then I'll go home if you don't mind. I think I need to be alone."

"Of course." Marina reached toward me and gave me a hug. "I understand what a terrible shock this is for you. And I'm sorry that yet again, you're bearing the burden of responsibility for the rest of the girls, but it was you he asked me to tell first. I don't know whether you find any comfort in that. Now, shall I go and ask Claudia to warm the soup? I think we could both do with a little comfort food."

After we'd eaten, I told Marina to go to bed and kissed her good night, for I could see that she too was exhausted. Before I left the house, I climbed the many stairs to the top floor and peered into each of my sisters' rooms. All were still as they had been when their occupants had left home to take flight on their chosen paths, and each room still displayed their very different personalities. Whenever they returned, like doves to their waterside nest, none of them seemed to have the vaguest interest in changing them. Including me.

Opening the door to my old room, I went to the shelf where I still kept my most treasured childhood possessions. I took down an old china doll which Pa had given to me when I was very young. As always, he'd weaved a magical story of how the doll had once belonged to a young Russian countess, but she had been lonely in her snowy palace in Moscow when her mistress had grown up and forgotten her. He told me her name was Leonora and that she needed a new pair of arms to love her.

Putting the doll back on the shelf, I reached for the box that contained a gift Pa had given me on my sixteenth birthday, opened it, and drew out the necklace inside.

"It's a moonstone, Maia," he'd told me as I'd stared at the unusual opalescent stone, which shone with a bluish hue and was encircled with tiny diamonds. "It's older than I am and comes with a very interesting story." I remembered he'd hesitated then, as if he was weighing something up in his mind. "Maybe one day I'll tell you what it is," he continued. "The necklace is probably a little grown-up for you now. But one day, I think it will suit you very well."

Pa had been right in his assessment. At the time, my body was festooned—like all my school friends'—with cheap silver bangles and large crosses hanging from leather strings around my neck. I'd never worn the moonstone and it had sat here, forgotten on the shelf, ever since.

But I would wear it now.

Going to the mirror, I fastened the tiny clasp of the delicate gold chain around my neck and studied it. Perhaps it was my imagination, but the stone seemed to glow luminously against my skin. My fingers went instinctively to touch it as I walked to the window and looked out over the twinkling lights of Lake Geneva.

"Rest in peace, darling Pa Salt," I whispered.

And, before further memories began to engulf me, I walked swiftly away from my childhood room, out of the house, and along the narrow path that took me to my current adult home, some two hundred meters away.

The front door to the Pavilion was left permanently unlocked; given the high-tech security which operated on the perimeter of our land, there was little chance of someone stealing away with my few possessions.

Walking inside, I saw that Claudia had already been in to switch on the lamps in my sitting room. I sat down heavily on the sofa, despair engulfing me.

I was the sister who had never left.

Don't miss any of the spellbinding

SEVEN SISTERS SERIES!

Or Lucinda's other "brilliantly written" (Historical Novel Society) novels!

Pick up or download your copies today!

CPSIA information can be obtained
at www.ICGtesting.com
Printed in the USA
BVHW080623160522
636791BV00001B/1